We at Jove Books are thrilled by the enthusiastic critical
acclaim that the Homespun Romances are receiving. We
would like to thank you, the readers and fans of this wonderful series, for making it the success that it is. It is our
pleasure to bring you the highest quality of romance writing in these breathtaking tales of love and family in the
heartland of America.

And now, sit back and enjoy this delightful new Homespun Romance . . .

COURTING KATE
by Mary Lou Rich

"Funny, honest, alive with crawl-off-the-pages characters,
Courting Kate is a warm, feel-good book to cherish."
— Vella Munn, author of *Spirit of the Eagle*

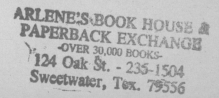

Titles by Mary Lou Rich

MOUNTAIN MAGIC
BANDIT'S KISS
COLORADO TEMPEST
THE TOMBOY
HEART'S FOLLY
COURTING KATE

Courting Kate

Mary Lou Rich

JOVE BOOKS, NEW YORK

COURTING KATE

A Jove Book / published by arrangement with
the author

PRINTING HISTORY
Jove edition / April 1997

The Putnam Berkley World Wide Web site address is
http://www.berkley.com/berkley

ISBN: 0-515-12048-0

A JOVE BOOK®
Jove Books are published by The Berkley Publishing Group,
200 Madison Avenue, New York, New York 10016.
JOVE and the "J" design are trademarks
belonging to Jove Publications, Inc.

PRINTED IN THE UNITED STATES OF AMERICA

10 9 8 7 6 5 4 3 2 1

In loving memory of my father, Grady Gammage

Mules should never be maltreated, but govern them as you would a woman, with kindness, affection, and caresses, and you will be repaid by their docility and easy management.

—John Mullen, *Miner and Traveler's Guide to Oregon, Washington, Idaho, Montana, Wyoming, and Colorado,* 1865

1

Oregon, 1868

ONLY A FOOL would risk his life to fell one last tree. Tanner Blaine didn't consider himself a fool, but he was that desperate. A cold rain saturated his clothing, ran off the brim of his hat and trailed down the back of his neck, making him shiver. He'd hoped the weather would hold until he had finished for the day. He hadn't been that lucky.

The late September storm lashing the tops of two-hundred-foot firs made them creak and moan like souls in torment. In the thick forest below, Tanner held his ax and eyed the frenzied branches warily. Icy drops stung his cheeks and blurred his vision. He impatiently wiped them away. Weather be damned, he had to work. Last winter he had quit too soon. Now, as a result, he had a mortgage at the bank.

He had thought he had his problems solved when he signed a contract with the Lucky Strike mine to supply timber for their flumes. Now he wasn't so sure. He needed that money to pay the bank and get him and his four younger brothers through another winter—if the blasted weather would allow him to get the trees cut and off the mountain by the deadline. If not, he would forfeit everything, the trees he had cut and the mountain he and his brothers called home.

Determined not to let that happen, he clenched his jaw and planted his feet more firmly on the springboard, an eight-inch wedge of wood driven into the tree trunk some twelve feet above the ground. He tightened his grip on the long, slippery handle of his ax and drove the blade deep into the tree.

He sucked in air made sharp with the scent of wet wool, rotting leaves and pitchy wood, then, muscles flexed, he swung again. A few more cuts and the tree would fall. Then, and only then, could he quit for the day.

Overhead, wood cracked.

A chill raced up his spine. He froze, his gaze shooting upward. Fear quickened his heartbeat and sent blood rushing in his ears.

He knew that sound. For good reason, the loggers called it a widowmaker—a dead treetop or limb that can break free from the force of ax blows on the trunk and fall on an unwary woodsman. Four years ago, one had killed his own father.

He squinted, but a thick gray mist tangling in the treetops made it impossible to see. The sound could have come from the dead snag two trees away. Or it could have come from the tree he was cutting. He hesitated, his better judgment telling him to get away and let the fir fall where it may. But in this wind, it could come down in the wrong direction, or worse, hit other trees and snap in half. Then he wouldn't be able to use it. He couldn't take that chance.

Grimly, he hoisted the ax and drove it into the wood.

The thousand-year-old monarch trembled. Two cuts later, it sighed, giving up the struggle for life.

Tanner tossed his ax into the brush, then gathered his legs beneath him, ready to hurtle from the springboard. A sound made him glance up.

A long, thick limb plummeted toward him—and the spot he had picked for his landing.

"Damnation!" He twisted to one side and threw himself into the brush, hoping he wouldn't land on the ax.

The limb whooshed by, grazing his cheek. It snagged his shirt, ripping off the sleeve.

The branch and the tree both crashed to the ground. Pine needles and wood chips exploded with the impact.

As the debris settled to earth, Tanner lifted his face to the falling rain and gave thanks that he had been spared. Shaking from his brush with death, he rolled to his feet and retrieved his ax. His arm stung. He rubbed the spot and felt something warm and sticky ooze over his fingers. Blood, turning pink as it mingled with the rain. The cut was deep, but it could have been worse. He could have lost his arm. Or his life.

He stared at the deadfall and shivered. Twice he'd been spared. At least this time, no one else had died. Guilt and sorrow riding heavy on his shoulders, he wrapped the tattered remains of his sleeve around the injury, picked up his tools and headed for his mules.

The pack animals and his gelding huddled together, tails to the wind, their coats dark with rain. For once the ornery mules gave him no problem, and it took little time to secure the tools and tie the packs. He figured the animals, too, would probably be glad to get home and out of the weather.

His own teeth chattering, clothes dripping wet, Tanner slid into his mackinaw jacket and topped it with a slicker. Then he mounted his horse, picked up the lead rope and started down the trail.

During the long trek home, Tanner's thoughts drifted back to earlier times. Times when they'd all been happy.

He couldn't remember his mother. He'd been told that she had been of Cherokee descent and had died when he was barely two. Soon after that his pa had left Kentucky and traveled to Oregon.

Instead of settling in the rich Rogue basin, Henry Blaine had chosen the high mountain valley in which to build a one-room log cabin for himself and his son. Folks below hadn't understood, but being a solitary man like his father, Tanner knew his pa had loved the isolation and the beauty. He couldn't imagine living anywhere else.

He'd been eight when his pa had married Maggie, an Irish lass who had taken to Tanner like he was her own. Over time, as the boys had been born, the cabin had been expanded, and while the place made no claim to being fancy, it suited all of them just fine. Growing up, they had been a rowdy bunch, and Tanner and his brothers had made the rafters ring with their laughter and their squabbles. But his pa had built the dwelling sturdy enough to last for generations, provided a wildfire didn't take it before its time.

Then, six years ago, Maggie had died in a diphtheria epidemic. Two years after that, the deadfall claimed their pa. Tanner had taken on the raising of his brothers, but the burden—and the responsibility—weighed heavy on his shoulders. Now, after losing both their parents, the mountain was all they had left. He would never allow them to lose it.

The rain had turned to sleet by the time he rounded the last switchback and crossed the creek. Beyond a large meadow, a welcoming beacon of light shone through the cabin window. Smoke, curling from the chimney, drifted on the wet air.

Pausing to rest the animals, he gazed past the house to the north side of the valley where a towering peak stood like a sentinel, sheltering the homestead from the deepest winter snows and bitter winds. Evergreens, surrounding a large meadow, shielded the place on the other three sides. In summer, that glen waved as an undulating sea of green grasses and wildflowers. Deer, elk and other wildlife roamed in abundance. Flocks of ducks and geese chose the quiet eddies of the creek in which to raise their young.

A short distance from the cabin, at the edge of the woods, he and his father had built a barn. Next to that a smokehouse held their winter's meat.

The place had everything a man needed, and Tanner knew if he looked his whole life, he couldn't find anywhere he would like better.

The gelding stomped restlessly, eager to get to this stall. Giving him his head, Tanner rode past the house, waving at eight-year-old John, who peered through the window, then hurried the mules on into the barn. Although he longed to dry himself in front of the fire and fill his belly with something hot for a change, his animals had to be cared for first. Then his tools had to be wiped down and oiled in preparation for the next day's work. It was pitch dark by the time he finished his chores.

He lifted the lantern from the hook and was leaving the barn when a gleam of white in a pile of hay caught his eye. Eggs. A whole pile of them. He'd wanted some for breakfast, but he hadn't gotten any. The boys had told him the hens had quit laying. Now he saw they had been too lazy to gather them.

Wondering what other chores still needed doing, he stuffed the eggs into his pocket then trudged through the rain toward the warmth of the house. "T-Tanner's here," John yelled through the open doorway.

"Are you announcing my arrival, or warning them I'm coming?"

"B-both, I r-reckon," John said, his blue eyes dancing.

Tanner reached out with his free hand and ruffled the child's blond hair. Shy little John was skinny as a stick and stuttered so bad you wanted to pull the words out of him, but he had a sunny disposition, something Tanner had never laid claim to.

It wasn't that Tanner intended to be grumpy, but it always seemed to end that way. With all he had to do, he had little time and no patience for more frivolous things.

His eyes narrowing, he took in his other brothers, Matthew, Mark and Luke, who sat warm and dry in front of the fireplace.

Lean and lanky, Matthew stood six-foot-three, the same height as Tanner. But even though Matt looked like a man, he was only sixteen. Most of the time he acted even younger.

Mark, fifteen, was half a foot shorter, a fact that irritated him. He was the handsomest—and most enterprising—of the bunch, with his dark hair, dimpled grin and dancing blue eyes.

Six feet tall at fourteen years old, Luke had grown to long legs, big hands, and even bigger feet. He couldn't take a step without falling over something. With his wild thatch of white-blond hair, he resembled a scarecrow who had outgrown his clothes.

"Clean your feet," Luke called out.

Tanner wiped the worst of the red mud from his boots onto a burlap sack by the doorway, then striding into the living room, he reached into his pocket and brought out an egg. "I found a pile of these in the barn. I take it none of you bothered to look for them."

"Dandy, just dandy." Matthew glanced up, a strand of shaggy red-blond hair clinging to the peach fuzz on his cheek. "You walk in the door, and already you're chewing at us." Scowling, he bit off a length of sewing thread, fed it through his needle, then bent toward the britches he was attempting to mend.

Tanner shot him a disgusted look, then went into the kitchen to unload his pockets. His stomach growled. He was so hungry he could eat one of the mules—hooves, hide and all. He sniffed, then glanced toward the cookstove. No skillets sizzling, no kettles steaming. Nothing. Then he saw a pile of raw meat sitting on the counter. "Matt, what have you been doing? Get in here and fix me something to eat."

"I've been patching your britches, that's what," Matt grumbled. "If you're that hungry, maybe you'd ought to fix your own damned supper." He threw the pants down and stomped into the kitchen.

"You watch your tongue, boy. Your poor ma would turn over in her grave if she heard you using that kind of language."

Matt gave him a mutinous look, then slammed a skillet onto the cast-iron range.

Knowing it would be a while before he'd be able to eat, and deciding Matt might cook a little faster if he left the room, Tanner retreated to the fireplace to thaw out. As he held his hands toward the crackling blaze, he noticed the empty woodbox. He turned toward Luke, who, as usual, had his nose buried in something to read—this time a well-worn newspaper.

"What happened to the kindling you were supposed to chop? And the wood?"

Luke lifted his gaze long enough to glare at him. "I had to do the dishes and scrub the floors, for all the good it did, considering the mud you tracked in. The way you act, you'd think I spent the day a-twiddlin' my thumbs."

"While you *weren't* cutting the wood, I was out there in the rain, working my rear off, dodging falling trees and doing my best to stay alive and keep a roof over your heads."

"You wouldn't have to work so hard if you'd stop being pigheaded and let one of us help you," Matt yelled out from the kitchen.

"You know my answer to that." Snatching up a towel, Tanner stalked toward the bedroom, stripping off wet clothes as he went. He couldn't make them understand how dangerous the woods could be. He hadn't understood either. His pa had warned him, but he hadn't listened. He hadn't even been aware of the danger he was in, until his pa shoved him aside. The limb had killed his father instantly. It had all happened so quickly. Tanner never had the chance to say he was sorry. Never had the chance to say goodbye.

Waves of grief and remorse nearly consumed him, and he forced himself to think of the present, to think of his obligations. He had learned the hard way, but his brothers weren't going to. It was the only way he could make amends.

He hung up the coat and wet clothes, and rubbed himself dry with a towel. Then he unwrapped the shirt and checked his bleeding arm. It needed stitches, but he couldn't do it himself, and he didn't want the boys to know. So he cleaned the wound, pulling the gash together as best he could, and tore strips from an old sheet and tied the bandage in place.

Shivering, he opened the bureau. Empty. Then he looked in the closet. Nary a stitch. "Where are my clothes?" He poked through the clothes basket. A sheet and two of John's shirts. Nothing of his. Finally he located a pair of tattered long johns beneath the bed. They made him itch and smelled of dust but they were dry, and he wouldn't have to run around naked. Dragging them on, he strode back into the main room. "I can't find any clean pants, or anything else. Mark, I thought you and John were going to do the wash."

"We d-didn't have any s-soap," John yelled back. "'S-sides it's been p-pouring rain all day."

"It wasn't raining yesterday. You could have done it then." Tanner lifted the water bucket. "Empty! Might have known it." He whirled to face them. "You haven't done a thing you were supposed to. What have you been doing?"

Luke grabbed the bucket from Tanner's hand and left the cabin, slamming the door behind him.

"W-why are you s-so mad?" John asked.

"He's mad 'cause it's raining, so he takes his temper out on us." Mark sighed. "Tanner, we work hard, too. I don't know of another boy in Oregon that has to sew, wash clothes and iron. It's plumb embarrassing."

"How do you think I feel?" Matt complained, slapping the steaks he'd floured into hot grease. "Every time I go into Jacksonville, all those old biddies stop me on Main Street to give me their recipes." He brushed a long hank of hair out of his eyes. "The fellers rib me. And the girls look at me funny—like I was peculiar, or something."

Luke kicked the door shut and plopped the bucket of water down on the end of the counter. "Yeah. You treat us like we're married to you, instead of like your brothers," he complained, his voice cracking in an exasperating falsetto. "May as well start wearing petticoats."

"At least you'd have *something* to put on." Tanner motioned toward his only article of clothing.

"What T-Tanner n-needs is a wife," John declared.

"Don't start with that again," Tanner warned.

"He ain't never gonna get married," Luke said with disgust. "Why should he? He's got us to do all the work."

"With that long hair and bad temper, who'd have him?" Mark asked. "'Sides, he'd have to court them, and he wouldn't take the time, nor the trouble."

"Who's got the time?" Tanner asked. He hardly managed to eat and sleep, let alone do anything else—much as he'd like to sometimes. Besides, that's all he needed—another mouth to feed. Another person to complain. Another responsibility.

Again he thought of his near accident. How could he make them understand? He stared at the four of them, wondering how they would manage if something happened to him.

He picked up the pants Matt had abandoned and pulled them on.

"I wasn't finished patching those britches."

"I've got to put on something," Tanner shot back. Every bone in his body aching, he sat down on the leather couch and stretched his bare feet toward the fire.

What would they do? He didn't know.

He prayed they wouldn't have to find out.

Soon the aroma of fried venison, beans and potatoes wafted through the cabin, and he could hardly wait until Matt set it on the table. When he did, Tanner quickly said the blessing so he could eat his fill. At the first mouthful, he sighed in appreciation. "Mighty good. Matt, you might make somebody a good wife at that." Tanner reached up and caught the biscuit that Matt immediately sailed toward his head.

When he couldn't eat another bite, Tanner rose from the table and washed his face and hands. His arm throbbed like blue blazes. Feeling his brothers' eyes on him, he clenched his jaw against the pain. "'Night, boys." He retreated to the bedroom.

Mark followed him. "What's that lump under your sleeve?"

"Had a little accident."

"Let me see," Mark insisted.

"I'm not one of your sick critters." Then deciding that Mark wouldn't leave otherwise, he rolled up his sleeve and took off the bandage.

A whistle of air slid between Mark's teeth. "The ax?"

"No. A deadfall. I don't want the others to know. Think you might be able to stitch it?"

"I've sewed everything else. Don't know why your hide should be any different." Mark left the room. He returned a minute later with an amber bottle, a needle and a spool of thread. "Had this rum left over from the fruitcakes." He pulled the cork and dumped the liquor into the wound.

Tanner bit back a curse and closed his eyes against the pain.

Mark pulled the flesh into place and stitched it, cutting the thread when he was through. His movements quick and efficient, he bandaged the arm. "Keep it clean," he warned. "We don't want it getting infected. I'll check it again tomorrow."

"Thanks, doc."

"You haven't seen my bill yet," Mark said, closing the door.

As his abused muscles melted into the feather bed, Tanner could hear the boys complaining—about his marital status and about not being allowed to help in the woods. He'd heard it all before, and no doubt would again. But he would not let their complaints sway him. He would not lose one of them the way he'd lost his father.

Trying to shut out their voices, he turned onto his side and pulled his blanket up over his ear. It must have worked. The sounds became distant and muffled. He grinned and snuggled deeper into his pillow. It was then he realized he hadn't muffled the sounds at all. His brothers were whispering.

Suspicious, he sat up and tilted his head, listening. Nothing. He couldn't make out one word. Flopping back on the bed, he glared into the darkness. They were up to something. He could feel it. Well, it didn't matter. He'd nip their shenanigans in the bud before they even began.

Just like he had the last time.

2

"*S*HE HAS TO go!"

"What would you have me do, Stephen? Kathleen is my cousin. She has no other kin. I can't throw her out into the street. She has no money. The poor dear has little more than the clothes on her back."

Kathleen Deveraux stopped midstride in the hallway, her arms wrapped around a pile of newly washed sheets. Her fingers bit into the worn linen. Dear God, she hadn't meant to be a burden. She had tried so hard to help. She should have realized. . . . She eased closer to the doorway, closer to the words that were tearing into her soul.

"Melody, darlin', I'm not trying to be mean. But I have to be practical." Stephen Courtney tried to reason with his wife. "You know how difficult it's been, how hard I've worked to feed the two—soon to be three—of us. Now I'm saddled with your spinster cousin as well."

"It's all Uncle Jason's fault. You'd think he would have had more foresight, especially where the future of his only child was concerned," Melody stated angrily.

"Well, he didn't. The fool gave everything he owned to the Cause, then mortgaged the rest. You can't blame the bank for foreclosing. He brought it on himself. Listen, I don't have time to discuss this now. I have to get to work, but we will talk about it later tonight."

"Lots of people lost their homes after the rebellion."

"But most didn't blow their brains out," Stephen said.

A surge of grief rushed Kathleen, then anger. They were right about her father. How could he have done this to her? To *them*? But she had to accept blame as well. She'd taken it for granted that Stephen and Melody would take care of her. Never once had she considered their position. As a struggling bank clerk, Stephen barely made enough to support his own small family and the baby soon to come. Their house was tiny, with only one small bedchamber and an alcove that would be the nursery. They had done everything they could for her. She'd done nothing but add to their burden.

Smothered by waves of guilt and hopelessness, she turned away and silently went into the alcove she'd been using for a bedchamber. She set the pile of sheets neatly on the end of the bed and dropped down beside them. Tears stung her eyes as she tried to think. She had no money, nothing of value. For goodness' sake, she barely had enough clothes to cover herself.

Massaging her temples, she knew there had to be something she could do. But what? The men who normally would have courted her were either dead or financially ruined, as she was, by the war. And she had no training of any kind, unless one would pay for smiling prettily at guests or dancing the latest steps. Somehow she doubted that many of those jobs would be available. Still, she could learn. She glanced down at her hands, rough and red from lye soap. She had learned to do laundry, hadn't she? Besides, she had no choice. She had to find work.

Rising from the bed, she checked her appearance in the cracked pine-framed mirror. Tucking a stray lock of ebony hair into the bun at the nape of her neck, she pinched her cheeks to bring a touch of color to her pale skin, then picked up her reticule and headed for the door.

Wanting to tell Melody her destination but knowing she couldn't without revealing what she'd overheard, she slipped silently from the house. She'd find either employment or other accommodations. She had to.

Striving to keep her hopes high in spite of the gray clouds overhead, Kathleen hurried down the dusty street. But it was hard to be cheerful when the gutted buildings and the charred tree stumps reminded her at every turn of the way things had been, but would never be again.

Before the war, elegant mansions with broad expanses of green lawns had lined the tree-shaded streets. Then Sherman and his Union troops had marched through, burning, looting, leaving Atlanta in smoldering ruins. Some buildings escaped the fire, but most had not. Despite a few attempts at rebuilding, she doubted that Atlanta would ever see prosperity again.

She pushed open the weathered door of a millinery shop, activating a bell that jingled merrily overhead.

Immediately a small, white-haired woman in gray dropped the bundle of lace she had been working with and hurried forward. "Hello. Can I help you?" she asked, her voice soft and Southern. Her blue eyes bright, the little woman smiled and clasped her hands together in front of her in a gesture of expectation.

"I wondered if you could use any help?" Kathleen asked, the words tumbling out in a rush of air.

"Oh." The smile disappeared and a trace of sadness etched its way across the milliner's face.

"I don't sew very well, but I could learn," Kathleen assured her. "I could wind laces onto spools, sweep, wash windows. . . . Anything."

The woman sighed and shook her head. "I'm sorry, dear. I sympathize with your plight. I wish I could help, but I, too, am in dire straits. I can't afford to feed a stray cat, let alone hire help." She moved to her window and adjusted a bonnet on the display stand, tilting the brim to a jauntier angle as if hoping that might lure someone into her shop.

"I don't sell many bonnets these days. The Southern ladies can't afford them. And those Yankees"—she confided in a hushed tone—"order French creations from that Northern Bloomingdale's catalogue."

It was then that Kathleen noticed the neatly mended but worn lace that adorned the cuffs of the woman's sleeves, the almost threadbare state of her dress. "I understand." She reached out and touched the older woman's hand in sympathy, then nodded toward the window where a woman in scarlet silk that boldly announced her trade had paused to peer through the glass. "It looks like you might have a customer, so I'll be on my way."

"Oh, I hope so. I do hope so," the milliner murmured softly almost as if in prayer. "Good luck, my dear."

Their eyes met, sending each other a message of understanding, of silent hope, then Kathleen nodded and went out the door.

She paused on the boardwalk next to the gaudily clad shopper and sent a prayer heavenward for forgiveness for what she was about to do. "That would look perfect on you," she fibbed. "The colors are exquisite, the workmanship superb." At least that was the truth.

"You really think it would look good on me?" the soiled dove inquired in a nasal twang.

"Madame's hats are lovely. I've heard the Countess Des Moines shops here when she is in the area."

"A real countess?"

Hiding her crossed fingers in the folds of her dress, Kathleen nodded. "One in the queen's own court."

"If a countess can wear her hats, they ought to be good enough for me." The woman glanced at the display again, then pranced into the store.

Feeling only a twinge of guilt, Kathleen squared her shoulders and headed down the street.

Passing several partially destroyed buildings, she entered the general store and approached the proprietor. "I was wondering. . . ."

"No! Don't ask." The thin, sour-faced man pointed to a posted sign: NO HELP WANTED.

"I would be willing to do most anything," Kathleen pleaded.

"You and every other female in town." He eyed her up and down in a way that made her want to slap his face. "I do know of one place that is hiring."

"Where?" she asked warily.

"I hear the Gilded Lily is taking on a few new girls." Again his gaze slid suggestively over her figure.

Whirling around, she slammed out the door. The Gilded Lily, a house of ill repute. Never. She would sleep under a tree and starve to death first.

Bypassing several burned and boarded-up buildings, she inquired at the mercantile and the laundry. The answer was the same at each. No work.

The restaurant owners said they hire only relatives and not even all of them.

Her hopes sagging, she made her way to the hotel, the only place besides the Gilded Lily where she hadn't inquired. To her amazement the owner, a Mr. Smythe, offered her a job.

"One day's work, that's all I can give you. Cleaning rooms, scrubbing slop jars. . . ." He paused to see her reaction. "I couldn't offer that if my wife weren't sick."

Kathleen clenched her teeth to hide her expression of distaste. "How much will you pay?"

"Pay?" The hotel owner ran pudgy fingers down one side of his drooping handlebar mustache. "I can't afford to pay hard coin, but I can give you some food."

"How much?" If she had to stoop to such disgusting labor, she intended that it be worth her while.

"A rasher of bacon"—he glanced at her—"and a loaf of bread."

"A slab of bacon and two loaves of bread," she stated firmly.

"Now hold on here. Do you want the job or don't you?"

She narrowed her eyes—and gambled. "You could do it yourself, I suppose."

His nose wrinkled. "A half-slab and two loaves. That's as much as I will go."

Better than she had hoped for. "Done. I'll be here first thing in the morning." Before he could change his mind, she whirled and strode through the door.

Outside the hotel, she sucked in a breath of air tinged with wood smoke, manure and mud. The rain that had threatened all day now drifted down in a soft, but steady, shower. A forgotten newspaper fluttered on a wooden bench. She picked it up, using it to cover her head from the droplets.

She couldn't afford to get sick, especially now that she had a job. Granted, it was a job no one else had wanted. A Deveraux emptying and scouring slop jars. Her ancestors would be spinning in their graves.

But then, they didn't have to worry about a roof over their heads. She quickened her footsteps and hurried down the street.

Upon reaching her cousin's, she urged Melody to lie down and quickly finished preparing supper, a meal of dried beans, salt pork and corn bread. She placed it on the table a few minutes after Stephen arrived home from work.

The meal was eaten in silence, and Kathleen sensed the tension between Melody and her husband, despite their halfhearted attempts to be congenial. Avoiding their eyes, Kathleen stared at the small portion of food on her plate. She would try to eat sparingly until she found more work.

Her cousins were unhappy because of her. She could not, would not, allow it to continue.

After doing dishes, she pleaded a headache and retired to her room. Too restless to settle into bed, she picked up the abandoned newspaper she'd brought home and began to scan the pages.

She read the society section, finding most of the names mentioned unfamiliar. Understandable, since most of her peers were almost as destitute as she. She poured over the classifieds, hoping to find an opening for a governess, or a lady's companion, but found nothing listed. She read and quickly dismissed an ad for a mail-order bride. She wasn't that desperate. She didn't know how any woman could consider marrying a man she had never met.

Finally, her head truly throbbing, she folded the paper and set it aside. She had a hard day's work waiting for her tomorrow. But at the end of that day, at least she would be able to contribute some food to Stephen's table.

And the day after that? Then what would she do?

The next morning, after telling Melody that she was going to the river in search of wild pecans, Kathleen donned her oldest clothes, tucked a much mended apron and a clothespin into a burlap sack, and left for the hotel. The day was cool but clear. That much at least was in her favor.

She pushed through the glass-paneled door and made her way to the heavy desk where the proprietor sat, going over his ledgers. "Good morning."

He scowled and peered at her over his glasses. "Oh, it's you." He removed his pencil from behind his ear. "Let's see, that was two rashers of bacon and two loaves of bread."

"No. We agreed on a *half-slab* of bacon and two loaves of bread." She stood, waiting.

"All right. I just wanted to see if you remembered." He handed her a ring of keys and motioned toward the stairway. "Better knock first. Some of the gents had a late night. They might still be abed."

"Where do I dispose of—of . . ." She flushed crimson.

He snickered. "In the privy—out back. There's two tubs in the alley, one for rinsing and the other for washing. You'll have to carry the water—and dump it when you're done."

"Of course." She had never entertained any idea that he might decide to help with anything.

"After you're done with that, you can clean the spittoons, make the beds, beat the rugs, sweep—" He shrugged. "And whatever else needs doing."

"You never mentioned any of that."

"You never asked." His eyes narrowed. "You didn't think I intended to pay you for less than a full day's work, did you?"

Full week's work was more like it. "You'll get your money's worth, Mr. Smythe." She tied on her apron and headed for the kitchen to put kettles on to boil.

The first three rooms were empty, but the chamber pots certainly weren't. Their stench permeated the very walls. Gagging, she rushed to the windows and threw up the sashes, hoping the fresh air would settle her stomach while airing out the place. She gulped in large quantities of clean air, then deciding she couldn't very well hang out the window all day, she reluctantly forced herself back inside. She clamped the clothespin on her nose and gingerly moved the containers into the hall; then one by one hoisted her smelly burdens and carefully made her way down the stairs.

As she worked, her thoughts turned to how to earn more money to help Stephen and Melody. Perhaps if she worked hard enough, did a superior job, Mr. Smythe would find something else for her to do. It was her only hope. There was nothing else in town.

After she'd placed the last beaten rug on the floor in front of a freshly made bed, she pressed a hand to her aching back and straightened. She had gained a new respect for her former servants. Brushing the dust form her skirt, she headed for Mr. Smythe's office, saying a little prayer as she walked.

Mr. Smythe glanced up from the figures he'd been adding and motioned to a chair across from him. "All finished?"

"Yes. Unless there is something else . . . ," she began hopefully.

He shook his head. "You earned your pay, I'll say that for you. But my wife is feeling better, and she'll be able to take over tomorrow."

"Isn't there anything?"

"You've done a good job, and if I could afford to hire anyone, it would be you. But the fact of the matter is, we barely make enough to keep ourselves and pay the cook." He shoved back his chair and got to his feet. "Now, let's go to the kitchen and collect your foodstuffs."

Mr. Smythe had been generous, adding five pounds of beans as a bonus. But as she carried her bounty home, the haplessness of her situation struck Kathleen anew. She had never worked harder, but the hotel owner had stated his position clearly. There would be no more work.

"Melody, I'm home," Kathleen called as she entered the house.

Wiping her hands on her apron, Melody stood in the kitchen doorway. "Thank goodness. I was afraid something might have happened to you. Did you find any pecans?"

"No, but I did obtain a day's employment."

"You worked? Where?"

"At the hotel."

"Doing what?"

"Taking over some simple chores that Mrs. Smythe was too ill to do. This was my pay." She removed the foodstuffs and placed them on the counter.

"Bacon!" Melody bent her cumbersome body, her soft brown curls sliding forward over her shoulders, and sniffed. "We haven't had any since the war. And the bread . . . mmm, smells heavenly."

"Shall we fry up some bacon for supper?"

"Yes." Melody clasped her hands together, as excited as a child. "Won't Stephen be surprised?"

Stephen arrived home later than usual and even though he tried to appear cheerful before Melody, Kathleen could tell by his manner that something was terribly wrong.

Insisting that Melody go to bed early, Kathleen finished the dishes, then went into the parlor to find Stephen staring out the window. "Would you care to talk about it?" she asked softly.

He stiffened, then lowered his head. "What would you like me to say? How Melody has sacrificed so much, yet she never complains? How happy she was over a simple piece of bacon I couldn't even provide? How I love her so and would give her the moon and stars if it were in my power? As it is, I can barely keep a roof over her head. Now with the child coming . . ." He broke off and covered his eyes with his hand. "I feel like such a failure."

"Stephen, don't." She placed a hand on his shoulder. "I don't know of anyone who works harder."

His face bleak, he turned. "The bank has cut my hours. I don't want Melody to find out. God knows how we will survive."

After Stephen left the room, Kathleen remained, staring out into the darkness. Her throat tightened with suppressed tears. She couldn't impose any longer. No matter what, she had to leave. Walking slowly into her room, she glanced at the paper lying on the bed, recalling the advertisement for the mail-order bride.

Now she was that desperate.

3

"*GIDDAP, YA FOUR-LEGGED* sons-a . . ." The pouring rain drowned out the rest of the driver's curses.

After leaving Yreka, the Concord Stage had crawled along the steep, muddy slope of the Siskiyou Mountains, its six horses blowing, scrambling for safe footing with every step. The storm had become even more fierce at the higher elevation. Thunder roared and the mountains trembled. Bright forks of lightning speared the earth, illuminating cloud-covered peaks.

Kathleen clung to the leather strap next to her seat and prayed the horses would be able to pull the heavy coach up the slippery grade.

The vehicle had been built to accommodate sixteen passengers, five on top and nine inside. At present, it contained herself and two other females, all of whom rattled around in its padded leather interior like stones in an oversized bucket. The two women sat in the forward-facing seat at the back. Kathleen had chosen the third seat in the middle, facing her traveling companions.

"Mercy sakes, I could walk and get there quicker than this," the elder, Bessie McGuire, complained.

Selina, Bessie's daughter-in-law, smiled and patted the

old woman's mitten-covered hand. "Now, Ma, you've been over this road enough times to know how long it takes."

The coach hit a bump and skidded sideways.

"I only hope that driver gets us there in one piece." Crinkling her mouth into a gap-toothed grin, Bessie raised her booted feet and braced them against the opposite seat, showing a good deal of flannel petticoat in the process.

In spite of her fear, Kathleen found it hard to repress a smile. Although she hadn't known Selina and Bessie long, they had her admiration. While their rough speech and clothing would scarcely qualify the pair as ladies, they, unlike herself, seemed to belong to this primitive land. Their leathery skin and red, calloused hands, now covered by thick wool mittens, told her they were not averse to hard work.

It would take more than meeting a stranger to frighten them, Kathleen thought, chiding herself for her own lack of courage. Her scolding didn't help. She admitted it. She was scared. Scared to death.

Why had she been so foolish? She should have waited until she found out more, but at the time the advertisement had seemed like an answer to a prayer. Now it loomed like an approaching nightmare. Before this day ended she would meet the man she had traveled over three thousand miles to marry. A man she wouldn't know if she ran over him in the middle of the street. She didn't know the color of his eyes, whether he had light or dark hair, or even if he had any hair at all. The only thing she had to go by was what the advertisement stated:

HANDSOME, PROSPEROUS LUMBERMAN REQUESTS LADY OF QUALITY TO SHARE SPACIOUS HOME IN OREGON'S BEAUTIFUL SISKIYOU MOUNTAINS—OBJECT MATRIMONY.

Not much to base a future life on. Not much at all.

They had corresponded—if you could call it that. She'd sent a letter asking for more information, along with a faded out-of-date photo. She'd been amazed that his return letter had arrived so quickly—then dismayed when she realized he'd answered none of her questions. His reply contained little more than a terse note saying, "You'll do," along with money for her train fare to Sacramento, the end of the railroad line, and a stage ticket from there to Jacksonville, Oregon.

She worriedly twisted the ties on her reticule. What if he wasn't handsome? Men had been known to have an exaggerated opinion of themselves. Looks weren't all that important, she decided, as long as he wasn't mean-spirited.

What if he was cruel and inclined to beat her? What would she do then? She was thousands of miles away from everything she had ever known.

Would her fiancé be in Jacksonville to meet her? What would she do if he wasn't? What if he hadn't received her letter saying she was coming? One of her stage companions had told her that the mail delivery this time of year was so erratic that sometimes the letters didn't arrive for months.

Kathleen was almost grateful for the distraction when a wheel of the stage slid off into a rut, catapulting the passengers upward to bang their heads on the roof.

"Mercy sakes, I swear that driver is tryin' to kill us," Bessie said, rubbing her palm over her thinning white hair. She retrieved a man's felt hat that she had discarded earlier and tugged it on, then anchored it in place with her muffler. "Now if he tries that again, maybe I can keep what few brains I've got left from gettin' addled."

Kathleen wished her own problem could be solved that easily. For the second time that day, she had ended up on the floor.

"Child, you might fare better if you moved back here with us," Bessie said. "At least you can brace yourself so's you don't end up black and blue."

"If you're sure I wouldn't be crowding you. . . ."

The old lady let out a whoop of laughter. "You're so little, it would take six of you to fill up the rest of this seat. Besides, you can share this lap robe. That outfit, while mighty pretty, don't appear like it's none too warm."

"It is a bit thin for the weather." Shivering in her black silk bombazine traveling costume and light wool cloak,

Kathleen settled in beside Bessie and gratefully tucked the quilt around her. While she didn't want to admit it to the ladies, that outfit was the warmest she had. Unlike Selina and Bessie, who wore boots, heavy dresses and flannel petticoats, she was ill-prepared for severe weather. Something she'd soon have to remedy, she decided.

"Suppose it'll snow?" Bessie said, peering eastward toward the higher Cascade peaks.

"Maybe if it gets colder, but right now it seems a bit too warm out for that. Thank God," Selina added under her breath. "In another couple of weeks the pass will be full of snow and ice. Then, even if a stage could get through, which is unlikely, it would be a hair-raisin' trip."

Thinking about the ordeal she had already experienced, Kathleen gave thanks that she had come when she did. But at the same time, anxiety made a knot in her middle when she realized that once she reached Jacksonville, if things didn't turn out as she had hoped, the winter weather would make it impossible for her to leave.

She imagined herself trapped, hemmed in by dark, inhospitable mountains, a stranger in an even stranger land. She shivered. *Get hold of yourself, Kathleen. It will be all right.* It had to be.

She forced her concerns aside and envisioned a rosier picture. She imagined herself being met by a well-groomed, fair-haired gentleman who would kiss her hand and solicitously ask about her journey. He would see her to her accommodations, and over dinner they would get acquainted. If they decided they were suited to one another, then, after a lengthy courtship, they would wed. After the ceremony, he would drive her to a stately, two-story house. The lawns would be spacious and tree-shaded, and the grounds well kept, with flower arbors. Of course his home couldn't be like the plantation she had left behind in Georgia, but still. . . .

"Whoa!" the driver yelled, pulling the horses to a walk.

"Are we there?" Kathleen asked hopefully, peering through the rain-dotted window.

"I wish we were," Selina replied. "We're pullin' into Robin's Roost to have a bite to eat and change horses."

"Robber's Roost is more like it," Bessie amended. "And as far as being there—" The old woman chuckled. "We've only made the summit. It's worse goin' down."

Worse? Before she could ask Bessie to explain, the door opened, and the buckskin-clad driver stuck his head inside.

"All out. And don't take all day eatin'. I want to get off this damned mountain before dark." He spat a stream of tobacco juice, then ambled toward the shotgun guard who was waiting for the hostlers to change the teams.

"My, isn't he a pleasant soul," Kathleen declared.

"Charlie Parkhurst ain't known for his politeness, nor his manners." Selina jumped down, then held up her hand for Bessie.

In spite of her advanced age, the spry old lady jumped flat-footed to the ground. Ignoring the drizzling rain, she set off in pursuit of the driver. "Wait up there," she ordered.

Parkhurst turned, his expression sour as his demeanor. "Yeah. What do you want?"

"What happened to the regular stage driver? He was a gentleman, not like another I could name," Bessie said pointedly.

"He had an accident. Stage rolled over. He'll be laid up for a spell."

"Sorry to hear that. Anybody else hurt?"

"Yeah. They sued the company. Cost it a lot of money." He narrowed his one good eye and picked up a slender chunk of iron. "You can bet it wouldn't happen to me. If'n I had an accident, I'd check out the passengers. Them that was dead, I'd leave alone. Them that weren't—" He hefted the wagon iron suggestively. "They wouldn't be filing no claims." He smiled maliciously, then walked away.

"Humph!" The old lady shot him a scathing glance then returned to the others.

"Would he do that?" Kathleen asked, horrified by the idea.

"I'd hate to put him to the test." Selina took Bessie's arm and escorted her inside.

After a dinner of scorched beans and tough steak, Kathleen and her companions had barely climbed aboard when the Concord lurched on its way. The stage kept to the mountain side of the road, when possible. Mostly it skittered over the slick surface like a drop of water in a hot skillet, coming all too near to the yawning abyss for comfort. Bracing their feet on the seat across from them, the other two women chatted. Kathleen stared straight ahead, too terrified to make any attempt at speech.

Now along with the usual chuckle of the axles, a steady click, click, click rose from the wheels of the stage. And another sound. Bells.

"What's that clattering noise?" Kathleen asked.

"Brakes," Selina replied. "The grade is so slick and steep that he is keeping them locked."

"And the bells?"

"He tied them to the harnesses. That's to warn anyone coming up to get out of the way."

The road was so narrow Kathleen shuddered to think of what might happen if they met another wagon, or even a horse and rider.

By the time the ground began to level out, Kathleen vowed no matter what happened, she would never go near that mountain again. Releasing a quivering sigh, she glanced at Selina.

"The pass is a sight better now than it used to be," Selina said, tongue-in-cheek. "If it hadn't been a-stormin', we would have had no problem at all."

Managing a doubtful smile, Kathleen stared out the rain-streaked window.

Now that they'd reached the valley floor, the horses stretched into an easy gallop, racing past cornfields, with their weathered stalks tied into upright bundles, and brown-grassed pastures. Kathleen stared at the lantern-lit farm-houses and wondered if one of them might belong to her future husband.

As suddenly as it had started, the rain stopped, and a brilliant rainbow lit the late afternoon sky. "Oh, it is beautiful," she cried.

"You ought to see it in spring. Everything is so green it hurts your eyes," Bessie said.

"We like it here, but the winters take some gettin' used to." Selina added with a smile, "However, some years we still have flowers bloomin' at Christmas."

"We never had much of a winter in Georgia. Might be a nice change." Especially if you were warm and dry and seated comfortably in front of a cozy fireplace, she thought, hoping her new home would have a large fireplace. Beyond the oak-covered foothills, the mountains loomed dark and menacing, their forest-crested tips covered with snow. Kathleen shivered. At least she wouldn't have to live up there.

After stopping to change horses again, they were quickly on their way. Now, instead of the slap of water and mud that had been the case, the stage wheels crunched in a thick layer of gravel, a definite sign of prosperity.

Kate peered out the window. By the increasing number of dwellings, she knew they must be coming into Jacksonville. Her heart drumming with both fear and anticipation, she was eager to get a glimpse of the place where she would make her home.

While Jacksonville was nowhere near the size of Atlanta, it appeared to be a thriving community. They passed several residences, one of which seemed so imposing that she craned her neck for a second look. Farther on, she noticed a newspaper office and a harness shop.

"Whoa," Charlie Parkhurst yelled, bringing the stage to a stop in front of a long, two-story white building. A sign dangling between two chains read UNITED STATES HOTEL. Much to Kathleen's amazement, the driver opened the door and courteously helped each of his three female passengers to the ground. "I hope you'll find the diggin's comfortable, ladies." After placing their luggage in the lobby, he returned, respectfully tilted a begrimed felt hat, then climbed atop the stage.

Kathleen and Selina looked at each other, then burst into giggles. "Was that the same man?" Kathleen asked, watching the coach disappear around a corner.

"Wouldn't dare be rude to us now. Too many people around," Selina said wryly. She glanced up and down the street. "I don't see your fiancé, but he might be waiting inside. Or he might be in one of the saloons." She pointed toward a group of buildings in the next block.

Kathleen blamed a blast of wind for the tremor that made her draw her cloak a little closer. The area in front of the hotel did appear deserted. No wagons. No horses. No Mr. Blaine.

Selina and Bessie waited expectantly. Still Kate hesitated. Now that she had arrived, she lacked the courage to go inside.

As if sensing her thoughts, Selina shot her a reassuring smile before turning to her elderly companion. "Come on, Ma. Let's get you out of the cold." She took her mother-in-law's arm and escorted her through the hotel's double doors.

The odors of manure, wet earth and freshly cut lumber scented the raw, cold air. Across the street, unpainted boards of a false-fronted building gleamed fresh and new against the more weathered, grey appearance of its neighbors. Down the block, an impressive brick building took up most of the corner, and Kathleen wondered if it might be a bank. Past that, the tinkling of a piano drifted through the swinging door of a brightly lit drinking establishment.

Taking in the sights and sounds, she wondered if she would ever feel at home in such a place. She dallied, thinking to delay her entry into the hotel a little longer.

Then, down the street, several men left the lights and noise of the saloon and strolled in her direction.

Fearing they might approach her, she gripped the brass doorknob and hurried into the lobby.

The combined stench of smoke, Macassar oil and un-washed bodies assaulted her senses, but the hotel itself seemed much better than other places the stage had stopped for the night.

Cream-colored lace curtains adorned tall narrow windows. Polished brass spittoons sat at strategic locations along the floor beneath pale blue damask–covered walls. Oriental rugs, mud-splattered but elegant, ran the length of the lobby. Off to one side, visible through open double doors, linen-draped tables denoted the dining room. He was probably waiting for her there.

Taking courage from this vestige of civilization, she moved to the dining room doorway and waited expectantly. Although a number of the tables were occupied, no handsome, smiling gentleman stepped forward to greet her. He had to be here somewhere. She signaled a waiter and gave him a message.

The man went from table to table, earning her several curious stares, then the waiter returned, shaking his head. "He isn't here, miss. You might check with the lobby."

"I'll do that, sir. Thank you." Gathering her composure, she moved toward the hotel desk. Except for a whisky salesman in a garish gold-checked suit, and the hotel clerk, this area, too, was empty.

Waiting until the salesman had left, Kathleen stepped forward and nodded at the bell clerk. "Good evening, sir. Could there by chance be any messages for Miss Kathleen Deveraux?"

The man checked various pieces of paper impaled on a brass spindle. "Nope. No messages."

While Kathleen felt disappointed that Mr. Blaine hadn't met her, she also felt relieved. At least this way, she would have a chance for a hot bath and a good night's sleep before he arrived. Tomorrow she wanted to look her best. She refused to dwell on the possibility that he hadn't received her letter and might not show up at all.

"I was expecting someone to meet me," she said. "Since it appears he's been delayed, I'll need a room for one night."

The man peered at her over his glasses. "You leaving on the morning stage?"

"No, sir, I'm not."

He gave her a suspicious look. "We don't cater to—"

Gracious me, he thinks I'm a . . . "My fiancé will be here to fetch me sometime tomorrow," she added primly, praying that would indeed be the case.

Her answer seemed to satisfy him. He shoved a ledger toward her. "That'll be six dollars for a first-class room. That includes your evening meal."

Kathleen gasped. "Six dollars? Don't you have anything less expensive?"

"We do have one we usually save for drummers and the like. It's two dollars."

"Does that include a meal?" she asked, determined to get the most she could for her money.

"Not usually, but if you'll settle for soup and bread . . ."

She'd hoped for roast beef and mashed potatoes, but soup was better than nothing. "I'll take it." She dug into her purse and counted out the correct amount of money. Even with the cheaper accommodations, she had less than two dollars left. Considering her strained finances, she gave thanks that her evening meal, however meager, came with the hotel's accommodations. Still able to taste that awful fare at Robin's Roost, she grimaced. At least they couldn't burn soup.

She signed the register and picked up the key. "I would like my bath water sent up as soon as possible."

"If you want a bath, it's a dollar extra."

While she was tempted to call him the thief that he was, she didn't wish to make a scene on her first night in town. "I do intend to have a bath, and for that price I'll expect the water to be hot."

"Second door upstairs, on the left." He peered at her trunk. "I hope you don't expect me to drag *that* up those stairs."

"Of course not, I expect it to fly up there all by itself." She could tell by the pained expression on his face that it was the only way her trunk would get there.

"I could send word to the saloon and see if one of the fellers—"

"No, that won't be necessary," she said quickly. Even if he did find anyone willing to help her, that person, too, would expect some payment for his effort. "The smaller bag will do for tonight." She frowned when he remained where he was. Apparently whatever luggage she needed, she would have to manage by herself.

She gazed at her trunk, uneasy about leaving it, especially since it contained everything she had of value. Small

miniatures of her father and mother in silver-backed frames,
frames that she had hidden rather than let them be sacrificed
for the Cause. A coverlet and a few bed linens she had
salvaged from the plantation. And most precious of all, her
mother's wedding dress and veil. "I want your assurance
that my trunk will be safe."

"If it's full of guns—or whisky," he said sarcastically,
"then I'd say you'd better not chance it."

"No. Only one revolver." She suggestively patted her
reticule. "I decided to travel light this time." Delighting in
the shock on the clerk's face, she leaned forward, waving a
finger in warning. "That trunk contains my wedding dress,
and I will hold *you* personally responsible if anything
happens to it."

His eyes shifted from her to the reticule. "I'll move it
behind the desk if that would ease your mind any."

"As long as it is safe." Grateful that he hadn't called her
bluff and made her check her nonexistent gun at the desk,
she picked up her smaller bag and waited until he tugged her
trunk out of the hallway. "By chance, are you acquainted
with Tanner Blaine?" she asked.

"Name doesn't sound familiar." He grunted and dusted
his hands. "It will take a while for that water to heat."
Before she could ask anything more, he pushed through a
curtain behind the desk and disappeared from her view.

She trudged up the stairs, found the right room number
and used the key to open her door. The stench of stale cigar
smoke and lingering body odors sent her scurrying in search
of a window. There was no window.

Using a gleam of light from the hallway, she lit a lamp
she'd found on a bureau, waved as much of the smell as she
could from the room, then closed and locked her door. "Two
dollars for this," she muttered, shaking her head. The whole
room appeared barely larger than a closet. Since previous
experience had taught her to be cautious, she stripped the
bed and checked the mattress for vermin. Satisfied that the
linens, although dingy, were clean, she remade the bed.
Then, weary beyond words and aching in every spot from
the jouncing she'd taken on the stage, she stretched out on

the coverlet. She was almost asleep when her rumbling stomach reminded her she had yet to eat. She also had to take a bath, if and when the water ever arrived.

Fearing the kitchen might close if she tarried any longer, she reluctantly rose and washed her face and hands, then patted a strand of hair into place. Tonight, she would eat her soup and bread, even taking seconds if it were permitted.

Tomorrow, she would find some way to send Tanner Blaine word that she had arrived.

Kathleen nervously paced the perimeter of her room. It was almost noon and she'd still had no word from Tanner Blaine. She'd risen early, dressed, and breakfasted on a slice of bread she'd saved from the night before, so that she wouldn't have to keep him waiting. Now she wondered why she had bothered. It had only given her more time to worry.

She'd asked around town and found that while a goodly number of people seemed to know Mr. Blaine, most hadn't seen him in over a month. And, while everyone knew he lived someplace outside of Jacksonville, nobody had been able to give her adequate directions so that she might seek him out on her own.

She'd thought he would be one of the town's leading citizens, but apparently she'd been wrong. It made her wonder how many other things she might be mistaken about as well.

Maybe he hadn't received her letter. Maybe he had received it, but was busy. The first she could excuse, but the second?

She'd traveled across an entire continent. How could he be too busy to take the time to come in and meet her?

Unless he'd changed his mind.

Last night she'd read and reread the advertisement and his letter. She hadn't been mistaken. Even if the man hadn't been inclined to flowery speech, the letter and the money he'd enclosed indicated that he'd been eager for her to arrive.

He'd come for her today, she told herself.

And what if he didn't? She'd left everything behind, all

on the promise in a letter. Now that she had taken the time to consider what she'd done, she wondered how she could have been so foolish. She knew next to nothing of her fiancé. And absolutely nothing of his family.

What if he had the inclination to drink? The town had a goodly number of saloons. Somebody had to keep them in business.

Her other fears resurfaced. What if he had a terrible temper? What if he beat her? It had been known to happen.

A knock sounded on the door. She opened it to find the maid standing in the hallway.

"You ready to leave yet, miss?"

Kate nodded, then put on her wool cloak and hat, picked up her small bag and went down the stairs.

"Any word from Mr. Blaine?" she asked the desk clerk.

"Nope. You want to pay for another night?"

"No, thank you. I'm sure he will be here soon." After placing her smaller bag on top of her trunk, she went to an alcove off of the lobby and settled herself on a chair in front of a window. Parting a lace curtain, she gazed out on the town.

Jacksonville, a hamlet surrounded by mountains, isolated in the winter because of those same mountains and impassable roads. It was almost winter now. The more she pondered her situation, the more agitated she became.

What if something had happened to Mr. Blaine?

What if he never came at all?

While one part of her wanted to give in to a fit of hysteria, another part, her pride, made her lift her chin and blink back the hot tears that blurred her vision. She was a Deveraux, born and bred a lady. She would not sit on a bench and weep like some orphaned waif.

But pride will not feed you, nor offer you a bed, a small voice inside her whispered. She swallowed a lump of fear.

A cold wind howled around the side of the building, making the window curtains flutter against the glass. Thinking of the night only a few hours away, she trembled. "Dear God, what am I going to do?"

4

"*T*-TANNER'S COMING B-BACK to the house," John warned, moving away from the cabin window.

"Dang it! I thought he'd be off to work by now." Mark brushed a hank of dark hair out of his eyes and gazed at his older brother striding through the front door.

"Mule threw a shoe," Tanner said, his voice filled with disgust. "I've got to take him into Jacksonville to get shod. Do we need anything from town while I'm there?"

"I think we've got enough sugar, but you could pick up another sack of flour," Matt said.

"How about beans?" Tanner asked.

"Gawd, no!" Mark exclaimed. "I can't stand to be in the same room with Luke as it is."

"You don't smell like no rose yourself," Luke countered.

"Flour. That's all?" When Matt nodded, Tanner turned on his heel and left the house. Moments later, riding his gelding and leading the mule, he headed down the mountain.

"Dang!" Mark said softly. "What are we going to do if *she* shows up today?"

"We ain't heard a word from her since we sent the ticket and the money," Luke said.

"We probably won't, either." Which, Mark decided, wouldn't be so bad. He and his brothers had experienced a state of panic once the letter telling her to come had been sent on its way.

Not wanting Tanner to find any incriminating evidence, they had burned the Atlanta newspaper and the woman's letter in the stove. Mark guessed that he and his brothers were destined to do women's work for the rest of their lives, or at least until they were old enough to get married. But dang it, he sure wished the idea of sending for a mail-order bride hadn't cost him that new saddle. Especially since it had taken him a whole year of cutting and peeling fence posts to earn enough money to buy the blamed thing.

"W-what if she d-does c-come?"

"Why would she? Especially since we sent her that other letter." Matt went back to his place by the fire.

"What if she didn't get it? What if she'd already left?" Mark asked, trailing after him.

"Yeah. What if she got it and decided to come anyway?" Luke added. "What are we gonna do then?"

"We told her Tanner had died. She wouldn't have any reason to come," Matt assured them.

"For the f-funeral? M-maybe she l-likes to look at d-d-dead people," little John suggested.

Matt snorted. "Don't be silly."

The more Mark thought about his saddle, the more he wished he still had it. Then he could sell it and use the money to get himself and the rest of them out of town. Now he and the boys were flat broke and winter was coming on.

Too agitated to settle, he gazed out the window and made a mental note to trim away the leafless limb that seemed intent on scratching a hole in the side of the house.

Winter.

With Tanner.

Bad enough under the best of circumstances. But with Tanner mad . . .

A chill not caused by the weather sent him back to the fireside where his brothers were still engaged in a morbid conversation about death and funerals.

Mark added his own comment to the glum observations.

"I've got a feeling death might be real pleasant compared to what Tanner will do to us if he finds out what we've done."

The storm from the day before had blown itself out during the night, and Tanner had hoped to get an early start. Heading down the mountain, he cursed the luck that made him waste valuable hours, especially on a day when the sun was shining. At least the mule wasn't limping and they were making good time. If it didn't take the smithy too long, he could still get back and put in a few hours' work before dark.

But when he reached the blacksmith's, he discovered that his usual bad luck still ran true. A freighter had left a whole string of animals that the man had to shoe before he could even get to Tanner's mule.

"Buford, I can't wait that long," Tanner protested. "Isn't there something you can do?"

"I'll try to get Jake in to help me, but he's been feelin' poorly of late," the smith said. "If not, I'll do a few of the wagon mules, then slip your critter in. Check back in a couple of hours, Tanner."

"Thanks. I'd appreciate it." Tanner had turned to leave, when a saddle hanging at the entrance of the smithy caught his eye. "That looks like Mark's rig."

Buford chuckled. "It is. He brought it last month, seemed in a real hurry to sell it. I couldn't give him what it was worth, but he took it anyhow. I figure I'll hang on to it for a while in case he wants it back."

"Mark skinned fence posts for a year to get that saddle. Couldn't see what he wanted with it myself. He doesn't even have a horse. Kids." Shaking his head, Tanner left the livery and strolled down the street.

Recalling a harness that needed mending, he turned in to J. A. Brunner & Bro.'s store and picked up a length of leather to do the job. After exchanging pleasantries with Joe Brunner, the elder Brunner's son, Tanner dug into his pocket and handed over the correct amount of coin.

The freckle-faced young man dropped the money into

the register. "By the way, Tanner, I hear somebody is looking for you."

"Who?"

"Don't know. One of the Britt boys mentioned it." Joe tied a string around the parcel and passed it over the counter.

"Thanks." Perplexed, Tanner left the store, taking note of new construction as he headed for the center of town. If the place kept on growing, it would soon be so crowded they wouldn't all have enough air to breathe.

That was one problem he and the boys didn't have. They didn't have a neighbor for miles.

He went into the Wells Fargo office and stepped up to the window. "Howdy, Lester. Any mail for the Blaines?" He doubted there would be. They usually picked it up once a month, and Luke had come into town after feed only the week before.

"Yeah. There was a letter, but I guess the boys already got that. And Mark came in to mail something several days back." The clerk squinted over his spectacles. "The boys order something special? One or the other of them have been in here pert' near every day."

"Is that right?" That explained the unfinished chores and the mysterious whispers. "They probably sent for something out of one of those mail-order catalogs." That might be why Mark sold his saddle. But the letter? Tanner didn't know of a soul his brothers could be writing to—let alone anybody that would be writing back.

"More than likely, that's the case. We get a lot of catalog orders through here." The clerk raised a finger. "Almost forgot. Heard somebody was looking for you."

"Yeah, I heard. Who was it?"

"I don't know. Another customer told me."

"Okay, Lester. See you next month." Frowning, Tanner left the post office and strode down the boardwalk. Whoever was looking, he hoped they didn't find him. He wanted to get his chores done and get home. He had neither the time nor the disposition for any distractions.

Besides, nobody had any reason to be looking for him—unless his brothers had gotten into mischief, and somebody was expecting him to pay the damages. It had taken him forever to replace that window they'd broken on the Fourth of July. They were good boys and hadn't done it on purpose, but it did seem that where his brothers went, trouble followed. And they had been hanging around town.

His frown turned into a scowl. "Damnation, that's all I need."

When his rumbling stomach reminded him he'd had no breakfast, and it was nearing noon, Tanner checked his watch to see if he had time to grab a bite to eat before he headed back to the blacksmith's. Deciding he did, he returned the timepiece to his pocket and strolled into the Stars and Bars, a local eatery. He picked a table near the window and gave the waitress his order.

She called it out to the cook and returned with a cup of coffee. "Ain't you Tanner Blaine?"

"That's my name," he said, almost reluctant to admit it.

"A woman was looking for you. Must be a stranger, 'cause I ain't never seen her before."

"A woman?"

His brothers weren't old enough to get into *that* kind of trouble. And he hadn't been with a woman since spring. He uneasily thought back to the last time and mentally counted the months. Seven. He'd been careful, but still . . . He stared up at the waitress. "You said she was a stranger?"

"Yep. I know everybody in town. She ain't from around here." Another customer came in and caught her attention. After that the place became so busy she barely had time to deliver his steak, let alone answer any more questions.

The meal was well-cooked and plentiful, and ordinarily Tanner would have really enjoyed the treat. But today, with his mind so preoccupied, he might as well have been eating sawdust.

A woman. A stranger. Since he didn't know anybody from anywhere else, she had to be a stranger to him, too. He chewed his steak. It could be somebody needing some work done. But usually the menfolk handled all those details. He shook his head, then sopped up the last of his gravy with his biscuit and popped it into his mouth.

He went to the register and paid for his meal, waiting while the waitress counted out his change. "She didn't say what she wanted?"

"Who? Oh, her. No, just asked for you."

"Miss, can I have some more coffee?" a customer called out.

"Got to go, Mr. Blaine. Hope you find her."

Not so sure that he *wanted* to find her, Tanner left the restaurant and crossed the street. He went into the mercantile, ordered the sack of flour and had the proprietor, Homer Ames, add it to his account. "Thanks, Homer, I'll pick up the flour on my way out of town."

"Go ahead, Tanner. It'll be here when you're ready."

Nodding, Tanner strode out the door. At least *she* hadn't been in the mercantile. Curiosity getting the best of him, he checked his watch. He still had a half hour. If some strange female was asking for him the banker would know. Nothing escaped Cornelius Beekman's keen ears or eyes. Tanner entered the bank and approached a gray-haired, bearded man seated behind a desk. "Can I have a word with you, Beek?"

"Hello, Tanner." The banker gave him a broad smile. "There's a young lady down at the hotel that will be mighty glad to see you. She came in on the stage last night."

"What does she want?" he asked, hoping the banker might know that, too.

Beekman chuckled. "Don't try to pretend with me. The cat's out of the bag, Tanner." The banker leaned forward. "But how you managed to keep *that* a secret is beyond me," he said in a whisper loud enough to draw the interest of everyone in the bank.

That? That what? While Tanner wanted to demand that Beekman explain, he had the feeling that he wouldn't want whatever it was told to the whole town. Noting the inquisitive looks he was getting from the other patrons, he uneasily ran a finger around his collar. "You said she's at the hotel?"

"Yes. And if I were you, I wouldn't keep a lady like that waiting," Beekman boomed out.

A lady like that?

Fearing the banker would blurt out more, Tanner whirled and pushed through the gilt-lettered doors.

Cat's out of the bag? Secret?

Tanner had the feeling he was in big trouble—even if he didn't have any idea what it was. The only person that could tell him was at the hotel, and he didn't even know her name.

Although he wasn't a drinking man, he wistfully eyed the saloon down the street. But the nearer he got to the hotel, the more he decided that it might be better if he faced whoever it was cold sober. He had a feeling he might really need that drink later on.

Pausing on the sidewalk in front of the hotel he checked his reflection in the glass window. Not exactly dressed for calling on a lady. With his patched britches, wild hair and heavy mackinaw, he resembled a scarecrow. Seeking to improve his appearance, he dipped his hands in the horse trough and slicked down his thick black hair.

He checked the window again, then snorted in disgust. He still looked like a scarecrow—with wet hair. Deciding there was no way he could make himself any more presentable, he opened the door and entered the hotel.

The lobby was empty. He picked up the brass bell on the counter and gave it a shake.

The ring brought the clerk to the front desk.

"Can I help you?" the small man asked, peering disapprovingly over his spectacles.

"Name's Blaine, Tanner Blaine. I understand somebody is looking for me."

The clerk smiled. "Yes, sir. She will certainly be happy to see you." He reached under the counter and took out a ledger. "The banker vouched for you, so I put Miss Deveraux's noon meal on your tab. I expect you'll want to take care of that now." He handed Tanner the bill.

Tanner stared at the paper, then shoved it back. "Two dollars? For one meal? I could feed my whole family for half that much."

"Somebody owes me for Miss Deveraux's lunch," the clerk insisted, waving the ticket.

"Who is this female? And how come she expects me to pay for her eats?"

"Mr. Beekman assured me you'd take care of it."

"Just because Beekman owns the bank don't give him no call to be so free with *my* money. He's got more than I do. Get him to pay for her meal."

The clerk drew himself up like an outraged banty rooster. "But Miss Deveraux said—"

"I've never heard of this Miss Dever—whatever her name is, and I'm not paying her bills. You can tell her that next time you see her."

"You tell her yourself." The little man twisted away and called, "Miss Deveraux, would you come in here?"

"What is it, Mr. Perkins?" a soft feminine voice inquired.

Tanner whirled.

A curvaceous vision in blue glided through the doorway and walked toward him. She was little. Her crown of ebony curls would barely reach his shoulders. Young, too, he decided. But not any schoolroom miss. Her features were delicate: a small, slightly tilted nose, a bow-shaped mouth, and bone structure that told him she would be beautiful even in old age. Her skin was pale as fresh cream and just as smooth. Clearly a lady of refinement. Certainly nobody from around here. He couldn't imagine what such a creature would want with him.

"It seems your feller's finally got here," the clerk announced.

Her feller?

He gave her a questioning look, but the gaze of her long-lashed violet eyes slid right past him.

She peered toward the hotel entrance. "Where is Mr. Blaine?" she asked, her voice soft and Southern.

"I'm Tanner Blaine."

She jerked her head and stared at him. The color draining from her face, she shook her head. "That's impossible. You can't be."

He scowled. "I *am* Tanner Blaine."

"Oh, my," she murmured. She studied him from head to

foot and back again, apparently finding him sadly lacking. "Oh, my."

Feeling more than a bit insulted, Tanner eyed her as intently in return. But unlike himself, she looked even better the second time than she did the first.

"Mr. Blaine refuses to pay your bill," the hotel man announced.

"Why?" she asked, tilting her head to meet his eyes.

"Why should I?"

"Surely you aren't refusing?" Her eyes widened. She swayed, as if about to swoon.

Tanner reached out an arm to support her. She smelled sweet, like summer flowers in a high mountain meadow. He drew her closer and took another whiff. She felt womanly warm and soft, reminding her he hadn't been with a female in a long, long time. It might be worth two dollars at that. "If I'd known you looked like this, honey, I'd have gladly paid your bills," he said, his voice low, husky.

She drew in a sharp breath, and moved out of his arms. Her eyes narrowed. "Then kindly do so, sir."

He crossed his arms to keep from grabbing her again. "Give me one good reason why I should—other than your looks, that is."

"Because it's expected, as you well know." She eyed him up and down. "Or should know, if you were any kind of gentleman."

Expected? "I can understand a lady being down on her luck and needing a handout. What I can't understand is how you happened to pick on me."

"Handout indeed!" She whirled toward the clerk, who was straining to hear every word. "There has to be another Tanner Blaine. That must be the explanation."

"I'm the only Tanner Blaine in these parts."

"Then how can you pretend not to know who I am?" she asked, her eyes filling with tears.

He frowned in confusion. "Lady, I'm not pretending. I don't know you, and I don't understand why you think I should."

"*You* don't understand?" She stomped her foot. "*I* don't

understand, either. After all I've gone through to get here . . . leaving everything—everyone. I wouldn't have believed you would desert me over one measly meal," she said in a furious whisper.

"All right, I'll pay for your damned dinner." He whipped two silver dollars out of his pocket and slammed them down on the counter. "There. Now, Miss— whatever your name is, unless there is something else, I'll be on my way."

"Kathleen Deveraux." she stated emphatically. She took hold of his sleeve. "And of course there's something else. We might not have formally met, but we have corresponded."

"Corresponded?" He was getting more confused by the minute. "Like in a letter?"

"Mr. Blaine, in case you have forgotten, you sent for me. I came all the way from Georgia to marry you."

"You—you what?" Tanner recoiled as though she had hit him. He couldn't have heard right. She couldn't have said what he thought she said. "Married? You—and me?"

She nodded.

Married? Somebody had to be playing a joke. *Beekman.* He started to laugh, but the sound died in his throat. The look in her eyes told him she was dead serious.

5

*L*OOKING *FURIOUS ENOUGH* to hit somebody, the man yanked the hat from his head and crushed it between his hands. "Lady, I think we ought to have a talk."

Kathleen swallowed and took a step backward. Tanner Blaine, or whoever he was, for she certainly had her doubts, was the biggest man she had ever seen. And although handsome in a wild, rugged sort of way, he was also most disreputable in appearance. His faded pants bore patches, and his coat showed frayed strands of cloth along the edges of the sleeves.

His hair, black as the devil's heart, hung straight to his shoulders, much too long to be fashionable. His eyes like cold, dark steel were narrowed. Above a square chin and shadowy growth of whiskers, his mouth appeared set and stubborn.

She shook her head. This had to be some sort of cruel prank. He couldn't be her intended.

"If you're through gawking, we need to have a talk."

"A t-talk?"

He glared at the curious desk clerk, who blanched and found something to do at the other end of the counter.

"Somewhere private. Your room?" he suggested.

"No!" She could not—would not—allow the man in her room, even if she still had one, which she didn't. Just the idea of being alone with him filled her with terror. "Some-where . . . outside?" she said, quickly dispelling any notion he might have that she had anything of *that* sort in mind.

"Outside it is."

She could have sworn he almost smiled, but decided she'd probably imagined it.

He strode ahead of her, not even allowing her to precede him through the hotel doorway, making it clear to her and anybody else that might be watching that Tanner Blaine made no claims on being a gentleman.

He took up a position smack in the middle of the wrought-iron and wood bench that sat a short distance from the hotel entrance. Extending his long legs out onto the boardwalk, with a calloused hand he patted the seat beside him. "I don't bite."

Not so certain, Kathleen spread her skirts and took a position as far away from him as she could manage. To hide her nervousness, she folded her hands in her lap. Good breeding had carried her through the Yankee occupation of Georgia. She had no doubt it would see her through a conversation with this backwoods lout.

"All right, Miss De—De—" He paused. "Hell, what was that again?"

"Deveraux. Kathleen Amanda Deveraux."

His hand closed over and swallowed hers. "That's quite a mouthful for a country boy. If it's all the same to you, I'll call you Kate—especially since we're *supposed* to be betrothed and all."

"Sir, I haven't given you leave to call me anything." She tugged her hand free. "And I haven't been called Kate since I was a child."

"Well, you don't look all that old now." He crossed his arms and gave her the onceover. "You look to be just about right—for the things I have in mind."

Heat rose to flood her cheeks. "Mister Blaine . . ."

"Don't be so stuffy, Kate. You can call me Tanner. That only seems fittin', us being so close and all." He grinned, flashing her a mouthful of white, even teeth.

She didn't find his expression comforting. She felt like a bird about to be eaten by a very large cat. "You don't seem to be taking this seriously."

His grin grew even broader. "Should I? Do you?"

"I wouldn't have come all this way if I hadn't."

The smile left his face. "Yeah. That's right. You mentioned something about a letter, and Georgia."

"The letter. Of course." She rummaged in her reticule. "Here it is." She carefully took out an envelope, unfolded it and held it toward him. "You can see it has your name on it."

Tanner scanned the newspaper clipping. He smoothed the letter and read it, too. "I don't know what you're up to, but I'm not going to marry you," he declared.

"What?" Confused, she stared at him.

"I didn't send for you, and I'm not going to marry you."

"What?"

"Are you deaf, or just plain stupid?"

"Sir, I'm neither 'deaf,' as you so quaintly put it, nor stupid. And I wouldn't marry you if you were the last man on earth. I'm certain there must be some kind of mistake. The Tanner Blaine who sent for me certainly could have no connection with you." She pointed to the advertisement.

"Handsome, prosperous lumberman?" He stared from the letter to her and back again. "There is no other Tanner Blaine. This thing has got my name on it, but *I* sure as hell didn't write it."

"If you didn't write it, sir, then who did?"

His eyes narrowed, he studied the writing again for several long seconds, then his eyes widened and he let out a growl. "Holy hell!" He crushed the papers in his fist. "Damn them! Damn them one and all!"

Kathleen sucked in a breath. "Mr. Blaine, must you curse?"

"I know who did this," he said, biting out each word.

"Who?"

"My lame-brained brothers. They were the ones who sent for you, not me. And if any one of them were old enough, I'd see to it that you got the bridegroom you expected. But the oldest featherhead is only sixteen, and that, I'm afraid, is far too young even for you."

"Even for me? How dare you, sir!" Kathleen jumped to her feet before she would lose the rest of her aplomb and physically attack the man. Even the Yankees had not insulted her so. "Even if you didn't write the advertisement, it is your responsibility just the same. Luring a poor woman thousands of miles. Why, you deserve to be shot!"

"I didn't lure you anywhere," he declared, eyeing her clenched fist. "But you're right, it is my responsibility."

"And as for marrying you, Mr. Blaine, or any of your kinfolk, I'd sooner be committed to an asylum." She gave him her most scathing look. "Although, sooner or later, I'd probably be sharing the establishment with you. I'd wager most of your kin are already there."

His face turned red then purple as if he were about to strangle in a fit of apoplexy, then a laugh burst from his throat and exploded into a hearty guffaw.

"Don't you dare laugh at me!"

"It's better than all that catawallerin' you're doing."

He took her hand and pulled her back beside him on the bench. Then he lifted a calloused finger and gently wiped away her tears. "All right, Miss Kate Deveraux, it seems we're both the victims of a misguided matchmaking attempt. Since you're already here, there's not much I can do about that part of it. The question is, what do we do now?"

The sun was sinking on the horizon when Tanner picked up the mule and headed home. His hands clenched on the reins, imagining them to be his brothers' necks. Of all the tomfool things they'd ever done, this was the absolute limit. He wondered when they had intended to tell him. A mail-order bride was hardly something you could keep a secret. Especially from the would-be groom.

If they were old enough I'd make one of them marry her, the thought repeated itself. But they weren't old enough. And this latest escapade only reinforced his notion of how young and irresponsible the boys really were.

Handsome, prosperous, lumberman . . .

What imaginations. Luke must have dreamed that one up. Prosperous?

Thanks to them, he didn't even have a penny to jingle in his pocket. After paying for her meal and the mule's shoeing, the little he'd had left he'd given to Miss Deveraux. He figured she had more need of it than he did. He was grateful he found her when he did, otherwise he might have had to sell the horse to pay for her room.

He had settled Kathleen Deveraux at Madame Jeanne deRoboam's boardinghouse and made arrangements for her room and board, on credit—with interest, of course, for even though Madame Jeanne was a friend, she was also a shrewd businesswoman.

Her boardinghouse, called the Franco-American, was probably nothing like Kate was used to, especially since it catered to all kinds of people—miners, loggers, drummers. Even the local soiled doves rented rooms on a permanent basis. Not exactly the kind of place to take a lady, but until he sold the timber and had the money to send her home, it was the best he could do.

He thought about the advertisement again.

Handsome?

He ran a palm over his unshaven cheek and pushed back a strand of long, shaggy hair. He'd needed a haircut months ago, but somehow never found the time. He'd seen tramps that looked better. No woman in her right mind would be willing to marry anybody as wild and unkempt as he was. Unless she was blind, she'd take one look and run the other way.

But Kate Deveraux wasn't blind.

She had the prettiest eyes he'd ever seen, like violets along a mossy creek bottom.

And she didn't run.

He frowned. In fact she seemed to warm up to him real good. Was she still hoping he'd marry her?

Pondering that question, he kicked the horse into a faster pace. But the memory of how good she felt in his arms pursued him.

"I'm not getting married. And that's that!" The sound echoed off the canyon, mocking him most of the way home.

"Boy, Tanner. It s-sure took you a long t-time," John said.

"Too long to just shoe a mule," Matt amended, hurrying to put the biscuits into the oven. "Did you have any trouble?"

"Depends on what you call trouble." Tanner dumped the sack of flour on the counter and hung up his coat. Then he stood there, arms crossed. He stared from one of them to the other, then back again.

Mark glanced at Matt, who had blanched white as the flour he was wiping up from the tabletop.

"Think I'll fill that wood box." Luke bolted for the door.

Tanner stopped him in his tracks. "Nobody's going anywhere." He removed the newspaper clipping and the letter from his pocket and placed them on the table. "They say confession is good for the soul," he said, his tone deceptively soft. "Anybody want to save their soul—or at least some of their hide?"

"She's here?" Matt whispered.

"Who's here?" Tanner asked.

"Tanner, I think you already know, but you'd better sit down anyway," Mark said.

Tanner pointed toward the table. "You sit."

The boys slid into their seats, each of them pale as death.

"All right, who wants to start?"

Matt snuck a look at him, then ducked his head and concentrated on the floor. "We sent for a wife for you."

"How could you do that?"

"We placed an advertisement for her in the paper, then when she answered, we sent her the money to come."

"I know that." Tanner flopped down in his own chair. "What I want to know is how could you do such a thing?"

"We were tired of doing all that female stuff." Matt shrugged. "So we just did it."

"Where did you get the money? She came all the way from Georgia."

"I sold my saddle," Mark confessed.

"I sold the gold watch Grandpa left me," Luke added.

Tanner frowned and looked at Matthew and John. "How about you two?"

"Remember those new pants you ordered that never came?" Matt asked.

Tanner sighed. "You sold my britches?"

"Not exactly. I took them back and got the money instead."

"John?"

"I only h-had that two d-dollars I got for C-Christmas."

Tanner ran a hand through his hair. "Let me see if I've got this straight. You sold everything you owned—including Grandpa's watch and my pants—and sent all the way to Atlanta, Georgia to get me a mail-order bride?"

"Yessir."

"Were you planning to let me in on it, or were you figuring to marry me off in my sleep?"

"We hoped she wouldn't show up."

"After you sent for her?"

"Well, when we'd had time to think about it, we got scared and wrote her not to come," Matt confessed. "We told her you had died."

"Of a heart c-cond-dition," John said.

"Because you were so overjoyed," Luke finished.

Tanner stared at them, not knowing whether to laugh, cuss, or murder all four of them where they sat. Never in his wildest imaginings could he have concocted such a scheme. What was worse, he had no idea how to unravel the mess.

Like it or not, Kathleen Deveraux had arrived. He couldn't send her back; he had no money. Even if she wanted to, she couldn't leave; she had no money either. Now she was in Jacksonville, waiting for him to decide what to do with her. And he didn't know what to do with her, especially since the woman had traveled better than three thousand miles, expecting to be his wife.

He didn't want a wife. Couldn't support one if he had one. But since it looked like he was going to have to support her anyway, it might probably be cheaper to marry her. Even the idea gave him a headache. He raised a hand to his throbbing temples.

A whiff of black smoke drifted past his nostrils. "Something's burning," he said absently.

"My biscuits," Matt cried, sprinting toward the stove. "Oh heck, the steak's burnt, too."

"Looks like beans again tonight," Mark said with a groan, glancing at Luke.

"I can't help it," Luke said.

"Then don't eat them," Mark yelled.

"There's nothing else to eat," Luke yelled back.

"Enough!" Tanner roared.

"Dinner's on the table," Matt announced.

"I've lost my appetite," Tanner muttered, as if anybody cared. The boys were already at it again. A body would have to be crazy to marry into this family.

Marry?

The very word gave him the shivers. But thanks to them, what other choice did he have?

"I won't do it. I'm not getting married."

Nobody paid any attention.

"I'm not getting married!" he yelled. Shooting a fierce scowl toward his brothers, Tanner put on his coat and went out to check on his mules.

6

THE NEXT MORNING things still hadn't changed.

"We're sorry, Tanner," Luke said, his face solemn.

"You said she's kinda pretty. Why, after you get to know her better, you might decide to keep her," Matt suggested hopefully.

"And if I had the money I might decide to send her back—like you did my britches!" Too furious to say any more, and unable to trust himself anywhere near his brothers for fear he'd end up murdering them, Tanner slammed his hat on his head and strode out the door.

A mail-order bride. He still couldn't believe it. Well, today Miss Deveraux was their problem. Not that making his brothers apologize to her would do any good. Maybe she might do them in, solve all their problems. She looked mad enough to do him harm yesterday despite their difference in size. Those purple eyes of hers shot sparks hot enough to singe a man's hide.

She was as foolish as they were. The very idea, a woman like her coming all the way from Georgia expecting to marry him.

No, not him, he amended. Some make-believe paragon the boys had dreamed up. He'd been quick to set her straight on that score.

She was a pretty little thing, but she looked puny. She

didn't belong here. It'd be like putting a butterfly in the middle of a hailstorm. She needed to be someplace refined, where she could have tea parties and such.

If he was in the market for a wife, which he wasn't, he'd want one who was strong, sturdy, one who could chop wood, milk cows and birth a half dozen children.

That's the kind of woman he'd need.

And she wouldn't have eyes like woodland violets.

He saddled his mule and headed for tall timber.

A knock on her door at the boardinghouse woke Kathleen from a troubled sleep. She ran a hand over her eyes, then threw on her robe and went to answer the door. Madame Jeanne, resplendent in a morning dress of rust-colored taffeta, stood on the other side.

"*Bonjour, ma petite.* I bring you the pitcher of warm water. Breakfast ees served een a few minutes." Her plump face crinkled in a good-natured smile, the Frenchwoman held out a steaming China water pitcher.

"Thank you," Kathleen said, grateful for the kindness. "Won't you come in?"

"Only for a minute." Madame Jeanne placed the pitcher on the washstand. "I hear about your leetle problem," she said hesitantly.

"By now the whole town probably knows about it."

The older woman patted Kathleen's hand. "Try not to theenk too badly of Tanner. He ees good man, and he maybe make good husband. But, like all men, he, too, ees reluctant when eet comes to the marriage."

"Especially when he didn't bargain for a wife in the first place," Kathleen said, twisting a lock of curly hair around her finger. "It isn't that I'm all that anxious to marry Tanner Blaine—or any other man for that matter. It's just that a woman in my position doesn't have much choice. I can't even pay for my own bed and board."

"After breakfast, we have leetle talk. You have more choices than you theenk." Madame Jeanne winked, then with a bustle of petticoats, she hurried out the door.

Choices. Although Kathleen tried to take encouragement

from the Frenchwoman's words, she knew those choices would have to exclude Tanner Blaine. The tall, rugged lumberman had made it quite clear that, while he felt obligated to pay her way for the time being, he had no intention of taking her on as a permanent responsibility as his betrothed or anything else. While she didn't disagree with that, for they certainly did not suit, it made her predicament even more tenuous.

She knew very little about the man and even less about his family. He was unmarried, and he had four brothers. He was also very friendly with several of the "ladies" down the hall. She blushed remembering the way they had fawned over him. They knew him, apparently quite well, as did the proprietress, Madame Jeanne deRoboam, who, though well past the bloom of youth, became almost girlish in his presence.

Tanner was a strapping figure of a man. She'd thought a good deal of his bulk was due to the heavy coat. She'd been mistaken, for at the boarding house he'd removed the mackinaw. She'd never seen such shoulders. A muscular chest filled out his red-checked work shirt, but his waist was narrow, his hips well formed. The sturdy black trousers that hugged his long legs had been tucked into heavy boots. Even dressed in rags, he could easily turn a girl's head if she wasn't wary.

She frowned. He could hardly be prosperous, not dressed like that. Four younger brothers to support. And now her.

She hurriedly finished her toilette and made her bed, then she paused in front of the window and lifted the edge of the lace curtain to gaze out on the town.

What would she do when the weather worsened? Feeling trapped, she brought a hand to her throat. She couldn't stay, not under the circumstances. She also couldn't leave. Apparently Mr. Blaine didn't have any money either. He had promised that as soon as he was able he would pay her way back home.

She picked up her brush and ran it through her hair, smoothing the curls into a simple French twist. She couldn't bring herself to tell him that she didn't have a home, that what family she had were glad to bid her goodbye. Couldn't tell him that she had no friends, or that he had been her last desperate hope.

Desperate.

He'd seemed desperate too—desperate to get rid of her.

But Madame Jeanne had come all the way from France. She was a woman alone, and she seemed to be doing quite well for herself, if the boardinghouse was any indication.

Kathleen gazed thoughtfully at the floral pattern of the pale blue and cream wall covering, the pristine white iron bedstead, the pastel-hued braided rug on the floor. The rooms were simple but well appointed, much like one would find in any modest home. And scrupulously clean.

And rented for her by Tanner Blaine.

She refused to just sit here and accept his charity. There had to be something she could do. Hoping Madame Jeanne would have the answer to her plight, she hurried from the room.

With the hubbub of breakfast ended and the dining area cleaned and made ready for the next meal, Kathleen and Jeanne sat alone at a small table in an alcove off the kitchen.

"I could be a governess," Kathleen suggested.

Jeanne looked at the list she had made and shook her head. "Eet has no future. Besides, no one in Jacksonville needs ze governess." She tapped a pencil she held between two pudgy fingers; then, sighing, she crossed another option off the list. Madame drew her mouth into a moue. "You can not sew. Or cook." She gave Kathleen a sidelong glance. "But you are pretty. And smart. You can be actress. Join one of the traveling shows that sometimes come to town. I help you with ze costumes, and ze girls, they help you with your makeup."

Horrified, Kathleen shook her head. She peered over at the paper where yet another item was being crossed off. "It seems I haven't many options after all." Pretty and smart seemed to be the only things left on the list, and in spite of Madame's insistence, Kathleen wasn't at all sure about those.

"Do not give up," the older woman admonished. "Let me think on it a bit."

"Thank you for trying." Knowing her landlady had things to do, Kathleen got up from her seat and left the room. This was her problem. It would be up to her to solve it. Maybe she could think better if she took in some fresh air.

After fetching her cloak and gloves, she left the boardinghouse and strolled along the weathered boardwalk. She smiled at an aging Chinese man, who shot her a look of alarm and darted into the nearest alley. She'd seen others of his country from the hotel window, always hurrying, always furtive, as if they were afraid to be discovered on the street. Strange, she thought.

Midway down the block she paused to chat with the handsome banker, Cornelius Beekman, who was heading to the Stars and Bars for lunch.

She also stopped at the *Oregon Sentinel* office and checked the help wanted column. Without success. Unless she was a miner or timberman, no work was to be found.

Madame had said Kathleen would do better to start her own business, but that took money. Besides, what kind of business could she do?

"Doggone it, they done sold out of pies again," a passing miner fumed. "I had my mouth set on apple, too."

"The bakery mostly makes bread, not pies," his companion muttered. "The ones they do make sell as soon as they come out of the oven."

The men passed on by, but their conversation stuck in Kathleen's mind. *Pies*. She'd made a few, but they'd barely been edible, certainly nothing anybody would be willing to pay for. Still . . .

Deep in thought, she strolled the length of Main Street, then cut through the alley and made her way back to the boardinghouse.

She paused in the vestibule to remove her cloak. Someone opened the door and entered behind her.

"Miss Deveraux?"

"Yes." She turned and saw four boys standing in the

boardinghouse entry. Their clothing, while shabby, was clean, their faces fresh-scrubbed.

"We're Tanner Blaine's brothers. We came to apologize. Could we talk with you for a minute?"

She knew before they spoke who they were. It wasn't because of family resemblance, because they looked nothing like their older brother. Tanner had black hair and eyes so dark a grey they, too, appeared black.

The boys' hair ranged from blond to dark reddish brown; their eyes were either blue or hazel. It was their manner, she decided. They held themselves erect, their bearing proud. The gaze they gave her was direct, appraising, and wary.

Well, she didn't intend to make it easy for them. They might think twice before pulling such a stunt again. She gave them a stern look. "Yes, I think we have a good deal to talk about. Won't you come into the parlor?"

They followed her through the doorway, each looking like he would like to bolt back the way he came.

She closed the door, then leaned back against it. "Now we won't be disturbed. Perhaps you'd better sit down." She motioned toward a rose velvet settee and a group of three chairs.

The three older boys each grabbed a chair, perching awkwardly on the edge of the seat. The youngest, a blond with big blue eyes, stood next to the eldest brother.

She gazed at them, and her earlier intention to chastise them vanished. They reminded her of puppies who had been into the larder and knew they were in big trouble. Judging by the look of them, Tanner had done everything but pin their ears to the wall. "Maybe you might begin by telling me your names."

"I'm Matthew." The oldest, a tall bashful lad, ducked his head and blushed furiously.

The next shot her a somewhat abashed smile, then leaned forward and stuck out his hand. "I'm Mark."

Holding out her own hand, Kathleen smiled at the dark-haired lad. *Nothing shy about this one.* "Hello, Mark."

"I'm Luke. And we've come to tell you how sorry we are for the mess we got you in. Dang it," the skinny, sandy-haired boy said in dismay when his voice rose from bass to soprano.

Her gaze shifted to the last of the group, a small youngster who looked so fearful she thought he might be about to cry. Unable to resist, she reached out and brushed a lock of hair out of his eyes. "And who are you?"

"J-J—J . . ." Shaking his head, he bit his lip.

"He's John. He's embarrassed 'cause he stutters," Mark volunteered.

"I used to stutter," Kathleen confided. John looked so wistful, so little, she wanted to gather him into her arms. She didn't. She didn't know him well enough for that. But one look into his eyes and he had stolen her heart.

"Y-you d-don't now, M-Miss D-Deveraux."

"Why don't you call me Kate. After all, we were almost related." She held out her hand and he slipped his into it. "You want to know how I stopped stuttering?"

John nodded.

"I learned to sing the words. Come over here and sit by me, and I'll tell you about it."

Several hours later, Matt and his brothers told Kate good-bye, and set out on foot through the woods for home.

"Man, she is pretty." Mark said, letting out a sigh. "I'd marry her if I had the chance."

"I'm the oldest," Matt said, staking his claim. "If she was to marry any of us, it would be me."

"And how would you support a wife? You ain't dry behind the ears yet, yourself," Luke crowed, kicking a rock ahead of him down the trail.

"I'm almost seventeen," Matt answered. "Lots of fellers get married that young."

"Tanner wouldn't let you," John sang with nary a stutter.

"You can bet on that," Mark added. "But I do wish we could help her. Kate was nice, even after we told her everything we'd done. Makes me feel real bad. Kind of responsible."

"It does seem a shame, her coming all this way to get

married and all." Matt wished he had some way to add ten years to his age.

"Maybe we can help her do that," Luke said.

"How?" Matt asked.

"Tanner won't marry her," Mark said. "He's dead set against it."

Luke grinned at them. "Who's talking about Tanner? Lots of single men around. She's awful pretty. I bet we'd have no trouble finding her a husband."

"No trouble?" Mark let out a whoop. "We're in enough trouble now, without buying more."

Matt strolled to one side of the leaf-strewn path and sat down on a fallen log. He studied on the idea for a minute. "It might work. Of course, we'd have to interview the fellers. Wouldn't want her getting no pig in a poke."

"Don't want pigs at all. It would have to be a man, somebody nice," John sang.

Mark laughed. "No pigs. And he'd have to have money, at least enough to support her."

"Everybody we know is darn near as poor as us," Matt said with disgust. "Except Beekman, and he's too tight-fisted."

"We could take turns watching the bank. See who puts money in. Then we could write down his name and find out if he's single," Luke suggested.

"Good idea. It could work, especially if Tanner is in the woods all day." Matt picked up a stick and drew circles in the dirt. "Mark, you take the first shift, starting tomorrow."

"All right, but you'll have to do my chores."

"You can do part of them before you leave, and I'll finish up." Matt got to his feet. "Now that that's settled, let's get on home. I've still got supper to fix, and you boys have got to chop wood and milk the cow."

"Remember, not a word to Tanner," Mark warned. "We'd better swear on it."

The boys stood in a circle, each of them clasping the right shoulder of the next. "I swear nothing we said will go beyond this circle," they said together.

"If I tell, I hope a chicken buzzard eats my rotten heart," Luke added, staring pointedly at John.

They waited until each of them had repeated the pledge.

"Amen," John said solemnly. He glanced up at the sky as if expecting some giant bird to swoop down and attack him. "I won't tell. I swear I won't."

"You've got him half-scared to death," Matt whispered accusingly.

"I'll bet he won't be the one to spill the beans," Mark said, watching his younger brother dash ahead of them.

"Well, I sure won't be the one to tell," Luke declared.

"I'll bet you will. You can't keep a secret for nothing."

"Can so."

"Can not."

His mind full of matchmaking possibilities, Matt quickened his step to avoid the argument, and hurried after John.

7

KATHLEEN HAD MADE a decision, several of them in fact. From now on she would call herself Kate Deveraux. Everybody else did. Calling herself Kathleen would only make her seem standoffish. And she couldn't afford that—not if she wanted to succeed in business.

After the boys had left she had discussed her idea of a pie shop with Madame Jeanne—Jeanne, she amended, for the Frenchwoman had insisted that Kate call her that. Jeanne had suggested that Kate set up her pie business in the small storage building that sat behind the boardinghouse—for the same rent as her former room, of course.

The place had been filled with odds and ends stashed there over the years. Some articles, Kate had been able to use, but most of it had gone to the local dumping site.

Jeanne had hired a handyman to repair the roof, replace the window glass, and do the heavier cleaning. He also built a few cabinets and shelves and installed a large cook range that had been stored after Jeanne had purchased a new one for her boardinghouse. She'd also had him install a small pot-bellied stove for heat and a bed.

After he had finished, Kate took over. Now, five days and several cooking lessons later, she glanced around at the small shanty and was pleased with what she saw.

Although small, the building was larger than the bedroom

she'd occupied at the boardinghouse, and even though it wasn't as fancy, Kate liked it even better because she had a part in the transformation. And now, if her business succeeded, she wouldn't be dependent on Tanner Blaine.

The stained walls now wore a fresh coat of white paint, and several colorful rag rugs dotted the board floors. Another of Jeanne's discards, an oaken chest of drawers and a mirror, gleamed after a thorough cleaning. Kate had given the rusty iron bedstead a coat of pale blue paint. Jeanne had supplied linens and several colorful quilts to keep Kate warm on the coldest nights, not to mention a small kitchen table and chairs, along with dishes and cooking items she thought Kate might need. The woman was a virtual saint in Kate's eyes, or, at the least, she was her fairy godmother.

Kate looked around her and nodded in satisfaction. Everything was ready. The cook stove was polished, the damper cleaned. Shelves and a discarded butcher table had been arranged to help display her baked goods. She had posted signs in the various businesses around Jacksonville, and had asked Jeanne and Mr. Beekman and others to pass the word. Starting tomorrow, Kate's Pie Shop would be open for business.

Only one more thing needed doing before she began her baking. She pulled a chair close to the wall and climbed onto the seat. In one fist she held nails and a clothesline strung through the top edge of a long curtain. Her other hand clutched a hammer. She stretched toward the ceiling, only to find the curtain still dragged on the floor. If only she were a tad taller. She stood on tiptoe.

"What are you trying to do, besides break your neck?"

"Oh-h," she squealed and twisted to peer behind her. The chair rocked, then tilted, launching her into thin air.

Tanner scooped her up before she hit the floor. "What were you doing?" he asked again.

"I was trying to hang that curtain before you scared me half to death."

"What for?"

"You can put me down now." She squirmed, pushed at his shoulder.

He sniffed, like he was smelling her, then he sniffed again.

She found it most disturbing. "Put me down. Now."

He held her a moment longer, then set her feet on the floor.

She straightened her clothing, and shoved a midnight black curl behind her ear.

"Well?" Arms crossed, he waited for her answer.

"I wanted to string a divider to separate my bedroom from the pie shop," she explained.

"Pie shop? What pie shop?" He frowned. "And what bedroom? You're supposed to be sleeping at the boarding-house."

"Well, I'm not. As of tonight, I will be sleeping right here." She pointed toward the sleeping area. "And tomorrow, I will open for business."

"Oh, no you're not," he said, shaking his head. "I won't stand for it. You're going right back to Madame Jeanne's." He took her arm and marched her toward the door.

"You won't stand for it?" She jerked free. "You can't tell me what to do. You're not my father. *Nor my husband*. You have no say in the matter. I am a grown woman, and I will do as I please."

His eyes narrowed. "If I were your father, or your husband, I'd turn you over my knee."

"You wouldn't dare."

"I might do it anyhow for being so sassy."

She eyed him warily, then backed away. She whirled and retrieved her hammer. "Don't even think about it," she warned, brandishing the weapon.

"You'd really hit me?"

"Not unless it became necessary."

He placed his hands on his hips and stared at her. "Why are you being so blamed stubborn? A woman back here— all alone. Why, anything could happen."

"The boardinghouse is right there." She pointed across the alley. "Besides, I can't go back. My room's been rented to someone else."

"What? Jeanne and I had an agreement. I've already taken care of everything."

"I don't want to be taken care of. I've made a different agreement. I refuse to be a burden. I am my own woman. Besides, Jeanne thinks this is a good idea."

"Well, I don't. Besides, Jeanne isn't going to be sleeping here, you are."

"I'll be perfectly safe."

"Oh, yeah? The only way you'd be safe is if I put you under lock and key." His mouth set, he took a step forward.

She took one look and raised her weapon. It only made him madder.

"You think that puny little hammer would stop some man intent on sampling a piece of you? It wouldn't stop him for a minute. He'd just throw that hammer away—like this."

The hammer clanged against the opposite wall.

"Then he'd just gather you close—like this."

He jerked her against his chest.

She pushed at him. "Let me go," she said between gritted teeth.

His arms tightened, so that she was unable to move. "Then, he'd do this." Like a hawk after a dove, he bent his head and captured her mouth. "And this—" When she gasped, he kissed her again, slowly, thoroughly, then his breath grew ragged, his mouth more intense, plundering hers. He kissed her as if he couldn't seem to stop.

More frightened than she'd ever been in her whole life, Kate began to fight in earnest. To no avail. He was heavier, stronger, and seemed intent on kissing the life out of her. His lips were cool and warm, fierce, then tender. He kissed her hair, her nose, her eyes, making her dizzy with his presence. He smelled like pine trees and wood smoke. And his hands made her feel things she never felt before. This was no innocent kiss like she had experienced behind the gazebo at sixteen. This was . . . She didn't know what it was. She only knew it opened doors to her imagination that she never knew existed.

A band of heat coiled in her middle, making her dizzy, confused. She wanted to shove him away, but she couldn't.

It was as if some outside force had taken control of her body. She was only aware of Tanner. Tanner . . . Even her heartbeat seemed to echo his name.

She wasn't sure when her arms went around his neck, or when she began kissing him back. She sighed and closed her eyes.

Breathing heavily, he stopped, removed his mouth from hers.

Dazed, she opened her eyes and saw him observing her.

"Convinced yet?" he asked huskily.

"That—that wouldn't happen," she somehow managed to say.

"Then he might get right down to this—" Tanner bent, slid an arm under her legs and lifted her off her feet. His expression hot and hungry, he took two steps and placed her on the bed. The next thing she knew, he was beside her, his weight pressing her down into the mattress.

Now really frightened, she tried to twist away from him. It was no use. "No. No, please . . ." Despite her best intention, a sob made its way past her throat. The sound seemed to bring him back to sanity. His assault stopped as abruptly as it had begun. But he didn't let go of her.

"Kate, I didn't mean to scare you. Kate?"

She couldn't answer.

Heaving a great sigh, he moved to the edge of the bed and sat up. He smoothed her hair back from her face, his calloused palm gentle against her cheek. "Are you all right?"

She stared at him, then turned her head away to hide her tears.

"Doggone, honey, don't cry." He carefully raised her to an upright position, then awkwardly patted her back. "I only wanted to show you what could happen."

He'd done more than that. She drew in a breath. "I'm not crying, and I'm not your honey." She slapped at his hand. "Don't touch me." She scooted away and got to her feet. Furious now, she whirled to face him. "And as for showing me what could happen . . . I think I got the idea, Mr. Blaine."

"I was trying to teach you a lesson," he said, as if such a lame excuse would explain his outlandish behavior.

"I don't need any lessons. And I certainly don't need you." She pointed toward the door. "Get out!"

He gave her a feeble smile. "I'll come back a little later, then maybe we can talk, after you've calmed down and all."

"Talk? Is that what you call it?" Her eyes narrowed. "You come anywhere near me, and I'll sic the dog on you."

"What dog?" He peered around the room.

"The one Mark's walking. He should be back any minute."

"Mark? What's Mark doing in town?"

"He's *your* brother. Why don't you ask him?" She shoved him through the door, then clicked the lock.

More shaken than he cared to admit, Tanner stared at the closed door. He didn't blame her for being upset. He didn't know what had gotten into him. If anyone else had tried such a thing, he would have shot him on the spot.

The ease with which he'd relieved her of the hammer gave him cause for alarm. And what followed . . . Another man wouldn't have stopped.

Worry gnawed at him, making his brows knot in consternation.

Maybe he ought to get her a gun.

On second thought, he'd better not. He'd probably be the one she shot.

She said she had a dog. *It had better be a mean son-of-a—*

"Tanner, what are you doing here?"

Tanner whirled, primed for a fight, then blinked. "I might ask you the same question." He stared at Mark, then at the ungainly critter beside him.

The thing was of an indeterminate color, a splotch of this, a streak of that, almost as if God had had a lot of colors left over and dumped them, letting them fall where they may. The rest of him wasn't any better. Big as a pony and shaggy as a yearling spring bear. The critter also looked like it had about as many teeth, all ready to fasten onto him. "That is about the ugliest varmint I've ever seen."

At that, the beast dropped to its haunches, ready to spring. A growl rumbled in its throat, low and menacing.

Mark took another half hitch on the already straining rope. "He don't appear to think much of you, either." He reached out and patted the stiffly bristled hair on the dog's head. "Easy, Fluffy."

"Fluffy?" Tanner stared at the dog, who snarled back. "His name is Fluffy? That's plumb ridiculous."

Kate named him, I didn't."

"No wonder he bites."

"Mark, is that you?" Kate appeared in her doorway. "There's my sweetiekins." She knelt and held out her arms. "Come here, Fluffy."

The big dog yanked the rope free of Mark's hand and galloped forward, slathered Kate with wet kisses, then threw himself at her feet.

"Good baby," she crooned.

Tongue lolling, tale wagging, the beast looked like a giant puppy—until Tanner took a step toward Kate. Then the dog had all the affability of an outraged lion.

"Call him off, Kate," Tanner warned.

"Maybe he thinks *you* need to be taught a lesson," she suggested, her eyes narrowing.

Lips curled, teeth bared, the dog trembled in anticipation.

"You've made your point," Tanner said with a calmness he certainly didn't feel.

"Good." She stood up and dusted her hands together. "And I didn't even have to manhandle you."

"Manhandle?" Like a feisty banty rooster, Mark stepped between them. "Tanner, what's she talking about?"

"Don't push it, boy. You've got some explaining of your own to do."

Uncertainty showed in Mark's eyes, but he didn't back down.

"Don't pay him any attention, Mark. You come on inside and have a piece of pie. You, too, Fluffy. Jeanne brought

Fluffykins a great big bone." She ushered Mark and her pet inside. She glanced at Tanner, then shut the door.

Tanner didn't care that he wasn't invited in. He figured he'd had enough temptation for one day. He was also grateful to have escaped in one piece.

He'd thought Kate might need a gun; now he knew better. She had *Fluffy*. And Mark. And probably the rest of his brothers, and Madame Jeanne, and no telling who-all else. He pitied any interloper who dared come near her. He'd be lucky to escape with his life.

Still, Tanner couldn't help but wish that she was bigger. He almost wished she had buck teeth or some sort of deformity. A woman alone, especially one who looked like Kate, even in a halfway civilized town like Jacksonville, was a walking invitation to trouble. Still, there wasn't much he could do about it. She had made that clear. After the way he'd behaved today, he'd be lucky to get within shouting distance.

He had thought to teach her a lesson, but it had backfired on him. He stared at the shack. He could still feel the heat, the warmth of her breasts pressed against his chest. Her hair, like fine silk, tangled in his fingers. And the way she'd smelled . . . She'd set his head reeling. He hadn't intended to take her to bed, but that's exactly what would have happened if he hadn't come to his senses.

He closed his eyes, his body throbbing with frustrated lust. Maybe he should have. From the way she kissed him back, maybe that's what she needed, too.

And afterward . . . He sighed, envisioning himself and Kate all warm with loving and cozy in the narrow bed.

Someone else appeared in the picture, and his eyes sprang open.

The sheriff, peering at him over the barrel of a shotgun.

And behind the sheriff, Mark glowered and hefted a chunk of stove wood.

And the preacher, license in hand, and the rest of the town, waiting just outside the door.

Along with Fluffy—and a whole pack of snarling dogs.

Sweat popped out on his forehead. It had been close. A

few minutes longer and it would have been all over but the singing. A few more minutes and he would have been either lynched or hitched.

A feeling of relief shook him right down to his boots. Then, remembering how warm and soft she was and how perfectly she fit in his arms, he decided it would almost be worth it.

Worth it? He swallowed. Amazed that he could even think such a thing, he turned on his heel and hurried toward his horse.

"Tanner? Hey, Tanner, wait up," a gruff voice demanded.

Expecting to see the sheriff, he turned and was almost relieved to see the owner of the Lucky Strike mine striding toward him. "Howdy, Tom."

"I'm surprised to see you in town, on a prime sunny workday and all. Have you finished cutting my timber yet?"

"No, but in another couple of days, I should have the first load ready for you."

"I have to have water to operate my hydraulic hoses. I need those logs, Tanner. That flume has to be in place by snow melt in the spring." Thomas Fuller's scowl deepened. "If you don't think you can get the job done, Sim Williams up on Stewart Creek has enough trees cut right now to pert' near build the flume."

"You have a contract with me," Tanner reminded him. "I'll meet the deadline. If I don't, according to that contract, I'll forfeit everything I've cut."

"I'm glad to see you remember. I won't abide any excuses, Tanner. I've got to have those trees." With that, the miner crossed the street and went into the bank.

With Tom's warning ringing in his ears, Tanner shot one more look toward the pie shop, then he mounted his horse and rode out of town. She'd said she didn't need his help. He hoped she was right. Until he had that timber contract finished, Kate would have to fend for herself.

"Here's the list. With the scarcity of pretty, single women, we sure don't lack for takers. I told the fellers we would look them over and give our approval. I also threatened them with Tanner and the dog if they didn't follow the rules." Mark placed the paper on the tabletop, and pointed to a long line of names.

"What if we don't like them?" Matt asked.

"Then we cross them off." Luke wet the end of the pencil and drew a line through one name.

"What'd you do that for?" Mark asked, grabbing up the paper. "He's as rich as Cornelius Beekman."

"Nobody's got that much money," Matt said, snatching it back. "Besides, Luke's right, he's too old. We're trying to find Kate a husband, not a grandpa." He ran a finger down the list. "Here's another one. He don't even have any teeth."

"But he seemed nice," Luke said. "I think we ought to let Kate decide."

"Decide what?" Tanner asked, coming through the doorway.

"Nothing." Mark yanked up a piece of paper from the table and stuffed it in his pocket.

Tanner looked from one guilty face to the next. "You aren't sending for any more brides, are you?"

"No, sir," Matt assured him, instantly joining a stampede for the door.

"I think I'll fill that wood box."

"I've got to milk the cow."

"I'm gonna check on the eggs."

Something is going on. Tanner blocked their exit. He put his hands on his hips and stared at them through narrowed eyes. "What are you all up to? And what was that about Kate deciding?"

"We wanted to give her some flower seeds," Mark said, giving him a sickly smile. "Luke thought we ought to let her decide what kind she'd like."

"Uh-huh." *And I'm a blue-eyed yeller dog.* Tanner glanced at John, who was staring at Mark in open-mouthed admiration. That look alone told him it was a flat-out lie. "You boys getting pretty cozy with Kate?"

"She's nice. And be-ootiful," John declared.

"That's quite a mouthful for such a little boy," Tanner teased, ruffling the youngster's hair.

"I'm not so little." The child stiffened with indignation. "I'll be old enough to get married before you know it."

"Thinking of getting hitched, are you?" Tanner studied him a moment. The child wasn't stuttering. He was . . . singing?

"If Kate would wait till I get big, I'd marry her," John sang.

"And what about that dog of hers? He'd eat you for supper."

"Who, Fluffy? He likes me. He lets me ride on his back," John boasted.

"Glad that varmint's got some use." Tanner turned toward the kitchen and rubbed his stomach. "Talking of eating, I'm hungry. What's for supper?"

"Potatoes, corn bread . . ." Matt began.

"And beans," Luke finished.

"Beans! Aww, no." Mark buried his head in his hands.

"Then let's eat." They all took their places and Tanner gave the blessing. No more was said about Kate, or the flower seeds. But when he happened to meet one of his brother's eyes, they quickly looked away. They didn't have any more money—that should have reassured him. It didn't. Especially when he knew that whatever they were up to had to do with Kate.

Mark looked from one to the other of the miners, cowboys and other assorted would-be suitors that had gathered in the clearing just outside of town. "All right, you boys draw straws to see who goes first. The shortest one wins, the next shortest goes second—and so on. If Kate doesn't cotton to you right off, then you drop out of the race. Agreed?"

Nodding, the men stepped forward, one at a time, each drawing a straw from a bucket of mud.

"I got a little bitty one," a skinny miner shouted, holding up an inch-long piece of yellow grass.

"Mine looks like a damn fir tree," a cowboy complained. "It's so long, I won't get to meet her before spring."

"That'll be way too late. She'll be married to me and carrying my babe by then," a lumberjack, a burly man in denims and a red-checked shirt, boasted. He held up a short straw.

"Now, hold on!" Matt warned, raising up a hand. "You're drawing for the *privilege* of *courting* Kate, not Kate herself, so don't get in such an all-fired hurry. She might not like any of you."

"What'll you do then?" the lumberjack asked.

"We'll pick a fresh batch for her to look over next spring."

"Don't forget," Mark warned, "Kate's a lady. Anybody trying anything funny will answer to Tanner."

So far, Tanner didn't know anything about it, and they'd all likely get their hides skinned if he found out. But Mark figured it was worth the risk, as his brother's size and reputation would scare the men into line, if nothing else did.

"Tanner shouldn't have any say one way or the other now. He's already had his chance." A miner with muttonchop whiskers spat a stream of tobacco, splattering a clump of Oregon grape bushes.

"She did come out here to marry him," Luke said.

"Then why didn't he marry her?"

"He's still undecided," Mark lied. "We figured we'd give you boys a chance while he's making up his mind."

"Undecided? I never heard tell of such a thing," a miner named Chauncey declared. "Poor little gal deserves better than that. Why, I'd treat her like a queen."

Mark gave the little miner an encouraging smile. Chauncey had just struck a rich gold vein; he could indeed treat Kate like royalty. If she married the miner, it would serve Tanner right.

"Has everybody got their days straight?" Matt waited until each man had marked his calendar. "Okay." He peered down at the scribbles. "Looks like Joe Bell is courting Kate tonight. Good luck, Joe."

"Thankee, son. I'll do my damnedest." His ruddy face beaming, the miner gave him a hopeful smile.

The men filed out of the grove of trees and headed back for town.

"We'd better hit the road, too, or Tanner will beat us home."

"Hold on, Mark. We can't all go," Matt said. "Somebody has to stay here and see how things go tonight."

Mark shook his head. "Matt, you can't stay. Somebody has to fix supper."

"Somebody else has to feed the stock and get the wood box filled—like you, Mark," Matt replied. "Besides, you've been in town every day this week."

"I'm too little," John said. "And I'm scared to go home after dark."

All eyes turned to Luke. It looked like he was elected whether he liked it or not. "What are you going to do if Tanner asks about me? I don't want to get into trouble, either."

They thought on it a minute.

"I know," Mark said with a grin. "We can tell Tanner you ate too many beans and are spending the night in the privy."

"What if he checks?" Luke asked.

Mark snickered. "Not likely."

"Maybe I could have supper with Kate," Luke said.

"No," Matt said quickly. "Don't even let her see you. Maybe Madame Jeanne would give you something. You don't want to spoil Kate's big evening."

"What am I supposed to do, anyhow?"

"Hide in that toolshed and watch her house," Matt said. "If the lights go off, or she yells, come a-runnin'."

"And if she don't?"

"You still watch and wait. After her suitor leaves, then you can come home."

"I don't know." Frowning, Luke stared at the mountains. "Those hills are awful wild at night. What if I run into a bear or a panther?"

"I'll leave you my rifle," Matt said.

"He won't need it," Mark said. "You eat so many beans nothing would want to eat you."

Luke shot Mark a sour look.

"You want me to come back in and watch?" Matt asked wearily.

"No. Just get on home before Tanner comes lookin'," Luke said. "He'd be twice as bad as anything I'd run into in the woods."

"See you tomorrow. And don't go to sleep."

"Get out of here." Luke watched his brothers head up the trail. The sun hung low in the sky; soon it would disappear behind the mountains. And when it did, no place seemed quite as black, or as scary. At least there would be a full moon tonight. He grinned. He'd see to it that Mark's turn at watch would come when it was pitch dark.

8

DESPITE HIS INTENTION to stay far away from Jacksonville and Kate, a lack of saw oil made it necessary for Tanner to make the trip into town. He had arrived shortly after the sun had risen only to find the mercantile still closed. Since he couldn't get the oil until they opened, he figured he'd stop in at the doctor's office, hoping the physician would have the answer to an illness that had been bothering the boys of late.

Dr. Frederick Thomas, who was also an early riser, invited Tanner in and poured him a cup of coffee. "I never get sick myself. Guess I've been exposed to so many germs I've gotten immune to them."

After taking a swallow of the coffee, Tanner didn't think immunity had anything to do with it. Even the strongest germ couldn't have survived a cup of Fred's brew. Not wanting to appear impolite, Tanner managed to finish his cup, hoping it didn't do any permanent damage to his innards.

"Ready for more?" The doctor hoisted the pot.

"No, thanks." He covered the cup with his hand. "One's plenty. Now about the boys . . ." He described his brothers' various complaints.

Across the desk, the silver-headed man nodded and made

notations on a pad he had in front of him. "All of them, you said?"

"Everybody except me and John. Whatever it is doesn't seem to affect us. We all eat the same things, the same stuff we've eaten all of our lives, so I don't think it could be that. We all drink from the same well." Tanner shook his head. "I tell you, Fred, it's got me stumped."

"When did this start?"

"About two weeks ago. one or the other of them has been sick ever since."

"Wonder if it could be something they are getting here in town?" the doctor said thoughtfully.

"In town?" Tanner straightened in his chair.

"Yeah. Ever since that courting business started, Jacksonville has been busier than a beehive in June."

"Courting business?"

"Surely you know about that?" Fred Thomas peered over gold-rimmed spectacles. "You don't." The doctor chuckled, his blue eyes dancing with merriment.

"No," Tanner said. "But I've got the feeling I'm about to find out."

"Why, those brothers of yours are running a regular matchmaking service. But so far, Kate hasn't favored any one man over the others."

"Kate?" Feeling the conversation getting away from him, Tanner gripped the arms of his chair and leaned forward. "What in tarnation are you talking about?"

Doc Thomas grinned. "The boys have been interviewing prospective husbands for Kate—she doesn't know it, of course. The whole town's been keeping it a secret, her being such a refined lady and all. Yes sir, a big, delicious secret. Well, anyway, after the boys weeded out the undesirables, the men left on the list drew straws. The shortest straw got to court her first. The men each get three chances, but if she doesn't like them right off, they are out of the running."

"The boys are doing this?" he croaked out. He knew they had been up to something that day when he'd come in and found them talking, but after he'd confronted them he figured they had thought better of the idea.

He should have known different.

Now that he thought back, he realized that lately there had been no fights, no arguments. The home place had been real peaceful.

Too peaceful. And he'd been worried they had something really serious wrong with them. Ha!

"I think I'm beginning to see the light. They've been faking it all along."

"I thought that might be the case." The doctor chuckled. "Your brothers have seemed perfectly healthy every time I've seen them. Although, with the hours they've been keeping, they can't be getting too much sleep. One or the other of them stays in town at night, watching Kate's house from that toolshed across the street. He remains there until whoever it is that's courting Kate that evening leaves. Then, after she retires for the night, the boy goes home. It's not bad here in the valley, but the nights must be freezing up on that mountain."

And that's not all, Tanner thought, picturing any of his brothers traveling that mountain trail after dark, alone. No telling what they might run into, and not only the four-legged variety. There had been a murder up Stewart Creek just last week. His brothers had guts, he had to give them that. But they sure didn't have any brains.

"You said Kate doesn't know about this?"

"No. She would have been courted anyway, by all the rutting bucks we've got loose in the county. But at least this way, it's happening in an orderly fashion, with someone looking out for her best interests."

"Her best interests?" He'd tried to look after her best interests and it had almost got him into more trouble than he could handle. "Why can't she stay home and cook, or whatever it is she's doing, then go to bed at night like a decent woman ought to?" Too agitated to sit, Tanner got up and paced the floor. "I don't like it. I don't like it one bit."

"Kate's a beautiful young woman. You can't expect her to stay unmarried just because you don't like it." Doc grinned. "Sounds to me like you might be jealous."

"Jealous? Me? Ha!" But as he envisioned some man all

duded up, knocking at her door, bringing her gewgaws, being invited in, maybe kissing her, holding her, getting lost in that flower scent of hers . . . and no telling what else . . . he clenched his fists, wanting to punch somebody in the nose.

"I'm not jealous," he repeated. "It's the boys' part in this I don't like."

"Uh-huh." The doctor filled Tanner's cup again.

"Why, I remember the time I had the boys watch over a cow in labor. I went to the barn the next morning and found every one of them sound asleep. Old Pet had birthed twin calves during the night, and they didn't even know it." Tanner ran a hand through his hair. "If they couldn't watch over a cow, how can they be expected to watch over a woman—especially one as tempting as Kate?" He picked up and downed the coffee in one gulp.

"You appear to know more about that than I do." The physician pointed a finger toward him. "You could do the watching."

"Me?" That would be like putting the fox in with the chickens. "Hell, I don't have time for this foolishness." Nevertheless, he knew he had to take care of it. It was his responsibility.

Tanner took his hat from the rack and jammed it on his head. "Nobody will be doing any more watching. And you don't need to worry about the boys' health, because I intend to put a stop to this nonsense right now."

"Good luck."

The doctor's laughter ringing in his ears, Tanner left the office and stalked down the street. As if they had a mind of their own, his feet automatically headed for the pie shop. He didn't try to stop them.

Maybe he should look in on Kate. No telling what might have happened during one of them courting sessions. See for himself if she was all right. His steps slowed. She was probably still mad at him, so he doubted if he'd be welcome for a visit.

Maybe he could buy a pie. At least that would get him in the door. He checked his pockets. Twenty-five cents.

Wonder if she'd sell me a piece of pie? He was still pondering his lack of finances, when a commotion down the street caught his attention. Curious, he stopped to watch.

"You get out of my flower garden," a hefty woman he recognized shouted.

Agatha Grimes waddled down her front steps and waved a broom at a tall, skinny cowboy, who was stretched out over her picket fence.

"Just one little rose?" the man pleaded.

"One rose?" Agatha brandished her weapon. "Not one leaf. I pampered those flowers all year. The frost got most of them. The rest of them are ending up at Kate Deveraux's house."

"I'll pay you for it." The man reached into his vest pocket.

"How much?" She eyed him skeptically. "Roses don't come cheap."

"I'll give you a dollar—for a pretty one."

The woman snatched up the coin. "All right. But I'll do the pluckin'."

One of Kate's suitors, no doubt. Tanner scowled and moved on down the street. A dollar for one flower. He didn't even have four bits for a pie.

When he reached Kate's, she was doing a booming business. Not only did she have customers, the line ran out into the street. Tanner hurried to beat another man also heading in that direction. "She must be a good cook," he said to the man ahead of him.

"She's getting better. At least they're eatable now. It ain't the cookin' as much as the cook," he confided. "It's worth a dollar just to see her smile."

"Her pies cost a dollar?" That sure let him out.

"Naw. Fifty cents, but most men buy at least two. They get to stay longer that way."

"Sorry, boys," a feminine voice called out. "That's all for today, but I'll have a fresh batch in the morning. Tomorrow's choices will be pumpkin and dried apple. Thank you for coming." She smiled sweetly, hung out a Closed sign and shut the door.

"Dadblame it. And I went and got a haircut and every-thing."

Murmurs of disappointment rose from the gathering, then the group broke up and the men went on their way.

Tanner fingered his own hair. Since he couldn't buy a piece of pie, he'd get a haircut with his two bits. He went back to Main Street and entered a nook with a red and white striped barber pole hanging over its entrance. Much to his surprise, he had to wait there, too. Finally his turn came, and he took a seat in the chair. "Something going on in town, Jake?"

"No more than usual," the barber said, tying a long length of cloth around Tanner's neck. He picked up his scissors and began whacking at a shaggy length of hair. "You mean having to wait?" The fat man smiled. "That's due to Miss Kate. I guess I ought to thank you, being as you're the one that brought her here. I hope she stays unattached for a while. All the courtin' fellers are getting haircuts, plus the ones that ain't even on the list. I've never cut so many heads of hair or shaved so many faces since I've been in the business. Heck, the way things are going, I might get rich."

Tanner scowled. "I suppose you're one of her suitors."

"Nope. My gal Bessie isn't as pretty, but she's a better cook. I like my vittles, you know." Jake patted his over-stuffed middle.

"I'd never have guessed," Tanner said wryly. "Better give me a shave while you're at it."

A while later, Jake removed the bib from around Tanner's neck and slapped a measure of bay rum between his hands and applied it to Tanner's cheeks. "There, all done. The cologne is on the house. I figure I owe you that."

"Thanks, Jake." Tanner paid the barber and started for the door.

"Are you going to give her away?" Jake asked.

"What?"

"Are you going to give Kate away when she picks a husband?"

"Has she picked one yet?" Tanner asked grumpily.

"Not that I know of, but I think she likes one or two."

"She does?" He hooked his thumbs in his belt loops. "Who?"

"Clint Beecher. He's the foreman of the Circle C. And then there's Hank Jordon; he owns the Tin Peak mine. And—"

"Since she hasn't settled on one, I don't need to worry about it, do I?"

"Guess not. You don't need to get mad at me, I'm not courtin' her."

Tanner shoved his hat on his head and left, slamming the door behind him. He wasn't courting her either, but apparently he was the only man in the territory who wasn't.

Next he went to the mercantile and purchased his saw oil, on credit. He still had time enough to get in a few hours' work if he left right now.

On the other hand, he still hadn't seen Kate, or any of the boys. How could he go home and leave this mess unsettled? He couldn't.

He strolled around town, passing the time of day with everybody of speaking acquaintance, talking with more people in one day than he ordinarily spoke to in a year. And even though he'd tried to avoid it, the subject of every conversation had been Kate.

She'd stayed cooped up in her house all day. He knew she hadn't gone anywhere because he'd been watching. Not on purpose, of course. It seemed like every time he went anywhere, his feet headed in that direction.

She knew he was in town. He'd caught her peeking at him from her front window. She didn't wave, or smile. She merely looked at him and dropped the curtain.

Dang it. He at least wanted to see her, talk to her a minute, make sure she was all right. Then, after he'd put his mind at ease, he'd head for home.

He glanced at the crimson sky. Sunset already. He hadn't seen any of the boys yet. Maybe they had already given up on the job. Maybe none of them were coming. If that was the case, then who'd watch over Kate?

The later it got, the more agitated Tanner felt. He still hadn't gathered up enough nerve to knock on her door. If that courting feller showed up, Tanner would never get the chance—unless he beat him to it. It was now or never, Tanner decided. Besides, it would be a shame to have gotten all slicked up for nothing.

He started toward Kate's, then his steps slowed. That other man would probably have flowers, or candy, or some other trinket. His own empty pockets wouldn't support a healthy flea.

Flowers.

He wheeled, making his way back to the yard he'd seen earlier that morning. He'd never been a thief, and looked down on anybody that was. He'd also never been quite so desperate.

It was full dark now; he might be able to get away with it. He looked both ways down the street. Nary a soul in sight. The gate was wired shut, but the fence wasn't too high. He vaulted over the row of pickets.

Two steps later, he discovered his feet had gotten tangled in something on the ground. He reached down and found his boot wrapped in a maze of wire and string. He yanked and set off a jangle of cowbells. He stepped the other way. Tin cans clattered. Booby-trapped. No telling what he'd step into next. He hoped it wouldn't be a bear trap.

Too late to hide the fact he was here. He'd better get what he'd come after and get out. "Where is that danged bush?" He groped in the darkness—and latched onto a clump of thorns. "Oww!"

"Clint Beecher, is that you again?" Inside the house, a lamp was lit. It moved toward the doorway.

He couldn't get caught like this. He'd never live it down. No time to pick and choose. He knelt, grabbed the base of the bush and yanked.

The plant whooshed from the ground, throwing dirt in every direction.

Tanner landed on his backside, the thorny bush on his chest.

"I've taken all I intend to," Agatha yelled. "I'm gonna fill your thieving hide with a load of rock salt. See how you like that."

He wouldn't. Tanner grabbed the bush and leapt over the fence.

A shotgun belched fire.

And pellets splattered across his backside.

His legs and bottom stinging like he'd sat on a nest of bees, Tanner clutched the bush to his chest and kept on running. When he figured he was out of range, he sprinted into a dark alley and stopped to catch his breath.

Better get rid of the evidence. He felt the bush. No roses. Not even a bud. But the blasted thing had more stickers than a cactus. He eased into a ray of light shining down from an upstairs window. "Aww, hell." No wonder it didn't have any roses. He'd stolen a dadblamed quince bush. He tossed it aside in disgust. The motion made him gasp with pain.

Agatha had nailed him good. A trail of warmth trickled down his leg. Blood.

He couldn't go to Kate's. He couldn't even sit his horse to go home. He couldn't get the salt pellets out without help. And he sure wasn't about to tell the boys what he'd been up to. The question was, what was he going to do?

Only one thing he could do. A few minutes later he knocked on the doctor's back door.

The bespectacled man peered out, then opened the door and motioned him inside. "Didn't think I'd see you again so soon, Tanner. What's wrong now? The boys sick again?"

"No. But I kind of have a little problem." His face hot with embarrassment, Tanner pointed to his backside. "Don't ask. Just get the blasted rock salt out."

A while later, much relieved, Tanner held out his hand. "Thanks is all I can give you until later."

The doctor grinned. "Don't worry about it." He pointed to Tanner's hole-dotted britches. "Looks like you've been attacked by a swarm of moths. I think I've got a pair of pants that might fit, if you're interested. They belonged to that gambler fellow who died last month. He won't be needing them anymore."

"I'd be much obliged, Doc."

Pants changed, Tanner headed out the door. "I don't suppose you've got any roses."

"So that's what happened." The physician gave him a broad grin. "I might. I do have one bush by the buggy shed. Take this lantern. It's hard to find even in the daytime. If there is a rose left in town, it will be on that bush."

Three yellow roses clutched in his hand, resplendent in his inherited striped britches and smelling of disinfectant and cologne, Tanner made his way to Kate's door, hoping one of her suitors hadn't beat him to it.

He knocked, then peered through the window. Except for Fluffy, Kate was alone.

She opened the door, and the smile left her face. "Tanner. What are you doing here?"

"Kate, could I talk to you for a minute? Please?"

She looked at him, hesitated, then she sighed. "All right—but only for a minute." She turned to the dog, who stood directly behind her. "Lay down, boy. He's a friend."

Friend. At least she hadn't sicced the dog on him. Nevertheless he couldn't help but wonder how many other 'friends' the dog had allowed to enter.

The animal gave him the onceover, then flopped down beside the stove and promptly went to sleep.

"I brought you these." Feeling as awkward as a school-boy, Tanner snatched off his hat and shoved the roses into her hand. Then he glanced around the room. There wasn't a flower in sight.

"Oh, dear. Not more." She eyed the blooms dubiously.

"Don't you like roses?"

"I like them fine—outside." She sneezed. "I'm allergic." She sneezed again.

"Figures." Tanner took them from her and tossed them out the door. "I just didn't want to come empty-handed."

She smiled. "I thought you might be avoiding me."

He followed her to a settee and waited until she was seated. "Whatever gave you that idea?" He took a seat beside her.

"You haven't been to see me—not since that day you . . ." She flushed crimson.

"Oh, that." He cursed the heat that rose in his face. "I guess I was too ashamed."

"Ashamed?"

"For the way I behaved and all."

She reached out and touched his head. "You got a haircut."

"And a shave." He drew her knuckles down his cheek.

"And new pants. You look quite elegant." When he released her fingers, she folded her hands in her lap. "Would you like a piece of apple pie?"

"That would be nice, but I thought you'd sold them all."

"I made more." She looked at him curiously. "How did you know I sold all my pies?"

"I—uh, heard it around town."

"Oh."

"Have you seen the boys lately?" he asked, mostly to keep from sitting there like a stump.

"They drop by from time to time. All of them except John. How is he?" She crossed the room to the kitchen, then returned with a slice of pie and a fork.

"Growing like a weed," Tanner said, taking a bite. "He doesn't stutter anymore. I guess we owe you thanks for that."

"He's very sweet." She gazed up at him, her expression wistful. "Would you bring him by sometime?"

"Sure. He'd like that." Tanner decided he'd like it, too: it would give him another excuse to visit. And he wouldn't have to buy a pie. He chewed, swallowed, then swallowed again. Maybe he wouldn't even have to eat one.

"You're very lucky," she said softly.

"Me? Lucky?" Good thing she couldn't see his backside.

"You have a family. People who care about you, who love you." She sighed. "Very lucky indeed." She took his empty dish and set it on the cabinet.

"I never thought about it. Don't you have any family?"

"Only a cousin," she said, taking her seat again. "Everybody else died in the war. It gets very lonely."

"Doggone. I had no idea." He reached out and took her hand. It was small, fine-boned and delicate. His calloused fingers held it gently. Like a hummingbird in a crow's nest, he thought. "You've got lots of friends around town. Besides, we consider you family."

"You do?" She peeked through a fringe of ebony lashes. "I thought you didn't want to have anything to do with me."

"How could you think that?" He wanted to have too much to do with her. That was the problem.

"You ever expected me. You can't wait until I leave." Her eyes grew shiny, like pools of glimmering sapphires. A tear spilled onto her satiny cheek.

"Aww, honey. Don't cry." Not knowing what else to do, he drew her into his arms. His motion released a floodgate of tears. "There, there, it's all right," he said, awkwardly patting her on the back. Feeling more inadequate than he ever had in his whole life, he cupped her silky head against his chest and felt his shirt grow damp with her tears. She was so soft, she smelled so sweet. A fire deep within him sprang to life. He fought his lust, forcing himself to remember that it was comfort she was seeking, nothing more. He held her until her heart-wrenching sobs subsided to a series of small hiccups.

She pulled away and rubbed her eyes.

"Feeling better?"

She nodded. "I'm sorry. I hate people that cry. I don't know what came over me."

He tilted her head and wiped her face with a clean handkerchief he'd found in the pocket of his new pants. "Maybe you're tired."

"I have been working hard lately," she admitted. "And I've had a lot of company in the evening."

"Oh? Who?"

"Just fellows from around town. They seem lonely, too. I'd invite them in, and they would talk for a while, mostly about family they'd left behind. I write letters for some of them. I don't have the heart to turn them away."

"They should know a lady needs her sleep," he said when she muffled a yawn. "What time do you get up of a morning?"

"Five. Sometimes earlier. I do most of my baking then."

"What time do you go to bed?"

"Ten or so. Depends on whether I have company or not."

"That proves my point. You're not getting enough rest."

"If I had a husband and children, I'd keep those long hours."

"Yes, but you'd also have somebody to help you."

Husband and children. Maybe she was thinking about getting married. Of course she was. She'd come all the way out here to marry him, hadn't she?

He lifted a damp curl off her cheek. So soft. He threaded his fingers through her hair. Like rippling silk. He breathed in her special fragrance. He rubbed her back.

She let out a sigh and arched into his palm. "Oh, that feels good." She yawned again. "I seem to be more tired than I thought. Maybe I will make an early night of it." She gazed up at him. Even with her eyes red and swollen, she was beautiful. "Would you mind?"

"Mind?" He saw her glance toward the curtained alcove. "You want to go to bed." Not daring to dwell on that thought, Tanner got to his feet. "I'll be back as soon as I can—maybe next week—if that's all right?"

"Of course." She followed him to the doorway. "Maybe you could bring John, too?"

"I reckon." The last thing he needed was his little brother tagging along, but if that's what she wanted, he guessed he could put up with it. He tilted her head and looked into her eyes. "Good night, Kate. Sweet dreams." He bent and placed a gentle kiss on her lips, then before he yielded to his baser urges, he put on his hat and went out the door.

He waited until she had pulled the curtain. He glanced across the alley at the toolshed, then strode over and opened the door. Spying Luke curled up in the corner, he nudged him with his boot. "Wake up, boy. You're going home."

Luke yawned, stretched, then opened his eyes. "Tanner!" He scrambled to his feet.

"What are you doing in here?"

"I—uh, come in after some fl— sugar, then I got tired and thought I'd take a nap." Luke peered through the doorway. "Why, look at that, it's dark. I must have slept all afternoon."

"In a pig's eye." Tanner peered around him. "I don't see any sugar, and I know what you've been up to. Not that it did any good, seeing as how you went to sleep."

Luke sagged. "I didn't go to sleep until after I ran that other feller off."

"What other feller?"

"The one whose turn it was. You were already in there, and I figured you didn't need any more company."

"You figured that right. What did you tell him?"

"I said Kate was too tired to have visitors tonight, so he left. He'll get two turns later."

"No, he won't."

"He has to. That's the way it works," Luke argued.

"Well, it doesn't work that way anymore. From now on anybody wanting to see Kate will have to go through me." He raised his finger and thumped his chest.

"Now she'll really end up being an old maid," Luke grumbled.

Tanner frowned. "Let's go home." He led the way to his horse and mounted, gingerly lowering himself into the saddle. When Luke was seated behind him, he nudged the horse toward the mountain.

Old maid. The term certainly didn't apply to Kate. She was warm, vibrant, loving. But Kate said she was lonely. She wanted to see little John, which meant she liked being around children. She also needed someone to rub her back after a hard day's work. Someone to hold her when she cried.

Much as he hated to admit it, Kate needed a husband. Somebody that wasn't dirt poor like him. He let out a long sigh. The Blaines were responsible for her being here. As head of the family, it was up to him to take care of her. He couldn't bring her to the mountain—or marry her. She deserved a better life than he could give her. A life that had already killed a stronger woman than Kathleen Deveraux: his stepmother, Maggie.

That left only one alternative.

He had to find Kate a husband.

9

"*I* HAVEN'T SEEN you around much lately, Chauncey." Kate carefully wrapped the dried peach pie and handed it over the counter.

The miner's usually amiable face wrinkled into a scowl. "Yeah. Well, it ain't because I wouldn't like to be, Miss Kate. Truth is, I'm not on the list no more. Things has changed since we have to go through Tanner."

"Go through Tanner? Tanner Blaine?"

"Yeah. He's plumb persnickety about who gets to court you." Chauncey slapped a hand over his mouth. He peered over at her.

Perplexed by the man's words, and actions, Kate started to ask him to explain—if he would. But taking note of the guilty expression on his face, she doubted if he would say a word. Maybe there was a better way. She smiled. "Since I don't seem to have any customers at the moment, how would you like to have a cup of tea with me? I might even have an extra piece of pie."

"I'd be plumb delighted."

A whole pie and pot of tea later, Kate knew all she needed to know. She shoved her cup aside and rose from the table. "And just where is Mr. Blaine holding these 'interviews'?"

"In Madame Jeanne's parlor, twice a week from three o'clock 'til five."

She glanced at the wall clock. Three-thirty. "Is he there today?"

"I imagine so," the miner said, his Adam's apple bobbing. "I saw quite a lot of fellers headed in that direction."

"Thank you, Chauncey. I hate to rush you, but it seems I have some business to take care of."

The miner put down his cup, and she took his arm and walked him toward the door. "By the way, tomorrow's pie is on the house."

"I'm real partial to dried apple with raisins," he said hopefully.

"Then that's what it shall be." After the man left, she locked the door, then went to change her dress. "Interviewing prospective husbands. For me!" She jerked a freshly ironed white blouse and a navy linen skirt from her closet and put them on. "Of all the nerve. As if I couldn't pick my own husband—if I wanted one. Which I don't. Especially one picked out by Tanner Blaine."

She yanked a brush through her hair to smooth out the tangles then twisted the mass into a knot. "He's gone too far this time." He didn't want her, yet he had the nerve to act as if she were his to pawn off onto somebody else. "I will not stand for it!" Feeling the need to vent her anger, she flung her brush across the room, where it bounced off the opposite wall.

The dog whined and tried to squirrel his huge body under the bed. The only thing he succeeded in hiding was his head.

Ashamed of her outburst, Kate knelt and patted his rump. "Fluffy, it's all right. Poor doggy. I'm not mad at you, sweetiekins."

His tail thumped the floor and a nose appeared, then large brown eyes peered at her from the bottom edge of the coverlet.

"Want a biscuit? Come on, puppy." She led the way to the warming oven and retrieved a biscuit left over from breakfast. After feeding it to her pet, she went out and shut the door. She didn't bother to lock it. Nobody in their right mind would enter her home with the dog there.

"Maybe I should have brought him with me. I could have

sicced him on Tanner." Right now, she'd enjoy watching the aggravating Mr. Blaine get his leg chewed off.

Her skirts swishing, she strode down the boardwalk. The faster she walked, the madder she got. By the time she reached the boardinghouse, she was in a white-hot fury.

She entered without knocking, then paused in the vestibule to catch her breath.

"Next," a deep voice called from inside the parlor.

Next? She shoved the parlor door open, then closed it behind her.

"Kate?" Tanner scooted his chair back from the desk. "Uh, what are you doing here?" Glancing at the doorway, he ran a finger around the inside of his collar and gave her a sickly grin.

"Why, whatever do you mean? I came to visit Madame Jeanne." She removed her gloves one finger at a time, then placed her palms on the desk. She leaned toward him. "Is there some reason I shouldn't be here?"

"Not at all. Jeanne's upstairs." He pointed toward the ceiling.

"Why are you here?" she asked, making no move to leave. "I thought you had timber to cut."

He didn't answer; instead he shot another look toward the doorway.

"Expecting company?" She took off her cloak.

"Uh . . . no. Not exactly." He came around the desk. "Have a seat. No, not there." He pulled her out of a chair facing the door and plopped her down in another. "This one is better. You can look out the window."

"Maybe I don't want to look out the window." She got out of the chair and followed him back to the desk, effectively blocking any attempt he might have made to escape. "Maybe I'd rather look at you." She placed her palm against his chest and backed him against the wall. He looked jumpy as an old maid on her first date. And she hadn't even started.

"Hmmm." She studied him a minute, then slowly walked around him. Stopping directly in front of him, she thoughtfully trailed her finger down his forehead, his nose and across his lips.

"What are you doing?" he asked warily.

She ran her other hand up his chest—and undid the top button of his shirt. Then watching his eyes widen, she undid the second button. Then the third.

He blinked. "Kate!" He grasped his shirtfront, trying to hold it together.

"Stand still." She slapped his fists aside, then slid her hands in next to his bare chest. His heart pounded like a trip-hammer against her palm. She nodded—and pulled out his shirttail.

He sucked in a breath. "Miss Deveraux?"

"No scars, that I can see—except this itsy-bitsy one right here." She touched a spot to the right of his nipple. "Oh, and one right here." She put the tip of her finger against the base of his neck. "And this one on your chin."

"A wood chip hit me."

"Poor baby." She stood on tiptoe, touched it with her lips, then traced the scar with her tongue.

"Kate," he breathed.

She brushed her lips against his and felt him tremble. She backed away, eyeing him speculatively. "Kisses okay. Nice lips, good teeth." She pointed to the open notepad on the desk. "You might want to take notes."

"Notes?" A bewildered expression on his face, he stared at the pencil she'd shoved into his hand.

"Uh-huh." She stepped close, lifted his shirttail, then moved her hands over his back, in a slow examining motion. "Back seems all right. No discernable lumps or knots."

"Hmm." She squeezed his buttocks.

He jumped. And dropped the pencil.

"Firm, nicely muscled."

Mouth open, he gaped at her, but she noticed he didn't make any attempt to move. She stooped and ran a hand down the outside of his leg, paused on his thigh, then continued past his knee and on down to his calf. "Seems sound enough, but you never can tell. You might be hip-shot or something. Why don't you turn around? I can't really inspect you properly from this angle."

He shut his mouth. "Inspect me?" He shoved her hands away, and jerked her to her feet. He released her at arms' length. "You want to tell me what you think you're doing?"

"That's the way my father used to buy horses. I figured a husband would be no different." She tilted her head and shot him a sideways glance. "But, I forgot, you're not one of the contenders—are you?"

She pointed toward the stack of papers on the desk, then tapped a finger against her teeth. "You might want to make him run a spell. I wouldn't want the kind that gets winded too easily." She raised her lashes and stared him in the eyes. "I would like a man with lots of endurance." She gave him a suggestive smile. "If you know what I mean."

He actually blushed. "Kathleen Amanda Deveraux! Why, I—I . . ."

"What's the matter, Tanner? Cat got your tongue?" She stepped toward him. "What kind of criteria are you using, if I might ask? Maybe I could suggest a thing or two." She ran a fingertip from the fiercely pounding pulse at his throat, all the way to his navel, moving slowly, seductively, making small lazy circles as she went. "Like, is he ticklish?"

He quivered like an unbroken colt. "Stop that!"

"You haven't answered my question."

His eyes appeared glazed, desperate. "What question?"

She smiled and moistened her lips with her tongue.

He groaned and closed his eyes.

"I'm waiting."

"I don't know. I can't remember the question. Oh, hell." He reached for her—pulled her against his chest.

She looped one arm around his neck and pulled his mouth down to meet her own.

"Kate. Oh, Kate."

Using her other hand, she threaded her fingers through his chest hair, tracing his ribs from the top to the bottom.

He moaned and pulled her against him.

Like that, do you?

He was breathing like a horse at the end of a grueling race.

Wonder how you'll like this? She clamped her teeth shut.

"Yeow!" He jerked his head back. "You bit me!" He touched his lip and stared at her. "What did you do that for?"

"Maybe you'd rather I did this?" She brought her heel down on his foot.

"Billy-be-damned! I think you broke my toe." He grabbed his foot and stomped in circles. "What's wrong with you, woman?"

The door crashed open. Three men burst into the room. "Tanner? Is one of us next? What hap——" Then they noticed her. "Miss Kate?"

She lifted her hand and wiggled her fingers in a little wave. "Hello, boys."

"Get out!" Tanner bellowed, pointing to the hallway.

"Looks like we came at a bad time, men."

"Sorry, Tanner. We'll let you get back to whatever it was you were doing."

The last man eyed Tanner's open shirt, then backed out and closed the door. "That looked like blood on his lip. Suppose she bit 'im?"

"He didn't look like he was complainin' none."

"Would you?"

"A little old love bite from a pretty woman like that? Hell no!" The voices faded then disappeared down the hall.

"Love bite?" He rubbed his lip, and looked at her. "Was . . ."

Her eyes narrowed. "Not in your wildest dreams. Now let's get back to business." She bent over the desk and picked up the stack of papers. "He's too short." She threw it in the trash. "Too tall." She thumbed through them. "Bad tempered." She shook her head. "Rich, but doesn't bathe." One after another she discarded, then sorting through the others, she sighed. "These won't do at all." Ripping the papers crosswise, she tossed them into the wastebasket. "I wouldn't marry any of them." She crossed her arms and looked at him. "Guess you'd better start over."

"How did you find out? What polecat told?"

"One of your rejects—a very nice man, I might add." She trembled with rage. "How could you do such a thing?"

He held up his hands and gave her a silly grin. It only served to infuriate her more.

"I have never been so humiliated in my life. If I wanted a husband don't you think I could get one on my own?" She whirled away and paced to the window. "Thanks to you, I must be the laughingstock of the whole town."

He eased out of the corner and stood in the center of the room, making sure she couldn't box him in again.

"Coward."

"Coward? You damn near bit my lip off. And all that other business? Unbuttoning my shirt and . . ." he waved a hand.

"Did you think I was trying to seduce you?"

He smiled and raised a brow.

Her mouth dropped open, and she slammed it shut. "You did. I can tell by the expression on your face. Of all the egotistical . . ." Outraged, she straightened and waved a finger under his nose. "You are the most impossible man I have ever met."

"Yeah, but you like me anyhow." He captured her hand and brought it to his mouth.

"Stop that!" She tried to pull it away, but he held her fast.

He kissed each fingertip and her palm, then ran his tongue over her pulse, taking tiny nibbles as he went. "Now it's my turn."

"Don't!"

"Don't?" He maneuvered her toward the desk, until she could retreat no further.

"What are you doing?"

"The same thing you did to me." He undid her top button.

"One more and I'll scream," she warned.

His dark eyes danced. "Go ahead."

"Hel—"

He swallowed the rest of her cry. His fingers traced the base of her throat, walking down to unfasten the buttons on her blouse. She gasped when he slid his fingers in next to her skin.

"Mmmmmmmm!" she cried, furiously, trying to twist away, but his lips held her fast.

"You wear too many clothes," he murmured when he allowed her to breathe. When her head cleared, she found she now lay on top of the desk, and he had her blouse unbuttoned to her navel.

Shocked, she stared up at him.

He gave her a lazy smile. "Let's see . . ." He nodded. "Scars?" He pulled the ribbon on her chemise.

"Let me up this instant," she hissed, pounding on his shoulders. She didn't dare scream now. She'd die of mortification if someone caught her like this.

"What's your hurry?" He caught her hands and bent his head. His hot breath, then his mouth, seared her flesh.

"Oh, my," she whispered. She couldn't move, couldn't breathe. Her heart pounded so furiously, she feared it would beat right through her body. Tears of humiliation spilled from her eyes.

Seeing them, Tanner froze, then abruptly released her. He pulled her upright and began fumbling at her clothes. "My God, Kate. I'm sorry."

"Sorry?" She slapped his hands away and yanked her blouse shut. "You're sorry all right. Sorriest human being it's ever been my misfortune to meet." Her hands were shaking too badly to redo the buttons, and she yanked at the fasteners in frustration.

"Here, let me." Despite her protests, he managed to redo her buttons, then tucked a loose strand of hair behind her ear. "There, that does it." He turned her to face a mirror that hung on the opposite end of the wall. "See?"

"Oh, good grief." Her lips were swollen, her hair stuck out every which way. Her clothes were wrinkled and her blouse had a large ink stain near the collar—and he'd skipped a button, making her whole top crooked. She couldn't have looked worse if she'd been drunk and dressed in the dark. She hurriedly undid and refastened her top, then tucked her blouse back into her skirt.

He gave her a pleased smile. "Good as new."

"Good as new?" She waved a fist under his nose. "Thanks to you I look like a harlot after a hard night."

"Now, darlin', don't get upset."

"I'm not your darlin', or anybody else's," she said between gritted teeth. "I'm me. Kate Deveraux. I'm my own person. I'll see who I please and do what I please. *And I don't need your help to find me a husband!*" Before she lowered herself to commit further violence, she snatched up her cloak and her reticule and headed for the door.

"I thought John and I might come visiting tomorrow night."

Eyes narrowed, she whirled. "John is welcome anytime. You, I never want to see again." She stepped through and slammed the door behind her.

"Howdy, Miss Kate."

She glared at the group of men gathered in the entry. "Don't you 'howdy' me. From now on the only time any of you will see me will be during business hours. Anyone coming around after dark will be greeted by my dog." She drew herself up primly and marched out the door.

That night, although several love-bitten swains strolled by and gazed longingly toward her window, not a one dared to stop. Tanner, watching from his seat in the toolshed, lifted her forgotten gloves to his swollen lip and remembered how good she felt in his arms. If she hadn't cried out his name, he'd be hunting up a preacher about now. Somehow that didn't sound so bad.

If he didn't have that mortgage hanging over his head; if he had more money; if he didn't have four younger brothers to support, then he'd marry her whether she wanted to or not and damn the consequences.

Judging by the way she kissed him, he didn't think she disliked him near as much as she tried to pretend. "Yeah, and if mules could fly, I'd be rich."

He waited until her lights went out, then he rose and stretched the kinks out of his muscles. As he stepped into the open, a layer of frost crunched under his boots. In the toolshed he hadn't noticed it had grown so cold. He eyed her house and thought of Kate snuggled up in a nice warm bed, and wondered what she would do if he tried to join her. He grinned, then ruefully rubbed his sore lip. He probably wouldn't live long enough to find out. After a moment of reflecting on that thought, he decided he wasn't about to go anywhere near her until she'd had a chance to get over her mad spell. He'd end up being fodder for that mutt.

His breath forming clouds of white mist, he shivered, then set out in search of his horse. A pale moon rising over the crest of the mountain showed the animal standing beneath a pine tree a short distance away.

Weary and more than a little melancholy, Tanner swung into the saddle. He wasn't any closer to finding Kate a husband, further from it, in fact. The only thing he had to show for his efforts was a sore lip and a throbbing toe. He had a long ride before he reached home, and a full day's logging to put in tomorrow. So far the weather had been holding. But if it was anything like the rest of his luck, he knew it wouldn't last.

10

A BARK AND a nudge from her dog made Kate open her eyes. Morning. Already. Groaning, she glanced at the window, then rolled over and covered her head. The little sleep she'd managed to get had been fitful. And because that sleep had been filled with dreams of Tanner, she ruefully thought she might have been better off with no sleep at all.

Someone pounded on her door, then Madame Jeanne called out her name.

Kate ran a hand over her eyes, hoisted herself upright and reached for her robe. Still tying the belt she answered her door.

"Hello, Jeanne. What brings you out so early?"

"Early?" Jeanne raised a brow. "Ees after noon." She pointed to the sun, which hung low on the horizon. "See?"

Late afternoon. In a few hours it would be dark.

"I must have been more tired than I thought." She motioned the woman in and shut the door.

"Are you all right, *cherie?* Some of your customers asked about you. I found you deed not open your shop."

"Oh, my goodness. I didn't even think about the pies. I don't have any to sell anyway." She pointed to a chair. "Have a seat, and I'll put some coffee on," she said, stifling a yawn.

"*Non.* You have a seat. I'll make the coffee."

A few minutes later Jeanne set a steaming cup in front of her. "You deed not sleep, and I weell bet I know the reason."

"I guess everybody knows." Kate managed a rueful smile. "Tanner and I didn't exactly try to keep our argument a secret."

"Ah, love. So many ups and downs, but never the dull moment, eh?"

Kate scowled. "Love has nothing to do with it. It's that—that man."

"Tanner Blaine ees quite the man, no?"

"He's an egotistical bully." But he could also be kind and gentle. Kate remembered the way he'd held her when she'd cried. She also recalled the concern he showed for his brothers, especially little John. She also remembered other things, things she'd be better off forgetting.

"He keessed you," the Frenchwoman said knowingly.

Kate remained silent. He did a whole lot more than that, but she wasn't about to tell a living soul, not even Jeanne.

"You love heem?"

"Of course not!" She took a gulp of coffee and burned her tongue. "How could I love a man like that? He's too big, too pig-headed, too stubborn."

"He ees a typical man." Jeanne nodded. "You love heem."

"I assure you I don't. And I don't want to talk about Tanner Blaine."

Jeanne grinned.

"Do you have any more pie recipes?" Kate asked, hoping to change the subject.

After discussing the finer aspects of pie creation, Jeanne left, then Kate dressed and straightened her quarters. She had a headache and didn't feel like baking. She'd remained closed one day, one more wouldn't matter.

She retired early, determined to make up for the lack of sleep from the night before, but once again she spent most of the night tossing and turning, finally getting up to spend the remainder of the night in her chair by the stove.

You love heem.

"She's wrong. I couldn't love him. I don't," she cried. Then why did she always end up in his arms? She closed her eyes, remembering the ecstasy, the passion. She wasn't a loose woman. Yet, she had come close to surrendering her virtue. She would have been ruined. And, God help her, she wouldn't have cared.

Fluffy came and put his head in her lap and gazed at her with soulful eyes.

The agonizing truth sent her to her knees. "I do. I do love him." She bent and buried her face in the dog's fur. "But he doesn't love me. Oh, Fluffy, what am I going to do?"

After tying the last of his tools on the mule, Tanner took a drink of water from the canteen and used the remainder to wash the sawdust from his eyes. He had worked long and hard, quitting only when it became too dark to see. He gazed up at the sky where stars now popped through the twilight. The number of trees he had felled today should have given him satisfaction. But the only thing he felt was tired.

He looped the canteen strap over the pommel and climbed into his saddle. "Damn it, Kate. Why can't you be reasonable?" He gathered the reins and clucked to the horse.

Reasonable? Women weren't known for being reasonable. Usually just the opposite. And Miss Kathleen Amanda Deveraux was no exception. In fact, now that he'd come to think on it, she was probably worse. He'd been trying to look out for her best interests. Why couldn't she see that?

Her best interests?

He'd almost seduced her—in Madame Jeanne's parlor. On a desk. With a bevy of would-be husbands waiting outside in the hall. Thank God none of them had opened the door.

Kate was pretty, but so were a lot of other women. And some of them had better figures. And they would be willing, if not eager, to have him make love to them. He had no problem keeping his hands off them. In fact, once he'd satisfied his baser instincts, they didn't affect him one way or the other.

Why was Kate different? What was it about her that made him want to strip her naked and make love to her every time he laid eyes on her?

He didn't know, but one thing was for sure. They would both be better off if he did stay away. Not that that would be difficult. She didn't want him anywhere near her. She'd stated that loud and clear.

He also remembered her confrontation with the men in the hall. She'd said she didn't want to see any of them, either. So until she changed her mind, he had nothing to worry about.

His mood greatly improved, he smiled, then he nudged his horse into a faster pace and headed for home.

After a successful season in San Francisco, the Gold Coast Players were booked to do a melodrama at Horne's new hall in Jacksonville. Almost everyone in the area would be attending the performance, and Kate found herself looking forward to the event.

After the fiasco with Tanner and her would-be suitors, she had rarely gone out in the evening and then only to see Madame Jeanne. She had attended a few functions, such as a quilting bee or a poetry reading, with some of the ladies from church, mostly to find out if she was the subject of any gossip. If she was, nobody had breathed a word.

Her pie business hadn't suffered because of her self-imposed exile. She had been busier than ever. Today she had baked right up until it was time to get dressed for the evening's gala. In fact, she'd worked so late that she hadn't had the opportunity to put her week's proceeds into the bank. Since this wasn't the first time the bank had closed before she'd made her deposit, she'd hidden the wad of bills in a crockery cookie jar, then placed it in the cabinet. The money would be safe enough, and besides, Fluffy would be there.

Tomorrow she would send a portion of it to Melody and her husband. The last letter she'd received from them sounded as though they could use it, especially now that the baby, a little girl, had been born. She bore her cousins no ill will. In truth they had done all they could for her.

She'd written to them upon her arrival. She'd explained that she and Mr. Blaine had disliked each other on sight, and had agreed it would be better to each go his or her own way. She had also told them that the West was filled with opportunities and she had opened a very successful pie shop.

They had written back eager to know more. Since then she had told them all about her life in Jacksonville, mentioning everything except that courting mess—and Tanner. She'd be mortified if they found out about that.

It had been almost three weeks since she had seen Tanner, and during that time she had been forced to face some hard and painful truths. No matter how much she might wish it different, there could be no future in their relationship. Accepting that, she'd made a decision. As soon as she had repaid Tanner and Madame Jeanne, she would leave Jacksonville.

She fastened a garnet clip into her hair, a Christmas present from Tanner and the boys. The boys had brought it in. Tanner hadn't come into town, probably afraid to show his face. She had sent presents back in return. A toy for John, books for Mark and Luke, a bottle of cologne for Matthew, and a pair of gloves for Tanner. Soon after that the weather had turned bad and she hadn't seen any of them since.

She studied herself in the mirror. Outside, she looked the same as she had when she'd arrived, but inside, she had changed. Now, she had confidence in her ability to survive on her own. She took pride in her new-found independence. Her pie business had proved that she could support herself. Why, farther north in a more populated area, she might do even better. And maybe there, in time, she could forget Tanner Blaine.

Thinking of Tanner made her sad and more than a bit wistful. "Put the man out of your mind," she scolded, adding a dash more Spanish paper to cheeks. "There."

The burgundy velvet dress hugged her waist and hips and flared around her ankles. The neckline dipped scandalously low. When she did reach the theater, she wondered if she would have nerve enough to remove her cape.

"Nonsense. If I'm doomed to a life as an old maid, I may

as well have some fun before I die." She gazed into the mirror. If she said so herself, she'd never looked better. Too bad Tanner wouldn't be there to see her.

A knock on the door told her that her escort for the evening had arrived. She hurried to let him in.

Dr. Frederick Thomas gave a whistle of admiration. "My word, Kate, you take an old man's breath away. Maybe I should have come armed. I daresay I'll have to fight men off by the droves."

She smiled. "Thank you. And you, sir, look so dashing, I fear I may be fending off a few heart-struck females of my own."

The doctor bowed and doffed a top hat. "The buggy's outside, if you're ready, my lady."

"I only need to find my gloves." She hurried back to her living quarters to seek her black gloves one last time. Where did she have them last? The day she went to confront Tanner. She hadn't seen them since. Giving it up as a lost cause, she pulled a pair of tan gloves from her drawer and returned to the other room. "I guess I must have misplaced them. Maybe no one will notice that these don't match."

"My dear, the last thing anybody will be looking at is your hands."

Tanner tied his horse to a hitching rail. Then, glancing around toward the theater, he removed his duster, folded it, then tied it behind his saddle. This was a tomfool idea. He didn't know why he let Jeanne talk him into it. He awkwardly straightened the stiff, scratchy collar, then bent and brushed the legs of his pants. The tie and tails had also been Madame Jeanne's idea. A former boarder, an actor, had left the suit in lieu of rent.

Tanner had never been so gussied up in his life. He felt like a monkey in a circus show. Or an undertaker. Well, at least it was dark. Maybe nobody would see him.

He tarried as long as he dared, then, squaring his shoulders, he entered the lobby of the theater.

"Tanner." Madame Jeanne, her voluptuous body encased in sleek black satin, left the group of people she was with and hurried in his direction. "I was afraid you were not coming, *cherie*." She placed her hands on her hips and gave him the onceover. "*Ooh la la,* you look so handsome."

"You look pretty scrumptious, yourself." He gazed around the gathering of people. "Quite a turnout for this shindig."

"They all come to see the new hall," she said, hooking her arm through his.

He glanced overhead, taking in the flickering crystal chandelier. "Looks real elegant. I doubt if even Portland has one so fine."

"I reserved you a place next to me. Oh, see, the lights are dimming already, I theenk we should take the seat." She tightened her grip on his arm and led him into the darkened theater.

"I hope you know where you're going," he whispered. "I can't see a blamed thing."

"Here." She led him down the aisle and preceded him into a row. "Sit." She tugged him into a vacant seat.

"Looks like a full house." He peered around at the people now taking up standing room along the walls.

"Everybody een town ees here."

Everybody? He craned his neck to look again. Then the stage lights came on, and the melodrama began.

Ten Nights in a Barroom captivated the audience and many a feminine eye was being wiped for tears, but Tanner found it hard to concentrate on the play. He was too busy scanning each row, although he couldn't see much. And if anybody had asked, he would have denied he was looking. Where was she? Maybe she hadn't come.

The curtain fell to a roar of applause, and the lights were turned up.

Tanner turned to Madame Jeanne. "Is it over?"

"No, no, *cherie*. Eet ees only the first act."

"Oh. What do we do now?"

"We could go eento lobby and have refreshments," she suggested.

"Yeah, let's do that. I don't know about you, but I feel plumb parched." Tanner stood, grateful for the chance to stretch his legs. He decided that whoever had constructed the seats must have been a midget. It sure wasn't built to accommodate anybody as tall as him.

"I need to powder my nose, *cherie*. You go ahead, and I meet you een a meenute."

Tanner followed the rest of the crowd into a large anteroom off the theater entrance. *Where is that punch bowl?* Spying a group of men in the corner, he headed in that direction, then stepped backward to avoid a man juggling three cups of cherry-colored liquid.

"Oh!"

Feeling something soft under his boot, he looked down, then shifted sideways. "Sorry, ma'am. I hope I didn't squash your foot."

"Only my toe," a familiar voice said.

Tanner jerked around and met a pair of violet eyes. "Kate?" He'd always thought her pretty, but tonight she fairly took his breath away. Her dress, what there was of it, fit her like a second skin. It was the part it wasn't fitting that made his eyes bulge. He frowned. "Aren't you afraid you'll catch a cold or something?" he asked, glancing around to see if anybody else had noticed.

They had. Every man in the room was getting eyestrain.

"Cold? Goodness no. I find it very warm in here." She opened a lacy black fan and waved it in front of her. The motion loosened tiny tendrils of gleaming black hair and sent them fluttering around her face.

"Here's your punch, my dear." The doctor handed Kate a cup. "Hello, Tanner. Kind of surprised to see you here. Didn't know you went in for this sort of thing."

"I don't, usually. Jeanne talked me into it."

"Here, Tanner, why don't you take this stuff? One of the boys offered me something a little stronger." He glanced at Kate. "If you don't mind, Kathleen?"

"Go ahead, Fred," she said. "You deserve it after the week you've put in." Kate brought the cup to her lips and took a sip. A bead of water dropped from the bottom of the cup and landed at the base of her throat, then, little by little, it inched lower, finally coming to a stop between the shadowy cleft of her breasts.

Mesmerized, Tanner watched, wondering if it would stay there or go lower still.

"What are you looking at?" she asked, fixing him with a frown of disapproval.

"Uh, nothing. Your cup was dripping." He congratulated himself for being able to drag his gaze back to her face. It took every bit of concentration he had to keep it there. "You said something about the doc putting in a hard week. Is it diphtheria?" Every winter the dread disease took a heavy annual toll.

"No. Smallpox." She sipped her punch. "You haven't heard?"

"Smallpox? No. Tell me about it."

"The first case occurred about two weeks ago. A man in Roseburg died. Then a few cases showed up locally. Everyone was worried for a while, but this week there were only two new cases. The *Sentinel* reported that the worst of it was over."

"Where did they put the sick people?" He didn't like to think of Kate being exposed to anyone that might have the disease.

"The Board of Health opened a pesthouse up on Kanaka Flats. They also opened a hospital for the overflow in that old store building outside of town, but so far there hasn't been any need for it."

"Kanaka Flats." It figured. Kanaka Flats, mostly a conglomeration of saloons and shanties, was home to most of the undesirable element in the area. "Guess they figured to get rid of the riffraff along with the victims."

"It's nothing to joke about, Tanner. I can't imagine a more horrible way to die."

"I'm sorry, Kate." Thinking of the array of people she came in contact with, he frowned. "Have you taken any precautions?"

"Of course. I've had the vaccination, and I also have a saucer of chloride of lime in my house."

"Is that enough?"

"Do I look sick to you?"

She had never looked healthier. His gaze dipped to her

chest. Almost too healthy. "You got a shawl or something? I wouldn't want you to catch cold."

"I told you, I'm fine. In fact I'm hot. Feel."

She took his hand and put it on her forehead, then on the base of her neck.

He jerked his hand back like he'd been burnt.

"Kate, are you all right?" the doctor asked, hurrying back to her side.

"For pity's sake. I'm fine. Do I look sick to you?"

"No, but I saw Tanner—"

"He wanted me to put on a shawl. I told him I didn't need it."

"Oh." The doctor peered up at Tanner and grinned. "She sure looks fine to me." He glanced down at Kate. "I think it's time to raise the curtain. Shall we go back to our seats?"

"Goodbye, Tanner. Enjoy the show." She hooked her arm through the physician's and went back into the theater.

Tanner scanned the emptying room, then spotted Jeanne. "I wondered where you went to," he said.

"I did not theenk you would meess me," she said, smiling. "Besides, I had beesiness to deescuss with Cornelius."

He led her back to her seat. "How is Beekman these days?"

"Looking forward to the new year; he plans to make even more money."

"New year? By golly, I had forgotten. Tonight is New Year's Eve. Speaking of money, I guess Kate's pie shop is still doing a booming business."

"Yes, eet ees a shame she weell be leaving us before long."

"Kate's leaving?"

Madame Jeanne didn't answer. The curtain had risen, the second act was beginning.

Tanner knew Kate wasn't in front of them, for he had examined the back of every head. None of them belonged to her. Trying not to be obvious about it, he swiveled and looked to the right and then to the left. Finally, he turned completely around and found her seated directly behind him.

"Sit still. I can't see," she hissed.

"Sorry." Feeling like a fool, he faced the stage and scooted down in his seat. At least now he knew where she was.

Toward the end of the act, he heard a man say in a loud whisper, "Doc, you're needed at the hotel. Looks like another case of the pox."

"Kate?" the elder man asked.

"Don't worry, I'll be fine," she said softly.

Tanner turned. "Go ahead, Doc, I'll see she gets home."

The rest of the performance seemed to go in slow motion and more than a few of the patrons began to nod. Others, mostly men, retreated to the lobby for a cigar or something to drink. But Tanner had no difficulty staying awake. He could actually hear Kate breathing. And with every intake he visualized the rise and fall of her breasts.

When the second act ended, the patrons again headed for the lobby.

By the time Jeanne stood and they started up the aisle, Kate was nowhere to be seen. Jeanne left Tanner and was soon huddled with Cornelius over a piece of paper, giving Tanner the opportunity to look for Kate. He found her in the midst of a group of women.

Telling himself he was glad she was unapproachable, he stepped outside to catch a breath of air. Several men in deep conversation drew his attention.

"I heard three more came down sick today."

"Thought the worst of it was over. At least that's what the *Sentinel* is telling us."

"Well, it appears that editor don't know everything, no matter what he prints in his paper."

"He left the shindig early. He's down at the paper now. Hear the *Sentinel* is putting out a special edition."

A knot of fear gripped Tanner's heart. Kate had been vaccinated, but his brothers hadn't. Maybe he should get them vaccinated, but that would mean bringing them into town and possibly exposing them to the disease. He'd talk to the doctor. In the meantime, he'd make sure the boys stayed clear of Jacksonville if he had to tie their feet to a stump.

"Mr. Blaine?"

He turned to see one of the Britt boys. "Howdy, son. What can I do for you?"

"Madame deRoboam said to give you this note." He handed Tanner a folded piece of paper, then ran off to join his chums.

Tanner went back into the lobby and opened it. Claiming a headache, Madame Jeanne had gone home by way of Cornelius Beekman's carriage. While he hoped she wasn't ill, Tanner couldn't help but be grateful that she had left. It gave him the opportunity to spend the rest of the evening with Kate.

When the curtains went up on the last act, Tanner took the seat that the doctor had vacated.

Kate looked up in surprise.

"Jeanne went home. I couldn't see any sense in both of us sitting alone."

Kate nodded, then directed her attention toward the stage.

He, however, couldn't focus on anything but her. He inhaled the scent of her, examined her profile by the dim lights of the theater. And since she couldn't see, him being taller, he drank his fill of the creamy, rising mounds of flesh he'd only dreamed of watching earlier. From his viewpoint, he could almost swear he saw dusky nipples, but then he always did have a vivid imagination. Whatever he was seeing, it looked mighty fine.

He heard her sniff, then saw a sparkling tear make its way down her cheek. "Kate?"

"It's so sad," she whispered, fishing in her reticule.

He took a handkerchief from his pocket and handed it to her.

Murmuring a thank you, she took it and dabbed at her cheeks. When she tried to return it, he took her hand and encased it in his own. He could have sat there forever, but long before he was ready, the curtain dropped.

Yells and whistles rose from the audience.

He gave Kate a startled look.

"They loved it. Wasn't it wonderful?" she sighed, her expression dreamy.

"Wonderful," he agreed. While Tanner had no idea what had happened on the stage, he wished the play could have lasted all night.

After several curtain calls, the house lights were lit and the audience filed out of the theater.

He helped Kate into her cloak and saw her to the buggy, then he retrieved his horse and tied it on behind. Two blocks. He wished it was two miles, but the night was cold and he didn't want Kate to take a chill.

A gun boomed, then another.

"Somebody's shooting." Pulling Kate down on the seat, he guided the buggy off the road and stopped behind the drooping branches of a pine tree.

Kate laughed. "It's midnight," she explained, easing upright. "Happy New Year, Tanner." She gazed up at him, her face pale, silvered by moonlight, her eyes shining like the brightest of stars.

"Happy New Year, Kate." Unable to resist, he took her in his arms. Her lips were soft and cool; he warmed them with his own. Discovering she was kissing him back, his kiss deepened; he pressed his tongue between her teeth. She tasted of punch and honeyed nectar, like the heart of a fragrant flower. He savored the core of sweetness, exploring every delicious crevice.

She shyly made a few explorations of her own. Sighing, she moved even closer, then her arms crept up and around his neck.

He kissed her chin, then her neck where the cloak had parted, then nibbled his way to the creamy tops of each breast. Her skin was soft as the finest satin, flawless as the most priceless pearl. He slid his fingers inside the velvet fabric, savoring the heat of her flesh against his palm.

She arched against him, and whispered his name.

His pulse raged like the rapids of a river, making him oblivious to everything but the woman in his arms. He bent his head to her rose-colored lips.

Her hands fastened in his hair. Her heart beat like the

wings of a hummingbird against the roughness of his fingers. She was so sweet, so perfect, and he wanted her more than he'd ever wanted anything in his life.

"Tanner, is that you?" a man called out from the street.

"Dammit!" Tanner moved in front of Kate, shielding her from the curious eyes of the caller. "Yeah, Ed. What do you want?"

"Doc needs his buggy. Got four more cases of the pox up Sterling Creek. Board of Health wants everyone off the street."

The ominous message cooled Tanner's overheated blood. Seven, maybe eight new victims, and who knew how many more. He gazed down at Kate, then tenderly kissed the tip of her nose. "Guess we'd better get you home, darlin'."

After seeing Kate safely inside, and kissing her good night, he returned the buggy to the doctor.

"Sorry, Doc, didn't know you'd be needing it tonight," he said, climbing down off the seat.

"I was hoping I wouldn't. If the circumstances were different, I wouldn't have cared if you hadn't brought the rig back until dawn." The doctor ran a hand through his hair. "Damn this pox. You never know when it will strike next, or who."

"Doc, are you sure Kate's safe?" Tanner asked, unable to bear the thought that she might contract the disease. "And what about the boys? Should I get them immunized?"

"Kate's been vaccinated. She won't get it. The boys will be safe enough if you keep them home." The physician set his black bag onto the floorboard, then he gripped Tanner's shoulder. "Don't worry, they'll all be fine." He climbed into the buggy.

Tanner swung into his saddle and followed the doctor as far as the cutoff, then headed toward the mountain.

A cold wind moaned down the canyon, and howled through the treetops overhead. It was a lonely, forbidding sound. Riding alone in the darkness, fear for Kate made him pull up his horse. Made him want to head back to town.

What would he do after he got there? She wouldn't come with him. And he sure couldn't stay.

She'll be just fine, the doctor had assured him. The physician knew his business. He wouldn't have said that if Kate was in any danger.

Reluctantly, Tanner headed up the trail. Thinking of the awful disease and how fast it was spreading, he only wished he felt that certain.

11

A RUMBLE OF wheels brought Kate to her window. Another wagonload of sick being taken to Kanaka Flats. Later, on the return trip, that same wagon filled with coffins would be heading for the cemetery.

She rubbed her arms against a sudden chill, and averted her eyes past the wagon to the street, where a choking cloud of dense smoke rose to cover the town. Pitch fires had been built at intervals down Main Street in hopes that the smoke would purify the air and therefore prevent the spread of the pox. Then, resorting to ancient traditions, sulphur had been added to the flames until the supply ran out.

The fires did nothing to quell the panic. Five people had died. Thirteen new cases had appeared. The Board of Health ruled Jacksonville was in quarantine. No one was allowed either in or out. She thought it ironic that when the vaccine was plentiful a number of people refused to have it. Now that the supply of vaccine had run out, people were clamoring to be immunized.

Since public gatherings were prohibited, Kate had closed her shop and remained inside her house, only going out for short periods to walk her dog. Even Fluffy appeared nervous, never straying from her side.

The bustling town of Jacksonville had become a tomb. Yellow flags indicating the presence of the disease were

seen on every side. Even more frightening, black wreaths
had now appeared on a few doors.

Although ineffective, the fires burned on, manned by day
and night. The editor of the *Sentinel* drew a vivid picture of
the eerie scene.

> By day the town is enveloped in thick smoke and by
> night the deserted streets are lit up by lines of fire that
> blaze and flicker among the shadows, and throw a
> ghastly and sepulchral light over everything. . . .

Kate stared through the haze, her gaze going to the
mountains. The boys hadn't been to see her in quite a while
now, and while she missed them, she also gave thanks. She
couldn't stand it if any of them contracted the disease.

Tanner had been in town. What if he had been exposed?

She thought about the theater and the large gathering of
people, some of whom were in the pesthouse now. Unable
to bear the thought that he, too, might get the pox, she
closed her eyes and bowed her head.

*Dear God, please keep Tanner and the boys safe. Please
don't let them get the disease.*

She added a few prayers for the victims and their fami-
lies. Some of them were church-going folks. Some that died
were devout Christians. And that poor little Love girl . . .
a sweeter child had never been born.

God hadn't helped them. Maybe he wouldn't hear her
either. She went back to look out the window. The scene
resembled a picture of hell. Somewhere a woman wailed
and screamed, the sound terrible, desperate. Was she the
wife, the mother of one of the victims?

How many more would be stricken and die? Kate drew
her shawl more closely around her. It was as if the Almighty
had washed his hands of the whole Rogue Valley.

Freezing rain, then sprinkles of snow, drifted down from a
cloud-filled sky, making Tanner put aside his tools and head
for the house shortly before noon. It had been three days
since he'd seen Kate. Three days that he'd been worried

sick. The doctor had promised she'd be all right, but Tanner couldn't rest until he'd seen her for himself.

After making sure the boys were all right, he checked the food staples, making a note to pick up whatever they might need. He knew this would probably be his last trip to town until spring. Not just because of the smallpox epidemic, but also because heavy winter snow would soon engulf the pass. Like it or not, they would be isolated for the rest of the winter.

Maybe the danger's past. Maybe Kate will be all right.

But his optimism died when, nearing Jacksonville, he paused to rest his horse on a rim overlooking the town. From there he noted the bonfires in the streets and the cloud of smoke covering the town. He also saw a campfire at the trailhead. A man with a rifle stood guard.

Finding the trail to Jacksonville blocked and guarded only increased Tanner's fears for Kate. It appeared that the town was in quarantine, which meant the smallpox epidemic had grown worse. Anxiety knotted his middle, and he fought the urge to race the horse down the hill and see if Kate was all right.

Common sense told him the only thing that would accomplish would be to get himself shot, or put in jail, neither of which would help Kate or the boys.

He stealthily retreated from the rocky ledge before he could be spotted. Avoiding the main trail so that he wouldn't leave tracks in the fresh snow, he kept to the trees and made his way down the hill. When he neared the trailhead, he led the horse into a draw and tied him to a sapling.

Kate's place sat in the middle of town, in the open. He couldn't possibly go there until full dark or else he'd be seen. Because it was closer and surrounded by shrubbery and trees, he decided going to the doctor's place would be his best bet. The physician could tell him the state of things, and also how Kate was—if the doctor was there. If he wasn't, at least it would be a good place to wait until Tanner could get to Kate's.

Like a shadow, he slipped from tree to tree until he reached the clapboard house. Relieved to see a light inside, but also afraid the doc might be busy with a patient, Tanner hugged the wall and peered through the window.

The doctor sat alone, dozing in a chair.

Tanner tried the door and found it unlocked. He quietly went inside. "Doc, it's Tanner Blaine," he said softly. "I need to talk to you."

"Tanner? What are you doing in town?" The gray-haired man's face was etched with weariness. He staggered from the chair and pulled the curtains. "Son, don't you know we're in quarantine? If anybody found you here, you wouldn't be allowed to leave."

"I don't intend to stay that long. I had to find out about Kate."

The physician gave him an uneasy look. "She's well, so far."

"So far?" Tanner gripped his arms. "What aren't you telling me?"

"Today a man came down with the pox, someone I gave the vaccine to a few minutes before I injected Kate."

A chill swept through Tanner's veins. "I thought you said she was safe. She couldn't get it."

"I thought she couldn't. Apparently something was wrong with the vaccine."

"Then she could get sick, too." An aching fear tightened his throat.

"She might. I'm not sure." The doctor let out a weary sigh, then peered at him through red-rimmed eyes. He motioned Tanner into the kitchen and poured them each a cup of coffee.

Tanner took his to the table and sat down.

Dr. Thomas took the chair opposite him. Ordinarily fastidious, the medical man's clothes were wrinkled and stained, making it apparent that it had been several days since he'd gone to bed. "How are the kids? Anybody feeling poorly?"

"No, they're fine." Tanner took off his hat and ran a hand through his snow-dusted hair.

"Tanner, you ought to know that Kate's volunteered to nurse the sick, although nobody has taken her up on it yet."

"You can't let her do it."

"She's a grown woman. I'm very fond of Kate, too, and much as I'd like to stop her, I have no say in the matter."

Tanner knew he wouldn't either—if he gave her any choice. A muscle jumped in his clenched jaw. He downed the coffee then shoved the cup aside. "That tears it. I'm taking Kate out of here, Doc, and God help anybody that tries to stop me."

"Do what you have to, Tanner. I, too, would feel better if Kathleen was away from here, at least until the disease has run its course."

His mouth grim with determination, Tanner held out his hand. "Take care of yourself, Fred."

"You, too, son," the physician called softly after him before shutting the door.

Tanner waited in the shadows and checked the street. Except for the men stoking the fires, there wasn't a soul in sight. Hoping it would stay that way, he crept from shadow to shadow until he reached Kate's.

He peered through her window and saw her sitting by the stove. Raising a finger, he tapped on the glass.

Fluffy raised his head and growled.

"Don't bark, dammit," he whispered.

Kate came to the window and peeped out, then she hurried to open the door. "Tanner! What are you doing here?"

He stepped inside. "Gather your things, I'm taking you to the mountain."

"You're crazy. I can't leave with you. The town's in quarantine. Besides, what would people think?"

"They'd think you've got some sense." He strode to her bed, stripped off a blanket and began throwing things inside.

"Stop it! I said I'm not going."

Frowning, he glanced toward the window. "You keep up that racket and neither of us will be allowed to leave. The boys need me at home. I'm not going without you, so make up your mind which way it's going to be." He stood, waited.

She sighed in defeat. "You leave me no choice. What about Fluffy?"

"He can come, if he stays quiet."

She stared at him a minute, then she nodded her head. "This is just temporary. As soon as the danger's over, I'm coming straight back to town."

"Fine. Get your stuff ready, and let's get moving." he waited for Kate to put on heavier clothes and boots, then she put night garments and a change of clothes into a carpetbag.

"Do you have any foodstuffs: flour, sugar . . .? The mercantile is closed, and under the circumstances . . ."

"Yes, I have both, along with a few other things we might need." She stuffed carbolic acid and other medical supplies into her bag, then wrapped the foodstuffs in a navy blue blanket and tied the corners shut. "I'm ready."

He extinguished the light, then led the way from the house.

"What if somebody comes by and finds me missing?" she asked quietly. "Shouldn't I tell someone I'm leaving?"

"Doc Thomas knows. Now be quiet and get a move on." He motioned Kate to go ahead of him until she'd reached a grove of bushy cedars. Tanner followed close behind, using a fallen limb to brush the snow free of their tracks.

After that, he led the way, keeping to the shadows. Kate, the dog beside her, stayed close by his side.

When they neared the trailhead, he motioned her to silence.

Now two men were there, one standing beside a campfire, the other sitting, wrapped in a blanket. "Damn, it's colder than a witch's tit." The man that had complained stomped his feet and held his hands out to the fire. "How long we gonna stay out here?"

"Nobody with any sense would be out on a night like this," the other man said, drawing the blanket closer.

"Nobody with any sense would be trying to get into a town that's quarantined."

"What are we sitting out here for, then?" He struggled to his feet. "I'm for going home."

"May as well die of the pox as pneumonia," the other man agreed. He kicked some snow on the fire, then gathered up his rifle and the rest of his belongings. Muttering to each other, the men headed back into town.

Tanner let out the breath he didn't know he'd been holding. "We wait a few more minutes, then we'll go find the horse."

When he was certain the men weren't going to come back, he hurried Kate across the clearing and into the trees. The horse stood, tail to the wind, where he'd left him. "We're in luck—with the snow falling like it is now, we won't leave a trail."

"That's good," Kate said, her teeth chattering.

He frowned. Although her cloak was wool, it wasn't all that heavy. She'd be half frozen before they reached the crest of the hill. Then he remembered the slicker he carried behind the saddle. It would keep the wind and snow off and help the cloak retain her body heat. He removed it and made her put it on. "How's that?"

"Much better. I'm warmer already."

He unwrapped his own muffler and tied it over her head, then helped her onto the horse and tied her carpetbag and food bundle behind the saddle. "Guess we're set."

"What about you?" she asked. "Aren't you gong to ride?"

"I'll walk. It will be quicker, and besides, I'm used to it." He didn't tell her that because of the snow, the horse couldn't carry double. He glanced up, where a flurry of white swirled from the sky. He also didn't tell her that the way it was coming down, they'd have to hurry or they wouldn't be able to get through at all.

Knowing they dare not tarry, he led the horse back to the trail and called to the dog, who was scratching around beneath a pine tree. "Come on, Fluffy. Let's go home."

The huge beast bounded past him and trotted up the trail, effectively breaking the way for the horse.

"You might be good for something, after all," Tanner said, watching the dog plow through the thick powder.

By the time they reached the summit, the storm had set in in earnest and, by the look of it, wouldn't let up anytime soon. In the mountain meadow where his cabin sat, it would be even deeper.

He wouldn't be able to fell timber, not for a while at least. Aside from doing a few chores in the barn, he'd be housebound, a condition that he normally detested. This time he looked forward to it, because he'd have Kate to keep him company.

He remembered the other night after the play when they'd been together in the buggy, and the kisses they'd shared before they'd been discovered. This time they wouldn't be interrupted, because it would be spring before anybody would be able to get up the mountain.

He envisioned long winter nights by the fire, with the boys asleep in their beds. Just him and Kate and the snow piling up around the house. Thinking of the possibilities, his blood grew hot, despite the freezing cold and snow. If it wasn't for the timber contract, he wouldn't care if it snowed until next June. From the way it was coming down, it might do just that.

For the first time in days, he smiled.

12

"WE'RE HERE," TANNER said, pointing across a snow-covered meadow.

Although Kate couldn't see anything but white, rimmed by snow-coated evergreens, she was happy to take his word for it.

A short time later, he stopped the horse in front of a large log structure that looked more like a barn than a house. He came to her side and lifted her down, supporting her until she could stand on her own. Then he guided her up a broad set of icy steps, across a covered porch and into the house. Although it was too dark to see much, the place was cozy warm.

"It's after midnight. The boys are in bed." He lit a lamp, then helped her out of her wrappings. He was being such a gentleman.

"I feel like I'm still on the horse," she said, attempting to straighten what she feared might be a permanent kink in her spine.

He chuckled. "You'll probably really be sore tomorrow. Come on in here and get thawed out. I'll stoke up the cookstove. You might want tea or something. Make yourself at home. I have to tend to the horse, then I'll be back."

Just when she was beginning to feel warm again, another

need made itself known. "There is one thing," she said hesitantly. "The privy?"

"Out back. I guess we should have gone there first. You'd better take a light." He lit a lantern and turned to the coatrack.

"The cloak will be sufficient this time," she said, donning it once again. She followed him outside and around the house to a small building. "I'll manage fine from here."

He nodded, then trudged away to care for the horse.

Kate tended to her needs quickly in the freezing weather, then left the tiny building. The snow had ceased to fall, and there was absolute silence. Overhead the clouds parted and a silvery moon appeared at the farthest horizon. It rose, tangling in the treetops, turning the mountain meadow into a wintery fairyland. Snow crystals gleamed and glimmered. Icicles dripped in spangles from the rooftops. It was spiritual, magical, and she had the feeling that if she moved the spell would be broken and all would disappear. She was unaware of how long she had stood there until Tanner appeared by her side.

"What are you thinking?" he asked, taking her hand.

"I've never seen anything so beautiful. Is it always like this?"

"Only when it snows," he said with a chuckle. "Look over there, see the deer?" He pointed to the edge of the trees, where a doe and two yearling fawns had appeared.

"No wonder you love it up here," she whispered.

"It's always pretty. At least we think so. You should see it in the spring. So green it hurts your eyes. And the wildflowers . . . And summers—flowers then, too, and wild berries. You can't imagine how sweet they are. We don't get the heat of the valley, so the air stays clear. At night the stars seem so close you could gather them in a basket."

Kate closed her eyes, picturing the scenes his words were painting.

"In the fall, the mountains are gold and crimson and every color in between. It is a sight to behold."

"It sounds like paradise."

He laughed. "And like paradise, we also have a few snakes."

The moment they were sharing was so special, so intimate, and it showed her a side of Tanner she hadn't been aware of. She didn't want it to end, but the cold air made her teeth chatter.

Noticing, he tucked her hand into the crook of his arm. "Well, right now we are both going to be in paradise before our time, if we don't go in and get warm." He picked up the lantern and walked her back to the house.

"It's warmer in the kitchen," he said. "The boys have the fireplace banked for the night." He fixed them both a cup of hot chocolate, then excused himself and disappeared down a narrow hall. He reappeared with his arms full of sheets, which he tossed into a basket in the corner.

"I don't want to put you to a lot of trouble," she said.

"No trouble at all." He slid into the seat across from her and drank his chocolate; every once in a while his eyes would meet hers, and he'd smile.

"What's so funny?"

"You've got chocolate on your upper lip. John does the same thing."

"Oh, my." Blushing, she brought her hand up and wiped it off.

"Don't be embarrassed. It makes you look younger. I was sitting here imagining you as a child. Bet you were feisty."

"My hair was always a tangled mess, and I was skinny as a stick. My mama despaired of me ever being a lady."

"She'd be proud of you now. All of your folks are gone?"

She nodded. "Except for a cousin. Mama died of a fever, then my father died shortly after the war."

"I lost my mother when I was young. Pa married again, then they had the boys. Maggie was really the only mother I ever remembered. She died when John was two. I guess I became the mother after that. Pa worked in the woods all the time." His face grew sad, tortured.

"What happened?"

"A limb got him. It would have gotten me, but he pushed me out of the way."

"It was an accident," she said, realizing he blamed himself for his father's death.

"Yeah. But I intend to make sure no such accident ever happens to the boys." He swallowed and looked away.

She wanted to go to him, hold him, comfort him. But it wasn't her place, and she sensed he wouldn't like it. Tanner Blaine was always so strong, stalwart, he wouldn't like anyone seeing his softer, more vulnerable side. Especially her.

"Guess we'd better go to bed or we'll meet ourselves getting up," he said gruffly.

A scratching at the door drew their attention.

"I forgot about Fluffy," Kate said.

"I'd better let him in before he knocks the door down." Tanner rose and let the dog inside. He laughed. "He looks like a white bear with all that snow clinging to him."

"If you have a rag or something, I'll clean him up, otherwise he'll drip water all over the floor," Kate said, dodging the dog's ice-crusted tail.

"Here, use this. Has to be washed anyway." He tossed her one of the sheets he'd removed from the bed. "Maybe I'd better help."

"He likes all the attention." She wrapped her arms around the dog's neck in an attempt to hold him still, but he wriggled free.

"Sit," Tanner ordered.

Fluffy obeyed.

"Minds better than the kids," he said, wiping the animal's fur free of snow. "There. That's good enough. At least he won't get your bed all wet."

"Thank you." She stood, undecided about where to go.

"This way." He picked up her carpetbag and the lamp and carried them down the hall. "Nothing fancy, but the bed sleeps pretty good." He set her bag on the floor and put the lamp on a pine dresser.

Curious about Tanner's home, Kate glanced around.

The honey-colored log walls gave the oversized room a coziness it wouldn't have had otherwise. "What a big bed!"

"My pa was tall, like me. He wouldn't fit in a regular bed,

so he built it special. Maggie said it was too big, claimed she got lost in it. After she died, Pa wouldn't sleep here anymore. Said it was too lonely." He pointed at a cedar chest at the foot of the bed. "After Maggie passed on, I packed away her curtains, best quilts and stuff. Figured to give them to the boys when they got married, so they would have something of hers to share with their own kids someday."

She traced the smooth pine footboard with her finger. "We had big sleigh beds on the plantation, but nothing of this size."

Worn, but clean, rag rugs were the rooms's only decoration. One lay beside the bed, a larger one was in front of the chest. A doorless closet containing heavy work clothes took up most of one end of the room. A straight-backed chair sat beside a rustic table. Above it was a shelf with a half dozen books.

"It looks very nice," she said.

"Probably nothing like you're used to, but at least I'm not cramped. I'll grab a pillow and some blankets, then I'll get out of your way."

"Where are you going to sleep?"

"I'll bunk in the front room. That old couch is danged near as long as this bed, so I'll make out just fine." He gathered up the things he needed, then gazed at her a moment. "If there's anything you need . . ."

"Only a little sleep," she said, stifling a yawn.

"Good night, Kate."

"Good night, Tanner."

He hesitated for a moment, then left the room, softly closing the door behind him.

She quickly changed into her nightclothes, climbed onto the bed and slid between sheets so cold they took her breath away. She doubled into a knot, wondering if she'd ever be able to warm a spot in the massive edifice; then about halfway toward the foot she located a lump of heat. Reaching down to touch it, she felt a hot rock wrapped in a thick towel. Tanner must have put it there after he'd changed the bed. How thoughtful.

Her toes touching the rock, she curled her arms around the pillow, knowing that only last night it had cradled Tanner's head. It rustled. Not feathers. She sniffed. It smelled of sweet grass and flowers, bringing forth images of a mountain meadow on a warm summer day. Much better than goose down, she decided.

She sighed in contentment. Never had she felt so cosseted, so protected.

She reminded herself that Tanner had brought her here out of obligation, to keep her from contracting smallpox. And as soon as the danger was over, he'd return her to town.

Nevertheless, as she lay there in his room, in his bed, breathing in his scent, she wished it could have been different. If only it could stay like this. If only it could last.

"What are you doing sleeping in here?"

Tanner opened one eye and peered up at Luke. "Go away."

"Something wrong with your bed?" Luke persisted.

"It's occupied."

"By who?"

"Kate. I brought her here last night. She's tired, so let her sleep."

"Kate? She's here?"

"Kate's here?" John yelled from the hallway.

"Shhh!" Tanner said, dragging himself to a sitting position.

"W-what's sh-she doing here?" John asked, stuttering in his excitement.

"She's trying to sleep, so keep it down."

"Did you de-decide to k-keep her?"

"Keep her? What are you talking about?" Tanner asked between yawns.

"K-keep her. Y-you know. Get m-married and have b-babies and stuff."

"We're not getting married, so don't get any ideas about that. There's a smallpox epidemic in Jacksonville. I didn't want her to get sick, so I brought her up here so she would be safe." He rubbed a hand over his eyes. "Any more questions?"

"Yeah," Mark said from the doorway. "Did she come willing, or did you kidnap her?"

"Damn! I feel like I'm in the middle of an inquisition." He shook his head and stared at his brothers. "Could you at least let me have a cup of coffee first, since it appears like I'm not going to get any more sleep."

"You didn't answer Mark's question." Matt stood, arms crossed, waiting.

"I didn't kidnap her. She came of her own accord. You can ask her."

"I'll do that—soon as she wakes up," Mark said.

Tanner stared at them in amazement. He was the oldest, they should be answering to him, not the other way around. Of course, they had always been protective when it came to Kate—which might be a problem if they kept it up. He'd just have to get them to mind their own business.

"Fluffy!" John yelled, running to hug the dog around the neck.

A very sleepy, tousle-headed Kate stood in the doorway. "Good morning. I can't believe it's daylight already. Seems like I just went to bed."

"That's because you practically did." Tanner shot accusing glances at his brothers. "I tried to keep these yahoos quiet, but you probably heard the results of that."

"We're sorry, Kate. I guess we were just excited," Luke said, blushing.

"I've always been an earlier riser. I probably would have been up before long, anyway."

"You sit over here by the fire," Mark insisted, tugging a large overstuffed chair close to the heat. "Get you warmed up in no time."

"What a big fireplace. I'll bet you could get a whole tree in there," she said in amazement.

"Not quite. We've got some pretty big trees, too," Tanner said with a grin.

"I'll fetch you some coffee," Matt said, hurrying toward the kitchen.

John gave her a hug, then squeezed in beside her. "What's smallpox?" he asked, singing the words.

"It's where your face turns black and your skin falls off," Luke said, taking up a position by her feet.

"Luke, for God's sake," Tanner admonished.

"It's a terrible disease caused by a bad germ," Kate answered. "Some of the people in Jacksonville are getting sick. But the doctor and the sisters of the Holy Names are working very hard to make everyone feel better."

"Everybody will be well, then?"

"Soon. Then I can go back home."

"I want people to feel better, but I hope they don't get well too quick," John said. "I want you to stay for a long, long time."

"She'll be here a while," Luke said with a snicker.

Tanner nudged him before he could say more.

Mark and Luke looked at each other, then at him. Tanner shook his head. He wouldn't let them tell her she was stuck here. He'd do it later when the time was right. Give her time to get used to the situation first. No sense getting her upset for nothing.

Luke gazed at Kate, his eyes full of adoration, then he frowned. "Kate, you're barefooted. Don't you have any slippers?"

"We left in such a hurry, I forgot to stick them in."

"I'll make you some," Luke promised. "I'll start right now. In the meantime you can wear a pair of my wool socks." He got to his feet and left the room.

"Here, try some of this, Kate." Matt handed her a steaming mug. "It's fresh and not too strong. I even scrubbed the pot."

"That's a first," Tanner muttered.

"Thank you." Kate sipped the brew. "Delicious, and different."

"I put a pinch of cinnamon bark in the coffeepot, thought you might like the taste better.

"It's wonderful, Matt. I would never have thought of it."

"You got another cup?" Tanner asked hopefully.

"It's in the kitchen," Matt said, not taking the hint. He

took the spot Luke had vacated. "I've got some canned huckleberries I've been saving. I might just make up a batch of my special pancakes."

"Umm. Sounds great," she said with a smile.

"I thought you ran out of them months ago. I remember the last time I wanted some——"

"I hid them. Been saving them for a special occasion," Matt said, gazing at Kate.

It didn't take a genius to see how he stood around here, Tanner thought. "Think I'll get the chores done. Work up an appetite," he said getting to his feet.

When Tanner reached the barn he discovered the mules had broken through the corral fence and, judging by their tracks, they were halfway up the mountain. Figuring he would eat before he looked for them, he tossed some hay into the manger for his horse, then he milked the cow and fed the chickens.

By the time he'd finished in the barn and returned to the house, the rest of them had already eaten. He didn't get any pancakes, nor any coffee. His breakfast, which he'd had to cook himself, consisted of an egg and a piece of leftover steak so tough he could have used it to resole his boot.

He didn't even get any conversation. With the boys chattering like magpies, he hadn't been able to get a word in all morning. He stared at the table where his brothers were gathered around Kate like pages waiting on a queen at court. He had the feeling with the boys hanging around her all the time, he'd be lucky to steal a kiss, let alone anything else.

He'd made a pot of coffee that, when it was done, tasted like dishwater mixed with barnyard mud. Grimacing, he dumped the pot. He didn't know why Matt's coffee always tasted better.

He yawned. Another hour's sleep wouldn't have hurt any, either. He shot a glance toward Kate.

Color bloomed in her cheeks; her eyes danced with laughter. The lack of sleep didn't seem to bother her. She looked fresh as a spring flower.

He felt and probably looked like something the dog had

found under the porch, which didn't help his disposition. He rubbed his unshaven cheek. He'd been shaving since he was fourteen. In two days he could grow a beard.

Matt was the only one of the boys who had to shave, and even then he could skip a week and nobody would ever notice.

No time for it now. He looked out the window and saw that the sky was once again intent on burying them in a blanket of snow. If he didn't get a move on, his mules would end up being cougar bait or so lost he'd never find them. "I've got to go find the mules," he said.

Nobody noticed.

Tanner put on his hat and coat and went out the door.

Fluffy sat, tail wagging, on the porch.

"Are you being ignored, too?"

The ungainly hound leaped up and licked Tanner's face, an act that both surprised and pleased him.

"Guess we'd better stick together." He bent and gave the dog's shaggy head a pat. "Hey, old son, how are you at finding mules?"

The dog let out a happy bark and trotted toward the woods.

Although Tanner knew he probably would have found the mules eventually, even though they were well hidden in a rocky draw, he had to give credit for locating them so soon to the dog, who not only discovered them but herded the temperamental critters back to the ranch.

It was shortly after noon when Tanner had the corral fence repaired and headed for the house for a bite to eat. Fluffy trotted alongside him. Although they had disliked each other at first sight, Tanner thought he and the dog had become pretty good friends, if one could say that of an animal.

At least the dog seemed to respect him, which was more than he could say of his brothers.

"Guess we'd better wipe our feet, or Matt will have us scrubbing the floors."

The dog looked at him and bared his teeth.

"My sentiments exactly." Tanner picked up an old sack and called the dog to him, then he brushed the snow from Fluffy's feet and fur.

When they entered the house, the dog trotted off to join John and Luke, who were playing checkers in front of the fireplace.

Tanner headed for the kitchen to see if Matt had made more coffee. When he reached the door he stopped dead in his tracks. "Get your hands off her!"

Matt, who had his arms wrapped around Kate, looked at him in amazement.

She looked at him like he'd lost his mind.

Mark glanced at the pair of them, then at Tanner. He began to laugh.

"Tanner, what is the matter with you?" Matt asked, but he kept his arms right where they were—around Kate.

"What do you think is the matter with me? I've been out working in the cold all morning, then I come in and find you hugging Kate."

"Hugging Kate?" Mark doubled over with merriment and ran out of the room. "Hey, Luke. You've got to hear this."

Matt and Kate stared at each other, then she shook her head. "The cold must have addled his brains. Now, where were we?"

"Take your hands off her. I'm not kidding," Tanner said, his tone deadly.

Matt removed his flour-covered arms from around Kate and dropped them to his sides. "She's right, you are addled."

"Tanner, stop it this instant," Kate ordered. "Matt was showing me how to improve my pie dough. I've had a problem with it being tough. He was showing me the right way to roll it out." Her violet eyes flashing, she raised a flour-covered finger and pointed to the door. "Now, if you would leave us be, we can get on with the lesson."

"Lesson? You weren't hugging her?"

"When you're hugging somebody, do you do it covered with flour?" she asked. "Really, Tanner."

Tanner looked at the flour-covered table, and the flour-covered Kate, and the half-rolled-out pie dough—and felt like a fool. "Well, if that was what you were doing, get on with it. I only came in for a cup of coffee anyhow."

"It's on the stove," Matt said coolly.

Tanner filled a mug with the potent brew, then left the room. He considered going to the living room until he figured out he was the subject of all the laughter. Having no place else to go, he put on his coat again and went to the barn.

He stayed there until Luke called him to supper. Still feeling a bit embarrassed, he took his place at the table and led the family in the blessing. He was relieved when no one poked fun at him for his earlier behavior.

The meal—venison steak, gravy, potatoes, dried green beans and fluffy biscuits—was done to perfection. He knew that for Kate, Matt had taken special pains with the preparation. For dessert they had pie, dried apple—or, in his case, humble. It, too, was out of the ordinary.

After eating his fill he decided Matt could give Kate all the cooking lessons he liked. He just wished his brother didn't have to get so cozy to do it.

John cleared the table while Mark and Luke started the dishes. Matt escorted Kate into the front room.

"Why don't you play something for us, Tanner?" Matt got the old fiddle down from the wall.

"All right, what would you like to hear?"

"Something we can dance to, right, Kate?"

"Sounds good to me," she answered, getting to her feet.

It didn't sound good to Tanner. "How about an Irish jig?"

"I was hoping for a waltz," Matt said.

I'll bet you were. It seemed to him like Matt was looking for another excuse to get his arms around Kate. Well, he wasn't about to give him the chance. He brought the fiddle to his chin and swung into a lively tune that had his fingers dancing over the strings.

Matt and Kate whirled around the room, his fair blond looks a perfect foil for her dusky beauty. The other boys joined the fun, each taking turns with Kate. With their youthful exuberance, the jig turned into a wild gallop that made Tanner glance at the rafters, wondering if they could stand up under such a din.

Barking, Fluffy raced around the room, anxious to join in the fun.

Finally when his fingers couldn't keep up the effort, Tanner reluctantly put his bow aside.

Kate's hair hung free to her waist, a riot of silky black curls. Her violet eyes sparkled, and her cheeks were pink with exertion. Her dishevelment gave her a wild, exotic look that heated his blood. He could almost imagine her dancing around a gypsy campfire.

The boys, gasping for breath, had collapsed in front of the fire. Tanner hoped that they would be so exhausted they would go to bed early. But Kate was the first one to bid them good night.

Disappointed, he watched her walk toward the bedroom. He'd hoped they might have some time alone, but with the boys around. . . . He shook his head.

John, rubbing his eyes, went next. The older boys, finding Tanner's company sadly lacking, followed close behind.

Tanner waited until the house grew quiet, until he was certain his brothers would be asleep, then he tiptoed down the hall and opened the bedroom door.

Kate lay sleeping, her palm tucked under her cheek, her long hair spilling over the pillow. She looked small, almost lost in the big bed.

Wonder if she'd mind some company? He'd taken only one step when, beside her, Fluffy raised his head.

"Good boy." He inched closer.

The dog let out a low growl.

"All right, don't get your fur in an uproar," he whispered. Apparently their new friendship didn't matter. The dog was Kate's guardian, and he wasn't about to let Tanner anywhere near. His show of teeth stated that in no uncertain terms.

Not anxious to have the whole household find him sneaking into Kate's room, he retreated and shut the door.

"Did you hear that?" Mark whispered.

"I heard him," Matt said. "For a minute I thought one of

us was going to have to go out and see what he was up to."

"He sure wouldn't like that," Luke said.

"We could pretend to get a drink of water or something," Mark suggested.

"There's a limit as to how much water we can drink. He'd catch on after a while," Luke declared.

"He's jealous. I thought he was going to punch me today," Matt said.

"And he's sneaky."

"He wants to pick the peaches, but he isn't ready to deal with the pits," Mark said.

"Peaches? Pits? What's that got to do with anything?" Luke asked, scratching his head.

"Tanner wants to bed Kate, but he's not willing to marry her," Matt explained.

"That ain't right," Luke muttered.

"Dang right it's not, and we're not going to let it happen."

"How are we going to stop it?"

They huddled together, talking softly, making one plan only to discard it in favor of another. Finally, unable to stay awake any longer, Mark and Luke went back to their own room.

Why couldn't I be older? Matt thought. He'd give anything just to be able to hold her hand. He'd be willing to die for a kiss. She considered him—all of them, except Tanner—younger brothers. But Matt didn't feel brotherly. He had hugged her; 'course she didn't know what he was doing. He'd hug her again if he got the chance.

But Tanner wanted more than a hug—that much was obvious to anyone who knew the ways of men and women. Tanner wanted— Picturing what Tanner wanted, Matt shoved a fist into his pillow, wishing it was his older brother's face. His own blood pulsing with the need to protect her, Matt stared at the ceiling.

After the whisper of voices grew silent, soft footsteps retreated down the hall. Apparently the Blaines were a restless bunch. First Tanner coming into her room, then the boys plotting across the hall.

Did one have anything to do with the other? Kate wondered.

She'd pretended sleep when Tanner had entered her room, even though it was hard to keep her eyes closed with him standing there looking at her. She would have sworn he must have heard her heart beating, it roared like a raging river in her ears.

If the dog hadn't growled, what would he have done?

Worse yet, what would she have done? Probably something they both would have been sorry for in the morning.

Would he have come to her bed, made love to her? And would she, could she have refused him? She didn't know.

She remembered the night in the buggy and what very easily could have happened. She loved him; it would be easy to surrender her virtue. It would also be the worst possible thing she could do.

He wanted her, he'd made that clear, and while she thought he was fond of her, she knew he didn't love her. And he certainly didn't want to marry her, otherwise he wouldn't have been so intent on finding her a husband.

She'd never been in love before, but other people had told her it was the most marvelous thing that could happen between two people. Somehow she doubted she would ever reach that state of euphoria. For as she lay in the dark, alone in the big bed, her love for Tanner Blaine was the most painful thing she had ever experienced.

13

"*W*AKE UP, TANNER. We need to talk."

His feet hanging over the arm of the horsehair couch, Tanner groaned and opened his eyes.

Matt, Mark and Luke stared down at him.

He glanced toward the living room window. "It's the middle of the night. Can't whatever it is wait until morning?"

"It is morning," Matt said firmly. "And it can't wait."

Tanner sighed, then pushed himself upright and put his feet on the floor.

Mark tossed a log on the fire and sent a haze of sparks into the room. He glared at Tanner, his eyes accusing. "We heard you last night. We know what you were up to, and we aren't going to stand for it."

Tanner looked from one to another of his brothers. Each of them appeared mad enough to punch him. "I don't know what you are talking about," he lied.

"You went into Kate's room. We heard you," Matt declared, daring him to deny it.

"So?"

"Don't do it again," Mark warned.

"Yeah. We'll be watchin'," Luke finished.

With that, the three of them marched back to bed.

"Well, I'll be damned. Sneaky little . . . They won't

stand for it? Who do they think they are?" He lay back down and pulled the covers back up over his shoulders, but guilt wouldn't allow him to sleep.

It wasn't as though he intended to force her or anything. He didn't plan to do anything she wasn't willing to do—regardless of what his brothers thought.

It isn't right, his conscience argued.

A woman needed a little loving, he argued. He'd be gentle. He'd never had any complaints so far. Some women had enjoyed it so much they begged for more.

Kate isn't like them. She's gentle-bred. A lady. She'd be ruined.

Ruined? Not in his estimation. A man appreciated a woman with a little experience. Besides, how did he know she'd never made love to a man? She was past the age when most women are married. She might have already been around the barn a time or two and didn't want to admit it.

Daisy, over at the Golden Spike saloon, had entertained half the men in Jacksonville at one time or another, yet to hear her tell it, she was pure as the driven snow. She'd gotten married, and her husband hadn't complained none. He'd said she taught him things he'd never dreamed of.

He tugged the blanket up again, uncovering his feet. The covers were too short. He couldn't keep one end of his body warm without freezing the other.

He drew up his knees and closed his eyes. Wasn't any sense worrying about something that probably would never happen. With that dog of hers and his brothers watching every move he made, he'd be lucky to get in as much as a "howdy do" before spring.

After cutting enough wood to replace what they'd used up in the storm, Tanner wiped his feet and went into the house.

He'd left Mark chopping ice out of the water troughs. Luke was shoveling a trail to the privy. Now if he could just get Matt and John out of the way.

He hung up his coat and gloves and had started toward the living room to warm himself, when a hammering sound drew his attention. He followed the noise and found Matt kneeling by Kate's bedroom door.

Kate stood beside him, watching.

"There. All done." Matt got to his feet.

"Something wrong with the door?" Tanner asked.

"Not now. I just put a lock on it." Matt glanced at Kate. "Anytime you feel like a little privacy, you just slide this bolt. That way nobody can bother you." He gave Tanner a pointed look.

"Isn't he thoughtful?" Kate said, giving Matt a smile.

"Real thoughtful," Tanner agreed. "Matt, I'll have to see what I can do for you sometime."

"Don't worry about it, Tanner. I'm glad to help out."

"Speaking of "out," I want you to clean out those stalls today. And then you can curry the mules."

"Can't do it today, Tanner. I promised to show Kate how to make bread."

"I'm really looking forward to it," she said brightly.

"Well . . . I wouldn't want to disappoint a lady. Matt, the barn will still be there—waiting for you—tomorrow."

Matt's face fell.

"Since you're set on giving cooking lessons, maybe I'll watch. Refresh my memory," he said smoothly. "It's been a long time since I've made a loaf of bread."

"Can you make bread, too?" Kate asked.

"Sure can," he said, sliding an arm around her waist. "Why, *darlin',* you'd be surprised at how many things I'm good at."

"We need to get started on that bread, Kate," Matt said, shooting him a look that would have driven nails.

"Tanner?"

"I'll be along in a minute, *honey.* I just want to inspect Matt's work. Wouldn't want you getting locked in so tight you couldn't get out, would we?"

After Matt took Kate off to the kitchen, Tanner inspected the lock. In truth, Matt had done a fine job. Neat, darn near perfect. The bolt slid easily. Not a chance it would jam. It was also stout enough to keep out a bull. Thinking of last night, he sighed. Well, he could scratch that possibility. But

Matt wasn't the only one who could play the game. A determined glint in his eyes, he headed for the kitchen.

Matt stood, arms around Kate, punching at a mound of dough. "We can pretend it's Tanner," he said, pummeling it with his fist.

Kate blinked when a puff of flour hit her in the face.

"I think it's safer over here. Besides, you can see better," Tanner said, freeing her from Matt's embrace.

"Yeah, but she won't learn how to do it."

"Sure she will. We'll use that bunch," he pointed to another mound of dough that hadn't been punched up yet. "Kate and I will do ours. You can show us how."

Matt scowled but remained silent.

"First," said Tanner, turning Kate to face him, "we'll get that flour out of your eyes." He took his handkerchief and wiped her eyes, then with his fingertip brushed a smudge from her nose. "Now, then." He sprinkled a handful of flour on the table, then placed the dough in the middle of it. "Let's see." He placed Kate in front of him and put his arms around her. "I think that's the way you were doing it, isn't it, Matt?"

"Since you know so much about it, from now on I'll leave the bread making to you." Matt wiped his hands and strode out of the room.

"Think I might enjoy bread making," Tanner murmured into Kate's ear. He took hold of her hands and pushed them in and out of the soft dough. "How about you, darlin'?"

"I think it could be real pleasurable," she said, sounding a little breathless.

"I thought you would," he said, hiding his grin.

"What happened to the bread?" Mark asked, trying to saw through a piece.

"Tanner made it," Matt said accusingly.

"I helped," Kate said, not wanting him to take all the blame. "Didn't we do it right?"

"It's okay. Actually it's quite tasty," Luke said, tearing off a chunk with his teeth. "Just a little hard in spots."

"I guess we need more practice," Tanner said softly, his eyes fixed on hers. "Lots more practice."

Thinking about that bread making, and the possibility that more would follow, she grew absolutely giddy.

That night when she'd gone to bed, that feeling still hadn't left her. She could smell the tangy pine and wood smoke scent of him, feel the strength of his arms around her, his breath warm against her cheek. His hands enfolding hers and the soft dough pressed between their palms, giving her the most erotic sensation she had ever experienced. And when they were finished, he'd wiped the flour from her face and neck. She could tell by the look in his eyes that he intended to kiss her.

Then John burst through the door.

Her face had flamed scarlet and Tanner had looked decidedly uncomfortable. They hadn't done anything wrong, yet they couldn't have looked more guilty if they'd been caught rolling on the floor. Thank goodness the child was too young to notice.

But the older boys weren't. Had they heard Tanner enter her room last night? Was that the reason Matt had put the lock on her door?

The lock. Matt would be insulted if she didn't use it. She crept out of bed and slid the bolt. Tanner wouldn't be visiting her room this night. As she climbed back into bed, she didn't know if that made her sad or happy. But at least she wouldn't be yielding to temptation.

It seemed Matt might be the wise one, after all.

A blinding snowstorm hit the next day. And John came down with a fever. Matt had awakened Tanner during the night and together they had watched over the child until morning.

"More than likely it's only a cold, but I think we should keep him isolated until we find out for sure," Tanner said.

Kate's eyes grew wide. "You don't think it could be . . ."

"Naw. How could he catch it?"

"Could I have brought him the germs?"

"No. If anybody brought him any germs it was me. I was at the doctor's office."

"But you came into town because of me. It would still be my fault."

"It wouldn't be your fault. Kate, the boy has a cold, pure and simple. But even with a cold, I think it might be a good idea if we made different sleeping arrangements, for the time being at least."

"Yes, you're right. What do we do?"

"If you don't mind, your bed being the biggest, we could put the three older boys in there. You could take Mark's room, and John could stay where he is. Is that all right with you?"

"Of course. I'll move my things right now."

Tanner took another look at John, then he went into the kitchen where Matt was busy with breakfast. "Maybe some soup might help him. I'll kill one of those old hens, and you could stew up a pot."

"You can't even see the barn. How are you going to find a chicken?" Matt asked.

"What if you get turned around?" Mark said. "You'd freeze before we could find you."

"You could use that new well rope," Luke suggested. "Tie it to the porch post and string it to the barn. That way you could find your way back."

"It's not long enough, but we could tie that length of clothesline on it," Matt said thoughtfully. "It might reach then."

Tanner gazed at Matt. "Yesterday I had the feeling that you wouldn't care if I froze or not."

"Hell, Tanner," Matt said angrily. "You're my brother. I might want to punch your gizzard out, but I wouldn't want anything to happen to you."

Tanner grinned. "I'll remind you of that next time."

"I'll go with you," Mark said. "Need to break the ice so the animals can get water. And that cow is probably bawling her head off to be milked. Besides, with both of us out there, we could get done quicker."

"I'd appreciate your help. Matt, keep an eye on John, but it might be a good idea if you don't go in there unless it's necessary."

"You don't think it's smallpox, do you?"

Tanner didn't answer. He didn't know. He did know John had never been this sick before. He put on his coat and hat and followed Mark out the door.

14

$\mathcal{I}$T HAD BEEN three days since the storm began. Tanner had hoped it would blow itself out, but instead it had grown in voracity, swallowing the mountain and everything on it in a swirling void of white. The wind intensified the cold, creeping in around the windows and the eves of the house, making it chilly despite the roaring fire. Praying the wood would hold out until the storm was over, he put another log on the fire and went to stare out the window.

The snow piled around the outside walls, mounding over the windowsills, reaching a depth of three feet, some places even more. The isolation he had hoped for had come to pass. Now, with John sick, he would have given his soul if he could exchange it for one bright, sunlit day.

A scent of flowers drifted to his nostrils. He shifted his gaze and found Kate standing by his side. "How is he?"

"No change." Her eyes were ringed with shadows from two sleepless nights. Like Tanner, she'd refused to leave John's side in case he might awaken and need her.

Tanner, too, would not leave John, for fear the angel of death would snatch the little boy if nobody was watching.

Even though Tanner hadn't allowed them to enter the sickroom, Matt, Mark and Luke also held vigil, pacing between the hall and the kitchen.

Matt continued to make meals that remained mostly

uneaten. Mark and Luke had taken over the tending of the stock, leaving Tanner free to care for their little brother. The family and Kate talked in hushed tones, moved slowly, quietly, and existed on copious pots of black coffee. It was as though they were locked in a place where time stood still, yet no one was willing to set the pendulum in motion.

Fighting overwhelming exhaustion of mind and spirit, Tanner poured another cup of the bitter brew and returned to the bedroom, setting the coffee on the bedside table, where it, like so many others, would remain until it grew cold.

He took the child's hand, holding it between his own. With the high fever John's skin had taken on the appearance of dried parchment paper. Tanner and Kate had bathed him with cool water and had attempted to force minute quantities of herbal teas, broth and other concoctions through the child's lips. Nothing they had been able to do had made the least difference. The fever raged on. John remained unconscious, hovering on that thin line between life and death, with each faint breath carrying him closer to the hereafter.

Unable to bear it any longer, Tanner lifted his little brother into his arms and held him close. He remembered John's first baby smile. His first tooth. His first hesitant step. The laughter and the mischief, the joy he had brought into their lives. *"Hang on, baby,"* he pleaded. But even as he spoke he could feel the child's life ebbing away.

His body shaking with silent grief, Tanner closed his eyes and bowed his head. It had been a long time since he'd prayed, and he wasn't sure the Almighty would even listen, particularly after the way he'd been behaving of late. He only knew John's fate lay with a higher power.

After exhausting every plea and listening for a reply, any hope for this dear little boy, Tanner finally had his answer. He placed John back on the bed and smoothed a lock of hair off the child's face. Glancing up, he saw Kate standing in the doorway.

"He's going to die, isn't he?" she whispered, her expression tortured, her face wet with tears.

"No! We won't let him. While I was praying, I saw my

father. He told me what to do." He took her hand and pulled her into the room.

"What did he say?" she asked.

"He reminded me of a story he used to tell of a miner who had a high fever. His partners had given up on him, left him alone to die. The Indians found him. Instead of scalping him, they cured him by packing him in snow."

"Snow? You're going to . . ."

"I can't just sit here and watch John die. I am going to either cure him or kill him. The cold might break the fever, or it might give him frostbite or pneumonia. It will be the Lord's decision whichever way it goes." He began to remove his brother's sleeping garment. The child's skin against his hands seemed hot enough to sear flesh.

John made a feeble attempt to open his eyes, then immediately lapsed back into unconsciousness.

Not even trying to hold back his own tears, Tanner scooped the wasted little body into his arms.

"Tanner?" Eyes wide, Kate stared at him. "I'm coming with you." She grabbed her coat and followed him from the house.

Instructing Kate to wait on the porch, Tanner waded down the snow-covered steps and a short distance away before he deposited John in an area next to the house where the dwelling would shield them from the cold wind. The snow was feathery light, and the heat of the fever melted it as soon as it touched John's body.

Tanner gently smoothed a layer over the child's skin, then added another, and another, until the boy was encased in an icy cocoon.

Please, let it work. Please, don't let him get any sicker. Scarcely daring to breathe, Tanner watched for a sign that the treatment was having an effect one way or another.

The child's body twitched as if becoming aware of the icy mound, but other than that there was no response.

What if it didn't work? What if he caused his brother to freeze to death? How could he ever live with that? Tanner hesitated. His gaze shifted to Kate.

Her face pale and drawn, her lips compressed and blue

with cold, she looked at him, and then at the little boy. Her eyes widened. "Look! He's moving."

He stared down at his brother.

John jerked, then began to shake. He moaned and cried out.

"Hold on, baby." His throat tight with emotion, Tanner fought the urge to yank his brother free of the ice and carry him back inside to the warmth. He couldn't do that, not yet. His own hands stiff with cold, he touched the feverish forehead. Still hot, but whether the fever was as high as before, he couldn't tell. Tanner was so cold that ice water would feel warm.

"Kate?"

"Yes, Tanner?"

"I need for you to feel his head. See if there is any change." He pushed his way to the porch and held out his arms. "No sense in you wading through this mess."

She gripped his shoulders as he hoisted her into his arms and carried her to where John lay. Her face intent, she removed her gloves and pressed the back of her hand against the child's cheek. "I think it's working. He doesn't feel as hot. Can we . . .?"

"Not yet. But I do have something you can do. Have Matt fill that washtub—tell him to make the water just warm enough to take the chill off." He carried her to the porch and set her on her feet.

"How much longer?"

He shook his head. "I have the feeling I'll know when the time is right."

Kate went into the house, and Tanner returned to watch over his brother.

Slowly but surely the flush of the fever retreated. Tanner still waited.

John coughed, then his eyelids fluttered. He shivered, then raised his arm and stared at the snow. His eyes big, he peered up. "T-Tanner?"

Thank you. Unable to speak, Tanner brushed the snow away and drew the child into his arms.

"W-what am I d-doing out here? Where's my c-clothes? I'm c-cold."

"Welcome back, baby." He carried the shivering child up the steps. His brothers and Kate waited by the door. "He's awake. I think he's going to be all right."

Tanner bathed his little brother, then put him to bed. Even though John seemed better, he and Kate remained at his bedside.

"You don't have to stay up," Tanner said, noting the dark circles ringing her eyes. "I'll watch over him."

"I want to stay. I love him, too," she said softly. She turned the lamp down to a soft glow, then pulled a chair close to the other side of the bed.

He knew she would stay there until morning. She did love the boy; her actions had proved that. Not even Maggie could have given John better care. He imagined Kate with a child of her own. She needed a child—children. She had so much love to give; she would make a wonderful mother. Yet, the idea of her creating those children with someone else was almost more than he could bear.

If there was any way, any way at all, he would ask her to marry him, to stay there on the mountain. But there wasn't. He refused to saddle her with his financial burdens. By the time he got his life in order and the boys were out on their own, years would have passed. He couldn't, wouldn't, ask her to wait.

John made it through the night without the fever rising. When dawn came, and the child was sleeping peacefully, Tanner knew the crisis had passed.

He rose, stretched to restore his circulation, then extinguished the lamp. He touched Kate's shoulder and saw that fatigue had drained the last of her willpower. She had fallen asleep.

Rather than wake her, he lifted her into his arms and carried her into her bedroom. There, he removed her shoes, then her dress, knowing she would be more comfortable without it. She'd lost weight, he noticed, but then they all had eaten very little. In Kate's case it only emphasized her fragility. He placed her in the bed and gently tucked the covers around her.

Weariness made Tanner's head reel, yet there was no place he could rest. He knew Matt was up: he'd heard pots rattling in the kitchen. And when he'd carried Kate past their bedroom door, he saw Mark and Luke were still in bed. After they woke, the living room would soon become too noisy for any attempt at sleep.

He ran a hand over his eyes. She looked so comfortable and the bed so tempting. Maybe she wouldn't care if he stretched out, just for a minute.

He pulled off his boots and lay down beside her. In seconds he was fast asleep.

"Do you see that?" Mark turned to Matt, whose brow knitted into a frown. "Suppose we ought to wake him up?"

"When he's that far gone the house could fall on him and he wouldn't know it."

"It ain't exactly proper, him being in her bed like that."

"Tanner's in no shape to try anything. Besides, he wouldn't make love to a woman who's sound asleep. We'll just leave them be." Matt pulled the door shut so that the slumbering couple wouldn't be disturbed.

He checked on John, then he and Mark returned to the kitchen. Matt loved Kate, but he also knew nothing would ever come of it. Although she appeared fond of him, she treated him no differently than she did the rest of his siblings. It was clear to everybody except his big brother that Tanner was the one who had captured her heart.

But Tanner would never do anything about it. Unless . . .

"I thought you agreed we would keep them apart," Mark declared.

"Do you want Kate to marry somebody else?" Matt asked.

"No. I want her to stay right here. But I also don't want him to . . . to . . ."

"Tanner's an honorable man, and if he did make love to Kate, he'd consider himself bound to marry her, whether he realizes it or not," Matt said. "And if he didn't make the offer, we could shame him into it."

"I don't know." Luke shook his head. "Somehow it don't seem right."

"We're not going to force them into anything," Matt said with exasperation. "We'll just give them the opportunity and let nature do the rest."

Lost somewhere between wakefulness and slumber, Tanner became aware of a cold draft on his shoulder. He tugged the covers up, then moved closer to the woman at his side.

With a soft sigh of contentment she shifted position, molding her body against his, until they fit together like a matching pair of spoons.

Savoring the intimacy, he put his arm around her waist, then sliding his hand up her rib cage, he cupped the soft mound of her breast. It seemed so real, he could feel the steady beat of her heart against his palm. Yet, he knew Kate wasn't really there, "It's only a dream" he murmured. It couldn't be anything else. Burying his face in a tangle of silky hair, he breathed in her fragrance and prayed he'd never awaken.

Kate, hearing his whisper, knew it wasn't a dream. She almost wished it was. For if it were a dream, she could control the outcome. The same way she had so many times before. In her fantasy, he would kiss her awake, then he would make slow, delicious love to her. But in reality she knew it would never happen, for when he awoke he would leave her, and later pretend it had never happened.

Tears crept from beneath her eyelids, but she would not allow herself to make a sound. For now she would hold on to the moment, lying next to Tanner, having him hold her, feeling the strength of his arms, the gentleness of his caress.

No, she would not wake him. Neither would she go to sleep. She, too, would lie there, tucking the moment away like a cherished memento, to bring out and examine someday when she was old.

15

"*Would you like* another piece of pie, sweetie?" Kate asked, hovering over John like a mother hen with only one chick. She fluffed his pillow and straightened his covers. He only had to sigh and she would be there by his side.

"I would like a little more snow ice cream," John said faintly.

Tanner, watching from the doorway, shook his head and grinned. "You're spoiling him."

"I'm doing no such thing," she replied indignantly. "I'm merely trying to make the poor little thing feel better."

The pitiful look John gave Tanner was so obviously put on that he was hard pressed not to laugh. In the week since the fever had dropped, that "poor little thing" had kept everybody running their legs off, including him. Although he hated to spoil John's fun, it was time the pampering came to a stop. "How would you like to get out of that bed for a while, Johnny boy?"

The child cut his eyes at Kate. "Well, I don't know."

"Absolutely not!" Kate declared, whirling to face him. "He's still not well enough for that."

"I'll play you a game of checkers," Tanner promised.

"You will?" John bolted upright in the bed and flashed him a wide grin. "I guess I could get up for a little while."

He peered up at Kate. "Please. Tanner hardly ever plays with me."

"You don't?" She frowned. "Why not?"

"Never seem to have the time. But that's all going to change, isn't it, squirt?" He leaned close to the bed and ruffled the little boy's hair. John's illness had taught him a lesson. He learned just how much his brothers meant to him. How devastated he would be if anything happened to one of them.

"Are you ready?" he asked, his voice husky with emotion. Never again would he allow work or anything else to make him forget the important things in his life.

"I'm ready," John said solemnly.

Tanner gently lifted the boy into his arms. John seemed weightless, fragile, and for a moment he wondered if he were doing the right thing. One look into Kate's fear-filled eyes told him he was. The family and Kate had to help John put the illness behind him. It was the only way he could truly be well.

Holding the child close, he strode into the living room. "Somebody set up the checkerboard. John has challenged me to a game."

"Gonna beat him are you, bud?" Mark said, going to fetch the game board.

"I don't know. Tanner's awful good," John replied doubtfully.

"Heck, he's so rusty, I'll bet Kate could beat him, and she's probably never played checkers in her life," Luke chimed in.

"I've played a few games," she said. "I might just challenge him later on."

"Won't do you any good," Tanner said, rising to the bait. "I'll never get that rusty."

"We'll see, Mr. Blaine. We'll see." She gave him a sly smile, then headed for the kitchen. "I almost forgot John's ice cream." She turned at the doorway. "Would anyone else like anything?"

"I wouldn't mind having a piece of that pie," Tanner said hopefully. "It sure did smell good cooking."

"It is good," Matt declared.

"Dee-licious," Luke agreed.

"Best pie I ever tasted," Mark said. "In fact, I'd like another slice."

"Sorry, but the remaining pieces belong to Tanner and John."

Surprised that she'd saved one for him, Tanner gave her a pleased smile.

She left the room, returning a few minutes later with John's ice cream and a large slice of dried apple pie. She handed it to Tanner.

It looked as scrumptious as it smelled, and it tasted even better. The crust was light and flaky, the filling mouth-wateringly delicious. "Oh, that's good," he said between mouthfuls. "I've never tasted any better." He licked his lips, wishing for a whole pie all his own. "Kate, you'll have people coming all the way from Yreka for a pie like this."

"Do you really think so?"

"I know so."

"I used Maggie's recipe, and Matt showed me how to improve my crust. Oh, I almost forgot your coffee."

"His pies have never been that good," Luke declared, watching her go back into the kitchen. "How come, Matt?"

"I think it's the cook, not the cooking," Matt said with a grin.

"He's never looked that pretty in an apron, either," Mark added. "Don't you think Kate's pretty, Tanner?"

Tanner looked from one of his brothers to the other. All of them were grinning like opossums. "I think she's mighty pretty."

"And she's a good cook," Matt added.

"That she is," Tanner admitted.

"Got a nice disposition, too," Mark said.

"Yes, she does."

"Then why can't we keep her?" John asked.

"You can't just keep a person like she's a pup or something," Tanner argued.

"You could if you married her," the little boy declared.

"We're not going into that again. We've got our reasons

for not getting married. Besides, you're too young to understand." He put the board in between them. "Now, let's play checkers."

Smiling to hide her hurt, Kate left the hallway and carried the cup of coffee into the living room. *Too young to understand?* Tanner had explained all about his brothers, his responsibilities, his obligations. She was a whole lot older than John, and she didn't understand Tanner's reasons, either.

After John and the rest of the boys had played checkers with Tanner, Kate took a turn. At first she played poorly, pretending to let him teach her the rudimentary elements of the game. In truth she had played since she was old enough to reach the board, and if she did say so herself, she was pretty darned good.

"Are you willing to bow to my superiority?" Tanner asked, after beating her for the third time.

"Not just yet. We'll try a couple more, unless you're too tired."

"Tired of playing checkers?" He gave a hoot. "I could beat you all night."

While Tanner was arranging the board she looked over his head and winked at the boys. "We'll see," she said, softly.

She quickly trounced him in that game and the next two as well, much to the boys' delight and Tanner's amazement.

"Do you give up?" she asked.

"Three and three, that makes a tie. One more, and this time I won't let you beat me," Tanner warned.

Kate smiled.

A little while later, a disgruntled Tanner conceded the game. "Where did you learn to play like that?"

"I had a bachelor uncle that did little else," she explained. "He taught me to play when I was four, and we played almost every day until he went off to war. I have gotten a little bit rusty these past few years."

"Did you let me win those first three games?" he asked with suspicion.

She grinned. "You'll never know, will you?"

"I'll bet you could teach me a thing or two about the game," he admitted.

"Could be." She could teach him a lot of things: how to love, how to trust, how not to be so pigheaded. If he would only give her the chance.

The next day the clouds parted and a brilliant sun lit the bright blue sky. Everywhere snow glittered like it had a covering of diamonds. Frustrated at being cooped up so long, Kate wanted nothing more than to go outside.

"Have you ever tried skiing?" Matt asked, coming up beside her.

"No. We never had that much snow in Georgia." She sighed wistfully. "It does sound like fun, though."

"What sounds like fun?" Tanner asked from the doorway.

"Kate's never been skiing. Why don't we show her how?"

"Would you like that, Kate?"

"I think so, if you'd teach me."

"How could I refuse?" He looked her up and down and frowned. "You'll need some britches."

"Luke outgrew a pair that might fit. And John's boots," Matt said. "I'll get them."

A while later Kate, dressed in the boys' clothes, followed Tanner to the barn and waited while he removed a pair of snow skis from the wall and fastened them to her boots.

"How does that feel?"

"Strange." She slid the boards back and forth, trying to get the feel of them, while Tanner put on a pair of his own.

"Ready?" he asked, handing her a pair of pointed slender poles. "Follow me. Do what I do." In a smooth gliding motion, he left the barn and headed toward the meadow.

Her heart hammering with excitement, Kate tried to follow his lead. While Tanner weaved gracefully across the snow, she moved like a duck with oversized feet. But after she began to get the rhythm, she decided it was more like sliding on air. She was so thrilled by her accomplishment she didn't notice she'd lost Tanner, until he yelled out her name.

"Kate, stop! That hill's too steep."

By the time she heard his warning it was too late, she was already over the crest and plunging straight downhill. The skis hissed over the ice-covered terrain, picking up speed with every foot. Hoping to slow herself, she leaned forward—and went even faster. She whizzed by trees, bushes. She ducked a snow-covered limb and felt it snatch her hat from her head. "Tanner!" she screamed.

"Fall down!"

Fall down? How? The more she leaned, the faster she went. Paralyzed with fear, she stared at a large clump of trees that suddenly loomed in front of her.

"Tanner! Help me!"

The trees drew closer and closer. Knowing she couldn't avoid the crash, she closed her eyes.

"I've got you, Kate." Tanner snaked an arm around her waist and jerked her off her feet. Snow flew as he skidded to one side.

She felt him release her, then she was flying through the air. She landed on her stomach, facedown in the snow. She jerked her head up to see Tanner tumbling end over end.

Tanner rolled to a stop several yards away. He sat up and stared at her. "Are you all right?"

"I think so."

He noticed that she'd lost her hat, but she didn't seem to be hurt.

She brushed at her hair, sending ebony ringlets spiraling through a crown of snow. She gazed at him and giggled. "You look like a snowman without a nose."

"I'm glad to know you're so concerned about me." Grinning, he raised his hand and slapped at the side of his head, shaking the white particles loose from his face and out of his ears.

"There's got to be an easier way to stop." She tried to get to her feet. Every time her skis made contact with the snow, they began to slide, carrying her with them.

"Stay put," he warned, afraid she might end up in an even worse predicament.

"How do I get up?"

Tanner reattached his own skis, then glided over beside her. "Maybe I should leave you there, keep you out of mischief."

"Thought you were going to teach me how to ski," she said, peering up like a dark-haired imp.

"I thought you might be ready to quit." He took her outstretched hand and hoisted her to her feet.

"Not on your life." She shook her head, tossing a lock of hair out of her face. The act set her skis in motion. They slid—in opposite directions. Her eyes widened. "Oh-h!" Off balance, she reached out and grabbed the front of his shirt.

"Whoa!" He tried to pull her upright, but it was too late. The momentum carried her backward, and him right along with her.

She plopped into a snowdrift.

He landed smack on top of her. Mouth open, he stared at her.

"Now what do we do?" she asked.

He peered over his shoulder at the tangle of skis and poles. "Danged if I know. Never been in this kind of situation before."

She gazed at him, then erupted in a fit of giggles.

"You wouldn't think it was so funny if you could see that cliff you almost went over," he said, laughing along with her.

"W-what cliff?" she managed to gasp out. "I was worried about the t-trees."

"The cliff on the other side of the trees."

He eyed her rosy cheeks and red nose. A riot of dusky curls framed her heart-shaped face, and a smudge of red mud streaked her cheek. She was a mess, but she never looked more appealing. "Your face is dirty. Think I'll wash it," he said, playfully scooping up a handful of snow.

"Don't you dare, Tanner Blai—"

He pushed the soft snow into her face.

She spat out a mouthful and swiped at the rest. "I'll get you for that." She dipped her hand into the drift, then pelted him with a snowball of her own.

"Ow-w, that's cold," he yelled, trying to remove a wad from inside his shirt. "Let's see how you like it." He stuffed a handful down her jacket front.

"Yeow," she squealed. "That's not fair. I can't reach it to get it out." She squirmed beneath him. "Oh-h. Help me."

He yanked off his glove and slid a hand beneath her shirt to try to remove the snowball. What he came up with was a palm full of warm, soft flesh. He froze.

She sucked in a breath. Startled violet eyes met his gaze.

"I, uh, I . . ." He couldn't remember what he was trying to say. Or what he'd been attempting to do. He swallowed, feeling himself being mesmerized by those deep, dark pools. Try as he might, he couldn't let go of her. And he was too far gone to make any attempt to get up.

She shyly lowered her lashes, then nervously moistened her lips.

God, she was beautiful, and soft. So damned soft. He felt every dip, every womanly curve of her body. He also felt every quiver, every stiffening awareness of his own arousal pressed into her. He fought the desire, even knowing as he did so that he was fast losing the battle.

Still, he struggled. He didn't want this. He didn't need it. It would change nothing. Snow and ice surrounded him, but it didn't help to cool the damnable heat burning inside him. He may as well have been lying in a current of molten fire.

She waited, her eyes locked on his. "Tanner," she whispered, then her arms slowly crept up and around his neck and Tanner knew he was lost.

A low moan rumbled from his throat as he reluctantly surrendered. The kiss was as inevitable as daylight following darkness and just as explosive. Once he started kissing her, it was impossible to stop. He kissed her fiercely, angrily, bruising her mouth with his fury. Yet he still felt her sweet response.

He raised his head. The gentle reproach in her eyes filled him with shame and unexpected longing. He kissed her again, this time with an odd tenderness. He didn't know where it came from, and he didn't welcome it. He didn't like feeling this helpless, this vulnerable.

His body trembled with desperate need, making him want to tear aside her clothes and bury himself deep inside her. But he wouldn't. Somehow this thing between them had become more than physical lust. It had opened doors long closed, releasing emotions filled with anguish and yearning. He didn't want to put a name to it. He refused to even try.

Tempted beyond reason, he bent his head to her full red lips. She tasted even sweeter than he remembered, and he remembered every single bit. He explored every sensitive crevice, then his tongue made slow, tentative love to hers. He kissed her lips, her nose, her eyelids.

Sighing with pleasure, she brought his mouth back to hers. This time their tongues mated with a fierce hunger. He bent his head and blazed a trail of kisses from her chin to the valley at the base of her throat.

Her pulse fluttered like a hummingbird's wings against his lips. Her breast, still held captive in his hand, swelled. Her nipple jutted into his palm.

She tugged at the fastenings on her shirt. One button, then another, flew off to be lost in the snow.

He slipped the others from their moorings, then parted the garment and bared their hidden treasures. High and proud, her breasts reminded him of coral-tipped mountains of snow.

She tightened her fingers in his hair and pulled him toward one rosy nipple. He took it between his teeth and teased it with his tongue. She moaned when he closed his mouth around the crest and suckled like a hungry babe. Then he moved to the other peak, conquering it, too. He kissed her tenderly, thoroughly, choosing this way to show her his feelings.

Purring in satisfaction, she rained kisses upon his head and murmured love words in his ear.

His breathing ragged, he raised his head to look at her.

Her eyes warm with passion, she raised a hand and touched his cheek. "Tanner . . ." The beguiling look she gave him was almost his undoing.

It would be so easy to make love to her—too easy. He

wanted her more than he'd ever wanted anything in his life. He also knew she could never be his.

Clamping down on his rampaging emotions, he shook his head. "I don't have the right. Someday when you go to your marriage bed, you'll be grateful I didn't. The man who claims you for his own will consider himself the luckiest hombre on this earth."

"What if I never get married?"

He gently smoothed a lock of hair back from her face. "That would purely be a shame." Avoiding her accusing gaze, he untangled himself and backed off of her. True to the vow he'd made in the snow that day when he'd prayed, Kate would leave the mountain the same way she came, a virgin.

Once he could remain upright, Tanner took off his skis. Then, after removing hers, he helped Kate to her feet.

Her nose and cheeks growing red from the cold, she tried to repress a shiver. "What happened . . ."

"Was a mistake," he said grimly. "Better get you dressed before you freeze to death." He reached to help her.

"Don't touch me," she said, jerking away. She buttoned the bottom of her shirt and tucked it into her pants. She lapped over the shirt top with its missing buttons and covered it with her coat.

He knew he had hurt her, and he felt bad about that. But if he had let things go any further, they both would have lived to regret it.

"Considering it's all uphill, it'll be easier if we walk back." He picked up the skis and handed her a set of poles. "These might help you keep your balance. I'll break the way, and you can follow."

She looked so small, so dejected, it was all he could do to not gather her into his arms. But it wouldn't help him, and it wouldn't help her.

Telling himself he was doing the right thing, he turned away. His boots crunching through the knee-deep snow, he made a trail toward the house.

16

*T*HE NEXT FEW days the sun shone brightly, melting the snow into scattered patches, and Tanner resumed his work. The unseasonable warmth would help him make up the days he hadn't been able to get into the woods. It also gave him a reason to avoid being with Kate.

She'd been quiet, withdrawn, since that day in the meadow snow. She'd watch him with haunted eyes, her face expressing such longing that it was almost more than he could endure.

Even though he wanted to take her in his arms, and beg her to stay, he wouldn't. He'd thought about it long and hard, marriage and all that it entailed. He'd seen the way she had reacted to John's illness. What if it had happened to a child of her own? Life on the mountain was lived close to the edge, with death only a breath away from life. How could he marry her, subject her to that?

He couldn't. He loved her, and because he loved her he would do what was best for her. In the long run, she would be grateful that he had. Sighing, he hoisted the ax and drove it into the tree. It was dealing with the present that was so damned difficult.

Of course there were blessings to be counted. John was back to being his impish self, and the bickering between the

three older boys was worse than ever. Everything had
returned to normal.

Everything but him.

Tanner knew with the snow melting as much as it had, he
could take Kate back to Jacksonville. Somehow, he couldn't
make himself do it. He would prolong the sweet torture of
enduring her presence, knowing she could never be his.
Storing up memories, memories that would have to last him
a lifetime. Rather that, than not having her here at all.

Kate didn't know she could leave, and Tanner had
instructed the boys not to tell her. His brothers had made it
plain that they wanted her to stay on the mountain. They
were also angry that he would not do something to keep her
there permanently.

They didn't know about the mortgage, or how close they
were to losing the mountain and their home. He'd never told
them. And he wouldn't, because there was nothing they
could do about the situation. If they knew, they would
probably do something foolish, something desperate, and
make matters even worse.

True to his promise to the mine owner, he had sent one
batch of logs down the mountain. But with the weather
delaying the cutting, he was behind on the work, far from
completing the contract. Too far. A knot of worry tightened
his middle, making him increase his pace. He'd pray for a
miracle, but figured his store of miracles had been used up
with John's illness. As long as he could put one foot in front
of the other, chip one more chip from the bark of the tree,
Tanner wouldn't bother the Almighty with his personal
problems. He would do it on his own.

He labored until full dark, then packed his gear onto the
mules by lantern light. After pausing only long enough to
use that same light to thaw his half-frozen hands, he
extinguished the lantern, saving the oil for another day.
Weary of body and spirit, he mounted his horse, picked up
the lead rope and headed for home.

A crescent moon spilled its pale light through the tree
branches overhead, dappling the snow-covered trail with
glitters of silver. The moonlight made the shadows even

darker, more impenetrable. Once, he caught the gleam of some forest creature's eyes. Deer, he decided, when his pack animals showed no fear.

Tanner raised his head and gazed at the narrow strip of sky revealed between the towering evergreens. Untold numbers of stars sparkled against the ebony canopy. The brilliance of the stars and the absence of clouds told him it would be very cold tonight. It would also be clear tomorrow.

The trail narrowed. Wet branches, and a tangle of wild blackberry vines, brushed the flanks of his horse. Tanner reached down to free his pant leg from one of the thorny lengths.

The gelding danced nervously, then came to a halt. The mules planted their feet and strained against the rope.

The critters had never liked this section of trail even when it wasn't overgrown with brush as it was now. Tanner knew their skittishness tonight had nothing to do with the thick undergrowth. Eyes squinted, he peered into the blackness. He couldn't see it. But he could smell it. Musky, rank. A bear.

The horse squealed and sidestepped.

"Whoa, son," Tanner crooned, hoping his voice would stop his gelding and the mules from bolting. He slid his rifle from the scabbard.

A deep *wuff-wuff* came from a stand of trees. Limbs swished. Cracked. A bulky dark shape left the shadows and came to a halt on the moonlit path.

A yearling, he guessed, judging the bear's size. The springlike weather must have made it leave the den.

The bear rose to its full height and peered toward him. It tilted its shaggy head to one side as if puzzled by what it saw.

The gelding and the mules, recognizing the scent of an old enemy, trembled and fought to run. Only Tanner's firm grip held them in check.

He'd hunted from the horse before: it knew the sound of a rifle. But the mules . . . If he fired the gun, they might break the rope. Besides, he didn't want to kill the bear if it wasn't necessary. "Go on. Git!" he yelled, waving his weapon.

The bear didn't git. It took a step closer.

Tanner couldn't back up the horse because the mules were behind him. Besides, the trail was too narrow. He couldn't just sit there and let the bear walk right up to him, either.

If his shot only wounded the bear without killing it, he would really be in trouble. Spotting a large, dead limb over the bear's head, Tanner hoisted the gun to his shoulder and took aim. He squeezed the trigger.

The rifle roared.

The mules hauled back on the rope and bucked.

The severed branch fell, striking the startled bruin on the head. The bear dropped to all fours. Then it wheeled and bounded into the darkness, crashing through brittle brush. The noise faded as the bear got farther away.

"Whew. Glad that's over." Tanner put the gun back into the rifle boot, then nudged his horse forward. He was anxious to get home. The boys would have heard the gunshot. One or more of them would be coming out to see what was wrong.

He'd covered about a mile when he saw a light bobbing toward him.

"Tanner? Tanner, is that you?"

"We heard a shot."

"It's all right," he shouted. When he got closer he saw Matt and Mark. Both were armed.

"Thought you might need help," Mark panted out.

"What was it?" Matt asked.

"A yearling bear," Tanner said, chuckling. "He was as surprised to see me as I was him. It was a standoff for a while, but the shot scared him off. He's probably still running."

"Kate wanted to come, too. Luke practically had to hog-tie her to keep her in the house."

"What did she think she could do?" Tanner asked. "She can't shoot."

Mark laughed. "Knowing Kate, if she thought you were

in any danger, she would have tried to whip that bear with a stick."

"She probably would have done it, too," Matt said ruefully. "Sometimes that woman scares me."

"Sometimes she scares me, too," Tanner admitted.

"Guess we'd better head for home." Mark glanced back down the trail. "If we keep her waiting much longer, she'll be coming after all of us."

"Just the other day," Mark continued when they'd begun to walk, "she boxed Luke's ears good."

"He deserved it," Matt said. "I was ready to wallop him myself for teasing her so much."

"I remember," Tanner said. "John told me. He sure got a kick out of it, especially since he's usually the one Luke picks on.

"Kate's temper kind of reminds me of your ma's," Tanner added after a pause. "Maggie didn't care how big or tough a fellow was, she'd cut him down to size. Kept Pa towing the line, that's for sure."

"I miss Mama," Mark said sadly. "It's nice having a woman around the place again."

"Don't get too used to it," Tanner warned. "Kate won't be here much longer."

After that the boys became silent.

When they neared the house, Matt and Mark took the animals on to the barn.

Tanner removed his rifle and his canvas lunch sack, then trudged through the slush toward the house.

Kate launched herself off the front porch and into his arms. "Tanner, are you all right?" she asked, her voice trembling. "I heard a gunshot." She patted his face, his head, as if searching for any telltale wounds.

"I'm fine, darlin'. I only shot to scare away a bear."

"A bear!" She stared at him in horror, then wrapped her arms around his waist and held on tight. "You might have been injured—or killed," she said, her face buried in his coat.

"It was only a little bear, and a scared one at that. After I fired, he high-tailed it!" He laughed, remembering the sight. "But I do appreciate your concern." He raised his hand and stroked her hair.

"My concern!" She twisted away, her eyes shooting blue fire. "Every day you run off into the woods, and you don't come home until after dark. You're doing it to get away from me. Don't try to deny it." She swiped at her cheeks. "Tomorrow, I want to go back to Jacksonville."

Tanner frowned. Somebody must have let the cat out of the bag. "Calm down, Kate. We still don't know anything about the epidemic. Why don't you stay on a while longer, at least until I find out what the situation is in town."

"What good would it do to stay? You've made it plain there's nothing for me here. I've accepted that. Now I have to get on with my life." She ran toward the door, then turned to face him. "Tomorrow." She disappeared into the house.

Tanner sighed. He knew he'd have to take her back eventually, but damn it, why did it have to be so soon?

Kate didn't appear for supper. From the accusing eyes that met his around the table, he knew his brothers put the blame for that squarely onto him. He'd hurt her. But he couldn't have done anything different.

The next morning the question of whether he would return Kate to Jacksonville or not was taken out of his hands. Tanner stood on the porch, wondering what to do about the situation, when he spotted a rider coming across the meadow. A rider leading an extra horse.

He set his coffee cup on the porch railing and went to greet the man.

"Howdy, Tanner." The visitor took off his hat and waved it. The long white hair and beard left no doubt as to the rider's identity. It was T. L. Long, the circuit preacher.

Just what I need. Tanner forced a smile and raised a hand. "Hi, yourself, T.L. What brings you up this way?"

The solemn old man drew his horse up and dismounted. "Could be I came to perform a wedding?" he eyed Tanner, waiting for an answer.

"Nobody up here getting married," he replied smoothly.

"Is Miss Kathleen Deveraux up here?"

"Yeah, Kate's here. In fact I was getting ready to take her back to town."

"I'll take her back—if she's wanting to go. But first I intend to talk with her."

"About what?"

"Tanner, that girl spent a whole month on this mountain. You haven't been known to be a saint where the ladies are concerned. I want to make certain that nothing happened that shouldn't have."

"I didn't rape her, if that's what you're implying."

"There's other ways for a woman to lose her virtue," the old man said, his own voice rising.

"What's all the shouting about?" Matt stood in the open doorway.

Kate stood directly behind him.

"This old coot wants reassurance that you're still a virgin," Tanner said, staring at her.

She gave a startled gasp, then turned crimson.

"Tanner, damn you!" His fists clenched, Matt strode down the steps.

"Don't bite off more than you can chew, boy," Tanner warned.

"You might whip one of us, but even you can't take all of us on," Mark stated furiously.

Luke and even little John glared at him.

"Don't bet on it," Tanner said coldly.

"Stop it!" Kate cried. "Stop if this minute." She looked at the old man. "Sir, I don't know who you are, or what's going on here, but won't you come in out of the cold?"

"I'd be obliged, Miss Deveraux. I'm T. L. Long, the circuit rider. I heard about you being up here, and thought it my duty to investigate."

"You're a minister?" Her gaze swept past the old man and focused on Tanner.

He held his breath. She was still mad at him. Now was her chance for revenge—if she decided to take it. She could get him lynched—or hitched. Or she could say goodbye and ride away. The choice was hers to make.

"It might be better if we talk alone," she said to the minister. She ushered the man inside and shut the door.

Tanner waited nervously for the verdict.

While T.L. was no match for him when it came to strength or muscle, Tanner would never raise a hand against him. He respected the elderly preacher too much for that. Whatever T.L. commanded he would be forced to do. It was either that or get out of this country.

A rueful smile twisted Tanner's mouth. Even if he did leave, the circuit rider would track him down. That old man was as tenacious as a bulldog.

A moment later the door opened and the minister motioned them inside. "I need to ask you boys a question. Did anything go on here that shouldn't have?"

Following along behind them, Tanner held his breath. He knew the boys wanted Kate to stay. What he didn't know was, would they lie to keep her?

"No, sir. We protected Kate like she was our own," Matt said vehemently.

"Well, there was that time— Ow-w!" Mark cried out, when Luke punched him in the ribs.

"What are you saying, boy?" T.L.'s hawk eyes fastened on Mark's.

Mark swallowed. "Nothing, sir. I was just joshing."

"Luke?"

"She's pure as the driven snow," Luke vowed, placing a hand over his heart.

A puzzled expression on his face, John stared from one to the other. "I don't know what you're talking about, but I want Kate to stay. I love her." He hugged her around the waist.

"We all love her, squirt, and we all want her to stay." Matt turned and glared at Tanner. "But it ain't up to us to ask her."

Every eye went to Tanner. Waiting, demanding that he make it right. He shifted on his feet. "Kate's a wonderful woman, and she deserves better than being stuck on this mountain. She's anxious to get on with her life so I say we wish her well." He held out his hand. "Goodbye, Kate. I'll be down to see you in a day or two."

Her face white, she looked at his hand, but she didn't take it. "Thank you for your hospitality," she said stiffly. She whirled and spoke to the minister. "Give me a moment to get my things." Then she ran from the room.

Tanner, his heart aching, picked up his hat and stalked out the door.

17

AFTER SHE'D SAID a tearful goodbye to the boys, T.L. helped Kate onto his extra horse, then mounted his own and led the way down the mountain.

Kate didn't look back. Couldn't look back. She felt as though she left part of herself behind.

Fluffy, too, had seemed confused, racing from her to the house and back again. Finally, he gave her a sad-eyed look and trotted along by her side.

Tanner hadn't waited until she had left. As usual, he'd grabbed his hat and taken to the woods. Bitterness tightened her mouth. He was probably glad to be rid of her. She thought of the hand he'd offered her. The hand she hadn't accepted. It had seemed so cold, so remote, especially after what they'd shared. Thinking of the rare happy times they'd spent together, her heart ached, her eyes blurred with unshed tears. She blinked, determined not to let them fall.

All too soon, the easy path was behind them and she was forced to concentrate on the steep descent ahead.

"Give the horse his head, Miss Kate," T.L. called back over his shoulder.

She certainly wouldn't attempt to guide the animal. Allowing enough slack, she knotted the reins and looped them over the pommel, then she wrapped both hands around the saddle horn and hung on tight.

The horse went to his haunches, trembling as he made it around one sharp, ice-coated switchback, only to be met with another.

Rigid with tension, Kate fought to maintain her seat in the saddle. She stared straight ahead, avoided looking over the outer edge of the seemingly nonexistent trail. She didn't need to see the chasm; she could hear from the clatter of rocks dislodged by the horses' hooves how far it was to the bottom.

Although the snow had begun to melt in some places, others were layered with thick coats of blue-green ice. More than once the horses lost their footing and only their inborn agility and a few murmured prayers kept them and their riders from skidding over the edge.

To think she hadn't realized the danger when she'd come up the mountain that dark, snowy night that now seemed so long ago.

The minister, having already made the journey once that day, took the return trek in stride.

But Kate, tense to the point of exhaustion, found the mountain trail with its slick surface and loose gravel completely unnerving. Nevertheless, she was grateful for the distraction. It helped her forget that every mile she traveled took her farther away from the boys. Farther away from Tanner. It also gave her an excuse not to carry on a conversation.

On the final descent into the valley, the trail widened. The minister pulled his horse over and rode alongside her.

Fluffy, pursuing a rabbit, raced ahead.

Although the temperature was warmer at the lower elevation, the air held a distinct chill, partly due to the lateness of the day, partly due to a layer of valley fog.

"'Spect you'll be glad to get home, now that the smallpox is over," the old man said.

"I will be happy to get my pie shop opened again," she affirmed. Glancing around, she noticed that the piles of rubble and burned timbers had disappeared from Jacksonville's streets, along with the stench of sulphur and smoke. The yellow ribbons had been taken down. A few wreaths denoting the passage of loved ones still remained on some doorways, and a number of new raw earthen mounds showed in the cemetery. Outside of that, it was as though the smallpox epidemic had never occurred.

A familiar buggy approached from the opposite direction. It belonged to Dr. Thomas. "Howdy, T.L. Welcome home, Kate," he called out, slowing as he passed them.

"Hello, Doctor," she returned, happy to see her friend.

Other townspeople, recognizing either her or the minister, called out a greeting. But some gaped at her in such a way that Kate knew she was certain to be the subject of gossip around their dinner tables that night.

She really couldn't blame them. In their eyes, she, a single woman, had left town in the middle of the night with a man to whom she was not related. And she had spent a month on an isolated mountain with him—a man who had made it clear to everyone that he had no intention of ever becoming her husband.

Kate found it hard to believe that she, a Deveraux, could ever become involved in such a scandal. She had no doubt that her poor mother must be spinning in her grave. The circumstances of her arrival had made it bad enough before, but now . . .

Catching more curious stares, heat rose to flush Kate's cheeks. Pride forced it away. She straightened in the saddle and held her head high. She'd done nothing wrong. Not really. Either way, she refused to behave as if she had. But remembering her scandalous behavior that day in the snowy meadow, she couldn't have felt more guilty if she tried.

She glanced at T.L., grateful to see that he apparently hadn't noticed her disquiet, then she switched her attention to her pet. At least the dog seemed glad to be home.

Fluffy raced ahead of them, examining every tree, every blade of grass to see if there had been any four-legged trespassers in his territory. The dog once again marked his boundaries, then sat tongue lolling, tail wagging, on her doorstep.

Kate and the minister pulled their horses up in front of the house and dismounted.

T.L. untied her carpetbag and carried it to her doorstep.

She inserted the key into the lock and opened the door, allowing the dog and the elderly man to precede her over the threshold. "Won't you stay for a cup of tea? It will only take a minute."

The minister declined her invitation, saying that his wife would be expecting him home. Hat in hand, he gazed at her, his eyes filled with sympathy. "Miss Kate, I sense that you and Tanner care for each other more than either of you is willing to admit. I don't know what the problem is. That's for the two of you to work out. But if I might say one thing in Tanner's behalf. He is a good man, hardworking, honest. There is scarcely a family in Jacksonville that he hasn't helped out in one way or another. Not with money, mind you; Tanner's never had much of that."

T.L. scratched his bearded chin and gazed at her. "Take for instance that time when old man Stevens broke his leg, and Tanner cut his family a whole winter's supply of wood. He helped build a barn for another family after a storm tore down the one they had. He sent milk in to the Widow Pearson's children after their cow went dry." The minister smiled. "I could go on all day and still probably not cover all the people Tanner has helped."

"I had no idea," Kate said in amazement. "He never said anything about it."

"He wouldn't." The preacher chuckled. "But, Tanner also has his faults. He's as stubborn as those mules of his, and so proud it's almost sinful. I know it's not any of my business, but I think he's gotten in over his head on that lumber contract. He's never said a word, but I heard some of the miners talking. I also know he would never ask for, or accept, any help."

"Tanner is a good man, and devoted to his brothers," Kate agreed. "I guess you heard how I came to be here."

"Yes. The boys meant well. Too bad it didn't pan out." He patted her hand. "Right now Tanner has a lot on his plate, and finding some of it too tough to chew. Just give him a little time—it might work out yet."

Kate knew she could wait forever and nothing would ever

change, but she couldn't tell the minister that. Tanner loved the mountain and his brothers. He had no room in his life for anything, or anyone, else.

"Goodbye, T.L., and thank you." She leaned forward and kissed the old gentleman on his cheek.

"If you ever need to talk to me, about anything at all, send word to my wife. She'll know where to reach me." He bent and rubbed the dog's head, then, leading the spare horse, the grizzled old preacher bid her goodbye and rode away.

"Well, Fluffy, looks like we're home again." She picked up her bag and moved it into the sleeping area, then she removed her cloak and hat and hung them on a peg. She sighed and looked around. Except for a thick layer of dust, everything was as she left it.

Quiet, neat. And lonely.

In the next two days Kate found herself too busy to dwell on her relationship with Tanner.

First she had a long visit with Jeanne, who brought her up to date on everything that had occurred in her absence. After that, she cleaned and polished her house until everything gleamed. Then she made a trip to the mercantile and restocked her larder. Finally, she posted notices that she was back in business.

The next morning as she removed the last of the golden-crusted pies from the oven and sniffed the cinnamon-scented air, it seemed as if she had never left. Her pastries had never looked, or smelled, more delicious. And judging from the line forming outside her door, she would be sold out before the hour had passed.

Filled with anticipation, she opened the door and beamed her customers a bright smile. "Hello, men. Today we have dried apple pie with raisins. We also have canned peach pie."

"What is your choice?" she asked a bearded miner who stood at the head of the line.

The man gave her a sly grin. "I'll take one of each." He leaned closer. "And I'll toss in ten dollars extra if you'll let me have a little of what you've been giving Tanner Blaine."

Kate drew back as if the man had slapped her. "I don't know what you've been led to believe, sir," she hissed, her face flaming. "I sell pies. Nothing else. If you want two pies, that will be a dollar and a half. Otherwise, please leave."

"Seventy-five cents apiece? Keep your damn pies. From what I heard they ain't worth eatin' anyway." A surly look on his face, the man shoved his way through the crowd and headed down the street.

Kate stared at the rest of the men. "My pies are now seventy-five cents each, and I think you'll find them worth it. Anyone wanting a cheaper variety might find some at the bakery down the street."

A few of the men left, but most of them stayed. Her old friend Chauncey stepped to the head of the line. "I'll take *four* pies, Miss Kate," he said loudly. "And I consider myself lucky to get them." He turned to face the rest of the men. "Some folks, like that fool that just left, don't have no manners. Act like they been raised by dogs." The little miner's eyes narrowed. "Miss Kate is a lady. Anybody treating her any different will answer to me." He drew three silver dollars out of his pocket and handed them to Kate.

Her vision blurring, she smiled at him. "Thank you," she murmured. She carefully wrapped his pies and handed them across the counter.

"If anybody gives you a bad time, you just let me know." The bristle-faced miner winked and turned to the crowd. "Oh, don't these smell good." Chauncey waved one under the next man's nose. "Glad I got mine first," he crowed, making his way down the line.

"I'll take two. Your choice." The next man stepped forward and paid her. While he didn't voice it, his lust-filled look told her that he, too, shared the first miner's opinion.

Avoiding his gaze, she handed him his pies, then went to the next person in line.

When the last of the pies had been sold, Kate sighed in relief, then closed—and locked—her door. She peered through the window at the snow-capped mountain. "Well, Tanner, I hope you're satisfied."

He claimed he'd spared her virtue, left her innocent. But somehow during the last hour, knowing how the miners felt about her sojourn on the mountain, she couldn't have felt more tarnished if she and Tanner had made love in broad daylight on Main Street.

It was nearing sunset when a knock brought Kate out of her chair. "Fluffy, come." She took the dog's collar and led him to the door.

"Who's there?" she asked, praying it wasn't one of the men returning to pay her a call.

"Eet ees me, *cherie*."

Trembling with relief, Kate unfastened the latch. "Jeanne. Come in."

The Frenchwoman entered the room, her expression curious as she watched Kate shut, then lock the door.

Kate motioned toward the sofa. "Sit down. The kettle is already on. I'll make us some tea."

With a rustle of black taffeta and petticoats, Jeanne settled her ample figure in the middle of the settee. "I had a veeseetor thees morning."

"Oh?" Kate frowned. "Who?"

"Chauncey. He ees worried about you."

Kate carried two cups across the room and handed one to her friend. "I did have a problem, but it was nothing serious. Besides, I'm not sure anything can be done about it."

Jeanne raised a brow. "Deed he?"

"What?"

"Deed Tanner make love to you?"

"No!" Hurt that her friend could ask such a thing, Kate set her cup down on the table. "Of course not!"

"Ah-h, I have offended you. I'm sorry, *ma petite*." Jeanne shook her head. "Your Tanner ees a bigger fool than I thought."

"He isn't *my* Tanner," Kate said vehemently. "He isn't *my* anything and never will be."

"*Cherie*, my heart aches for you. I, too, gave my heart to one who never wanted eet. I got over heem eventually, and you weell, too."

"How?" she asked, her throat tight with unshed tears. How could she ever get over Tanner, forget his touch, his kiss, and what it was like to be held in his arms?

"Find someone new," Jeanne suggested. "Only next time, choose someone weeth your head and not your heart."

"I doubt that a decent man would have anything to do with me. Especially since everyone in town believes I spent the last month warming Tanner's bed." She sipped her tea and grimaced. "And as for the other, I'm afraid my head has even less reliable judgment than my heart."

She raised her head and met Jeanne's knowing gaze. "Before the epidemic struck, I had decided to leave Jacksonville. Now I know that was the right decision. I don't see that I have any alternative."

The Frenchwoman frowned. "Maybe that ees for the best. You could do eet now, *cherie*. Get by on your own. You have changed, become more confeedent. A broken heart seems to do that to a woman."

Jeanne placed her empty cup on the table, then rose and smoothed her skirts. "Een a way, I almost envy you. A deeferent town. A new life. A whole future of possibeeleet-ies." Her dark eyes gleamed. "Who knows what adventures await you? Could be very exciting."

"I think I've had my fill of adventures for a while." Kate walked her friend to the front door, then after Jeanne had returned to her own establishment, Kate sat on her front step and waited for Fluffy to finish his rounds.

It was easy to make plans. It was carrying them out that was difficult. She'd need money.

If she were to get up earlier, make a few more pies each day, she could soon get her rent caught up and have enough saved to leave. She almost had enough in the bank now to repay Tanner. The question was, how could she get it to him? And how could she make him accept it when she did?

Stubborn as one of his mules, T.L. had said.

She had to agree, Tanner was that and more. But she had been known to be stubborn, herself. She'd find a way somehow.

Fluffy bounded back to her and took up a position at her

feet. Raising his shaggy head, he stared toward the mountain and whined.

"You miss them, too, don't you?" She removed a burr from his ear, then reluctantly got to her feet, opened the door and led him inside. The dog hated being cooped up. He needed room to exercise, room to roam.

She remembered how her pet had taken to John, sleeping at the foot of his bed after the boy had recovered from his illness. The pair had become constant companions. Although he'd tried hard not to, John had cried when the dog left.

Kate locked her door, then moved across the room to her chair.

Fluffy plodded across the floor and plopped down in front of the fire.

Her mood somber, Kate gazed at the dog and knew what she must do. When she was ready to move on, she would arrange for Fluffy to be taken back to the mountain, back to John. The child would take care of her pet. And Fluffy would be happy there.

And she, once again, would be all alone.

18

"*D*ANG IT!" TANNER glared at his ax handle as if it had broken on purpose just to spite him. He'd hoped to get another tree cut before dark, but now that wouldn't be the case. He didn't have a spare ax, and he had neither the time nor the patience to make and season a handle like he ofttimes did. He gathered up his gear and packed it onto the mules.

"Nothing left but to make a trip to Jacksonville." Somehow that didn't fill him with the despair that it should have. In fact he found himself grinning like a fool. Even though there was no one around but the animals to see, he wiped the expression from his face.

He told himself that Kate was still his responsibility. Besides, he'd promised he'd look in on her.

He hurried toward the homestead and, once there, he made Mark and Luke see to the animals while he took a bath and shaved.

"Aren't you gonna eat?" Matt asked, watching Tanner comb his hair.

"I'll get something later. Got to get to the mercantile before they close."

"Tell her hello," Matt said, grinning.

"Who? Kate? Doubt if I'll even see her." Ignoring his

brother's smart-alec smirk, Tanner grabbed his coat, putting it on as he headed out the door.

Although it was past closing time when he reached town, the mercantile was still open. Homer, the proprietor, was unpacking a new shipment of goods. Tanner made his purchases, then he ambled toward the pie shop.

He knocked on Kate's door, then feeling awkward as a schoolboy, he stepped back and wiped his boots on the back of his pant legs.

"Who's there?" she called out, peeking through a crack between the curtains.

"It's Tanner."

"Step into the light so I can see you," she ordered, pulling one of the curtains to the side.

He took off his hat and moved so that the light revealed his identity. "Kate, it is Tanner. See?" He bent and peered directly at her.

Something screeched across the floor; a moment later Kate cautiously opened the door. "Come in."

Tanner stepped inside.

Fluffy eagerly greeted him by jumping up to lick his face.

His own gaze hungrily devouring Kate, Tanner absently ruffled the dog's fur.

She quickly pulled the curtain shut, then locked the door. Observing her odd behavior, he frowned. "Kate, what's going on?"

"Nothing," she said, motioning him to a chair. "Like you said, a woman alone has to take precautions."

Her behavior seemed more than precautionary to him. She looked jumpy as a bug in a pen full of chickens. "Has anybody bothered you?"

"No. Don't be silly," she said, too quickly for him to think it was the truth. She touched the dog's shaggy head. "I have Fluffy, remember?" She turned toward the cookstove.

Tanner dodged the dog's tongue. "The way he's behaving right now, I'd say he'd be more inclined to lick someone to death, rather than bite anybody."

"He's just happy to see you." She handed Tanner a cup of steaming tea.

Taking the tea, he locked onto her violet eyes. "Are you happy to see me?"

She blushed and lowered her lashes. "Of course. Why wouldn't I be?" She cast a glance toward the doorway, then raised her cup to her mouth. Her hand shook. When she saw that he had noticed, she set the cup back onto the saucer and clasped her hands in her lap.

"Am I making you nervous?" he asked, determined to get to whatever was bothering her.

"Whatever gave you that idea?"

"Kate, something is wrong. Don't try to deny it. I'm not about to leave here until I find out what it is."

"All right, if you must know, I was trying to figure out how to tell you that I am leaving Jacksonville."

"What?" Feeling like she'd knocked the pins from under him, he shook his head. "You can't go anywhere until I finish that contract. Then, if you're still determined to leave, I'll pay your fare back to Georgia."

"It's not a matter for discussion. I have no intention of going back to Georgia. I'm moving farther north—to Portland, or maybe Seattle." She raised her chin as if daring him to try to stop her. "And I don't need you to pay my fare. I have my own money. I have earned enough selling my pies to repay the money you spent in my behalf. I only need to get it out of the bank."

"Keep your damn money. You don't owe me a dime." Tanner got to his feet. The idea that she thought she could just run off on her own . . . "I've got to get out of here," he muttered, struggling to keep hold of his temper.

"Don't let me keep you." She followed him to the door and unlocked then jerked it open.

He stopped on the threshold.

"Well, what are you waiting for?"

"We've got to get something straight first."

She stared past him, her jaw set.

He cupped her chin and made her meet his gaze. "You're not to leave Jacksonville until I say you can go."

Her eyes shot violet fire. "You can't tell me what to do," she said furiously.

"On second thought, I might not let you go at all." He pulled her into his arms.

"You can't stop me," she said defiantly.

"Oh, can't I?" He bent his head, capturing her mouth with his.

Her lips were stiff and unyielding.

His were fierce and determined. He forced his tongue between her teeth and hungrily plundered her honeyed sweetness.

She struggled, pushing against him.

He tightened his grip. He wouldn't set her free. He couldn't.

He cupped her breast and felt the nipple knot beneath his circling thumb. He kissed her long and thoroughly, his tongue mimicking the movements his body longed to make.

She swayed toward him, her body molding to his. She was soft and warm and smelled of cinnamon and spice.

He slid his fingers into her hair, loving the feel of it. Like strands of finest silk. His kiss grew more gentle, his mouth conveying everything he was loathe to speak aloud. Finally, knowing things were bound to get out of hand if he continued, he forced himself to break away. There were so many things he wanted, needed, to tell her. But not now.

"Oh, Tanner." Her eyes like dark pools, she gazed up at him. Her trembling hand caressed his cheek.

He brought it to his mouth and kissed her palm. "You will not leave." Satisfied that he'd made his point, he broke away and strode down the steps and into the darkness.

She was still leaning against the edge of the door, staring after him, when he rode out of sight. Dazed, she fought to regain her composure. She had wanted to scream at him, tell him he had no right to interfere in her life. Instead she'd melted in his arms. Allowed him to take liberties—again. "Damn him. Damn him to hell!"

He hadn't kissed her because he loved her. He was only trying to show her he was boss.

"Well, he isn't *my* boss. And he can't tell me what to do."

A noise in the alley made her aware that she was

silhouetted against the lantern-lit room. She squinted into the darkness. She knew it wasn't Tanner. She had watched him leave.

And it couldn't be Fluffy. When she'd opened the door, the dog had seized the opportunity and raced off in the other direction, in pursuit of a stray cat.

Feeling vulnerable without her pet, she clapped her hands together, hoping he would come. "Fluffy. Come on, boy."

A noise sounded again, closer. This time from the darkness at the side of the house.

She whirled. "Fluffy?"

The dog bounded up behind her, coming from the opposite direction. Panting, he stopped at her side. He raised his head and sniffed the air. A growl, low and deep, rumbled from his throat.

She touched his back and felt the ruff on his neck rising. It's probably the cat again, she told herself.

But what if it wasn't? What if it was something—someone—else? Someone skulking in the darkness. It might be one of the Chinese going home, but they were always off the streets before dark. They were too afraid for their own safety to cause a problem for anyone else.

Could it be the miner from that morning?

What if there were more than one person? One man could easily overpower her. Two, and she wouldn't have a chance.

Except for a tinkling of music from the saloon down the street, the streets were silent—and empty. No one could hear her if she cried out. If the dog took off again she would be left all alone.

She wrapped her hand around Fluffy's collar and tugged the resisting dog into the house. Once they were inside, she released him and slammed the door. She threw the bolt, then twisted the lock. Then she dragged the kitchen chair across the room and wedged the back of it under the doorknob.

A sound that could have been a man's laugh drifted on the clear night air.

Could he see through the curtains? She went to the table and blew out the lamp. She stood in the darkness, staring first at the door, then at the windows.

Was it her imagination? Or was someone out there in the darkness, watching, waiting?

God help her, she didn't know, and she wasn't about to go outside and find out.

The dog moved to her side. He, too, was tense, uneasy.

Seeking comfort, she tangled her fingers in his thick fur.

She didn't know how long they stood there. Five minutes? Two hours? More? She only knew she was frozen with fear, the metallic taste so strong in her mouth she found it hard to swallow, almost impossible to breathe.

The dog finally broke the spell. He stretched and yawned. Then he licked her hand. He left her side and flopped down in front of the fire.

Kate took a few wobbling steps and collapsed on the settee. When she finally did go to bed, she took the stove poker and placed it beside her. She did not undress, and she did not close her eyes.

She stared into the darkness, longing for the strength, the protection of Tanner's strong arms. He'd told her he wouldn't let her leave. But he also didn't give her any reason to stay.

Loving him the way she did, she didn't dare remain in Jacksonville. Tears seeped from her eyelids and made wet patches on her cheeks. Each bittersweet parting only made her miss him that much more.

It was dawn when exhaustion finally claimed her, dragging her into a restless sleep.

Kate awoke determined to put her fright of the night before behind her—until she discovered boot prints in the mud beneath her window. A chill crawled over her, leaving her faint and trembling. She hadn't imagined it. Somebody had been here.

She whirled, her gaze examining every bush, every building, anything large enough to conceal a man. She saw nothing.

Stop it! He's not here now.

Forcing a calmness she did not feel, she walked to the mercantile and purchased the spices she needed. As she turned to leave she noted a display of firearms. *A gun? Don't be ridiculous.* With her luck she'd probably end up shooting herself instead of the prowler. She shuddered, doubting that she could ever bring herself to fire the weapon if she had it. The idea of spilling another person's blood filled her with horror.

Still, a gun would be protection.

No. But as she turned away, one of the guns caught her eye. It had a mother-of-pearl handle and was small. It would easily fit into a purse or a pocket. It didn't look dangerous, or big enough to kill anybody. But it might make enough noise to scare a person off.

"Howdy, Miss Kate."

Lost in contemplation, she hadn't known anyone was there until she heard her name. She whirled. Recognizing Chauncey she managed a shaky smile.

The miner's bushy gray eyebrows drew into a frown. "Are you thinking about getting yourself a shootin' iron, Miss Kate?"

"Uh, no. Not really."

He stepped to the case and gazed down at the weapon. "Pretty little thing, ain't it? Might be kind of handy for a lady to have around." He eyed her intently.

"Do you think so?" She bit her lip and looked at the gun again. "I wouldn't know how to shoot it."

"I could teach you," he offered. "But if you really wanted to protect yourself, it might be better if you had something bigger—like a shotgun. You wouldn't have to be accurate. You could just point it and shoot. Be impossible to miss. You'd blow a hole clean through anything that aimed to bother you. Why, I remember one of doc's patients had all his innards . . ."

Kate's stomach rolled. Bile rose in her throat. "Thank you, Chauncey. I'll think it over." Before she disgraced herself, she clamped a hand over her mouth and fled from the shop.

19

$\mathcal{A}$LL THROUGH THE night, Tanner pondered Kate's behavior. The next day it was still foremost on his mind. She had appeared scared, uneasy, and he didn't think it had anything to do with him, or worry about her reputation. When he'd arrived at her house he'd heard a noise inside. Later he'd realized she'd had a chair wedged against her door. Before she'd allowed him to enter, she had returned it to its place by the table.

Why? What was she so afraid of? And why didn't she want him to know?

The more he thought about it the more certain he became that he had cause for alarm.

Instead of working until dark as had become his custom, he quit early and headed for the house.

"Tanner, is something wrong?" Matt asked when Tanner strode through the door.

"I'm not sure. I think I need a second opinion." Tanner removed his coat and hat and hung them on the rack, then he poured himself a cup of coffee. "Why don't you and Mark gather round the table here and see what you think."

When they were settled on either side of the long wooden table, Tanner told them about the visit he'd made to Kate and her strange behavior. He also told them she had been planning to leave Jacksonville, but that he had managed to change her mind.

He didn't tell them about the argument they'd had.

And he certainly didn't tell them about the kiss.

Not only because he considered it none of their business, but also because he didn't want to rile them up when he needed their help.

"The weather's nicer now, and it's not so cold at night. I think it might be a good idea if we take a turn or two staying in that toolshed across from her place," Tanner said. "Keep a watch on her house at night. See if anybody's bothering her."

"From what you've told us, that might be a good idea," Mark said, glancing at Matt. "What do you think?"

"Something's spooked her. Tanner, since you're working so hard these days, let me and Mark take care of this. If anything serious comes up, we'll let you know. Otherwise, we can handle it."

"I would feel better," Tanner said.

"Are you gonna talk all night? I'm hungry," Luke complained from the kitchen doorway.

"Keep this between us," Tanner warned, knowing that Luke would insist on helping out. He also knew that, as before, Luke would fall asleep.

"You've got it," Mark said softly. "I'll get my gun and be on my way."

"I'll pack you a sandwich," Matt said, rising from the table. "Give you something to do while you're watching."

"Watching for what?" Luke asked. "Where are you going?"

"Hunting." Mark flashed Tanner a grin. "Who knows what kind of varmint I might catch."

Tired of her own cooking, Kate went across the street to sample some of Madame Jeanne's excellent French cuisine. After a meal of coq au vin and a glass of wine, Kate spent a few moments in conversation with her friend. Then, saying goodbye, she returned to her own dwelling.

She'd put in a hard day with scarcely any rest the night

before; now she was practically asleep on her feet. She'd made a point to be home before dark, but now the long night stretched out before her.

She'd let the dog loose before she left, hoping that by allowing him a good run, he would be content to spend the rest of the night inside. But now, having reached her doorstep, she wondered at the wisdom of that decision. Fluffy wasn't waiting on the steps as was his usual custom. In fact her pet was nowhere in sight.

"Fluffy. Here, boy," she called, first in one direction, then another.

He didn't come.

She waited for a few minutes, uneasily noting that the sun was fast disappearing behind the horizon. When it set, night would fall like a black shroud. As a child she had been afraid of the dark. As an adult she liked it even less. Now fully aware of the dangers that might be lurking just out of sight, she was terrified.

"Fluffy. Come on, puppy," she called, louder this time.

Still no response. Either he was out of earshot or too preoccupied to pay her any mind.

Her nervousness made it impossible for her to remain outside any longer. She inserted the key into the lock.

The door swung open of its own accord.

Gasping, she jumped back. Then, her heart pounding, she cautiously peered into the room. Had she forgotten to lock it?

No. She'd checked it. The house had been secure.

A faint smell of cigarette smoke lingered in the air. Someone had been here. She swallowed. Could still be here. "Hello. Is anyone there?" she called, hating the tremor in her voice. "Hello."

"Miss Kate, something wrong?"

"Oh-h!" Kate wheeled. "Dr. Thomas." She clasped a hand over her thundering heart. "I'm so glad to see you. I locked my house and went to supper. When I returned a few minutes ago, I found my door open."

"Hmm. Better let me take a look." The doctor opened his medical bag and removed a pistol. He stepped to the doorway. "If anybody's in here you'd better show yourself right now," he called out in a no-nonsense tone. He entered the house and lit the lamp. He checked the corners, the closet and under the bed. Then he came back to the door and motioned her inside. "Nobody here now. You'd better take a look around and see if anything is missing."

"I don't have anything worth stealing." She checked her meager store of belongings. She had deposited all of her money in the bank. Everything else seemed to be in place. "Maybe it wasn't locked after all. Maybe the latch didn't catch."

"Let me have your key, and I'll check it." He inserted the key into the lock and tried it several times. "It seems to be all right." He frowned. "I don't want to scare you, but could be somebody else has a key."

Her eyes widened. "Would that be possible?"

"It's an old building. The lock is a standard size. Most any key of the same type would fit it."

"Oh, my. That never occurred to me." The idea that anyone could break in was bad enough. But the knowledge that they could enter and leave at will . . .

She thought about all the nights when she'd been asleep, depending on the security of the lock. Of course, she'd also had her dog to give warning.

Remembering her pet, she glanced up at the physician. "Have you seen Fluffy tonight?"

"No, can't say as I have. Is he missing?"

"Not really. I let him out for a run, and he hasn't come back yet." She forced a smile. "I'm sure he'll return most any time."

The doctor frowned. "I hate to leave you alone like this, but I have a patient that I have to see."

"I'll be fine," she said, with a lot more assurance than she felt.

"Lock up tight," the elder man ordered. "On the way back if I run into your dog, I'll bring him by."

"Thank you. But I'm certain he will have returned home before then."

"Good night, Kate."

She followed the doctor to her doorstep, then she called her dog again. Finally, when the night closed around her, she scooted back inside. As she turned the key and slid the bolt, she wondered why she bothered. If intruders really wanted to get in, the flimsy fixture wouldn't keep them out. And once inside, without the dog, she would be at their mercy.

Mark had barely made it into the tool shed when the doctor and Kate came out the door. Was Kate sick? Maybe that was why she had been so uneasy. Taking a seat on an upended barrel, he peered from the edge of the doorway, listening to her call the dog. She didn't look sick to him. Maybe it was some female complaint. While he didn't know much about that, he had heard other people talk about them.

Finally she went back inside and closed the door. Then the house plunged into darkness.

It seemed strange she would go to bed with her pet still outside. The dog hadn't come when she called. Where was the mangy critter? Fluffy was very protective of Kate. Even on the mountain he rarely left her side.

Could something have happened to him? Mark scoffed at that idea. He had the feeling that beast could have gone up against a bear and come out the winner.

Then what?

He grinned. A lady dog, of course. The worthless mutt had gone courting.

Kate must be scared to death, he thought. When she'd been on the mountain, he remembered, she had always tended to the outside necessities before it had gotten dark.

Even though he didn't relish spending the night in an uncomfortable toolshed, Mark was glad he was there. He only wished he could reassure Kate, tell her he was watching over her and that she had nothing to fear, but he didn't dare. Not just because Tanner had told him not to, but because he knew Kate was too proud to admit to a little thing like fear.

He shifted to a more comfortable position to avoid a nail that was sticking up between the barrel staves. Sleep tugged at his eyelids, but remembering Tanner's comment about Luke, Mark fought back a yawn. If he'd known he would be expected to stay awake all night, he could have sneaked a nap that afternoon. As it was, he'd spent the day chopping stove wood. Now his muscles ached, and he was not only exhausted, but bored.

Maybe if he ate something . . . He was poking about in the grub sack when a faint movement caught his eye. Nothing that he could really see, more like sensing a vague change in the alley shadows. *Wind in the trees? Or maybe the dog?*

All thoughts of food forgotten, Mark narrowed his eyes, trying to penetrate the gloom.

Whatever it was seemed intent on blending with the darkness. It moved again. *Too tall for an animal. A man.*

Mark slid his hand down and picked up his rifle. Silently he eased from the shed and crept toward the observer.

The man stood in a patch of shrubbery, his gaze riveted on the pie shop.

While he couldn't see the man well enough to identify him, the smells seemed familiar. Pipe smoke, garlic, wool and . . . whoever it was could have stood a bath.

Mark edged closer. He planted the tip of the gun barrel in the man's back. "One move and you're dead," he said softly.

"Mark? That you, boy? For God's sake, don't shoot. It's Chauncey," the old man said in a hoarse whisper.

Mark lowered the tip of the gun. "What are you doing sneaking around Kate's?"

"I might ask you the same thing!"

"Tanner sent me. He was worried about her."

"Shh!" The miner glanced around. "Can't talk here. Let's go over yonder." The old-timer pointed to the toolshed.

Once they were inside, Mark asked for an explanation.

"I ran into Doc Thomas earlier. He said somebody broke into Kate's house tonight while she was out to supper. Scared her pretty bad. Doc had to go out to see a patient, and I promised I'd keep an eye on things. Make sure whoever it was didn't come back. On top of that her dog's missin'."

"Somebody broke into her house?" Mark's fingers curled around the gun stock.

"'Pears so." The miner sighed, then shuffled his feet. "I don't know how you're going to take this, but things ain't been the same for Kate since she came back from the mountain. Some of the fellers got the idea that she and Tanner had been carryin' on."

"That's a damn lie," Mark said vehemently. "Who were these fellers? Maybe I ought to have a word with them."

"I already did, and I thought I had the matter settled. I love that little gal like she was my own. I let it be known that I'd kill anybody that messed with her." The old man patted his waistband, letting Mark know that he, too, was armed.

"Somebody broke in. And now the dog's gone. I wonder . . ." Mark put his hand on the old man's shoulder. "Chauncey, would you mind sitting here for a spell? I want to see if I can locate that hound of hers."

"Take all the time you need, boy. She shore sets a store by that critter."

His rifle cradled in his arms, Mark left the shed. Moving in the silent way Tanner had taught him, he stayed to the shadows and made his way down the street.

Mark checked every street, every yard, calling softly so that he didn't have all the animals in town setting up a din. He looked everywhere he could think of, even venturing into Chinatown, a place most white men wouldn't go after dark. But there was no sign of the dog.

Maybe the animal had returned to Kate's on his own. Then again, maybe not.

"Fluffy. Fluffy. Come on, boy."

Still no answer.

He stood at the end of the street, debating what to do next when an odd noise caught his attention. "Fluffy?"

It came again, so faint that if he hadn't been listening, he wouldn't have heard it.

Didn't sound like a dog. Didn't sound like anything he'd ever heard.

He stared into the darkness and made out the shadowy

bulk of an abandoned barn. Whatever it was, was in there. Holding his rifle ready, he followed a path through the tall dead grass, trying to make as little noise as possible. Although half the building was in a state of collapse, somebody had secured the latch. Mark slid the timbered draw bolt and opened the door enough to slip inside.

He stood in the darkness, tense, ready. He hard the sound again. Now he knew it was an animal in pain. "Fluffy?"

He eased forward, tracing the sound to a boarded-up stall. He set his rifle to one side, then ripped off the boards. Wary of what might be waiting inside, Mark lifted the gun. He stepped through the opening.

A bulky, light-colored shape lay against a pile of dark straw. The stall smelled of old manure, mold, wet fur—and blood.

"Fluffy?"

The animal whined and made an attempt to rise.

"Damn!" Mark lay the gun aside and reached inside his coat pocket and removed a match. He struck it, filling the air with the scent of sulphur, then he looked down.

Fluffy, his fur covered with blood, his eyes glazed with pain, peered up at him.

"Oh, damn." Sick, Mark knelt and ran his hand over the matted, russet-tinged fur. Shot. From the amount of blood he guessed the dog was more dead than alive. "Easy, boy," he crooned, when the dog made an attempt to get up.

The match burned the ends of Mark's fingers, and he blew it out. He needed more light. He ducked back through the boards and felt an upright timber at the edge of the stall. Hanging on a nail at head height, he found a rusty lantern. He shook it and heard a faint slosh of oil. He felt in his pocket for the last of his matches, lit it and touched it to the wick.

The light flickered, then flared, smoke rising through the already black chimney. He turned it to a steady glow and went back inside the stall.

He dragged his boot in a circle and scratched out a bare place to set the lantern. He sure didn't want to catch the hay on fire. Then he got down on his knees and examined the dog's wounds. Lots of blood, but except for a deep furrow atop the dog's shaggy head and a bullet graze along his rump, he could find no actual bullet holes.

"Looks like you got lucky this time, fella." He wished he could clean up the animal and examine him a little better first, but he decided it was more important to get the critter back to town. The question was, how? This horse of a hound weighed almost as much as he did.

He hesitated, not wanting to leave the dog, but also knowing he had no choice. Whoever left Fluffy there probably thought the animal was dead. If so, they wouldn't be coming back anytime soon.

Praying that was indeed the case, Mark bent and blew out the light.

Fluffy rustled the hay and whined.

"Stay, boy." He gave the dog one last pat then hurried from the barn.

"Shot you say?" Chauncey shook his head.

"I need some way to get him back to town," Mark stated. "Any ideas?"

The old miner thought a moment. "Hmm. Might work. Madame Jeanne used to have an old pushcart out back. If'n it's still in one piece, it might do the job. I'll have to go with you. Dog's too heavy to handle on your own."

"Let's get it done then. I don't like the idea of leaving Kate unprotected. After we get him loaded, you come on back here. I'll take Fluffy to the doctor's. If Doc's back, I know he'll help."

Although the cart wobbled, it proved sturdy enough to carry the animal. Chauncey helped Mark load the dog on, then hurried back to the toolshed while Mark took the dog farther down the street.

The doctor, having just arrived home, was happy to treat Kate's pet.

"Best leave him here overnight," the physician said, applying antiseptic to the head wound. "That way I'll have time to clean him up before Kate sees him."

"Good idea. No sense scaring her worse than she already is. I'll head back and relieve Chauncey. Tomorrow, it might be a good idea to have a talk with the sheriff."

"I'll handle that little chore myself," the doctor said grimly. "Seems like things have been getting a little lax around here of late. Pretty sad state of affairs when a woman is scared to leave her home, let alone that breaking-in business. Then this. Whoever did this should be hanged."

"Doc, I think it might be better if we didn't say anything to Tanner," Mark warned. "He'd probably end up killing somebody. You know how riled he gets. If he found out, he'd go plumb crazy."

"I thought he didn't want anything to do with Kate."

"How could you think that?" Mark asked in amazement. "Tanner's a fool for the woman. When he isn't working himself to death, he just sits and stares into space with a silly look on his face. Oh, he likes her, all right. He's so crazy in love, it's plumb pitiful."

"Then why doesn't he marry the girl?"

Mark shrugged. "I guess he thinks she's too good for him. Being stuck on that mountain is a far cry from living on a plantation in Georgia." He studied a knot in the floor. "And then there was Mama. I remember how hard she worked. She was a big, strapping woman. Make three of Kate. After she caught diphtheria and died, Tanner vowed not to bring another woman to that mountain. He hasn't, either—until Kate."

"The mountain didn't kill Maggie," the doctor said gruffly. Your mother loved it there. If you recall, a lot of people died of diphtheria that winter."

"I don't remember much about that. I guess I was too wrapped up in my own loss." Mark swallowed. "I sure wouldn't want the same thing to happen to Kate."

Dr. Thomas shook his head. "Sometimes I wonder if the lot of you boys has the sense God gave a goose. Living up there, breathing that clear, fresh air, would be a whole lot healthier than living down here in the valley. So it gets a little cold. You've got a house, haven't you? You don't have to spend the winter outside."

"No. The house is warm enough." He smiled. "Kate liked it there. She laughed and sang all the time."

"There's your answer. The problem isn't with Kate, it's Tanner." The elderly man gave him a sly look. "Perhaps it's the marrying thing. Some fellows don't want to be tied down."

"With the four of us to look after, Tanner couldn't be any more tied down if somebody chained an anvil around his neck." Mark frowned. Could they be the obstacle?

The doctor finished with the dog, gave him a drink of water and made sure he was comfortable. Then he carried the lamp back into the other room. "Fluffy should be better tomorrow. After I get him halfway presentable, I'll take him back to Kate."

"She'll be glad of that, doting on that critter the way she does. Pays him more attention than she does Tanner."

"Is that a fact?" The white-haired man grinned. "A little competition might be what Tanner needs."

After the doctor showed him to the door, Mark melted into the darkness.

Troubled, Mark thought about the break-in, then he thought about the attempt to kill the dog. Anger pulsed through his veins, making him shake with the need for vengeance. Whoever had shot Fluffy wanted Kate to be alone. Wanted her vulnerable. Helpless. And God knows what might happen to her if that ever came about.

Well, it was up to the Blaines to see that didn't happen. Whether Matt came or not, Mark decided he would be spending all of his nights in town.

His gaze searching the shadows, he made his way down the street.

20

$\mathcal{A}$LTHOUGH TANNER HAD tried to concentrate on work, his mind continued to stray to Kate. A feeling of foreboding rode heavy on his shoulders. What if somebody had been bothering her? What if Mark couldn't handle it? Realizing that he might have put both Kate and his brother in danger, Tanner quickly packed his gear and headed for the house. After a few terse words to Luke and Matt, Tanner rode down the mountain.

It was nearing midnight when he reached Jacksonville, and except for the saloons, most of the town was dark. He stealthily guided his gelding to a patch of grass behind the toolshed, then dismounted. His feet had barely touched the ground when the felt a gun barrel press against his back.

"Hold it right there, mister."

"Chauncey? That you?"

"Tanner?" The old miner let out a long sigh.

"What are you doing here? What's going on?" Tanner listened while Chauncey brought him up to date. His anger built with every word; by the time the old man had finished, Tanner was shaking with rage. He took his rifle from the saddle boot and turned toward Kate's, peering into the shadows for any intruders.

"Don't go off half-cocked," Chauncey warned. "You

might end up shootin' your brother. Or worse yet, Kate might shoot both of you."

"I didn't know she owned a gun."

"I got her one. She ain't very good at shooting yet. No tellin' what she might hit."

Mark slid from the alley and hurried toward them. "I thought you were going to wait at home. What about the timber?"

"The hell with the timber," Tanner hissed. "You think I'd risk Kate getting hurt for the sake of some damned trees?"

"How's the dog?" the old miner asked.

"He'll be okay." Mark glanced toward the house. "Anything happen?"

"Not yet, but when it does we'll be ready." He put his hand on Mark's shoulder. "You go across the street to Madame Jeanne's. Watch from the alley. If you see anything suspicious, hoot like an owl."

After Mark vanished into the darkness, Tanner started across the street.

"Where are you going?" Chauncey asked.

"In there." Tanner pointed to Kate's. "With the dog gone, I doubt she's asleep. And like you said, I don't want her to end up shooting one of us."

He hurried across to Kate's and softly knocked on the door.

"Get away or I'll shoot!"

"Kate. It's Tanner. Let me in."

A chair scraped, then she slid the lock and opened the door.

Tanner pushed her back and stepped inside. Then he closed and locked the door.

"What are you doing here?"

"I heard you had some trouble. I came to take care of it." By the swish of petticoats, he could tell she was still fully dressed.

"I have a gun." She waved it under his nose. "I can take care of myself."

"Put that thing down before it goes off." He took the palm-sized gun out of her hand and tucked it into his waistband. "We had better be quiet. We don't want to scare them off."

"Who?"

He took her hands in his. "Somebody tried to kill your dog tonight."

"No-oo. Where—"

"Fluffy's all right. Doc is looking after him. Whoever did it wanted him out of the way."

"You think they'll—"

"I'm sure of it. You go to bed." When she started to protest, he held a finger to her lips. "Open your window a little bit. I want you to listen for an owl hoot."

"An owl?"

"Mark. He's across the street. The hoot will be his signal that we have company." He felt a tremor go through her body. He took her into his arms to ease her fears. "Don't worry. We won't let anything happen to you."

"I know. I was thinking about my dog." She stepped away. "I hope they do come. I can't wait to get my hands on them."

"Okay, lady, to your window. Let's catch some varmints." He heard the soft rustle of cloth as she moved across the room. Tanner took up a position by the side window, figuring that would be the most likely point of entry. Crouching on the floor, he parted the edge of the curtain and gazed into the alley.

For a time all was silent and Tanner had begun to think no one was going to show up at all. He shifted positions to ease his cramping legs, then he heard Kate whisper that she'd heard Mark hoot.

"Okay, be quiet now." He removed his gun from his waistband and held it at the ready. Then he placed it beside his rifle on the floor. He had never shot anybody and didn't want to start now. Besides, getting shot would be too easy on whoever was trying to harm Kate.

Two horsemen entered the alley, then leather creaked as they dismounted.

Easing back from the window, Tanner waited, hidden from sight behind the couch.

Something struck the window and glass tinkled onto the floor. A gloved hand came through the opening, released the lock, then slid the window open.

"Boost me up," a man whispered. "I'll get the girl and hand her out to you."

The man crawled through the opening. A sickly sweet smell accompanied him. Chloroform.

Rage rushed through Tanner's veins, making him tremble with the need for action. He wanted to strike out, to punish, but cold reason forced him to remain still.

The man straightened, and the silent way he moved toward the bed told Tanner the intruder was wearing moccasins.

Muffled sounds from the alley drifted through the window. Mark and Chauncey were taking care of the other man.

Tanner eased upright and crept across the floor.

When the intruder hovered over the bed, Tanner launched himself toward him. Capturing the man in an iron grip, he flung him back into the other room. "Kate, are you all right?" He reached out to touch her, but she wasn't there. The quilt covered only pillows. "Kate?"

"Here." Kate rose from the floor on the other side of the bed. "Look out!"

Tanner whirled, and ducked a bit too late. A thrown chair caught him on the shoulder. "Want to play rough, do you?" Only too glad to oblige, he strode toward a burly man silhouetted against the window.

Kate scurried behind him and rushed to the kitchen to light the lamp. "It's him. The man who insulted me before."

"Blaine!" The man held up his hands. "We didn't mean her no harm." He tried to back away.

Tanner wouldn't let him. "No harm? Chloroform? Kidnapping?" Fury blurred his vision. "I know exactly what you meant." He snaked one hand out and gripped the miner's shoulder. The other hand, doubled into a fist, smashed the man's nose. Blood sprayed across the floor. Tanner hit him again, this time in the belly with a force that lifted him off his feet. He hit him again, and again, until Kate's cry of anguish brought him back to sanity.

Tanner staggered to his feet and stared down at the blood-drenched man stretched out on the floor. Sickened by the sight, he turned to look at Kate.

She was pale as death, her eyes wide with horror.

Mark stood in the doorway, looking green enough to vomit.

"Right in here, sheriff." Chauncey escorted the lawman into the room.

"My God! Who is it?" The sheriff stared down at the prostrate miner.

"Toddy Dobbs," Chauncey answered. "He and his brother have a claim out on Sterling Creek." He knelt and lifted the man's eyelid. "Still alive, but I don't reckon he'll be pestering any more women anytime soon."

"You all right, Tanner?" Mark asked, coming to stand beside him.

"Yeah." He was covered with blood, but it wasn't his. He was shaken by the realization that if he'd continued the way he was going he would have beaten the man to death.

"Jeanne's coming to take Kate home with her," Mark said solemnly. "I think it might be best if we headed home ourselves."

Tanner turned toward the lawman. "Sheriff?"

"Go along, Tanner. While I can't legally condone what you did, I can certainly see your reason. If the mangy curs had tried something like that with any of my womenfolk, I probably would have killed them."

Tanner looked at Kate, but she seemed to be in a daze. He couldn't blame her for being shocked. Most women would have fainted.

He nodded to the sheriff and Chauncey, then followed Mark out the door.

The next day, Tanner, unable to face Kate, had stayed on the mountain. Mark rode into Jacksonville alone.

When Mark returned that night, Tanner, noting that Luke and John were engaged in a game of checkers in the front room, motioned the older boys into the kitchen.

After pouring himself a cup of coffee, Mark began to relate the day's events.

He told Tanner that the sheriff had reported that he and his deputy were keeping an eye out for any more trouble. Not that they expected any. The men in town seemed to be giving Kate's place a wide berth.

Doc had returned Kate's dog to her and Fluffy was already up and around. Doc also said that it would be some time before Toddy Dobbs would be going anywhere, even if he could get out of jail.

Madame Jeanne insisted that both Kate and her pet spend their nights at the Franco-American, at least until things were back to normal.

Mark also said that when he went to talk to Kate, he was told she had been given a sedative and was asleep.

Then he had hung around town until he had talked to Chauncey. It was only after the old miner promised that he wouldn't let Kate out of his sight that Mark had decided to come home.

Mark told them that apparently Chauncey had embellished the tale of the night before until Tanner appeared like an avenging angel. Knowing how miners' gossip traveled, not a soul in the whole country wouldn't hear about what had happened to Dobbs. Mark said he could guarantee that anybody who cared about his hide would be certain to treat Kate with nothing but the greatest respect.

"And don't forget, she's got Fluffy back," Matt added. "I don't imagine he's likely to forget that somebody shot him."

"If that dog ever got ahold of anybody else bent on mischief, there probably wouldn't be a greasy spot left," Mark said with a laugh.

Tanner stared at each of his two brothers in turn. "Mark, I want to thank you for being there last night. And Matt, I want to tell you that I appreciate your holding things together here at home. I know I haven't been the easiest person to live with lately."

"Heck, Tanner, we know you've got a lot on your mind. 'Bout time we grew up and helped out a bit," Mark said, holding out his hand. "Right, Matt?"

"Right." Matt held out his hand as well.

Tanner shook their hands, then much to their embarrassment he pulled both his brothers close and gave them a hug. "God, I'm proud of you. Maggie and Pa would be, too."

"Aw, cut it out, Tanner," Mark said, blushing crimson.

Tanner laughed and ruffled his hair as he'd done so many times when Mark was little. "Don't let it go to your head, boy."

"I think it's time I scared up something for supper," Matt said gruffly, rising to stoke up the stove.

"I'd better tend to the stock," Mark said.

Tanner watched him stride from the room. It might have been his imagination, but it looked like his brothers walked a little straighter, held their heads a tad higher. He was proud of them. They would be fine men some day.

A few minutes later, catching wind of the squabble going on in the front room, he wondered if the other two would ever grow up. Shaking his head, he reminded himself that they were young yet. They still had a few years to go. He only hoped he'd live through it.

The ordeal of the last couple of days and nights only enforced Kate's determination to leave Jacksonville. Even though she knew no one would dare try anything after learning how Tanner had dealt with the intruder, she found it difficult to feel secure in her own home. And as ferocious as he was, the dog had been no deterrent to the men who had terrorized her. Fresh tears welled as she thought of what had befallen her poor pet.

She had wanted to be independent, had thought she'd reached that goal. Instead, once again, she had men looking after her—the sheriff, the deputy, Chauncey, the doctor, and Tanner—men who had better things to do with their time.

Tanner. She would never forget the stricken look on his face when he realized how near he had come to killing a man with his bare fists. Would he ever forgive himself? Could she ever forgive herself for being the cause?

Yet, she'd thought about it long and hard and knew she couldn't have done anything different. She certainly hadn't given the Dobbs brothers any encouragement. And the pie shop was her home.

Jeanne had told her to put the incident out of her mind, and Kate had tried. But even though the present danger had passed, how could she ever be sure that someone wasn't lurking around the corner, waiting for the chance to get her alone?

She couldn't, but she could take precautions. She had a gun now. Two guns, she amended. The boys and Chauncey had insisted on it. And they had also made sure that she learned how to use them. She had the dainty, but deadly, Colt derringer that she had seen in the display case at the mercantile, a present from Chauncey. She also had a long-barreled Remington .44, compliments of Dr. Thomas.

Even though she could now hit a target with some degree of accuracy, Kate knew she could never bring herself to shoot a man. The idea of taking a life . . . She shuddered. Not only did she consider it a mortal sin, she knew she wouldn't be able to do it.

But to put her friends' minds at ease, she continued to take her daily shooting lesson.

"She's still set on leaving town," Matt said, staring at Tanner across the table he was clearing.

"Well, she can't go," Tanner stated. He thought he'd already settled the matter, but apparently he hadn't.

"There's only one way you're going to keep her here," Mark replied from his place at the sink. He lifted his hand from the dishwater and pointed at Tanner. "And you know what that is without me saying."

Tanner stared at the coffee grounds floating on the surface of his brew. He knew, all right. He'd just hoped to have a little more time. He glanced up at Matt. "Do you know when she's planning to leave?"

"She didn't say for sure. But I got the feeling she's anxious to get on her way. Maybe as soon as next week."

"What?" He hadn't expected her to go so quick. That put a different light on the matter. As long as she remained in Jacksonville, she had him and his brothers and her friends to watch over her. Dobbs and his brother were still in jail and would be for some time to come. Since there hadn't been any more trouble, Kate had insisted on moving back into her shop, but the sheriff and his deputy, upon Tanner's and the doctor's insistence, continued to patrol her house every night.

But if Kate moved to Portland or Seattle—or anywhere else, for that matter—anything could happen to her, and he wouldn't even know. He scowled.

He couldn't just let her wander off and get into no telling what kind of trouble.

What if she left, and he couldn't find her?

What if she liked it up there?

What if she found somebody else?

He thought about Kate and some other man. She had no sense when it came to men. She came all the way across the country to marry someone she had never even met. What if it hadn't been him? What if it had been somebody like Toddy Dobbs, or worse—if that was possible. Even if she met somebody decent . . . That's what he wanted, wasn't it?

No, dammit. That wasn't what he wanted. That wasn't what he wanted at all.

Tanner shoved the cup back. He needed to get his financial responsibilities squared away before he could think about committing to anything. But it didn't look like he was going to have that option.

"Since I'm the one who caused the problem, I should be the one to pay the price. I guess I'd better marry her. I think that would be the right thing to do." He looked at them, expecting their approval.

Matt looked at Mark and rolled his eyes.

"We wouldn't want you to put yourself out, or anything," Mark replied dryly, vigorously scrubbing at a dirty spot on the table.

"I thought you wanted me to marry her."

"Tanner, if you go into town with that attitude, I can guarantee she won't have anything to do with you," Matt said.

"Yeah. To hear you tell it, you're doing her a favor by marrying her. She sure ain't gonna stand for that."

Tanner mulled that over. Maybe they were right. "What do you think I should do?"

"The same as anybody else. You have to court her. Bring her presents. Quote poetry and stuff."

"Presents? Poetry?" The only kind of poetry he knew, he'd learned from the working girls at Madame Jeanne's. Sure wasn't fit for a lady's ears. "I don't know. . . ."

"Do you want to marry her or not?" Matt asked, shooting him a look of disgust.

"Yeah, but . . ."

"We may as well forget it. Besides, somebody else is sure to beat him to the punch." Mark hung up his dish towel and started to leave the room.

Tanner moved in front of him. "Hold on, now. What somebody else are you talking about?"

"You think you're the only man around?"

"Has she been seeing somebody else?" Tanner thought she didn't want to be courted. He'd heard her tell them that.

"Could be." Mark smothered a yawn with his hand. "I'm going to bed." He darted from the room.

Tanner whirled. "Matt, is she?"

"Come on, Tanner. Courting Kate has been every bachelor's goal for months now."

"Is that right?" Apparently she had changed her mind.

Matt looked him up an down, then shook his head. "You need a haircut."

"Anything else wrong with me?" Tanner asked dryly.

"Well, it wouldn't hurt if you tried asking her something, instead of trying to boss her around all the time".

Tanner opened his mouth, then shut it.

Matt had already escaped from the room.

Had Kate told Matt about the kiss that night at the door? He didn't think she would, but . . . He rubbed his chin, then ran a hand through his hair. It had grown some.

The boys said he should court her. The problem was, Tanner didn't know how. He had brought her flowers—once. That hadn't worked out too well.

Court her?

Every time he got near her, they ended up in a fight. Mostly it was his fault. He'd always ended up kissing her even when she didn't want to be kissed. Thinking back on it, she hadn't complained much. In fact, as long as they were kissing, they got along fine. It was the talking that always got him into trouble.

If he could get to the kissing without having to say anything . . . then he could explain the rest of the stuff later, why he'd rejected her and such. Kind of ease into it, . . .

Pondering the strategy of that, he headed off to bed.

After quitting work early and going to the barber shop, Tanner went to Kate's only to find she wasn't there. She also wasn't at Madame Jeanne's. He strolled down Main Street, thinking he might run into her.

He didn't.

And now, hours later, she still wasn't home.

Tanner paced in front of her house, sat on her doorstep, then got up to pace again.

Where was she?

Who was she with?

He lit a match and checked his pocket watch. It was way past her bedtime. Didn't she know she had to work tomorrow?

When he finally heard a buggy approaching, he sprinted for the toolshed. He didn't want her to think he had nothing better to do than stand around and wait for her.

Dr. Thomas pulled the horse up in front of the house. Then he hopped out of the buggy and went to help Kate down. He walked her to the door. "Thank you, Kathleen."

"Thank you, Fred. The meal was delicious, and I really enjoyed the buggy ride."

Buggy ride? What was she doing out riding around in the old coot's buggy—in the moonlight? He clenched his fists when Kate stood on tiptoe and kissed the doctor on the cheek.

"My dear, being with a pretty woman like you makes this old man feel like a schoolboy," the physician said.

"You're not so old. More like in your prime, I'd say," she retorted with a smile.

Prime! Doc Thomas is old enough to be her father, Tanner fumed inwardly.

"Well, guess I'd better get along home," the physician said.

"Good night, Fred."

"Sweet dreams, Kate." After she was safely inside, the medical man got in his buggy and drove off down the street.

Tanner brushed the dust from his clothes and strode toward her door. He knocked. Once. Twice. Couldn't she hear him? Finally he pounded on the door with his fist.

"Get away from there or I'll shoot," she called out.

"Kate. It's Tanner. Open up."

He heard the latch click, then she opened the door, a gun clutched in her hands. It wasn't the little derringer he'd taken away from her before; this one looked as big as a cannon. He stepped back.

"What do you want?" she asked.

"Put that thing down, and I'll tell you." He eyed the weapon nervously.

"Still giving orders, are you?" She looked him up and down. "You may as well come in. I don't want to wake the whole neighborhood."

He took off his hat and stepped inside.

She closed the door.

He waited, expecting the usual amenities.

But she didn't offer him a seat or anything else. And she still held the gun, although it wasn't pointed at him—at present.

"Well? What do you want?"

"I came courtin'," he said, shoving a box of candy at her.

"C-courting?" She looked at the candy then at him. "It's been opened."

"I got hungry," he explained. "Aren't you going to ask me to sit down?"

"Why? It's late, and I want to go to bed."

He looked at the bed, then he lifted a brow and looked at her. He smiled.

She frowned—and raised the barrel. "I want you to leave—right now."

"But I came courtin'."

"I doubt if you even know what the word means. When you court a woman you don't show up on her doorstep in the middle of the night. And you don't give her a half-eaten box of sweets."

"If you had been home instead of out gallivanting around *half* the night, I could have done it right."

"A *gentleman* would ask a lady ahead of time. Then, when and if she accepts his invitation, a *gentleman* would take her out to supper, or a play, or whatever."

"What kind of 'whatever'?" he asked, not liking the sound of that.

"I can guarantee it's not the kind of 'whatever' you're thinking about," she said, drawing herself up primly.

"All right, since I'm already here," he grumbled, "How about a walk in the moonlight?"

"At this hour?" She shook her head.

"It's not my fault you got home so late."

"It's also none of your concern what hours I keep."

"A *lady* would be home at a respectable hour," he countered.

Kate's eyes narrowed. "Are you implying I'm not a lady?"

He could tell by the glare she shot at him that he'd stepped into that with both feet. "Damn, I knew this talking business would get me into trouble." Well, he just wouldn't talk any more. He reached for her.

She backed away—and cocked the gun. "Get out!"

"You are the most aggravating female I ever met." He jammed his hat back on his head. "I don't know why I ever decided to court you in the first place." He jerked the door open and stomped outside.

She followed him over the threshold. "Well, I'm sure I don't know why, either. I certainly didn't ask you to."

He locked his gaze onto hers. He could have told her he

loved her, but staring down the barrel of a loaded gun didn't exactly appeal to his romantic nature. This wasn't going right. Not right at all. "Good night, Kate. *Sweet dreams,*" he said, mimicking the doctor's phrase.

She glared at him, then whirled and got the candy box from the counter. "Don't forget this. You might get hungry again." She threw the box at him, then stepped back inside and slammed the door.

A stray dog crept from the shadows. He eyed Tanner cautiously, then ravenously devoured the spilled candy.

His own stomach rumbling, Tanner shot a resentful look toward the cur. She could have handed him the box. She didn't have to throw it in the dirt.

A gentleman would ask a lady ahead of time.

Maybe he . . . He glanced at the house and saw the lights go out. Pondering the perversities of women, he headed for his horse.

Inside the house, Kate eased away from the window. So he wanted to court her, did he?

Why?

It wasn't like she hadn't given him ample opportunity. He'd had months, and he hadn't said a thing. He'd had no objection to fondling her at every opportunity. He would have gone even further if she had give him the least encouragement. But he had certainly never given any indication of making a commitment.

That day on the mountain the preacher had practically asked him over the barrel of a shotgun.

Tanner hadn't said a word.

Had he changed his mind?

And, if he had, why now?

Why now?

21

THE NEXT NIGHT, Kate went to a play at Horne's hall with Hank Jordon, the owner of the Tin Peak mine. The night after that, she attended a church social with Dr. Thomas. Then last night, when she had supper with Madame Jeanne, some man, apparently a salesman, sat with them most of the evening.

Tanner knew this because he had been watching Kate, first through the boardinghouse window, then from the toolshed across from her house.

Every day, after quitting work early, he'd come into town, planning on doing the gentlemanly thing, only to find somebody else had beaten him to it. He'd intended to knock on her door, pass a few pleasantries, then ask her out—ahead of time, like she'd said. But, dang it, he had never had the chance.

Then when she did get home, it was too late to do any courting. And with the attitude she'd had the last time he'd tried it, he figured she would have to be softened up a bit before she'd ever consider going anywhere with him.

Tanner scowled, wishing he could run off with her, marry her and be done with it. But if he tried such a thing, he'd probably end up at the end of a rope.

He was getting tempted to try it anyway, but before he could act on the impulse, the same man who had been such a nuisance at the boardinghouse pranced up the alleyway and knocked on her door.

Dressed in a fine checkered suit, a bowler hat, his shoes polished, and his hair slicked back and reeking of Macassar oil, the salesman cut a fine figure—if you cared for that sort of thing—which most women did.

He hoped that Kate had better sense, but, all smiles, she answered the door.

The man gave her a bouquet of daffodils—which Kate accepted. After she stuck them in a vase, she and the slicker walked across the street to the Franco-American.

Tanner followed from a distance, spying on them from behind the boardinghouse until the cook came out to dump the garbage.

Afraid he might be recognized, Tanner went back to Kate's, where he prowled the alley, waiting for them to come home. He checked his pocket watch for the umpteenth time. What could she be doing? He could have eaten three meals in the time it took her to eat dessert, and they'd been eating that an hour ago.

The tinkling of her laughter alerted him to her presence. He darted into the toolshed, and peered from behind the half-opened door.

"It was a divine evening, thank you, Daniel," she said upon reaching her doorstep.

"Not half as divine as the company, my sweet."

De-vine? Tanner rolled his eyes. He'd never heard such hogwash in all his life. He almost bolted from the shed when the scoundrel kissed her hand. Then her wrist.

Before Tanner could act, Kate reclaimed her arm and opened her door.

Fluffy poked his nose out and growled.

Tanner grinned. He knew he liked that critter.

The salesman took one look at the dog and retreated down the steps. "Good night, Kathleen."

"Good night, Daniel." She slipped inside and closed the door.

Her suitor released a regretful sigh, then with one last wistful look at the house, he strolled away.

Tanner stepped from hiding. "Hold up, there."

The man whirled, startled. "What . . ." He hoisted his arms, thinking he was being robbed.

"Put your hands down, you fool." Tanner took the salesman's arm and pulled him out of earshot of the house. "Look here, *friend*. We need to get some things straight. That's *my* woman you've been stepping out with. *My* woman you've been kissing." Tanner drew himself up, looming over the smaller man. "I don't like it," he bit out, his tone full of menace.

The man held up his hands and backed away. "Sorry, mister, I didn't know."

"You know it now." Tanner gripped the front of the stranger's suit. "See that it doesn't happen again."

"No, sir. You have my word."

Tanner released him.

The man hurriedly moved away, then broke and ran toward the saloon.

"One down." Tanner dusted his hands together and smiled. Now if the rest of them would scare off that easy.

It was nearing sunset and Kate had just removed a fresh batch of pies from her oven when she heard a knock on her door. "Now who could that be?" She wasn't expecting company. After the late hours she'd been keeping, she'd decided to go to bed early for a change. She wiped her hands on her apron and peeked through the window glass. *Him again*.

She opened the door. "What do *you* want?"

"Same thing I wanted last time," Tanner answered, as if determined not to be put off by her frosty attitude. "I've come courting. And since you insist on it, I've come to ask you ahead of time."

"I don't think so." She went to shut the door.

He stuck his foot in the crack, then thrust a wilted bouquet through the opening. "Here."

"Flowers?" She pinched her nose, but the pollen had already done its work. She began to sneeze. "Get them— achoo—out of—achoo-achoo—here!"

He tossed the wildflowers into the street.

When she turned to grab a handkerchief, he took the opportunity to sneak inside.

She glared at him, tears flowing from her eyes.

"Sorry, Kate. That other feller brought you flowers. I though maybe you were over your allergy."

"Ah-choo! What other feller—fellow?"

"That duded up salesman." He scuffed his boot on the floor. "Yellow flowers, remember?"

"I tossed them out after he left." She blew her nose, then looked at him. "How did you know about that?"

"I—uh, somebody must have told me."

A lie if she'd ever heard one. "Oh?" She tapped her foot. "And what else did they tell you?"

"Nothing much. Only you haven't been home much lately."

"Anything else?"

"Only that you've been staying out till God only knows when every night."

She smiled. "I have been keeping rather late hours." She stifled a yawn.

"Yeah." He leaned close and lifted her eyelid and stared into her eyes. "Just like I thought. Bloodshot."

She pushed him away. "They are not. Even if they are it's none of your concern—or 'your friend's,' either."

"You're the one who said you weren't getting enough sleep."

She hadn't said that, had she? "Well, maybe I could take a nap, if you'd quit pestering me."

"I'll leave—when you agree to go out with me." He crossed his arms and leaned back against her door.

"Is that the only way I'm going to get rid of you?"

He nodded.

"All right then, I will."

"When?"

She bit her lip, then lifted her hand and began counting on her fingers. "I have an engagement then, and then, and, oh yes, then, too." She glanced up at him. "How about two weeks from next Sunday?"

"What? That's dang near a month away."

She shrugged. "Sorry, but that's the best I can do. Take it or leave it." Mimicking his stance, she crossed her arms and smiled.

His brows drew into a scowl. "Since I don't have any choice, I guess I'll take it."

"Good. Now that we have that settled, you can leave." She moved toward the door. She couldn't open it because he was still leaning against it. You'd think he was holding the wall up.

"How about a piece of pie first, or maybe a cup of coffee, or tea?" He shot a hopeful look toward the kitchen area, where the scent of cinnamon and peaches hung heavy in the air.

"Those are for my customers—my *paying* customers," she added. "They're too hot to cut tonight. Besides, they are already spoken for. I will be making some peach pies tomorrow."

"I won't be here tomorrow."

"I know. Isn't that too bad?" She peeped at him from beneath her lashes. "You could have Matt make you a pie. Or for that matter, you could make your own. I seem to remember you're rather handy in the kitchen."

"Don't have the fixin's." He could be handy in other places too, if she'd give him the chance.

"Mercantile is still open—if you hurry." She pointed toward the door.

He sighed, then hoisted himself to an upright position. "I guess I can take a hint."

"Tell the boys hello for me," she said, almost shoving him through the doorway.

"I'll do that." He untied his horse and went down the alley.

Curious, she watched from her bedroom window and saw him amble across to the mercantile and go inside.

"Kate, are you busy?"

Recognizing Dr. Thomas's voice, she dropped the curtain and hurried to open her door. She knew a guilty flush tinged her cheeks, but the physician didn't seem to notice.

"Hello, Fred. What can I do for you?"

"I wanted to show you something," the doctor said, his blue eyes sparkling. "Olson's mare had the prettiest twin fillies I've ever seen. Thought you might like to see them."

"I'd love to." Her fatigue forgotten, she grabbed her bonnet and shawl and followed him to the buggy.

Leaving the mercantile with a gunnysack full of canned peaches, Tanner glanced up when he heard a buggy coming down the street. Recognizing it as Dr. Thomas's, he raised a hand in greeting.

"Howdy, Tanner," the silver-haired man said, nodding to him.

A woman, her face partially shielded by a bonnet, also waved. "Goodbye, Tanner," she called back over her shoulder.

Tanner whirled. "Kate?"

He watched the buggy until it rolled out of sight, then he hoisted the sack and tied it to a piggin string behind his saddle.

She'd told *him* she was too tired to go anywhere. Told *him* she wanted to take a nap.

She'd had no intention of taking a nap. And she didn't look tired at all. Her cheeks bloomed with color.

It would be three weeks before she would even go out with him. Anybody else showed up, and off she'd go.

He swung onto the saddle.

Three weeks? He shook his head. He had no intention of waiting that long.

The next day Tanner showed up in Jacksonville at dawn. He staked his horse out behind Dr. Thomas's, hoping the critter had sense enough not to eat too much of the sweet green grass and make itself sick, then he strolled down Main Street and went into the Stars and Bars for a cup of coffee. By the time he ambled back to Kate's, a crowd had already gathered there.

"Good morning," she called to her customers as she hung the Open sign on a peg by her front window. In her blue calico dress and with her hair pulled back and tied with a matching ribbon, she looked pretty as a mountain wild-flower. He had the feeling she could be selling empty pans and the men would still line up to buy them.

Smiling, she took orders at the door. She collected her money and wrapped each pie, passing a moment of conversation with the buyer before going on to the next customer.

The pies disappeared like snowflakes in July. Judging by the number of the crowd remaining, Tanner knew he would be likely to do without unless he took matters in hand.

When he saw she was nearing the end, he stepped forward. "I believe that one is mine. Remember, you promised it to me yesterday?"

She looked at him, then nodded. "I didn't think you would make it." She glanced down at the next man in line. "I'm sorry, but I did promise this one to Tanner. I'll make sure to save you a special one tomorrow," she said.

"All right." The miner glared at Tanner, who gave him a broad grin in return. "I'll pay for it right now, just to make sure. I purely love peach pie."

The miner and the rest of the men filed away.

Tanner held out his money and collected his pie. Then he took off his hat and sat down on her front step.

"What are you doing?" she asked, frowning down at him.

"Eatin' my pie."

"Here?"

"This will do—unless you want to ask me inside."

She shut the door.

He finished the pie and leaned back against the doorway. The sun warming his body and the pie filling his stomach proved more than he could resist. Soon he found himself nodding off.

Is he still here? Kate wondered. If he'd left, she hadn't seen him go. She eased the door open to check outside.

Tanner toppled onto her floor, sprawling backward across her rug.

"Oh!" She peered down at him. "Tanner, are you all right? Are you hurt?" Her heart thundering, she knelt to see if he was breathing. Was he unconscious or was he dead? Maybe he'd choked on a peach pit. She'd checked the fruit, but nevertheless . . . She unbuttoned his shirt and pressed her head to his chest. He seemed to be breathing all right. What was it, then? "Tanner?" Then she heard him snore.

She jumped to her feet. "Tanner! Tanner Blaine," she hissed, nudging him with the toe of her shoe.

"Humph?" He snored again.

"Tanner, you wake up this minute."

He opened one eye a slit. Just as quickly, he shut it and went back to sleep.

"You can't stay there. I can't even shut the door."

She glanced up the alley toward the street. Was it her imagination or was half the town out for a stroll? What if somebody saw him? "Tanner, get up this minute."

He didn't move.

She jerked his arm. Why wouldn't he wake up. Maybe something really was wrong with him. Should she go for the doctor? Then she remembered seeing the physician's buggy leaving town earlier.

She bent and lifted Tanner's eyelid.

A steel gray eye stared back at her.

His eyeballs weren't rolled back in his head. He seemed to be simply asleep.

She refused to leave him where he lay. And she couldn't move him. She studied the rug and freshly waxed floor.

Or could she?

She bent, grabbed the edge of the rug and pulled.

It, and Tanner, slid across the floor.

She tugged again until his feet cleared the threshold; then, snatching up his hat and the pie tin from the doorstep, she hurried inside and closed the door.

She turned to see Fluffy nuzzling him, then, apparently satisfied, the dog yawned and went back to his place in the corner.

"Big help you are," she scolded.

The dog merely cocked his head to one side and wagged his tail.

"What now?" she asked herself. After checking Tanner's

pulse, she didn't think there was anything physically wrong with the man. Then she remembered Matt having once said that his brother was prone to these episodes, especially when he was exhausted. Matt had also said that, once asleep, the house could fall on Tanner and he'd never know it.

That explained the situation. But why did he have to go to sleep here? Now?

She smoothed a lock of dark hair out of his eyes. He did look tired, and she knew he had been working awfully hard. She didn't know anyone who labored more diligently.

Nevertheless, she'd have a hard time explaining Tanner's presence if some of the ladies from church dropped by, as they were prone to do from time to time. She pulled her front drapes, hoping they would think she wasn't home.

She eyed the curtain strung across the room, and the bed beyond it. Did she dare? Her reputation would be ruined if anyone discovered him. But at least if she could get him that far, he would be out of sight. She'd feed him coffee, strong black coffee. That should get him on his feet.

She pulled the rug; then, noticing his boot heels were marking her floor, she bent and removed them. She pulled again. This time, without his boots dragging, he moved more easily.

When she had him out of view behind the curtain, she returned to the kitchen and made a pot of coffee. When it had boiled, she poured a large cup and carried it to the bedroom.

He lay just as she'd left him. He hadn't moved a finger.

She couldn't give him the coffee lying down, she might choke or scald him if she tried. She set the cup on the bedside table. Then, getting down on all fours, she pushed him into a sitting position and propped him against the bed.

She reached for the coffee.

He slid back onto the floor.

"Drat!" She moved the cup closer, then propped him up again. Realizing the coffee may still be too hot, she took a swallow herself, then held it to his lips. "Drink," she commanded.

He took a sip, and another, and looked at her through half-shuttered eyes.

She forced some more of the brew past his lips, praying it would do the job. When the cup was empty, she shoved it to one side.

"Tanner, stand up. That's an order," she said gruffly.

"Yessir," he mumbled thickly, making a feeble attempt to rise.

She pulled, hoisted, tugged and lifted until she had him on his feet. Her apron had fallen off, and somewhere during the struggle she'd lost her top dress button. Lost her hair bow, too, she noticed, tossing her head to throw her hair back out of her eyes.

Tanner yawned, stretching his arms overhead. Then his eyes slammed shut. He swayed.

"No, you don't." She grabbed him around the waist and held on tight. But he was too big. It was like hugging . . . a falling tree.

He toppled backward, taking her along with him. Another of her buttons shot across the room and ricocheted off the wall. The next thing she knew, she was entangled in Tanner's long limbs. And they were both lying on the bed.

"Oh, good grief," she cried, trying to pry his arm off her neck. It was like trying to move a dead weight. When she had managed to move that arm over her head, he turned onto his side. His other arm fell across her breast.

He snored, his warm breath tickling her ear. Mumbling, he snuggled even closer. One leg slid over hers.

She couldn't get free of him; he was on top of her skirt. She couldn't turn. His leg had her pinned to the bed. With his arm stretched across her middle, she could barely breathe.

"Tanner. Tanner, wake up."

He snorted, then exhaled.

"If this isn't a fine kettle of fish," she muttered, staring at the man by her side. She sighed in resignation, knowing she wouldn't be going anywhere until he either rolled over or woke up. Both seemed highly unlikely anytime soon.

Since she'd never had him this close, or this still before,

she began to examine his features. She studied the long, slightly hooked nose, the square chin. In sleep he looked younger, less fierce, almost boyish.

She'd never noticed what long eyelashes he had. He'd always glared at her with those steel-colored eyes. His high cheekbones and bronzed coloring told of his Indian heritage. As did his glossy black hair. He was sinfully handsome— and he knew it. Arrogant, too.

Her gaze traced the contour of his mouth. She could feel the short puffs of air that drifted between his lips. He smelled of peach pie and coffee.

She remembered how those same lips had felt when he kissed her. Unable to resist, she tilted her chin and pressed her mouth to his. His lips were warm and smooth. She kissed him again, glad he was asleep, but at the same time wondering what would happen if he should wake. A warmth spiraled inside her.

She ran a finger down his arm and traced his muscles, hard, sinewy. She trailed her hand across his muscled torso, tangling a matt of silky chest hair around her fingers. She touched his nipples and was surprised to see them harden. She eyed them curiously, wondering what he might be feeling. She probably should button his shirt, she decided, but with him lying on it, she couldn't pull it together.

Her gaze drifted downward to where his flat middle disappeared into his pants, paused a moment. Blushing at her wanton thoughts, she forced them away. His long legs dangled over the end of the bed. Strong, capable of covering great distance. For a man his size, he moved with the grace of a cat.

He moaned, drawing her attention back to his face.

She kissed him, then tasted his lips with her tongue. Nice. Slightly peachy. Intrigued, she tasted him again. Something she'd never wanted to do when he was scowling.

Now in sleep, he smiled.

What was he dreaming about, she wondered. The mountain? The wildflowers in the meadow? Or was he dreaming about her? Hoping the latter might be the case, she closed her eyes and nestled against him.

*   *   *

Tanner forced himself to stay still, even though the arm stretched unnaturally over his head tingled with lack of circulation. Those kisses of hers had almost been his undoing. The little minx. It was all he could do not to pull her into his arms and kiss her back.

As long as he was awake, she pretended not to have much use for him. But when she thought he didn't know what she was doing . . . A smile tugged at his mouth. Even though his eyes had been shut, he'd felt her gaze even when she hadn't touched him. He'd gritted his teeth and fought his body's natural response.

Who would have thought she would do such things? She'd been curious as a cat.

Her soft, even breathing told Tanner she had fallen asleep. He smiled and pulled her even closer, content for the first time in weeks. It had taken some playacting on his part, but he had her where he wanted her.

He imagined going to bed with her each night, making love by the firelight. Curling his body around hers, shielding her from the cold. Then waking with her in his arms and making love by the dawn's earliest light.

Envisioning that joining, his body hardened against hers. He inched away, afraid she would awaken. He contented himself with feeling her softness, her sweetness, inhaling her cinnamon scent. If they lived to be one hundred, he might never get enough of her. If he had his way they'd never get out of bed.

Her dress gaped enticingly where she'd lost her buttons. He undid one more and carefully slid his hand inside. He cupped her breast, and felt it swell to fill his hand. He could see her pregnant, her body swollen with his babe. That same babe suckling at her breast. She'd make a wonderful mother—if he could ever convince her to be his wife.

Cursing himself for the time he had wasted, he kissed her forehead and brushed a damp curl from her cheek.

He guiltily thought of his deception. She'd despise him if she ever found out.

He had slept like this once. It was after his pa had died.

He'd spent weeks working from dawn to dusk with hardly any rest. He'd avoided sleep, because with it came the reliving of the nightmare, and the part he'd played in his father's death.

When he finally had collapsed, he'd slept for two days and nights, oblivious to everything around him. He'd scared his brothers to death, but the doctor had assured them he would be fine when he awakened. And he was.

With Kate cuddled next to him, he'd never be too sick or tired to know she was there. In fact, he never felt more alive in his life.

If she found him in her bed come daylight, she'd probably have a conniption fit. But it would be worth it.

He nuzzled her cheek.

She sighed, murmuring his name.

She must be dreaming about him. He grinned. She'd told him it would be three weeks before she'd even go anywhere with him.

He had accomplished much more than he had ever hoped for and it had only taken him one day.

He snagged a quilt from the end of the bed and pulled it over them. Lost in oblivion, she didn't even know it.

He closed his eyes and hugged her close.

Now that he had her where he wanted her, he intended to keep it that way.

22

A NOISE REACHED into Kate's dreams and tugged at her consciousness. She ignored it and snuggled closer to the warmth at her side. She'd been dreaming about Tanner, dreaming they were married and she was sharing his bed. She nuzzled her pillow.

It let out a snore.

She blinked. Then blinked again, unable to believe what she was seeing.

It wasn't a dream. Tanner was here. In her bed. Snoring in her ear. And his hand . . . She jerked it from inside her dress.

He snorted, then exhaled on a long whistling sigh.

"Ka-ate? Kate, are you there, dear?" a feminine voice called from nearby.

Oh, no! Nellie McGruder—and Hester Hamilton! The worst gossips and busybodies in Jacksonville. The pair were also organizers of the sewing circle at the church.

Her heart hammering against her ribcage, Kate stared at Tanner. She thought she'd locked her door, but apparently she hadn't. And now it was too late, the women were here, inside her shop.

Maybe she could pretend she was asleep. Maybe they would go away.

Mrs. Hamilton might. Nosey-body McGruder would be

more likely to peek behind the curtain. If she did . . . Her gaze shot to the man peacefully sleeping by her side.

She couldn't let them find Tanner here—in her bed. Kate twisted, yanking frantically at her dress to remove it from under his legs. She heard the fabric tear, but didn't have time to worry about it. And at least she was free.

She jumped from the bed and slid her feet into her slippers, wondering how they came to be off her feet. She tried to fasten her dress. Most of the buttons were missing. She did up the ones that were left, thinking maybe she could cover it with her apron. She scanned the bedroom. Drat! She must have lost it in the kitchen.

Tanner moaned, patted the bed beside him, then sleepily opened his eyes.

Why did he pick now to wake up? She shot a glance toward the curtain, expecting to see the women any minute.

Maybe she could hide him.

Not likely, with his feet sticking over the end of the bed. She tugged at his legs, then bent his knees. So far, so good. She covered him with the quilt.

"What . . . What?" he mumbled. He raised his head. "Kate?"

"Shh!" She shoved his face into the pillow. "Go back to sleep." She yanked the covers up over his head and prayed he'd keep quiet.

"Kate?" Mrs. McGruder called from near the other side of the partition.

Knowing she dare not delay any longer, Kate pushed her hair out of her eyes and slid from behind the curtain, pulling it shut behind her.

"Mrs. McGruder. Mrs. Hamilton," she said brightly, hoping she didn't wake Tanner in the process. "I was asleep."

Mrs. McGruder, the heavier of the two women, stared at her curiously. "Asleep?"

"In the middle of the day?" Mrs. Hamilton peered over the wire-rimmed spectacles that were perched on the end of her long, thin nose.

Kate's gaze shot to the window where the sun was indeed beaming brightly. "Uh, . . . Headache. I had a headache," she said quickly.

The women stared at her gaping dress. She tried to pull it together. "Mending. I was doing some mending."

"I thought you were sleeping," Mrs. McGruder stated.

Fluffy yawned, then Kate heard the dog's toenails click against the floorboards as he came up behind her.

He probably wants out, Kate decided, until she saw the women's eyes widen.

"What's that he's eating?" the fat woman said, taking a step forward so she could see better. "Why, it's a man's boot."

Kate whirled.

The dog was chewing on a boot—what was left of it.

"He's cutting teeth," Kate explained. "So I found him that old boot to chew on."

"Doesn't look that old to me." Mrs. Hamilton eyed her suspiciously. "Did you buy him a pair, dear?"

"A pair?"

"Look, Nellie, isn't that another boot under the settee?"

"Why, so it is."

The women stared at each other; then, their eyes bright with curiosity, they turned to Kate.

"They were on sale," she said, feeling herself sinking deeper by the minute.

"Hey, darlin', you got any coffee?"

Kate closed her eyes and muttered a curse.

Both of her callers uttered shocked gasps. They stared at the back of her shop.

Afraid of what she might see, but unable to stop herself from looking, Kate whirled.

As if on cue, the curtain slid back. Barefooted, his hair tousled, his shirt open and shirttail trailing over his pants, Tanner sleepily scratched his bare middle and yawned.

"Oh, my." Mrs. McGruder covered her mouth with her hand and let out a high-pitched giggle.

"Oh, no!" Kate cried. This couldn't be happening. It had to be a nightmare. Her entire body flushed crimson.

Not having the good grace to be embarrassed, Tanner rubbed his eyes and stared back at them. "Mornin', Nellie. Hester." He smiled at Kate. "Sorry, darlin', I didn't know we had company."

"Tanner. Tanner Blaine!" Her eyes bright as a bird's, Mrs. Hamilton looked at Tanner's bare feet, then at the boots. Arching a brow, she peered at Kate. "On sale indeed. Looks like we might have interrupted something."

"Yes, it appears we might," Mrs. McGruder said, a delighted smile dimpling her chubby cheeks.

"Tanner wasn't feeling well, so I let him lie down," Kate tried to explain.

"And you were taking a nap, too. How cozy."

"No, dear, she was mending, remember?"

"She said she was asleep," Mrs. McGruder snapped.

"And sewing."

They looked at Kate's missing buttons and the ripped dress dragging the floor behind her. Then they eyed Tanner, who looked as smug as a cat that had been into the cream.

Kate shoved her hair out of her eyes and glared at him. He was enjoying this!

"This isn't what it looks like, ladies," Tanner said, coming up behind Kate and wrapping his arms around her.

Kate stiffened. Leave it to him to make things worse—if that was possible. She tried to wriggle free.

He squeezed her tighter. "Miss Deveraux has just accepted my proposal of marriage."

"What proposal?" Kate asked, before she could stop herself.

"Did you forget already, darlin'?" His eyes twinkling like quicksilver, he winked. "You promised to be my wife." He nuzzled her temple.

She twisted her head to face him. "I did no—"

His mouth came down on hers.

"Oh, my. How romantic," Mrs. McGruder said with a sigh. "Hester, I think we'd better leave and let these two young people get back to whatever they were doing."

The tall, skinny woman glanced toward the bedroom, then eyed them with disapproval. "Most people have the decency to wait until after the wedding."

Still captured in his embrace, with his lips locked on hers, Kate fought to have her say. "Nmmm," was all she could manage.

Tanner waited until the two women had left the shop before he set her free.

Trembling with fury, she backed away. "How could you?"

"I don't know what you're so mad for." He gave her a playful swat, then went to stoke up the cookstove, adding a few chunks of wood. "I just saved your reputation."

"You just ruined my reputation, you mean. Coming out of there like that . . ." She waved a hand toward him. "Heaven only knows what they thought."

"Yeah." He grinned. "Got any coffee?" He peered under her cabinet.

"Nothing happened," she insisted.

"No, nothing happened." He yawned again and stretched his arms over his head. "Now, about that coffee?"

"Coffee! How can you think of coffee at a time like this?"

"I thought it might help me wake up."

"It's right in front of you." She whirled toward the stove and picked up the blue enameled pot. She shoved it into his hands. "Here's your coffee. Now get out."

"It's cold," he complained, feeling the side of the pot.

"You want me to heat it?" she asked between gritted teeth.

He smiled. "That would be real nice." He looked around the room. "Do you know what happened to my socks?"

She slammed the coffeepot down on the stove. "How should I know? It didn't look like you were wearing any when I pulled off your boots."

"I was wondering how I came to be barefooted." He pointed to his shirt front. "You did this, too?"

"You needn't look so pleased. I was checking to see if you were dead."

"Do you always put dead men in your bed?"

"You weren't dead."

"Well, at least that's one thing we agree on." He sauntered toward her. "Darlin', I'm very much alive."

"You won't be if you come any closer," she warned, wrapping her fingers around the handle of a large cast-iron skillet.

"Now, is that any way to talk to your intended, darlin'?"

"Stop calling me 'darlin'.' And you aren't my intended. You aren't my anything."

"That isn't what the ladies think." He wondered how far he could bait her before she threw the frying pan. Since the thing weighed almost half as much as she did, he decided he was safe. "They think we already celebrated the honeymoon."

"You . . ." She tried to hoist the skillet—and dropped it on the floor.

"Be a shame to disappoint them." He moved closer.

She retreated until her back was against the wall. "Don't!"

"What's the matter, honey?"

She shoved at him. "You're what's the matter. You get up out of my bed and come in here looking like—like that. Why couldn't you stay under the covers? Why didn't you go back to sleep?"

"I wasn't sleepy. Besides, I missed you," he said, telling her that he knew she had been sharing the bed with him. "How did I get in your bed, anyhow?" he asked, pretending innocence.

She glared at him, but didn't answer.

"Since I don't remember getting there on my own, I guess you must have put me there."

"I did—not." She frowned. "Not on purpose."

"Then how did I get there?" he asked, stroking the base of her throat with his thumb.

"You were asleep. And . . ." She slapped at his hand. "Quit that. I can't think."

Placing one arm on either side of her, he nuzzled her cheek, then nibbled at her ear. "Go on."

"I, uh, . . ." She shook her head. "What was I trying to say?"

He chuckled.

"Stop. How do you expect me to concentrate with you doing *that?*" She twisted her head away from his tongue, which only gave him more access to her neck.

He kissed her earlobe, and the soft spot where the nape met her shoulder, then trailed his tongue down to the base of her throat and tasted the flutter of her pulse. "Hmm, so sweet." He kissed the sensitive hollow, then deftly undid the remaining buttons.

"Tanner, stop it right . . . Oh."

He covered her mouth with his, swallowing any protest she might have made. His roaming hand slid inside her chemise and curved around her swelling breast. His own heat rising, he felt the rosy-crested tip thrust against his palm.

She moaned and arched against him.

Just when things were really beginning to get interesting, an annoying drumming sound caught his attention. "Now what?" He raised his head and listened.

Somebody was pounding on Kate's door.

The front curtains were drawn so the visitor couldn't see inside, but the latch wasn't locked. Whoever it was could enter at any time.

"Honey?" He looked down at Kate, who appeared about to swoon. Her lips were pink and swollen, her eyes hidden by long, silky lashes. Her creamy skin was reddened by his kisses. Not counting the fact that she was half undressed. He had caused her enough problems. He couldn't let anybody else see her like that.

He scooped her into his arms and strode across the floor. He shoved the partition aside and lay her on the bed. Her glossy hair streamed back over the pillow. Wishing whoever was at the door would give up and go away, he gazed at her for a moment.

Torn between wanting to join her and a desire to protect her, he swallowed and covered her with the quilt. Then he left the bedroom, pulling the curtain shut behind him.

The coffeepot steamed, hissed, then boiled over, filling the air with an acrid stench.

He snatched the kettle from the fire, burning his hand in the process.

The pounding came again, insistent, demanding, telling him that whoever was outside wasn't about to go away. "Kate, are you in there?" a gruff voice called.

Tanner couldn't answer the door barefooted and half-dressed. Determined not to shame Kate more than he already had, he snagged one boot, then took the other one away from the dog. Fluffy seemed content for the moment with the chunk he'd torn off.

Tanner stuffed his feet inside the boots, then hastily buttoned his shirt and stuffed his tails into his pants. Running a hand through his hair to smooth it, he went to answer the door.

Bob Rutledge, the foreman of the Lucky Strike mine, stood on the other side.

"Tanner Blaine! What are you doing here?" The ruddy-faced man shifted to one side and tried to peer into the room.

Tanner moved with him, blocking his view. "What do you want?"

"Where's Miss Deveraux?" the man demanded angrily. "We were supposed to have supper this evening."

Tanner took note of the man's broadcloth suit, his boiled shirt and string tie. "Yeah, I wondered why you were so duded up," he said, feeling scruffy as a stray dog by comparison. The only thing that soothed his ego was the fact that he was inside the house with Kate, while the miner was left outside, standing on the porch.

"My *fiancée* is indisposed," Tanner answered smugly.

"Your fiancée?" Rutledge's eyes narrowed. "Since when?"

"It became official earlier today."

"I don't believe it." The man stepped up to the threshold as if to force his entry. "She would have said something."

Tanner didn't move.

"I want Miss Deveraux to tell me herself," the miner insisted.

Tanner's eyes narrowed. "The future *Mrs. Blaine* isn't feeling well. She has a headache. I won't allow her to be disturbed." He took a step forward, forcing the other man to retreat down the step.

Blustering, Rutledge straightened his suit and glared. "What are you doing in town, anyhow? You're supposed to be cutting timber."

"I told you. I was busy getting engaged." Tanner smiled

into the man's almost purple face, then he closed—and locked—the door.

"You'd better have that timber ready. If you don't . . ."

More worried about Kate than the foreman's threats, Tanner hurried across the floor and into the bedroom.

When he approached the bed, Kate stared up at him with wide violet eyes. "Who were you talking to?"

"Nobody special. I sent him away."

She groaned and rolled over, burying her face in the pillow. The movement of her shoulders told him she was crying.

He sat down on the bed and gathered her into his arms. "It will be all right, honey. I'll take care of everything."

She gave a strangled gasp and raised her head, the look on her face incredulous. Even with her hair tangled and her eyes red, she was the most tempting sight he had ever seen.

"If you take care of anything else, I'll kill you," she hissed. "You've ruined my reputation. By now those good ladies will be discussing my wild carryings-on over every tea table in town. No telling what whoever that was at the door thinks. Thanks to you, I'll be scorned, mocked. Even if we were to wed, she added, frowning, "I'd never be able to face anyone in Jacksonville again."

"Everything will be fine after we get married. You'll see." He trailed a finger down her cheek and brushed away a teardrop. "Besides, we wouldn't be the first couple in town to get the cart before the horse." He absently twisted a long, silky curl around his finger. "I'll admit I would have preferred to have waited a bit to get married."

"Waited a bit?" She snatched her hair from his grasp. "You can wait until perdition. I have no intention of marrying you."

He frowned. "I meant, I do have to finish cutting that timber first. After today I don't think Tom Fuller will allow any more excuses." He rubbed his chin. "I should be done with that by the end of April. We could get married the first of May?" He glanced at her, waiting for her decision. "Unless you'd prefer June."

"Oh, there's no talking to you because you apparently

haven't heard a word I've said." She planted both palms against his chest and pushed.

He landed on the floor. He gazed up in surprise. "What did you do that for?"

She slid from the bed and stood, hands on her hips. "Now, do I have your attention?"

He focused on the area where she was about to spill out of her dress. "You sure do, darlin'."

Noting his distraction, she glanced down and gasped. "You—you scoundrel!" She jerked her dress front together.

He chuckled. "It's not like I'm seeing something I haven't seen before." He raised a brow. "Remember that day in the meadow?"

"You would remind me of that." She turned away and buttoned her dress.

Tanner got to his feet and came up behind her. He took her in his arms. "You're cute when you're mad."

"Flattery will get you nowhere." She broke free of his embrace and moved away. "Haven't you got something else to do—in California, maybe?"

He cupped her chin and forced her to meet his eyes. "I do have a few things to take care of. But I'll be back."

"It won't do you any good," she said firmly. "The door will be locked."

He shoved his hands into his pockets and shot her a predatory grin. "I'll be back, Kate," he promised. "Don't expect a little thing like a locked door to keep me out."

Fluffy whined and followed along behind him.

"Want to go with me?"

The dog wagged his tail.

Kate might lock him out, but she'd never leave her dog outside. Tanner opened the door, allowing the dog to escape. "Me and Fluffy will see you in a bit."

"No! Fluffy, you come back here," she yelled, from the threshold.

Ignoring her, the dog quickened his pace and trotted alongside Tanner.

He reached down and stroked the mutt's massive head. "Fella, I think you might come in real handy tonight."

While Fluffy raced around doing his business, Tanner checked on his horse and hobbled him in a grove of trees closer to Kate's, so that the gelding would be nearby when he left later that night.

Then, hoping he might find a dress to replace the one Kate had ruined, Tanner stopped by Lottie Martin's dressmaker shop. He figured he owed Kate that, since it was his fault her frock had gotten ripped.

Lottie had one that would suit Kate to perfection: it was a deep sapphire blue with lace trim. The blond who had ordered it claimed the dress was too dark for her fair skin. Glad to get the garment off her hands, Lottie told Tanner she would sell it to him for a fraction of its original cost.

When Lottie added that she would settle for firewood instead of hard coin, Tanner was quick to accept the deal. The dressmaker promised she would alter it to fit Kate and deliver it to her the next day.

Tanner whistled for the dog and headed back toward the pie shop.

"Blaine, I need to have a word with you," a man called from across the street.

Wondering who could be wanting him, Tanner turned and recognized the speaker as Thomas Fuller, owner of the Lucky Strike mine. Fuller left the group of men he was with and strode toward him.

"Hello, Tom," Tanner said. They shook hands and exchanged small talk. And even though Fuller's manner seemed friendly enough, the chill in his eyes told Tanner that he was not as congenial as he seemed. Apparently Rutledge had wasted no time in getting to his boss. Tanner waited for the man to speak his piece.

"Come on over to the hotel bar and join me in a drink, Fuller insisted. "These town meetings always leave me dry as a bullfrog in a drought."

Tanner shot a look toward Kate's, knowing she would be there waiting. He also knew their future might depend on his answer. "All right," he said, hoping that after a few drinks he could persuade the man to give him an extension on the timber contract.

They crossed the street and entered the lobby of the United States Hotel.

Tanner remembered the last time he'd been there, the day he'd met Kate, and how determined he'd been that she wouldn't disrupt his life. Now she was as much a part of him as the air he breathed, even though she didn't yet see it that way.

Not wanting to keep the mine owner waiting, Tanner quickened his step and followed Tom into the bar.

Fuller chose a damask-covered table in the corner where they could talk without being disturbed.

Tanner, more familiar with the rowdy atmosphere of the local saloons, found the place too elegant for his taste. Even Horne's new theater wasn't half so fine. He had the feeling that a man drinking at the United States bar should be clean-shaven and wearing a suit.

Catching a glimpse of himself in a mirror running the full length of the wall behind the gleaming, brass-railed, cherry wood bar, did nothing to dispel that notion. He felt as out of place as a skunk at a Sunday school picnic. As he took note of his shaggy hair, his battered hat and his shadowed jaws, he gave thanks that his pant legs covered his chewed boots.

Large, gold-framed paintings of smiling, gauze-draped nudes adorned the brocade-covered walls. Crystal chandeliers flickered overhead. Brass spittoons took up strategic spots around the perimeter.

Heaven help the man that spit on that polished oak floor or on the thick Oriental rug, Tanner thought wryly. Glad that he neither smoked nor chewed, he shifted uneasily in the padded leather chair.

Except for himself and Fuller and a well-dressed foursome playing cards, the place was empty. Maybe nobody else felt comfortable there, either.

The bartender looked up from the glasses he was polishing and called out a greeting to the mine owner. Then he reached beneath the bar and removed a bottle, apparently private stock, and brought it and two crystal tumblers to the table. With a flourish, he poured them each a hefty shot, then stood waiting.

"Thank you, O'Dell. Just leave the bottle," Tom instructed. "We've got some business to discuss."

The bartender nodded and returned to the counter.

Tom hoisted his drink. "Here's to your health." He swallowed his drink. "Hah-h, smooth as silk. Prime bourbon." He glanced at Tanner.

Not wanting to offend the man, Tanner downed his own drink, only to have Tom immediately pour him another.

"My foreman told me you've been hanging around town all week. I presume that means you've finished cutting the timber."

"Not quite," Tanner hedged. "It won't be long now, though."

"How long?"

"By the end of the month." Only if he worked night and day, and was god-awful lucky, Tanner thought.

"Since this is March first, that's almost a month yet. You're already over the deadline I gave you."

"The snow delayed me some," Tanner said, downing the second drink.

"Among other things, from what I hear." Tom filled their glasses again. "I understand from Rutledge that you're engaged to Kate Deveraux."

Tense, Tanner waited. If the man said one derogatory word about Kate, contract or no contract, he would put his fist in Fuller's elegant mouth.

But the mine owner only extolled Kate's virtues. Apparently she was very well-liked around town. He knew from the man's comments that Fuller hadn't heard the latest gossip, yet.

The mine owner offered Tanner a cigar, which he declined.

Fuller stuck a cigar in his own mouth and lit it. He took a puff, filling the area around his head in a circle of smoke. "I think my foreman was hoping he might persuade Kathleen to marry him. Somehow, I never really thought she was your type."

"She's much too good for me," Tanner agreed, a little resentful at the man's implication. "But nevertheless, we'll be getting married before summer." Sooner than that if he had his way.

"Well, Blaine, your private life is your own concern—as long as it doesn't interfere in our business arrangement." He leaned forward and placed his palms on the table. "We have a contract, and I've been more than lenient. I won't abide any more delays. I need that flume, and I need it now." He scooted his chair back from the table. "I'll give you until the fifteenth. Not one day more."

"The fifteenth?" A knot tied in Tanner's middle. He nodded.

"May as well enjoy the rest of this. The hotel will charge me for it anyhow." He sloshed the remains of the bottle into Tanner's glass. Then he abruptly left the saloon.

Two weeks. Tanner stared into the amber liquid. To do more than six weeks' work. There was no way. He couldn't do it.

He had to do it. He had no choice.

He could rig lanterns to see by, work until he dropped. It wasn't the work that bothered him. It was the realization that during those two weeks, there would be no time for coming into town—or seeing Kate.

She hadn't yet agreed to marry him.

Other men with a lot more to offer were knocking on her door. Men that wouldn't hesitate to take advantage of his absence.

He couldn't lose her. Not now.

But it might very possibly happen.

Needing to vanquish his sense of foreboding, he turned up his glass and downed his drink. It didn't help. It only made him dizzy.

"We're closing now, sir."

Tanner glanced around the room. Except for him and the barman, the place was empty.

"I'm finished." He bid the man good night, got to his feet and staggered from the hotel.

When he reached the boardwalk, Tanner leaned against the hitching rail and gulped the cool air, hoping it might help clear his senses. He wasn't much of a drinking man, never had been. And he hadn't had anything to eat since that pie this morning, which fact only added to his intoxication. The two combined made a potent combination.

After a minute, he glanced up the street, surprised to see that the town, except for the saloon on the next block, had grown dark. The only light came from a three-quarter moon directly overhead. Most of Jacksonville had retired for the night.

He pushed away from the hitching rail. His head spun. The way his legs were wobbling made Tanner wonder if he'd even make it to Kate's. *The dog.* He didn't dare go back without him. He sure didn't feel up to hunting for the animal either. He called a few times and when he neared the pie shop, he managed a whistle. He sighed in relief when Fluffy emerged from the shadows.

With the ultimatum the mine owner had given him, he had to get things settled with Kate. Tanner hoped that if he explained the situation, she would understand that the rest of that courting business would have to wait.

He wondered if he'd still have to court her, if she'd still consider it necessary. It seemed kind of silly under the circumstances. By being caught in her bedroom, he'd already compromised her reputation—even if nothing had happened.

Those old biddies didn't know that, however. If he could judge by the look on their faces, they thought he and Kate had been having an orgy.

And while he hated to be the cause of damage to Kate's good name, he also had the feeling that Bob Rutledge wouldn't care if Tanner had slept with Kate or not. Rutledge would steal her just for spite.

That fact, and not being sure how she felt about him, or about Rutledge, left Tanner apprehensive about the state of their future. He also recalled that when he'd left, Kate had been fit to be tied.

Not knowing what to expect, he went up her steps and knocked politely.

She didn't answer.

He tried the knob. It turned easily. At least she hadn't locked him out, but it didn't seem like her to leave the door unlatched either. For all he knew she had that frying pan waiting on the other side. He let the dog in first, then cautiously followed.

He looked around. When he didn't see her, he felt safe in closing and locking the door.

Fluffy walked to the settee and began wagging his tail.

Tanner, following the dog's cue, found Kate there, curled up, one palm under her cheek. Asleep, she didn't look much older than Luke. He knew she'd had a difficult day, but he'd hoped that they could talk. He'd hoped that if he couldn't get her to agree to marry him right off, at least he might persuade her not to marry anybody else. At least not until he had time to advance his own cause.

But since she was asleep, he wouldn't have the chance. Besides, he hated to burden her with his problems.

She moaned in her sleep.

She didn't look too comfortable all scrunched up that way, and she would be cold before morning. Maybe he should carry her back to the bed. He slid his arms under her legs and lifted her into his arms. She felt so good, smelled so sweet, he was tempted to pack her right out of there, take her back to the mountain.

He took a step. Staggered from too much to drink. Dropped her back onto the sofa.

Jolted awake, Kate opened her eyes to see Tanner looming over her. "So you're back." She sat up. "Where's Fluffy?"

"He'sh all right. See." Swaying, he pointed toward the corner.

"It's about time," she said, crossly. She sniffed. "You smell like a moonshine still."

"I had some bus-i-ness to take care of at the hotel bar."

"Humph." He was drunk. "Monkey business, I'd imagine."

"It'sh true. I'da been back hours ago, but I ran into Tom Fuller. . . ."

"Was he driving a whiskey wagon?"

"No. He was walking. Scoot over, I gotta sidown."

Kate managed to move just in time.

Tanner's knees buckled. He flopped onto the sofa, then buried his head in his hands. "I don't feel so good."

"You look even worse." He was an inebriated mess. He couldn't stand, couldn't walk, and appeared to be about to pass out on her couch. "I think I'd better make some coffee."

She put the pot on and returned to find he was dead to the world. At least this time he wasn't in her bed. She stared at him, started to shake him awake. She hesitated. Even if she did manage to get the coffee down him, she doubted if he would be in any shape to ride.

Removing the coffeepot from the fire, she thought about the treacherous mountain trail, about the wild animals that lurked in the brush. If he did ride out and something happened, in his present condition he'd be helpless. He might get hurt—or killed, and it would all be her fault.

On the other hand, if she allowed him to stay here, her reputation would be tattered beyond repair. But knowing how gossip spread, she imagined the good ladies had already taken care of that.

What did she have to lose?

Her virginity?

Somehow she thought men set more store by that virtue than did women. Otherwise, why would they demand that their women remain chaste and pure, while they prowled around like alley cats?

She looked at Tanner, who snored in oblivion. At least she'd find out what she'd been missing.

Scandalized by the direction her thoughts had taken, she quickly fetched a quilt form the bedroom and covered him.

Tanner didn't even move. And from the look of him, he wouldn't until morning.

Her virginity was safe. That should have made her happy, but it didn't. It only made her annoyed. She checked the door and adjusted the blanket on Tanner, then she blew out the light and went to bed.

23

$\mathcal{K}$ATE CHANGED INTO her nightgown and climbed into bed, her thoughts filled with the man asleep on her couch, and what he had come to mean to her. She loved him more than she'd ever thought possible.

Months ago, she had arrived in Jacksonville expecting to be Tanner's bride, only to have him tell her in no uncertain terms that he had no intention of marrying her. To prove that fact, he'd attempted to marry her off—to anybody that expressed any interest.

Then, during the smallpox epidemic, he'd practically kidnapped her and taken her to the mountain—because he felt obligated to take care of her.

Had he also felt obligated to kiss her, to make love to her in every way but the one that would leave him no choice but to marry her?

Then, recently, he'd decided to court her, even though it was obvious that he had no idea of what the term entailed.

Why? Was it because he didn't want anybody else to have her? Since he had been so determined to marry her off, that didn't make sense either.

But thinking back on it, she realized that it was shortly after Tanner had decided to court her that most of her other gentleman friends had ceased to call. Did Tanner have something to do with that, too?

She thought of his marriage proposal. No, she corrected, he never asked her to marry him. He'd simply announced it, as if she had no say at all in the matter. And he'd only done that after the ladies had caught him coming out of her bedroom.

Obligation again, she was sure of it.

How could she ever trust his motives? Especially when she doubted that he really knew what he wanted himself.

If only he really cared.

She closed her eyes and hugged her pillow, imagining what might have happened if the ladies hadn't arrived when they did, if their lovemaking had had a whole different ending. . . .

Awakening with a headache, his mouth feeling like he had been eating fuzzy caterpillars, Tanner wondered why his feet were dangling on the floor, and what had happened to make him feel so bad. Holding onto his head, he sat up. Then he remembered. He was at Kate's. Before that he'd been drinking with Tom Fuller.

Still half tipsy, he felt his way to the kitchen, located a pitcher of water and dumped a portion of it over his head. He used the rest to rinse his mouth.

He lifted the curtain and peered out the window. It had been late when he'd left the saloon. By now it must be the wee hours of the morning. He should leave. Kate had probably gone to bed hours ago. Considering what happened earlier that day, she probably wouldn't take it too kindly if he was still there when she got up in the morning.

He gathered his coat and hat, then hesitated. After what had happened with the Dobbs brothers, he didn't like leaving her door unlocked. And he couldn't latch it from outside. He had to wake her so that she could lock up behind him.

When he neared the bed, he heard her mumble in her sleep. She thrashed about as if she were having a nightmare.

Thinking to comfort her, he sat down on the edge of the mattress, then reached out and touched her shoulder. "Kate? Are you . . ."

"Are you going to kiss me or not?" she whispered.

"What?" He couldn't have heard her right. He leaned closer.

Her eyes were closed.

Was she asleep, or wasn't she?

Before he could decide, she locked her arms around his neck and pulled him over in the bed. She mumbled something in his ear.

"Kate, are you asleep?"

She didn't answer. She also didn't let go.

He kissed her, gently, hesitantly. "Sweet, so sweet." Knowing she must be dreaming, but unable to resist the pleasure, he kissed her again.

She kissed him back with a passion that curled his toes.

Still feeling the effects of the night before, he was lost before he'd begun. He couldn't resist her now if the whole town stood there with loaded shotguns.

But she apparently didn't intend to be resisted. She kissed his ears, his hair, anything she could reach.

His heart thundered, and his blood roared in his ears. He tried holding Kate in one arm while yanking off his boots with the other. He couldn't balance long enough to do it. He did manage to unbutton his shirt, but before he could attempt anything else, she tangled her hands in his hair and pulled his head to her breast.

He came up with a mouthful of nightgown. She pulled him down again and he nuzzled the damp cloth until he found what he was seeking. Beneath his lips, her breast rose full and warm, its tip sweet as sugar candy. He drew it into his mouth, wishing the garment wasn't between them.

She smelled like flowers, tasted like cinnamon. Both he found more intoxicating than the bourbon and also more addicting. She filled his mind, took his senses. He fumbled with the neck of her night garment. Buttons. Tiny buttons. He groaned.

She opened her eyes. Blinked. "Tanner? What . . . ?"

He kissed her into silence. That was when she became aware that it was no dream. He was really here. A coil of heat spread through her belly. Was this desire? This awful aching?

"Tanner," she whispered. The moonlight slanting through her bedroom window showed him as clearly as if she had lighted a lamp. His tousled black hair drooped onto his forehead. Eyes dark as night burned with an inner fire. A fire for her. An answering glow blazed inside her. "Tanner," she said softly, raising a hand to touch his stubbled cheek.

"Darlin', you're not asleep." It wasn't a question. His expression, what she saw in his eyes, spoke of his desire, told her what he intended to do. And heaven help her, she wanted him to do it.

His gaze moved over her face, caressing each feature. Then it settled on her mouth.

She moistened her lips, then his mouth descended to claim hers. This time there was no hesitation; his kiss was fierce, demanding. His tongue slipped between her teeth, coaxing, entreating. She welcomed it, teased it, shyly, then eagerly, exploring with her own.

He moaned, his lips moving along her face, down her neck, to her breasts.

She tugged at the damp nightgown, wanting nothing between them. "Help me."

Sensing her urgency, he pulled her to her feet in a sudden, swift movement. Buttons flew, then he whisked the nightgown over her head. He looked at her a moment, making her shy in her nakedness. "Kate?"

Her hands rose to encircle his neck.

He kissed her again, then gently lowered her to the blankets. His hands and lips dispelled the last of her resistance, and she surrendered with all of her being. He stroked her wonderingly, making her quiver with eager desire. He suddenly stopped and moved away from her. Thinking he meant to abandon her, she cried out in protest.

He yanked off his boots, his shirt, then unfastened his pants. He stood, fully aroused, his body pulsing with his need. He waited, giving her a chance to change her mind.

She smiled and held up her arms. "Tanner, love me."

"Oh, I surely will, darlin'."

She took his hand and yanked him down on the bed, then she straddled him.

"I must be dreaming," he gasped, when she leaned over and smothered his face with kisses. Her hair, losing its pins, fell forward. She brushed it aside and kissed his mouth, his whiskery chin, his neck. Then, sliding lower, she tasted the skin around his nipple and felt it harden. She licked his salty flesh.

She was a virgin. And she knew he would expect her to be timid, fearful, especially this being her first time. Instead she felt like a pagan goddess, intent on setting his blood on fire.

His eyes raked hers, telling her this was the last chance she would have to stop him.

She couldn't. She wouldn't. Whatever happened, she would welcome it with no remorse. She savored the glorious feel of him, his sleek hard body, his musky masculine scent. She slid her hand down his abdomen, lower. He swallowed when her fingers curled around his arousal. She caressed the hard swollen length that told her of his desire. He was so hard, so hot.

Tanner trembled and drew in ragged breath. "No. Don't." He quickly untangled her fingers and held her hand to one side.

"Why? Does it hurt?"

"It feels too damn good, and I want to make it last. I already feel as if I'm about to explode."

She pressed her body to his, her hungry lips seeking his mouth. She moved restlessly, her breasts creating delicious friction against the mat of hair on his chest.

He drew in a sharp breath. A quiver shook him from head to foot. Last? He'd be lucky if he made it through the next minute.

"Take me," she whimpered.

Her desperation fed his own. He rolled her onto her back. His fingers sought her inner core, touching her in a way that made her cry out with urgent need. Then, knowing she was ready, he shifted his weight, entering her slowly, letting her grow accustomed to the fullness. Afraid he might hurt her, he pressed against a veil that would not yield. He kneaded her breasts and kissed her, his touch gentle, hesitant.

As if sensing his reluctance, she arched toward him, impaling herself on his body.

Trembling violently, he gripped her hips and pulled her home.

She surrounded, enfolded him in her tight, hot heat, taking all that he gave and demanding more. She caught his rhythm and made his body sing her sweet siren's song.

Kate knew this was the moment she had been born for, and when he suddenly thrust deep inside her, the pain was over before it began. She had lost her virginity, but she only felt blessed relief. Tanner filled her deeply, moving in a way that brought surge after surge of sweet desire. An explosion of heat spread through her veins, bringing an aching that increased with every thrust. Then pleasure grew, becoming so intense that it was almost unbearable. She strove to meet the fevered crest. Then waves rushed through her, sweet shocks rocked her body, flooding her until she was left weak and trembling.

Tanner loved her long and well. If he was asleep he prayed he'd never awaken. Kate already had his heart. Now, in this moment, she'd also claimed not only his body but his soul as well. Passions spiraling, he led her to the crown of the wave and felt her ride it to fulfillment. He felt her stiffen as the tremors of her climax shook her body again and again. Her eyes wide with wonder, she grew still, her gaze locked on his.

His own muscles taut with self-denial, and thinking not to impregnate her, he tried to withdraw.

She cried out in protest and pulled him back. She moved against him. That was his undoing.

Desperate need overriding judgment, he drove into her again and again, until finally he arched, straining against her. He shuddered, his body and his mind crying out her name. He erupted in a mighty burst and spilled into her welcoming womb, flowing on a current as old as time.

Finally, his body spent, he withdrew and collapsed at her side. He gathered her to him and smoothed the damp, dark curls that clung to her face. He gazed at her in wonder. He still couldn't believe it had really happened. He had known many women, all knowledgeable in the ways of the flesh, but he had never felt such rapture, such a feeling of completion as he'd experienced in the arms of this sweet woman.

She smiled at him, her lips swollen with his kisses. Her breasts rose full and coral-tipped. A sheen of perspiration made her skin glow in the moonlight.

"Are you all right? Did I hurt you?" he asked.

"You didn't hurt me," she whispered, snuggling against him.

He cradled her tenderly, kissing her forehead, her nose, her cheeks.

She sighed, closed her eyes and immediately went to sleep.

Shortly before dawn Tanner woke, reluctant to let go of the best dream he had ever had. He opened his eyes and glanced around; then, propping himself up on his elbow, he stared at the woman by his side. A fierce joy bubbled inside him. It hadn't been a dream. He was here, in Kate's bed, and he had made love to her.

Or rather she had made love to him.

He wasn't quite certain how it had happened. Nor did he intend to ponder the fact. That would be like questioning a miracle.

He only knew that now she truly belonged to him, and he would never let her go.

He gave thanks that he hadn't left last night, that he had awakened her so that she could lock the door. And what an awakening. . . . Just thinking about it made his heart thunder. No halfway measures for Kate. She had given all of herself, as in everything she did. And she had demanded the same of him in return.

As he studied her tousled beauty, he felt a pride of possession, of conquest. He smiled. There would be no more dilly-dallying. He wouldn't stand for it. They would be married as soon as possible. And while he might have preferred to wait a while before starting a family, last night had pretty much taken care of that. Remembering the intensity of their joining, a quiver of heat surged through him. She could right now be carrying his child. Strangely pleased by the idea, he slid his hand over her flat stomach, imagining he could feel the flutter of a new life inside.

Kate frowned and moaned in her sleep.

When he kissed her, she opened her eyes. "Oh, my." She met his gaze, then blushed and ducked her head.

"Good morning, darlin'."

"It really happened? It wasn't a dream?" she asked in a whisper, drawing the sheet up to her chin.

"No dream." He kissed her nose, her eyes, then landed on her lips. "You're mine now. All we have to do is tie the knot."

She sucked in a breath. "I don't remember you asking me to marry you."

"I told you yesterday we were getting married. I only wanted you to decide when. Considering what's happened, I think it should be right away." He grinned, then pulled her over on top of him. "Until then . . ."

She shoved him away. "What I recall of last night was wonderful. But I never said I would marry you. Besides, it isn't necessary."

"It damn well is necessary. I could have made you pregnant." He frowned. "After last night you don't have any choice, and neither do I."

"I do have a choice. And I won't have you marrying me out of some misguided sense of obligation." She tossed back the covers, then, suddenly aware of her nudity, she snatched up a blanket.

"Obligation?" He reached out and reclaimed the blanket. "If I didn't want to marry you, I wouldn't. But you're right, it is my obligation, and my responsibility. It's time I lived up to it."

"See. You admit it." She drew herself up primly, but considering her sate of nudity, it only made her more tempting.

She was still arguing when he snagged her arm and pulled her back into the bed. "Talking again. Never fails." He kissed her mouth, swallowing her furious words. His hands roamed her tense body. "That's better," he said when she began to relax.

"Let me up," she demanded, between kisses.

"Uh-uh." He fondled her breasts until they were full and heavy, their tips like rosy pebbles. Then his palm slid lower and cupped her womanhood. He watched her eyes widen when he teased her bud of desire.

"Damn you, Tanner." She closed her eyes, giving in to her passion. His kisses smothering her protests, he continued his ministrations until she rocked against him.

Her hands roamed his back, inflicting pain as she demanded fulfillment.

He brought her to the edge; then, almost mindless with desire himself, he claimed her, using his mastery to make them whole once again. She clutched his shoulders. A keening cry tore from her throat.

He pounded her body, conquering her slick, satiny flesh. This time he didn't try to withdraw; if anything, he drove even deeper. If that's what it took, he would get her pregnant—that way she'd have to marry him.

He loved her long and well, holding himself intact until he felt her tremble.

"Tanner. Tanner," she cried, quivering like a bowstring in his arms.

He cupped her hips, then he, too, strove to reach fulfillment. He plunged one final time, burying himself deep within her, his body pulsating again and again, spilling his life-giving forces.

When it was over and she sagged against him, he withdrew and collapsed by her side. Her breathing evened, and he looked down to see tears on her cheeks. He tenderly wiped them away. "I'm sorry, Kate. I didn't mean to hurt you."

"You didn't hurt me, but I don't want us to do it again," she said, knowing even as she uttered the words that they were a lie. She did want to do it again and even now, gazing into his steel-gray eyes, she felt herself weakening. She should have been satisfied, but a flicker of desire sparked again. She determinedly tamped it down before it could flame to life. "I don't want us to do it again," she repeated.

"You sure have a funny way of showing it." He turned and picked up a boot. It was then she noticed his back where her fingernails had raked his flesh.

"Oh, Tanner, I'm sorry." Her fingertip traced the blood-edged welts. "Does it hurt much?"

"It was worth it." He raised a brow and grinned. He found his shirt and put it on.

She saw the garment was missing most of its buttons. She pursed her lips and peeked up at him. "Did I do that, too?"

"I'll lap it over. Nobody will notice."

"Where are you going?" she asked, noting he sure seemed in a hurry to leave.

"We can't have everybody thinking you're a fallen woman. If I get out of here before daylight, no one will be the wiser."

"Oh." *Fallen woman.* She wished he had used a different expression. "It's a little late to be thinking of my reputation."

"Better late than never," he said, kissing her as he retrieved his other boot.

When he was fully dressed, he grabbed his hat and walked back to the bed. Even needing a shave, his hair uncombed, and his shirt lapped over his middle, he took her breath away. He bent and gave her a kiss. "Better lock the door behind me, then go back to sleep. I'll try to come back later."

After he had left, she stared at the pale star-speckled sky. Fallen woman. She was that and more. She had willingly surrendered her virginity. She couldn't blame him for taking what was offered, especially when she'd practically attacked him.

Still, it was no reason to get married. She frowned, thinking about that marriage business. Tanner had admitted he would be marrying her because he considered himself obligated, responsible. He'd feel even more so, now that she might be carrying his child.

What if she did say yes? Would he still feel the same if it

turned out she wasn't pregnant? Would he change his mind when it was time for the ceremony? And if she was pregnant, would he resent her and the child later on? She didn't know what to think, what to believe.

He had made love to her, not once, but twice, introducing her to passion that she could have only imagined before. Now that she knew what rapture awaited in his arms, she doubted if she'd have the strength to refuse him again.

She had already lost her virginity. Her reputation had gone before that. She certainly had nothing else to lose.

Even now in the dawn's first light, her flesh warmed with the memory of the night they'd spent. He had caressed her body and made it sing with joy.

But he had never said he loved her.

24

$\mathcal{K}$ATE DIDN'T GO back to sleep. Instead she heated water and took a bath, removing all telltale traces of their lovemaking. Then, after hurriedly dressing, she stripped the bed. She stared at the blood-dotted sheet. She didn't dare send that to the laundry. It would be like hanging a sign on her door for everyone to see. She used her bath water to wash it by hand, then hung it by the stove to dry.

She reheated the coffee left over from the night before and poured herself a cup. It was thick, black, and bitter as gall, but she drank it. At least it would keep her awake.

Then, for the first time that morning, when she picked up the brush to take the tangles out of her hair, she looked at herself in the mirror. Her lips were swollen from Tanner's kisses, and her cheeks were red from his whiskery caresses. She critically examined the rest of her appearance and wondered if anyone could tell. She didn't see anything much different, until she gazed into her eyes.

Guilty. Plain as day.

All trace of innocence was gone. Looking back at her were the eyes of a woman. A woman who knew what it was like to be loved by a man. She put the mirror down and quickly walked away.

She couldn't open the pie shop, even if she had dozens of

pies baked, which she didn't. She'd never be able to face anybody again.

"Drat!" She had to open the pie shop. She had promised the miner Tanner had beat out yesterday, claiming the last pie for his own. She couldn't disappoint the man, especially since he had paid in advance.

She tied her apron around her waist and stoked up the stove. There would be questions enough about herself and Tanner without her giving cause for more. Besides, keeping busy helped; it gave her less time to think.

When it was time to open her shop, she had some pies cooling and others coming out of the oven. Not as many as the day before, but not so few as to arouse suspicion.

The pies went quickly and by the time she'd sold the last of them, she had a raging headache. If anybody noticed anything different about her, they had been too polite to say. And if they had mentioned her reddened complexion, she would have calmly attributed it to having worked over a hot stove all morning.

After depositing her proceeds in the cookie jar, she pulled her shades and locked her door. Then she staggered to the back room and fell across the bed. She was almost asleep when Fluffy hoisted himself up on the edge of the bed and licked her face.

"Oh, no." She rubbed his head. "I suppose you can't hold it?"

He whined.

"All right." Shielding her eyes from the light with the back of her hand, she opened the door and let her pet outside. But, remembering the night he was shot, she sat on the steps and watched him carefully, calling him back when he started to wander out of sight.

The day was warm, and pine-scented breezes sent the green grass nodding in the field behind the toolshed. She gazed at the mountain and wondered when wildflowers would be blooming in the meadow. She thought of the flowers Tanner had brought her and wished she had them back. She wouldn't put them in a vase, her allergy wouldn't allow that. But she would press them between the pages of a book, preserving them and her memories. When she was old, she would bring them out and show them to her children and her grandchildren.

Children? Grandchildren?

Until this morning she had never thought of having any. She absently rubbed her palm across her middle.

"Penny for your thoughts."

Kate glanced up and saw the doctor watching her. Blushing, she jerked her hand down by her side. "Hello, I didn't hear your buggy."

"That's because I walked. Too nice a day to ride. Mind if I sit down?" He motioned to the step beside her.

She scooted over. "No, but wouldn't you rather go inside?"

"Naw. I saw you rubbing your middle. Got a stomach-ache?"

"No. But my head feels ready to split," she confessed.

"I know the very thing for that." He reached into his bag and removed a packet of headache powders. "Take these and sleep for a bit. In an hour or two, I'll come by in my buggy and take you for a ride."

"Could we see the fillies again?"

"Don't see why not. I bet they've grown some by now." He patted her hand, then got to his feet. "Get some rest now. Think I'll visit Madame Jeanne, see if she can scare us up something for a picnic."

After the doctor left and the dog had finished his business, Kate went back into the house. Fred Thomas was a wonderful man, kind, considerate. A true gentleman. She wondered why he'd never remarried.

Thinking of marriage reminded her of Tanner and his outrageous proposal, and her head pounded with a vengeance. Why couldn't Tanner be uncomplicated like the doctor? Why did he have to be so . . . She shook her head and went to get a glass of water.

In the mountain's dense forest, the sun had gone down an hour ago and darkness had settled into the shadows. Reluctant to call it a day before he had filled his quota,

Tanner lit the lantern and kept on working. Two more trees, he vowed, then he could quit for the night. He hoisted the ax. His muscles quivered and his back throbbed, but he forced the pain away and drove the blade into the tree. He couldn't quit even for a minute, for if he did, his muscles would become so stiff he wouldn't be able to continue.

With the impossible deadline Tom Fuller had set looming ever nearer, Tanner no longer returned home at night. Instead he had set up camp in a nearby clearing. Finding it saved not only time but effort, he wished he had thought of doing it sooner. He told himself the winter weather would have made it impossible anyway. Although the nights still dropped to freezing, a canvas strung over a frame protected him from the dampness and blocked the cold wind.

He didn't have to worry about cooking, since Mark or Luke brought his dinner out every night and usually stayed to chat a while before returning home. Matt, at Tanner's insistence, stayed close to home with John.

Although the boys pleaded, begged, then demanded to help with the trees, Tanner stood firm. He could not, would not, allow them to take the risk.

He drove the ax home again and again, until the trunk was severed. He waited for the telltale crack, then leaped from the platform.

He was safely on the ground when the towering giant groaned, then with a whoosh of air crashed to the ground, showering the area with wood splinters, dust and pine needles.

Tanner nodded in satisfaction. "One more."

"Are you trying to kill yourself?" Mark asked angrily. "I've been watching for the last hour, thought you'd quit when it got dark. But no, not you." He yanked the ax from Tanner's hands and stared at the dark stain on the handle. "Tanner, are you stupid or just plain crazy?"

"Give me back the ax, boy." He held out his bleeding hand.

"No. I won't." Mark stepped back, still gripping the tool. "And you haven't got the strength to make me."

"One more tree and I'll quit. I promise."

"Not one tree. Not one limb," Mark said, backing away. "Whether you like it or not, you're done for the night."

Tanner took one step, staggered, then nodded his defeat. "All right, you win. Blade's dull anyhow." He doubted if he would have been able to cut another tree even if Mark had given him the ax. He had been driving himself, becoming more exhausted each day, and now he had little or nothing left in reserve. Maybe a good night's rest, he thought. His stomach growled, reminding him that he hadn't eaten since last night. Truth be known, he wouldn't have bothered to eat now if Mark wasn't here. He would have gone straight to his bedroll.

Mark picked up the lantern and led the way back to camp. He set the light on a stump, then lifting a kettle he'd put on to boil earlier, he poured hot water into a pan. "After you wash up, you'd better soak those hands. I stuck some of that salve Doc left us in my pack in case you had blisters. But I sure didn't expect anything like that. Don't you have any gloves?"

"I did. They wore out a couple of days ago. I forgot to ask you or Luke to bring any more."

"You can have mine. They're in my pack."

Gritting his teeth, Tanner forced his raw flesh into the hot water. The pain made him gasp, but Mark was right. He had to soak the dirt out or they would get infected. He couldn't afford to have that happen. When the torment subsided, he washed them thoroughly, then lifted them from the water and examined his palms. They looked like raw meat, but they were clean. After he'd dried them, Mark applied the salve and wrapped them with a fresh towel he had torn into strips.

"Can you eat?"

"Nothing wrong with my stomach." Tanner took the tin bowl Mark handed him and began awkwardly ladling the stew into his mouth. "Good," he said between bites. "When did you get the rabbit?"

"On the way home yesterday."

"Yesterday? Luke was here, not you."

"I went into town."

"And . . . ?" Tanner prompted.

"And I saw Kate."

"And . . . ?" Getting anything out of Mark when he didn't want to tell it was like trying to pull teeth out of a closed mouth.

"Then I came home."

"Tell me about Kate." Tanner set his bowl aside and waited.

"Oh, all right." Mark dug his boot toe into the dirt. "She's leaving."

Tanner felt like Mark had punched him in the stomach. "When?"

Mark shrugged. "She might already be gone."

Why? Why now, when he thought they had things settled? Maybe she was upset because he hadn't been in to see her since that night they had made love. It wasn't that he hadn't wanted to. He wanted that more than anything. He also knew if he did, he wouldn't be able to leave her house until dawn. And with Fuller breathing down his neck, he simply couldn't spare the time. He'd thought she'd understood.

"She sent the dog back with me."

"Then she really is leaving." His appetite gone, Tanner got up and walked into the darkness, his mind pondering what Mark had told him. Maybe he could stop her, if he had the strength to saddle his horse. But exhausted as he was, he'd probably fall off the saddle before he got ten feet down the trail.

He cursed himself for not asking more questions. Was she pale? Was she upset? Had she said where she was going? Had she left any word for him?

Tanner returned to camp, but his questions remained unanswered. Having done the dishes, Mark had already left for home.

He crumpled onto a stump and stared into the dancing flames of the campfire. How could she leave like that? How could she throw everything away, rejecting not only him and his love, but all chances for a life together?

She'd said she wouldn't marry him. That it wasn't necessary.

It was necessary—to him. Why couldn't she see that?

Maybe she just didn't care.

After she had talked to Mark, Kate had waited, hoping against hope, praying, straining to hear that one familiar footstep. That one familiar voice calling out her name, asking that she stay.

More than a week had passed since the night they had spent together, two more days since she'd talked to Mark.

Tanner hadn't come.

Not that it would have done any good, she told herself. Things wouldn't have changed. She wouldn't marry him to ease his conscience, or because he felt an obligation. At least she wasn't pregnant—her monthly had arrived right on time. She wouldn't have to marry because of a child. She would only marry for love. And it would have to be a two-way love. Even though she loved him more than life itself, the feeling wasn't returned.

Tanner had shared her bed, shared her passion. But he had never told her—or given her any reason to believe—that her affection was returned. And even if they did wed, she was certain that later he would resent having made the sacrifice.

She had been waiting until the last moment, but now, fearing the Wells Fargo office might close, she left her house and hurried to the building. Gathering the last of her courage, she stepped up to the scarred wooden counter. "One ticket to Portland, please."

"One way or round trip?" the agent asked. Thin and pinch-faced, the man looked sour as he waited for her answer.

"One—" Kate swallowed, hoping he didn't notice the break in her voice. "One way," she said softly.

He told her the price.

She placed the required amount by the window, then waited until he slid the ticket over the counter.

"Schedule's on the wall," he said, anticipating her question.

"Thank you." She placed the ticket in her reticule and checked the timetable. Tomorrow morning at six. Her heart leaden, she left the building. It was done.

Now all she had to do was to say her goodbyes to the doctor and Jeanne. She dreaded that final meeting.

She'd bid Chauncey goodbye yesterday and the occurrence had left both of them in tears.

The crusty old miner had sobbed like a baby, then he pleaded with her, begging her not to go. When he'd seen she wouldn't change her mind, he'd accepted the news with silent reproach.

Overwhelmed with guilt, she had promised she would return for a visit. He'd vowed to come to Portland and see her; but both of them knew that neither would be the case, that this would be the last time they would ever meet.

She headed back to her house and went inside. Her footsteps echoed on bare floorboards, resounded off the unadorned walls. Already the place had a sense of abandonment, a sense of loneliness, especially now that she'd sent Fluffy to the mountain.

Her trunk was packed, ready to be picked up at dawn tomorrow and taken to the stage station. Other containers, holding cooking utensils and the like, would be stored at Madame Jeanne's. After Kate was settled, she would send for them. Taking one last, long look around, she picked up her carpetbag, then closed and locked the door.

She paused on her steps and raised her eyes to the mountain, saying a final farewell to the boys—to Tanner. She had thought the boys might come in to say goodbye, but then she hadn't told them exactly when she was leaving, only that she was. Now, remembering her goodbye to Chauncey, she was glad they hadn't. She might not have found the strength to leave.

She inhaled the pine-scented air, only vaguely aware of a freight wagon rumbling behind her, its harness jingling as it progressed down the street. Somewhere in the distance a mule brayed, a peculiar melancholy sound.

In contrast, from a nearby yard, children's voices raised in a squabble, then quieted at a mother's scolding.

The savory smell of onions and boiled corned beef and cabbage drifted on the air. Not from Madame Jeanne's, she thought. The Frenchwoman considered such fare common. Her dishes were basted with wine, topped with delicate sauces. Always delicious, always served with elegant French flair. She would miss Jeanne's cooking, and her friendship.

If only things had turned out different, she mused. But they hadn't. She could stand here and drown in self-pity, and make herself late for the supper she would be sharing with Dr. Thomas and Madame Jeanne, or she could wipe her eyes and get on with her life.

Turning her back on the brooding mountain, she picked up her carpetbag, walked down the alley and crossed the street.

25

*T*HREE DAYS HAD passed since Mark had told Tanner that Kate would be leaving, three days in which Tanner hadn't done anything about it, because, in spite of his bandaged hands, he'd been forced to continue felling trees. Even though he was powerless to prevent her from going, Kate was always on his mind. And it wasn't only Kate that worried him. He couldn't get rid of Mark. Tanner had asked his brother to go home; when that didn't work, he'd ordered him.

Mark had left only long enough for Tanner to get over his anger, then like a bad penny, when Tanner was busy working, Mark had turned up again.

Because he had neither the time nor the inclination to beat his brother into submission, Tanner had reluctantly accepted his presence. Then, afraid Mark would get hurt if he continued to stay underfoot, he had grudgingly allowed the boy to strip the fallen trees of branches. Tanner also vowed that at the first sign of carelessness, the first mistake, he would send Mark packing if he had to tie him to the mule.

But Tanner was gratified to see that, unlike Luke, who still hadn't grown into his feet, Mark was not only agile, but cautious. Mark took no chances and accomplished the job with a minimum of excess movement.

Feeling somewhat better about the idea of allowing Mark

to help him, Tanner knew his brother would be a good woodsman someday. And having Mark with him had proven one more advantage: Tanner still didn't have to do the cooking, and he didn't have to eat cold food.

With Mark's help, the felling was going smoother and quicker, and Tanner began to hope he might meet the deadline after all.

Higher up on the mountain, in the other area where Tanner had been working, it had been necessary to drag each tree to a logging deck. Here, after the trees were cut and bare of limbs, the mules would pull each of them to the skid trail, where the logs would be released and allowed to slide down a long muddy ravine to the water. If everything went as it was supposed to, the downed timber would float downstream and end up in a dammed-up area on the creek. When Tanner had gotten the logs that far, his job would be done.

Workmen hired by the mine would collect them from the pond and load them onto the huge lumber wagons. Teams of stout oxen would pull them to the mill.

His task had been long and arduous, and knowing what he knew now, Tanner wondered if he would have the courage to commit himself to do such a thing again. It had been the means to an end, he decided. The bank held his mortgage, and the timber contract provided money to pay it. Simple as that. He'd really had no choice. It had been a matter of survival.

Today he and Mark had risen at dawn and paused only for lunch. It was now midafternoon, that time when the woods grew quiet, as if its inhabitants were napping, waiting for darkness. It was also a time when the slanting sun rays struck Tanner straight in the eyes. He squinted against the glare and drove the ax blade into the tree, shooting chunks of bark and pitchy wood into the brush below. He made the last cut on the big fir, then tossed the ax off the platform. He waited.

The tree didn't fall.

Shielding his eyes, Tanner stared upward to where the tops of the lofty branches brushed the sunlit sky. Although he couldn't see for certain because the timber was so thick, he thought one of the other trees must be holding it. His heart pounding, he extended his hands and pushed against the trunk, hoping it wouldn't ricochet back and trap him on the springboard.

It didn't move.

A gust of wind caught in the lofty tops and whipped the upper branches. The tree swayed, tilted, swung on its axis. But it still didn't fall.

Tanner held his breath and waited. On a bet, he'd once driven stakes into the ground with his falling trees. He'd been that accurate in his cutting. But this one was different. He knew the fir would fall—eventually. What he didn't know was which way it would go.

"Tanner, I'm done skinning this one. You want me to do something else, or fix supper?"

Mark. Tanner swung his gaze from the tree to his brother. Ordinarily where Mark was standing would have been safe, but not now. Not with this tree. It could very easily fall right on top of him. "Mark, get out of here!"

Another gust of wind lashed the branches into a violent frenzy. The tree swayed, sighed.

Mark froze, staring at the treetop as if mesmerized by the tree's motion.

"Run!" Tanner yelled.

Coming to his senses, Mark whirled.

Tanner jumped from the springboard and raced after him.

With an agonized groan, the giant fir tree twisted free. It plunged to earth.

Tanner felt a rush of air, heard the cracking of wood. Stinging, needle-tipped branches whipped his back, his neck, his face. Then a crushing blow drove him to the ground. Wind left his lungs as a heavy weight slammed down on him. A bone snapped. Pain shot up his leg.

The ground vibrated beneath him as the giant settled over and around him. Wood chips, dust and debris sifted to earth, pelting his body, filling his nostrils and his eyes.

Then silence.

Tanner fought the dizzying pain and tried to raise his head. "Mark?" He prayed his brother had made it free.

"I'm all right," Mark called back. "If I can get loose from this mess. How about you?"

Tanner couldn't answer. A wave of red-rimmed agony carried him into darkness.

"Tanner?" Mark untangled himself from the last of the branches. He ran along the length of the tree. His gaze searched frantically. Then he saw his brother under the dense foliage, pinned to the ground by a heavy limb. "Tanner!"

Tanner didn't answer. Didn't move.

"Tanner!" Mark tore through the sharp-needled limbs. Yanked a branch aside. He bent and felt Tanner's neck for a pulse. A faint heartbeat fluttered against his fingertips. His own heart began to beat again. He was alive. But how badly hurt?

Tanner wasn't bleeding from the mouth or ears, but the limb lying across his back might have broken some ribs. Heaven only knew what else might be wrong. Mark knew he had to free him before he could tell.

He located the ax, then returning to Tanner's side, he quickly removed the smaller limbs. Only when he was certain he could cut the big branch without dealing his brother even more injury did he sever it from the tree and pull it aside.

Now that Tanner was uncovered, Mark noticed the unnatural angle of his right leg. Broken for sure.

He took out his pocket knife and slit Tanner's pant leg, then carefully removed his boot. The leg was already swollen and discolored. Even though the bone hadn't punctured the skin, it was still a bad break. Mark pulled Tanner into the open, then he straightened the leg and pulled the bone until he felt it snap into place. He splinted it between two sticks. Realizing Tanner would be unable to ride, he rigged a travois using two stout branches and ropes, then covered it with a bedroll. He tied the contraption behind the calmest of the mules. Grateful that Tanner was still unconscious, he pulled him onto the travois and anchored him into place.

Mark saddled the gelding, then freed it and the other mule. A swat on the rump sent the animals running down the trail. He hoped that when they reached home, somebody would come looking. Then Mark would send him for the doctor.

Mark lit the lantern, holding it in front of him so he could see the trail. Saying a silent prayer for his brother, he took hold of the second mule's harness and led it toward home.

The travois jolted over a tree root. Tanner groaned.

"Hang on, bud." Mark wished he had something to give him for the pain, but he didn't. Since Tanner wasn't a drinking man, there was seldom any whisky in the house.

The path was uneven, full of ruts and rocks. He tried to avoid the worst of them, but it was going to be a long, tortuous journey.

Tanner drifted in and out of consciousness, and his skin had taken on a grayish tinge that made Mark uneasy. Anxious to get his brother home, Mark took advantage of the lapses into unconsciousness to make up for lost time.

It was only when they were some distance down the trail, and the darkness had closed in around them, that Mark remembered the rifle he had left in camp. Thinking of the bear that Tanner had encountered before, he stared into the shadows and hoped they wouldn't come across anything he couldn't scare off with a stick. He breathed a sigh of relief when they broke through the dense brush and into the meadow.

Hearing hoofbeats, he raised his head and waved the lantern. When the rider grew nearer, he saw it was Luke on the gelding.

"What's wrong?" Pulling the horse up, Luke peered at the stretcher. "Tanner?"

"He's got a broken leg, and no telling what else. Get the doctor."

"I'm gone." Luke whipped up the horse and headed for the pass.

* * *

Matt didn't know if Tanner had for some reason turned the animals loose, or if they had broken their ropes and run away. A sense of foreboding made him hope nothing was wrong. A sense of urgency had made him send Luke out to check. After watching Luke race off into the night, Matt and John stood silently on the front porch and waited.

A bobbing light appeared on the edge of the meadow. It stopped a moment, apparently to greet Luke, then came on toward them. *Mark or Tanner. Maybe both.*

When the light grew nearer, Matt could make out Mark leading the mule. Tanner must have sent him home. Matt let out a sigh of relief, until he realized that Luke wasn't returning with him. "Everything all right?" he called out.

"Accident. Tanner's hurt."

"Stay here," Matt told John. Fearing the worst, he ran down the steps. "How bad . . ." Then he saw the travois, and the unconscious man strapped to it. Everything in him shouted denial. It couldn't be. Tanner had been indestructible. Tanner had never even gotten sick. Now to see him lying there helpless. . . .

Matt met Mark's solemn gaze. Fear knotted his middle.

"Is he d-dead?" John whispered.

Matt turned toward the doorway. Even in the dim light he could see the child's face had drained of color; his body shook with silent, racking sobs.

Fluffy frantically licked the little boy's hand.

"H-he's d-dead, isn't he?" John asked again.

"No, he's not dead. And he's not going to die," Matt said, unable to bear such a thought.

"He'll be fine. We're going to take good care of him," Mark said reassuringly. "He does have a broken leg." He moved closer. "And no telling what else," he added to Matt under his breath.

"How serious is it?" Matt asked, almost afraid to voice the question. As he stared at the litter, another accident flashed through his mind. That time his father had died. It couldn't be happening again. He swallowed against the pain.

"I did the best I could, but he's in a bad way," Mark said, his voice husky. "Luke's gone for the doctor. Until he gets here, the best thing we can do is to make Tanner comfortable—then we just have to wait and pray."

"Hold the light, John, so we can get him inside," Matt instructed. "Then go turn down his bed."

Mark cut the tracings and took one side of the frame; Matt took the other. They carefully carried Tanner up the steps and into the house.

John ran ahead of them to prepare the bed, then, eyes wide, he waited while they placed Tanner on top of the covers. "He's awfully d-dirty," the boy said solemnly.

"Suppose we could wash him up some without hurting him?" Mark asked. "That way the doctor could see what he was examining."

"Good idea. Probably make Tanner feel better, too." Matt hurried to the kitchen and returned with a pan of warm water. Carefully, they removed Tanner's clothing and began to sponge the dirt and tree sap from his body. He untied the shirt Mark had tied around Tanner's middle and traced the discolored ribs with his fingers.

Tanner groaned then opened his eyes. "I see I made it home." He grimaced, his face contorting with pain. "Where's Mark?"

"Right here."

"Are you all right?"

"I'm fine. You'd be fine too, if I hadn't stood there like a stump." A tear made a mud trail down Mark's dirt-caked face. "Damn, I'm sorry, Tanner." He turned away and wiped his eyes.

"Don't go beating yourself up, boy," he said with obvious effort. "I didn't know which way to run, either. Guess we both picked the wrong direction." Tanner glanced down at his leg. "Broken?"

"Yeah. I tried to set it. That limb whacked your ribs pretty good, too. Couple broke, maybe more. They're so bruised it's hard to tell."

"Luke's gone for the doctor," Matt said. "Until he gets here can we do anything to help you feel better?"

"Getting the dirt off helps a heap." Tanner tried a smile but didn't quite make it. His eyes shifted to John, who stood silently by the bedside. "Hi, sprout." He let out a jagged breath. "Think I'll take a nap." He closed his eyes.

Matt knew it was no nap. Tanner had lapsed into unconsciousness, and he hadn't wanted John to know. His gaze shot to Mark.

"Probably better this way." Taking advantage of his brother's comatose state, he finished washing Tanner's chest, then wrapped his ribs with strips from an old sheet and tied the bandage in place.

"What if he d-don't get b-better?" John asked, his eyes wide and stricken.

"He'll be fine." Mark walked over and looped his arm around the little boy's shoulder. "Hey, Johnny, think you can rustle me up some grub while I put the mule away?"

"Got some b-beans I could heat," the boy said eagerly.

Matt waited until they had left the room, then he turned his attention back to his older brother. He stripped off Tanner's pants and examined the splinted leg. From what he could tell, Mark had done a good job. He wouldn't have expected anything less.

Ever since he could remember, Mark had dragged home one hurt critter after another. He'd been good at setting bones, healing wounds. He seemed to have a gift for it. Matt was grateful that Mark had been with Tanner when the accident happened, instead of himself. While he was good at cooking and other things, Matt had never been good at doctoring.

Matt finished bathing Tanner and covered him with a blanket. Then, not knowing what else to do, he pulled up a chair and sat down to wait.

Luke sent the gelding down the treacherous grade at a pace that threatened both their necks. When he reached the outskirts of town, he whipped the lathered horse into a gallop. Sliding the animal to a halt in front of a small white house, he jumped from the saddle.

Lights were on. That meant the doctor was home.

Luke crossed the yard in two leaps, then raised his fist and pounded on the door. "Doc. Doc Thomas."

"Hold your horses," a gruff voice yelled from inside. The silver-haired physician opened the door. "Wha— Luke?"

"It's Tanner," Luke gasped out. "He's hurt. Tree fell on him. Broken leg and . . . I don't know what else."

Doc's gaze slid past the wide-eyed boy to the lathered horse. "That animal is done in. Take him to the livery and have them saddle a couple of fresh mounts. I'll finish with this patient and be ready by the time you get back."

Frowning, the doctor returned to his office and began stuffing medical supplies into his satchel.

"What's up?" Chauncey asked from his seat in the corner.

The doctor told him about Tanner.

"This old carbuncle can wait," the grizzled miner muttered. "It ain't the first time I've had one."

Doc took a tin from a shelf and dumped some ground-up leaves into a paper. "Make a poultice out of this. It won't be as quick as lancing it, but it should bring the boil to a head and make it drain."

"Thank ye." Chauncey took the paper and stuffed it into his shirt pocket. "Wish Miss Kate was here."

"I was thinking the same thing." The doctor paused. "If Tanner ever needed that woman, he needs her now."

The crusty old miner wrinkled his face. "I bet if she knew, she'd come a-runnin'."

"Well, since she's halfway to Portland, there's little chance of that."

"Too bad." The old miner scowled. "I'd best get out of your way, Doc. If I can help out, let me know." Still muttering to himself, Chauncey left the house.

Luke strode in immediately after. "Horses are outside."

"Let's go, then." The doctor picked up his black medical bag plus another satchel containing surgical knives, laudanum, splints and bandages, then he went back into the bedroom and stuck in a change of clothing. He didn't know how bad Tanner was hurt. He thought it best to be prepared.

After a final look around to see if there was anything he

might have forgotten, he extinguished the lights and closed the door.

Luke tied the bags behind the saddles, then held the bridle while the doctor climbed onto the prancing horse.

Doc lifted the reins, then kicked the horse into a gallop and followed Luke out of town.

When they passed the pie shop, he thought of Tanner and Kate. The two could make a go of it. If they weren't so blamed stubborn. In his opinion they were made for each other. Even if they couldn't see it, they needed each other.

Now more than ever.

As they rode past the cemetery, the rows of markers gleamed silver in the pale moonlight. The doctor thought of his many friends, his family, and his patients who had died in the smallpox epidemic. All now rested on the hillside.

Luke's urgency told him that Tanner was seriously hurt.

What if Tanner didn't make it?

What would happen to those boys?

Damn it, Kate. Why did you pick now to run away?

26

THE CONCORD STAGE had been delayed in the Siskiyou Mountains because of a fractured wheel spoke. As a result, the coach, scheduled to leave Jacksonville at six that morning, hadn't departed until early afternoon.

Kate had been eager to be on her way, but as the familiar landmarks rolled by and she realized she could be seeing them for the very last time, doubts began to enter her mind.

Once on the road, sitting for hours in the swaying stage had given her time to think, time to reflect on her actions. Had she been unfair to Tanner? Had she expected too much? She didn't know. The only thing she was certain of was the feeling that her heart had been ripped out by the roots.

The doctor had asked her to wait, to give Tanner a chance to finish the logging contract, then see what would happen. But she had let pride get in her way, certain that if Tanner had loved her, he would stop her from leaving.

He hadn't. He hadn't even come to say goodbye.

Of course, she hadn't told Mark exactly when she would be leaving. She hadn't known herself until the night she had bought the ticket. If Tanner had been aware of her departure date, would that have made a difference? Would he have been there then?

Whether he would have come or not, she'd never know.

She'd made her choices, and she would live with them. It was time to look forward, not back.

The driver cracked the whip and the stage leaned into the upcoming curve. A range of evergreen-clad mountains loomed ahead. Behind their snow-tipped crests, clouds scudded frantically across the sky, telling her a storm was in the offing. Alongside the road, trees tossed in the frenzied lashing of the wind.

Inside the stage, Kate gripped the leather strap to keep her balance and tucked a woolen lap robe around her, grateful for its additional warmth. But as she settled back into her seat, she couldn't stop her thoughts from returning to the night she and Tanner had spent together. She closed her eyes, remembering the ecstasy, the passion. The feel of his lips, the strength of his arms, and the moment when he'd claimed her. Then later, when he'd awakened and taken her again.

Now it seemed even more dreamlike than it had then. And like a dream it had vanished in the light of day.

She heaved a wistful sigh; catching herself, she opened her eyes, glad that she was alone in the coach. How could Tanner make her feel those things, behave that way himself, if he didn't care? She remembered the tenderness of his touch, the look of wonder on his face. Maybe he did love her and simply wasn't able to tell her. Some men were like that, saying with action what they couldn't put into words.

Their joining had been fierce, joyous, combining hearts and souls in that one moment when they had truly become one. If she had become pregnant, would she have still been so determined to be on her way? Somehow she doubted she would have had any say in the matter. Family was everything to Tanner. She knew that from seeing him with his brothers. A child—his child—would be no different. He wouldn't have allowed her to leave. He would have made her stay, married her. And because she loved him, she wouldn't have had the strength to resist. Then, for the rest of her life, she would be forced to live with the knowledge that Tanner had married her simply because of the baby. She couldn't, wouldn't allow that to happen. Was she selfish to want him to love her for herself?

The first time they had made love, she'd been foolhardy, living only for the moment, the passion. It was a wonder she hadn't gotten pregnant. She might not be so fortunate if it happened again. And it would have happened again if she'd stayed. She loved him too much for it to be otherwise. That was one of the reasons she had to leave.

Well, she had left, so that was no longer a problem. She had a whole new life waiting for her just up the road. Then why did she feel such sorrow, such an overwhelming sense of loss?

The stage slowed on the rising grade. The whip cracked and the horses blew as they labored up the hill, but Kate paid little attention to the sounds or the scenery. Her thoughts were still on Tanner.

The wind whipped and whined around the stage windows, making Kate glad she was inside the coach and not on top with the driver. The steady chuck-chuck of the wheels and the rocking of the coach finally lulled her into closing her eyes. Exhausted from the late hours she'd been keeping, her mind retreated, seeking a place where there was nothing but peace. Even there, Tanner filled her dreams. And peace was not to be found.

The stage jolted to a stop. Kate, yanked from a troubled sleep, sat up and rubbed her eyes. A sense of unease drew a wrinkle to her brow and made her wonder if something might have happened to the coach without her being aware of it.

She peered out the window and saw a two-story white building beside the roadway. She recognized it as a way station and knew they had stopped to change horses. A sign swinging crazily from a rafter over the steps of a wide front porch read WOLF CREEK INN.

A jingle of harness bells drew her attention to the opposite window, and she saw a long string of mules and a freight wagon pull up beside a corral.

The freighter, a burly man in plaid shirt and black denims,

shouted a greeting, his breath forming white clouds against the cold air. He climbed down to join Uriah Jones, the stage driver, and the hostler, who were in the process of changing teams. They welcomed him jovially, as if they were all old friends.

Nothing seemed to be amiss. But the sense of foreboding wouldn't leave her. If anything it grew stronger.

A stiff gust of wind picked up the dust and swirled it about the coach. A shiver skittered down her backbone, leaving goosebumps in its wake. Her palms grew clammy. Her heartbeat quickened.

"Miss, are you all right?"

"What?" Disoriented, she whirled toward the open door and stared at the driver.

"Are you sick or something?" Uriah asked, his weather-beaten face mirroring his concern.

"No, I'm all right," she shakily assured him. She raised a trembling hand to her cheek. Her face was wet with tears. She hastily wiped them away.

"Wolf Creek Station," he said. "We'll be going on to Canyonville to spend the night, but I thought you might like to get something to eat while I change teams. Don't take too long, though, I've got a lot of time to make up."

She allowed him to help her to the ground. "Thank you." She managed a feeble smile, but was grateful when he left her to return to the other men. She took a moment to get the kinks out, then, anxious to be out of the cold, she walked toward the building.

Overhead, a trace of crimson tinged the purple sky. Beneath it, ever-deepening shadows infiltrated the evergreen hills.

Sunset. Soon it would be dark. She shivered with dread. She had no reason to be so anxious, she told herself. She was overtired; she must have had a bad dream, even though she couldn't remember it. That was all it was, that and her imagination.

But a sixth sense told her it had been something else—a premonition. Her footsteps slowed. She had experienced that same kind of feeling before—when someone she loved had died.

A familiar face, etched with pain, flashed through her mind. "Kate," she heard him cry.

She froze. "Tanner!"

She whirled and ran toward the driver. "Mr. . . . Mr. . . . Uriah—"

"Yes, miss?"

"You must turn the stage around. I have to go back."

The driver shook his head. "Afraid I can't do that. This stage is Portland bound. I have a schedule."

"Please," she begged. "I have to return to Jacksonville."

"Sorry, but there's nothing I can do."

If she couldn't go by stage . . . There had to be another way. She turned to the hostler. "Can I rent a horse?"

"All the horses belong to the stage line."

"Miss, Jacksonville is on my route," the brawny freight driver broke in, running a hand over his unshaven face. "But I don't know if you'd care to ride with me, and the seat on that wagon ain't exactly the place for a lady."

She hesitated. The man's rough appearance certainly didn't inspire confidence. But if she had learned anything these last few months, it was not to go by first impressions. And with her growing fear for Tanner, she would have accepted a ride with the devil himself. "You could take me?"

"You would be safe with Jules," Uriah assured her. "But like he said, it sure would be uncomfortable."

"When can we leave?" She managed a grateful smile. "I do need to get there as quickly as possible."

"The mules have to rest. And I'm a bit tuckered myself. But I will be leaving at dawn tomorrow."

"Tomorrow?" Frustration threatened to choke her, but she tried not to let it show. So much could happen in that length of time. Something had happened to Tanner; she knew it. And she knew he needed her. More than anything she wanted to be at his side.

It also looked like she would need wings to get there before tomorrow.

Trying not to appear ungrateful, she looked at the teamster and nodded. "I'll be ready."

Dr. Thomas rubbed the sleep from his eyes and shuffled into the sick room. "Any change?" he asked softly.

Matt shook his head. "Coffee's on the stove. Looks like you could use it."

"Thanks." He went back to the kitchen and poured himself a cup. He twisted his back to remove the stiffness. It was hard to find a spot that didn't hurt. He was getting old, and that ride up the mountain had just about done him in. After that, he'd been with Tanner most of the night, until Matt had forced him to lie down for a while.

After assessing that Tanner had a concussion, two broken ribs, two more cracked, and the broken leg, he had rebandaged the injuries.

He still found it hard to believe that Mark had come up with the same conclusions, or that the youngster had set the leg. A practicing physician couldn't have done any better.

Remembering all the times Mark had come to him with questions about some hurt varmint he had found gave root to an idea. It was a shame for the boy to be stuck up here on this mountain, especially when he had such talented hands. If somebody, say an aging medical man like himself, took the boy under his wing, Mark would make a fine doctor someday, if that was what he wanted to be.

Examining the notion, he poured a second cup and carried it back to the sick room. He handed it to Matt. "Don't you think you could use some rest, too?"

Matt shook his head. "Mark ran me out after you left. He's the one who stayed here all night. I got up a little bit ago."

"Where is Mark?"

"He's down at the barn, tending to the stock."

"He did a good job on Tanner."

"Yeah, I know. But all the doctorin' in the world isn't going to do a lick of good if we can't keep Tanner from frettin'." Matt looked over at his brother and frowned.

Tanner was sleeping, due to the laudanum they had forced

down his throat. Even though they had given him enough to put a horse to sleep, he had continued to moan and toss and call for Kate. Finally, afraid he might hurt himself if they didn't, they had tied him to the bed.

Now they had to wait, let nature take its course, and pray that no infection set in.

Doc sipped his coffee. If Kate were here, that would ease one part of the problem.

Although Doc was certain Tanner would deny it, he had called out for her in his sleep. He had also fought against taking the drug, saying that he had a contract to finish. It had taken not only the doctor, but Matt and Mark to hold him down, while Luke administered the drug.

"This contract, . . ." the doctor began.

"After I heard him muttering about it, I went to find the papers. I also found some notes he'd made. Tanner didn't tell us, but he has to get it finished right away. If he doesn't, he will lose all the work he put in. He'll also lose the mountain."

Doc let a whistle slide between his teeth. "No wonder he's worried." He looked at Matt. "What are you going to do?"

"I don't know. Mark and I could try to finish it ourselves, but I doubt if we would make the deadline. If Tanner woke up and we weren't here, he'd get out of bed if he had to crawl."

"In his condition that could kill him." Doc downed another gulp of coffee. "Damned shame." He rubbed his chin thoughtfully. "Looks like Tanner's going to be out for a while. Is Luke up yet?"

"I'm up," Luke said through a yawn, peering through the doorway.

"Come on into the kitchen, son. I've got some things that need doing in town. Maybe you could take care of them for me."

"Sure thing, Doc."

"First, we could all use some breakfast." Matt followed them into the kitchen and put the skillet on the fire.

Several hours later, Luke sat in Madame Jeanne's parlor,

his hat wadded in his hand while she read the letter Doc had given him to deliver.

"Relax, Luke," the Frenchwoman said with a smile. "Would you like a cup of tea?"

"No, ma'am." He couldn't tell her he couldn't abide the stuff. That wouldn't be polite.

"Maybe a piece of Kate's pie?" she asked, her dark eyes merry.

"I thought Kate had left."

"She has. I saved these."

"That would be right nice, ma'am."

"Jeanne. I inseest," She got to her feet. "Come eento the kitchen. I theenk we will be more comfortable there."

Two pieces of pie and a cup of chocolate later, Luke bid her goodbye.

"Tell Dr. Thomas not to worry." She fanned herself with the letter. "I take care of eet. I am certain Chauncey weell help out, too. Geeve heem sometheeng to do besides wear a hole een my carpet."

"Thanks, ma'am—Jeanne."

Luke mounted his horse and headed for home. Although his curiosity had been killing him, he still didn't know what was so important in that letter. And neither the doctor nor Jeanne had volunteered to tell him. "Guess they figured it wasn't none of my business." Which it wasn't. Nevertheless, he couldn't help but wonder.

He wondered all the way home.

The freight wagon rumbled into Jacksonville shortly after noon. Kate had the driver unload her things at Madame Jeanne's, then thanked the man and bid him goodbye.

Jeanne, surprised and happy to see her, told Kate about Tanner, then sent someone to find Chauncey. Kate was nearly hysterical by the time the old miner arrived at the boardinghouse door.

"Kate, honey, I'm so glad you came back," he said. "Now I know Tanner is gonna get well."

"Can you take me to him?" Kate asked, trying to keep the desperation out of her voice.

"I've already got the horses outside."

He tied Kate's carpetbag on behind the saddle, plus several things Madame Jeanne thought the doctor might need. Within minutes they were heading up the mountain.

Although Kate tried to be optimistic, she knew Tanner's injuries were serious. She took comfort in the fact that Dr. Thomas was with him. She was also determined to do what she could to aid his recovery.

Seeing riders ahead of them, Kate frowned. She had never seen anyone up here before. At the switchback, she turned to glance behind her. A steady stream of men were coming up the trail. "Chauncey, who are all these men, and where are they going? Is there a new gold strike?"

The old man chuckled. "They're going to Tanner's."

"To Tanner's? Why?"

"Honey, Tanner has helped out pert' near everybody in these parts. Now they are going to return the favor."

"I don't understand."

"The timber contract." Chauncey grinned. "We found out it has to be finished right away or Tanner will lose the mountain. He didn't tell anybody. The boys found the papers. That man's so danged proud he probably wouldn't stand for it if he knew what we were doing. But we ain't gonna give him a say in the matter. It was Doc's idea to get him some help. I've jest been passing the word."

Tears stung Kate's eyes. The boys and the mountain meant everything to Tanner. The loss of either of them would destroy him. She knew he had been worried about the contract, but she didn't know the situation had been so desperate. And she, unknowingly, had put even more pressure on him. Now her actions seemed vain, petty. With the loss of his home hanging in the balance, no wonder he hadn't come to see her. She wouldn't blame him if he never wanted to see her again.

At least now he wouldn't have to fret about the contract. Now he could concentrate on getting well.

Although the trip up the mountain seemed to take forever, Kate knew they had made it in record time. When they finally arrived at the house, little John and Fluffy burst through the door to greet her.

"Kate, you d-did come b-back," the boy cried, wrapping his arms around her. "I kn-knew you w-would."

She gave John a big hug and kiss, then patted the whining dog's head. "How's Tanner?" she asked, almost fearing to hear his answer.

"Sleeping." John frowned. "He got hurt, you know."

"I heard."

"I'll put the horses up, Kate," Chauncey said. "You go on in and check on your man."

My man. Needing no encouragement, Kate raced up the steps.

Matt and Luke met her at the door. After giving her hugs of welcome, Matt took her to Tanner's room. Luke went to help Chauncey. She found out that Mark was out guiding an earlier group of men into the woods.

When she entered the sickroom, Doc Thomas looked up from the bedside. "Thank the Lord. How did you know?"

"I sensed he needed me. That's why I came back." She moved to the bedside.

Tanner lay unmoving. His pallor and the bandages sent a bolt of fear tearing through her chest. She stared at the strips of cloth running from the bedposts to his hands and feet. "How is he?"

"Holding his own. He'll get better now that you are here. He's been calling for you. Every time he regains consciousness, he tries to get out of bed. That's why he's tied down. He's been fretting about the timber."

She smiled. "Thanks to you and Chauncey, and every able-bodied man in the area, I hear that's being taken care of. Dozens of men are on their way here now."

"Tanner's got lots of friends. They are glad to help out when they can." He looked at her and smiled. "He's also got a woman that loves him. That makes him pretty lucky, I'd say."

"I do love him, but I'm not sure the feeling is returned."

"Words don't come easy to a man like Tanner, but he loves you. You have my assurance of that." The doctor rubbed his neck, then yawned and got to his feet. "Now that you're here, I think I'll take a little nap. Oh, if you'd like you can untie him—he's sleeping sound enough that he won't be going anywhere."

"What if he does wake up?" she asked. "Is there anything I'm supposed to do?"

"Seeing you here would be the best medicine I could prescribe. Just make sure he doesn't try to get out of bed."

"Don't worry about that. Tanner Blaine isn't going anywhere until I tell him he can."

Chuckling, the doctor left the room.

Kate took the seat he had vacated and pulled it close to the bed. She untied the straps, then lifted Tanner's hand. Scarred, rough—and those blisters . . . She bent and pressed her lips to his palm. Once she would have thought such a hand denoted commonness, a lack of breeding. Now it represented strength and integrity, as well as gentleness—everything she could ever want in a man.

As she stared at Tanner, she wondered how she could ever have imagined she could leave him. "I love you," she whispered.

As if she had reached into his consciousness, Tanner opened his eyes. "Kate," he called weakly.

"I'm right here." She smoothed his hair back from his forehead and gently kissed his brow.

"I'm not dreaming?" he asked, trying to raise his head.

She pushed him back against the pillow, then touched her mouth to his cracked lips. "Does this feel like a dream?"

"You're here. You're really here." He closed his eyes, then opened them again. "Don't leave me, Kate."

Tears welled in her eyes. "I'll never leave you again."

Several more times that day, Tanner opened his eyes, searching the room until he found her. Then, apparently satisfied, he went back to sleep.

Kate stayed by the bedside even though both Matthew and the doctor urged her to get some rest. She had given Tanner a promise. She would not leave his side.

Despite her good intentions, in the wee hours of the

morning exhaustion claimed her. She was still asleep when Matt carried her to the other room and tucked her into bed.

The next day, Tanner seemed to gain strength, his lucid periods growing longer. Twice Kate even managed to get him to swallow some broth.

"He's getting well," Dr. Thomas said from behind her when Tanner had gone back to sleep.

"He seems better, but I was afraid to hope," she said, taking comfort from the physician's words. "How long will it take him to completely recover?"

"The bones have to knit, and he will probably have headaches for a while. Couple of months and he ought to be good as new." The doctor took a swig from his coffee. "He's darn near worked himself to death, so the rest will do him good. The problem is keeping him down until he gets healed."

"That doesn't seem to be a problem," Kate said, looking at the man on the bed.

"Right now the laudanum is keeping him asleep. But I am cutting back on that so he can get some nourishment. The next time he wakes up might be a problem."

Two hours later Kate saw what he meant.

Tanner fought to raise himself in the bed.

Kate gripped both shoulders and tried to push him back. "Doc. Help me!"

"I've got to get up," Tanner insisted.

"You are not going anywhere."

"Kate? What . . ." Dr. Thomas took one look and rushed to hold Tanner down.

His brow beaded with sweat, Tanner sagged back against the pillow. "Damn it."

"Curse all you want. I won't have you undoing all my work, young man," the doctor said sternly. "You are going to stay in this bed—and you are going to behave yourself."

"And I'm going to see that you do," Kate assured him.

"Bossy," Tanner mumbled.

"You haven't seen anything yet, Mr. Blaine." She tucked

the covers back around him. "First you are going to eat some broth, then you are going to take a nap. And you are not going to think about getting out of this bed."

"Broth? Uh, Doc? . . ." Tanner glanced at the doctor, then at Kate. "I need to . . ."

The doctor chuckled. "Kate, I think we need a little privacy."

She glanced at Tanner, taking note of the almost pleading expression on his face. "Oh. . . ." Her face flaming, she left the room.

She entered the kitchen to find Chauncey and Matt sitting at the table. "How are things going in the woods?"

"The men sent a batch of logs down the skid chute this morning. They should be all finished in a day or two."

"Wonderful. Tanner will be glad to hear that."

"Uh, Kate. I don't think we ought to mention it yet," Matt said. "If Tanner finds out someone else is doing his work, he's sure going to try to stop them."

"He's got to know sooner or later," she insisted.

"We'll tell him," Chauncey said. "Just as soon as the work is done."

"That might be best at that," she agreed. By that time, it wouldn't do him any good to get up. There wouldn't be anything left for him to do. "Has Tom Fuller said anything about the contract?"

"His men are up here helping skid the logs. Tom's a good man, and he figures it's partly his fault Tanner had the accident," Chauncey said. "He had no idea Tanner was trying to do the whole thing all by himself."

"Tanner is proud—and stubborn."

"Yeah, and right now, I hear him yelling for you," Matt said with a grin. He handed her the tray he had prepared.

Kate carried it into the sickroom. "Your broth, sir."

Tanner scowled. "Again? There's nothing wrong with my stomach, Kate. Can't you get me some solid food?"

"You must be getting better. You're cranky. That's a sure sign you're getting well."

"I'd get well a lot sooner if you'd give me a kiss," he said huskily.

She leaned forward and pressed her lips to his, then she moved away and filled his spoon. "Eat all of this, and I'll give you more."

"More broth, or more kisses?" he asked.

"Both."

"Like I said, I'd get well a lot faster if I had something more substantial."

From the look in his eyes, she knew he wasn't referring to food. "For now, sir, you'll settle for broth and a kiss. I won't have you making promises you aren't able to keep."

He gave her a wicked grin. "Bring on the soup, Kate. I have a feeling that I'm going to need my strength."

Her heart fluttering wildly, she shoved a spoonful into his mouth.

27

"*IS EVERYBODY DEAF?*" Tanner yelled, pulling at the ropes that had him bound hand and foot, strapped down like a calf ready for branding. "A man can't even break a leg without somebody taking advantage of him."

"I can see you're feeling better," the doctor said wryly from the doorway.

"Cut me loose, Doc. I can't stay here. I've got work to do."

"No, you don't." The doctor felt his forehead. "No fever. That's a good sign."

"Then I can get up?" Tanner said hopefully.

"Not on your life. I didn't ride all the way up this mountain to have you end up killing yourself."

"You don't understand."

"I know all about the timber deadline. And it's being taken care of." The doctor smiled.

"Did you get an extension?"

"No, better than that. It's being cut right now as we speak. The boys—"

"No!" Frantic, Tanner yanked at the ropes. "Please, Doc. I've got to stop them."

"The kids are fine. They aren't the ones doing the felling. But Mark and Luke are helping strip the trees. Matt has gone out to take the men some food."

"What men?"

"Only every able-bodied man that can swing an ax." He named off several people Tanner knew, and some more he'd never heard of.

"I don't accept charity, Doc."

"Charity, hell. You didn't think it was charity when you helped them out."

"I was only being neighborly."

"They appreciate the chance to return the favor."

"Tanner! You're awake," John cried as he and Fluffy burst through the doorway.

"Hi, squirt." Tanner looked from the boy to the doctor. "Cut me loose—please."

"All right, as long as you promise to stay put. You've had a concussion, along with broken ribs and that broken leg. I don't want you undoing all the doctoring Mark and I have been doing."

"Mark?"

"He set your leg and got you back here to the cabin. I want to talk to you about that boy later, but right now I expect you could do with something to eat."

"You've got that right." Tanner hesitated. "Doc, where's Kate?"

"Sleeping. I gave her a dose of laudanum. It was the only way she would leave you."

"She's still here," Tanner said softly.

"Yes, she's here. And this time if you're smart, you won't let her leave." The doctor shook his head. "Although what she wants with anybody as pigheaded as you, I'll never understand." Still grumbling, the doctor left the room.

After he'd eaten, Tanner had Dr. Thomas bring him up to date on everything that had happened since the accident. Afterward, the physician insisted that he take a nap.

"Is Kate still sleeping?" Tanner asked.

"That's what I said." The doctor studied him. "When are you going to marry that girl?"

"I asked her once, but I've been thinking about that a lot these last few days. I thought about how close I came to dying. And about what would happen to her if I did. She'd be stuck on the mountain, taking care of the boys, maybe little ones, too. I couldn't put her through that, Doc." He shook his head. "I've got nothing to offer a woman like Kate."

"Do you love her?"

"Of course I do. Don't you see? That's why I can't marry her."

"Humph!" Kate eased back down the hall to her own room. Tanner did love her. But he wouldn't marry her. She sighed in exasperation.

"Kate, are you awake?"

"Yes, Doc." She opened her door. "How's our patient?"

"Mule-headed as ever."

"Yes, I know."

"You heard?" He frowned. "What are you going to do?"

"I'm not certain yet, but I do know he's not going to get rid of me that easily."

"Good for you. At least one of you has some sense." He patted her shoulder. "I've got to go back to Jacksonville. A patient of mine is getting ready to have a baby."

"What about Tanner?"

"Tanner will be fine as long as he behaves himself. He can start getting up, but I don't want him to do anything— especially any lifting. He should stay in the house." he grinned. "If he gets ornery, tie him to the bed."

"I'll do that."

After the doctor left, Kate thought about the conversation she had overheard. So Tanner wasn't going to marry her. She shrugged. Lots of people lived together without benefit of clergy. If that's what it would take, so be it. He couldn't forcibly evict her; he hadn't the strength.

By early the following week the crew had finished the job and left the mountain, and the mortgage had been paid. Although the words hadn't come easily, Tanner had thanked each one of the men and shaken his hand. He later confessed to Kate that they had made him realize there was no weakness in asking for help.

Lying in bed had also given him time to realize something else. His own accident made him relive the day his father had died. Made him remember things he had forgotten.

That day, too, a tree had been falling. The limb that struck his father had broken off from the top. Tanner could not have known which way it would go—and neither could his father. Thinking back on the event, Tanner knew he couldn't have prevented it. His father's death had been bad luck, an accident.

All these years Tanner had blamed himself; now he knew it wasn't his fault. While the grief would always be there, now it seemed easier to bear.

The long period of convalescence following his experience had also allowed him to look at his brothers in a new light. Mark and Matt were almost grown men. He had decided it was time for them to make their own decisions.

Because Tanner had refused to accept the money Kate had deposited in his name at the bank, she insisted on giving it to the boys. Part of it she put aside for Luke and John's education. The rest she divided between Matt and Mark.

The older boys, realizing that Kate and Tanner needed time alone, had made some changes in their own lives. Matt had taken over the pie shop, and while he didn't have as many customers as Kate, he was building a thriving business. In the afternoons he went to school. He blushingly confessed to Kate that he had even met a special girl.

At Dr. Thomas's urging, Tanner had allowed Mark to move into town with Matt. He, too, attended school, and on weekends he made the rounds with the doctor. Mark also studied medical books at night. They all agreed that someday Mark would be a fine physician.

Luke, John and Fluffy had remained on the mountain, and even though Tanner missed the older boys, he was glad to have the time with Kate. During the period he'd been hurt, she had brought a bit of springtime into their lives, but now he was almost well. Soon, like that all too brief season, he knew Kate would pack her bags and be gone.

He could prevent her from leaving. All he had to do was ask and she would stay. But he wouldn't. He'd decided the best thing he could do for Kate was to do nothing at all. While he couldn't bring himself to send her away, sooner or later she would give up and go on her own. She would forget him and find someone who could give her a better life.

In the meantime, he would take joy from her presence, but he wouldn't kiss her, or hold her, or take her into his bed. No matter how much she enticed him, he would not yield to temptation.

Kate had been biding her time, waiting for Tanner to heal. Now his ribs were back to normal, and although he still wore the splint on his leg, the doctor would be removing it at the beginning of next week.

Now with the older boys moved to town, Kate continued to take care of Tanner as well as Luke and John. Day after day she waited for Tanner to declare himself, to no avail. Even though she gave him ample opportunity, he had yet to confess that he loved her. He'd told the doctor, so why couldn't he say it to her? Outside of a few comments about the mountain or the boys, he rarely spoke to her at all.

He had done little else, either. They had exchanged a few kisses—at her initiative—but he acted almost like he was kissing an old friend or a sister. Although he had been unable to hide the hunger in his eyes, he'd never tried anything else.

Lately, his behavior had grown downright aggravating, and she was fast reaching the end of her patience.

He seemed to be waiting, expecting her to leave.

But she had no intention of going anywhere. She had other plans.

When Chauncey had volunteered to take Luke and John into Jacksonville that evening to see Tom Thumb and his traveling troupe of little people, Kate had eagerly accepted his offer, not only because she knew the boys would enjoy the theater, but mainly because it would give her a chance to be alone with Tanner.

After the performance, since it would be too late to return home, the boys would be spending the night with Matt and Mark. Tomorrow, they all planned to attend church and would pass the afternoon visiting. Mark would bring them home the next morning.

With one full day and two nights at her disposal, Kate figured to make good use of her time. She'd get Tanner's cooperation one way or another, or her name wasn't Kathleen Amanda Deveraux.

For their first meal alone, she'd fixed all of Tanner's favorites: hot biscuits, venison steak smothered in gravy, whipped potatoes and dandelion greens. He'd eaten like a condemned man at his last meal—to avoid conversation, she suspected.

Unbeknownst to Tanner, she'd added a little something extra to his supper—just enough laudanum to put him to sleep. When he woke up, she planned to make him see things her way—or suffer the consequences.

She checked the mantel clock. Everything was ready. Soon the drug would be wearing off. There would never be a better time to make her point.

She slipped into Tanner's room, taking note of the soft snores coming from the region of the bed. "All right, Mr. Blaine, we will see how long you will sleep." She bent close and gently blew in his ear. "Tan-ner," she whispered.

A soft voice reached into Tanner's dream and tugged him from sleep. "Hm-m?" Warm lips touched his, then playfully nibbled at his chin.

He sighed in contentment.

"Tan-ner, wake up," she said in a sing-song voice.

She kissed him again, slowly, teasingly, then eased her tongue into his mouth.

He opened his eyes. *Kate?*

Surprised and shocked, it took him a moment to come to his senses. He felt a bit woozy, but he wasn't dreaming. Kate was kissing him. He tried not to kiss her back but couldn't seem to summon the will. Besides she tasted so good. Too damn good.

What was she up to?

She nibbled his neck, his ears, then pressed her lips to his. "Kiss me, Tanner." She leaned closer, her bosom thrusting against his chest.

Dang it! She was trying to seduce him. And he had to put a stop to it before it got out of hand. He tried to push her away—and found out he couldn't move. She had tied him to the bed again!

Maybe if he pretended he was asleep, she'd go away and leave him alone. She couldn't see him. It was dark in the room.

But she sure could feel him. He trembled when her hand trailed down his body and caressed the part of him that immediately sprang to life. That was when he discovered he wasn't wearing any clothes.

So much for pretending sleep. "Kate?" he breathed.

"Are you awake, darlin'?" she cooed.

"You know I am. I'd have to be dead not to be." He pulled at the straps. They didn't give. His legs were tied, too. "Let me loose."

"Not on your life. Doc told me if you got ornery to tie you to the bed." She kissed him again. "And that's just what I'm doing."

"Ornery?"

"Ornery."

"But I haven't done anything. . . ."

"Exactly my point."

He heard the splash of water. "What are you doing?"

"I'm going to give you a bath."

"In the dark?" He swallowed. "I can take my own bath."

"Not like this one, you can't." She washed his face, his neck, his ears, much like any mother would a wayward child.

He grinned. "You didn't have to tie me down to do that."

"I've only started." She kissed the spots she'd washed—his face, his jaw, pausing to nibble his earlobes.

He didn't move. He didn't dare—and he tried not to think about what she might do next.

But his traitorous mind wouldn't cooperate.

She rinsed the cloth and started on his chest. Then she bent and dried it with the same teasing motions.

By this time he was a quivering mass of raw nerve endings.

When she rinsed the cloth and dipped still lower, he knew he was in deep trouble.

"Kate, what are you . . ." He groaned when her cloth caressed that part of him that was demanding attention. Then her mouth closed over him. . . . Kate . . . don't. . . ."

Much to his relief, she left that region and washed his thighs and his legs.

"You can let me up now," he said, straining to see in the darkness.

"Nope, I've got you right where I want you." She trailed a finger from his toes to his groin and back again. She paused, then continued on up his middle to his chest, then to his forehead.

He gritted his teeth, but couldn't stop trembling.

She stood there in the darkness.

Even though he couldn't see, he could feel her studying him. She must have eyes like a cat.

Her palm closed around him.

He swallowed. "What are you doing?"

"I'm checking to make sure you're not damaged, but it appears like everything is working just fine."

"Damaged?" That part of him that had caught her interest was definitely unscathed. If it got any more undamaged, he was likely to bust something.

She lit the lamp and turned it down to a soft glow.

He sighed with relief. At least if he could see, he could prepare himself to resist her. He heard a soft rustling.

Then she stepped into the light.

Resist her? Ha! She wasn't wearing a stitch.

He groaned. He almost wished she had left the room dark.

With a smile as old as Eve's, she pulled the pins from her hair and shook it free. It tumbled in a shining mass over her shoulders. She walked toward him. "Now, where was I?"

Under her questing lips and mouth, Tanner thought he

would surely lose his mind. "Kate, honey, please have mercy."

"Mercy?" She straddled him and leaned forward. "I understand you don't want to marry me now, and that's all right." She kissed him, long and deep.

His head reeling, Tanner tried to concentrate on the rest of what she was saying, but it wasn't easy. Especially when the cherry tip of her breast jutted, tempted, teased him—just out of reach.

"But I'm not leaving this mountain, Tanner Blaine. If you take me to town, I'll come right back. Whether you like it or not, I intend to be your woman. I'll cook, clean your house, wash your clothes, and take care of your brothers.

"I'll also be warming your bed each night," she whispered. She lifted her hips and settled over him, taking him deep inside her. She kissed him again, her tongue moving in rhythm with her body.

"And I'll be bearing your children. So you may as well get used to having me around."

"Don't I have any say in the matter?" he managed to croak when she gave him the chance.

"Talk away." But she didn't stop what she was doing to listen.

He couldn't talk. He couldn't even think. He'd probably be better off keeping his mouth shut. It was always the talking that got him into trouble, anyway. Besides, if he said anything, she might quit. He didn't plan to say a word.

She brought him to the pinnacle, then she stopped. "Well, Mr. Blaine?"

"Kate, I'll do anything you say, just untie me."

"I thought you'd see things my way." She leaned forward and untied his hands, then she twisted and loosened the straps holding his feet. "One's caught on your splint."

"Never mind about that," he said. Unable to wait, he pulled her down on him and loved her as well as he was able to under the circumstances. But he noticed she wasn't voicing any complaints.

When it was over and she snuggled next to him, he

ondered how he could ever have thought he could let her
o. It would be like cutting out his heart.

He had been wrong about Kate. Despite her size and
ragile appearance, she had proved to be a woman of both
trength and determination. He nuzzled the top of her head
nd grinned. And since she seemed so determined to have
im, how could he refuse?

He kissed her forehead. "I'm no prize, you know."

"I know. But you'll learn," she said, flashing him an
mpish grin. "And when you get ornery . . ."

"Two can play at that game, Miss Deveraux." Before she
ould move, he had her hands and feet tied to the bed. Then
e slowly, thoroughly tormented her the same way she had
im. His heart filled with love, he gazed at the panting
voman beneath him.

"Tanner, please."

"Not until you agree to marry me."

"Anything."

"When?"

"Whenever you say," she gasped.

"How about Sunday?"

She frowned. "That's day after tomorrow. I need more
ime than that."

"Sunday week, then."

"Fine. Now—"

"Sunday week it is." He untied the fastenings. "Now
ome here, woman, and give me some proper loving."

"Proper?" She arched a brow. "All of this is highly
mproper, Mr. Blaine."

She sat up on the side of the bed. "I have to make plans.
et's see we . . . need to make invitations, and maybe
eanne would bake the cake. . . ."

"Talkin' again." He silenced her with kisses. "Now about
hose children . . ."

"What about them?"

"I'd like at least six. Three boys and three girls."

"I was hoping for a dozen," she murmured, pulling him
own on the bed.

His passion rising, Tanner hoped those children didn't

come along too soon—he wanted some more time to hav Kate all to himself. *And when they do come . . .*

She kissed him.

. . . I'll have to add on to the house and . . .

She kissed him again.

. . . Make a few improvements. . . . What else? . . .

She let out an exasperated sigh.

First, I'd better send for the preacher before she change her mind.

"Thinking again?" she asked, peering up at him.

He grinned.

"You can think tomorrow." She pulled his head dow and whispered against his lips. "Now about that prope loving . . ."

"Bossy female." Tanner took her in his arms, content t let her have her way.

Dear Reader,

I hope you enjoyed *Courting Kate*.

The town of Jacksonville has retained much of its earlier charm, and many of the buildings mentioned in the story are still standing. The smallpox epidemic, the pesthouse, the fires in the streets—sadly all are part of the town's history.

As for the characters, Jacksonville had more than its share. Cornelius Beekman did indeed charge people to keep money in his bank, and he did not loan any of it out. Madame Jeanne deRoboam ran the Franco-American until it burned. Determined not to let that happen again, she married a man who owned a brickyard. She agreed to see to his comforts if he would build her a new hotel—of brick. Apparently it was a happy venture, for they were together many years. The stage driver, Charlie Parkhurst, was later discovered to be a woman. Since Charlie cast a ballot in the election, she was actually the first woman in Oregon to vote.

Kate, Tanner and his family, the doctor and Chauncey were all figments of my imagination even though they became very real to me as the story unfolded.

I love to hear from my fans regarding this and other books I have written. You may write to:

Mary Lou Rich
P.O. Box 101
Murphy, OR 97533

For an autographed bookmark and newsletter of future novels, please enclose a stamped, self-addressed envelope.

Until next time, happy reading.

Mary Lou Rich